praise for
THE LOST QUEEN

"Did you know that King Arthur's favorite wizard, Merlin—or, more accurately, the real man he was based on—had an equally important twin sister? Get hooked on her story in Signe Pike's *The Lost Queen*."

—*Redbook*

"Mystical, epic, and captivating. I couldn't put it down."

—Hazel Gaynor, *New York Times* bestselling author of
The Girl Who Came Home and *The Lighthouse Keeper's Daughter*

"Building on the fascination of Camelot and other Arthurian tales of nobility and magic . . . A story of bravery and sacrifice."

—Associated Press

"An extraordinary historical page-turner . . . *The Lost Queen* is more than a book; it is a profound experience."

—Patti Callahan Henry, *New York Times* bestselling author of
The Bookshop at Water's End and *Becoming Mrs. Lewis*

"An engrossing debut . . . Pike's narrative blends court intrigue, romantic interludes, and gritty violence into a literary brew worth savoring to the dramatic finale."

—*Booklist*

"A gripping tale . . . You won't regret losing yourself in this fast-moving story."

—*Charleston* magazine

"Deeply researched as well as entertaining."

—*Library Journal*

"An unusual take on Dark Ages drama."

—*Kirkus Reviews*

"*The Lost Queen* rocks."

—*Charleston City Paper*

ALSO BY SIGNE PIKE

*Faery Tale: One Woman's Search
for Enchantment in a Modern World*

THE LOST QUEEN

QUEEN

❧ A NOVEL ❧

SIGNE PIKE

ATRIA PAPERBACK

New York London Toronto Sydney New Delhi

ATRIA
PAPERBACK

An Imprint of Simon & Schuster, Inc.
1230 Avenue of the Americas
New York, NY 10020

First Atria Paperback edition June 2019

ATRIA PAPERBACK and colophon are trademarks of Simon & Schuster, Inc.

For information about special discounts for bulk purchases, please contact Simon & Schuster Special Sales at 1-866-506-1949 or business@simonandschuster.com.

The Simon & Schuster Speakers Bureau can bring authors to your live event. For more information or to book an event, contact the Simon & Schuster Speakers Bureau at 1-866-248-3049 or visit our website at www.simonspeakers.com.

Manufactured in the United States of America

10 9 8 7 6 5 4 3

The Library of Congress has cataloged the hardcover edition as follows:

Names: Pike, Signe, author.
Title: The lost queen / Signe Pike.
Description: First Touchstone hardcover edition. | New York : Touchstone, 2018. |
Series: The lost queen ; 1 |
Identifiers: LCCN 2018002985 (print) | LCCN 2018008974 (ebook) |
    ISBN 9781501191435 (ebook) | ISBN 9781501191411 (hardcover) |
    ISBN 9781501191428 (softcover)
Subjects: LCSH: Queens—Fiction. | Scotland—History—To 1057—Fiction. |
    Kings and rulers—Fiction. | Nobility—Fiction. | BISAC: FICTION / Historical.
    FICTION / Sagas. | FICTION / Cultural Heritage. | GSAFD: Historical fiction. |
    Fantasy fiction.
Classification: LCC PS3616.I425 (ebook) | LCC PS3616.I425 L67 2018 (print) |
    DDC 813/.6—dc23
LC record available at https://lccn.loc.gov/2018002985

ISBN: 978-1-5011-9141-1
ISBN: 978-1-5011-9142-8 (pbk)
ISBN: 978-1-5011-9143-5 (ebook)

For Eric and Asa

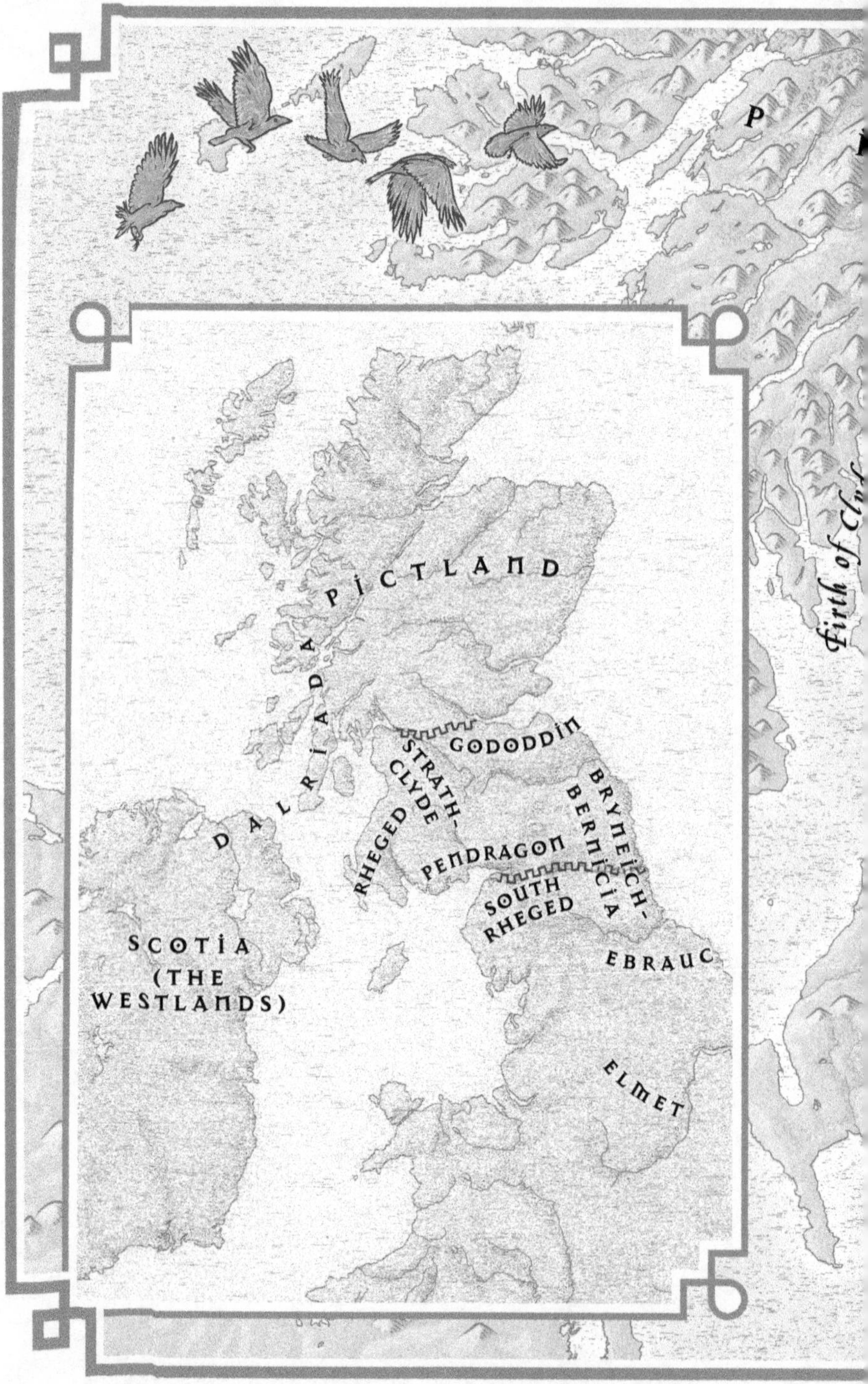

P
Firth of Cly
PICTLAND
DALRIADA
GODODDIN
STRATH-CLYDE
RHEGED
BRYNEICH-BERNICIA
PENDRAGON
SOUTH RHEGED
SCOTIA (THE WESTLANDS)
EBRAUC
ELMET

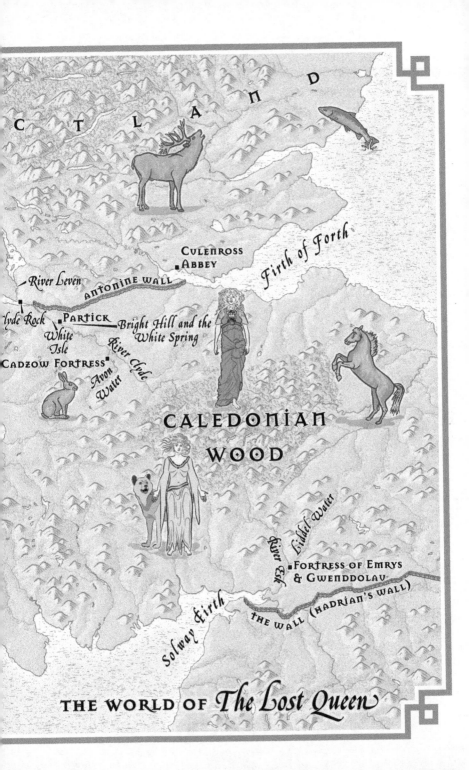

THE WORLD OF *The Lost Queen*

THE PEOPLE

Kingdom of Strathclyde

House of Morken

Ariane: Wisdom Keeper

Brant: warrior, Morken's nephew, older brother to Brodyn

Brodyn: warrior, Morken's nephew, younger brother to Brant

Cathan: head Wisdom Keeper of Strathclyde, counsellor to Morken

Crowan: nursemaid to Lailoken and Languoreth

Desdemona: servant

Herrick: servant

Languoreth: daughter of Morken, twin sister to Lailoken

Lailoken: son of Morken, twin brother to Languoreth

Macon: groom

Morken: petty king/high chieftain of Goddeu, halls in Cadzow and Partick

House of Tutgual

Angharad: daughter of Languoreth

Cyan: son of Languoreth

Elufed: queen of Strathclyde, a Pict

Gladys: daughter of Languoreth

Gwenfron: daughter of Tutgual

Morcant: son of Tutgual
Rhydderch: son of Tutgual
Rhian: wife of Morcant
Rhys: eldest son of Languoreth
Tutgual: king of Strathclyde

The Borderlands
Ceidio: former king of Ebrauc, Gwenddolau's father
Emrys: the Pendragon, leader of the Angle resistance
Gwenddolau: Emrys's second-in-command, "Uther" Pendragon
Maelgwn: warrior, general of Pendragon's army

Kingdom of Ebrauc
Eliffer: brother to Ceidio, king of Ebrauc
Gwrgi: king of Southern Ebrauc, brother to Peredur, son of Eliffer
Peredur: king of Northern Ebrauc, son of Eliffer

Kingdom of Gododdin
Pascent: son of Vortigern
Vortigern: king of Bryneich, Southern Gododdin

The Christians
Anguen: monk in Mungo's order
Fergus: monk in Telleyr's order
Garthwys/Mungo/Kentigern: Christian monk, bishop of
    Strathclyde
Telleyr: Christian monk

The Scots of Dalriada and Manau
Aedan mac Gabhran: nephew of Conall, king of Manau
Conall mac Comgall: king of Scots of Dalriada

PHONETIC PRONUNCIATIONS

House of Morken

Ariane: "AH-ree-AH-nee"

Brodyn: "BRO-din"

Cathan: "CATH-an"

Crowan: "CROW-an"

Kingdom of Goddeu: "Goth-thew"

Lailoken: "LIE-lo-kin" (*Nickname "LIE-el"*)

Languoreth: "Lang-GOR-eth"

Morken: "MOR-kin"

House of Tutgual

Angharad: "An-HA-rad"

Cyan: "KY-ann"

Elufed: "El-LEAF-ed"

Gladys: "GLA-diss"

Rhian: "REE-AH-n"

Rhydderch: "RU-therk"

Rhys: "REEse"

Tutgual: "TOOT-gee-al"

The Borderlands

Ceidio: "KAY-dee-OH"

Emrys: "EM-riss"

Gwenddolau: "GWEN-tho-lye"

Maelgwn: "MILE-gwinn"

Kingdom of Ebrauc

Eliffer: "El-LEAF-er"

Gwrgi: "Ga-WHERE-gi"

Peredur: "PEAR-REE-dur"

The Christians

Brother Telleyr: "TELL-er"

Brother Anguen: "AN-gew-en"

In the 1830s, a group of quarrymen discovered a body buried on a hilltop two miles east of Dunipace, Scotland. The skeleton had been laid to rest in an ancient coffin of unhewn stone. No weapons, jewelry, mirrors, or combs were found in the grave. The only accompanying artifact was a large earthenware vase, and inside it the decayed remains of parchment. A report was published in *The New Statistical Account of Scotland*, and the skeleton was removed so quarrying could continue.

The body, the coffin, and the earthenware vase have all since been lost.

Along with the parchment and whatever was written upon it.

I.

I have been a drop in the air.
I have been a shining star.
I have been a word in a book.
—"Cad Goddeu" ("The Battle of the Trees"),
translated by Robert Graves, *The White Goddess*

CHAPTER 1

Cadzow Fortress, Strathclyde
Land of the Britons
Late Winter, AD 550

I was dreaming of the forest. This time no rustle of wind, no bird-call, no sliver of light penetrated the thick canopy of trees. Silence thundered in my ears like a band of warhorses. And then, through the gloom, I heard my mother call my name, her voice soft and hollow-throated as a dove's.

Languoreth.

I woke with a start as my brother tugged back the covers and a rush of cold air met my feet. Lailoken's sandy hair was unkempt. He watched impatiently as I rubbed the sleep from my eyes and reached for my dress, but as I tugged the wool over my head, my mind quick-ened and the memory came rushing back.

Mother was dead.

Nine days had passed since the sickness took her. Sleep—when it came—brought some relief, but each morning when I woke, my wound tore open anew.

"I dreamt of her." I looked at my brother. "Mother was calling my name, I'm certain. If only I could have seen her . . ."

I waited a moment, hoping for a response, but Lailoken only frowned and handed me my cloak. The purple rings beneath his eyes told me he'd been up through the night again, seeking her spirit in the

Summerlands. For a moment, Lail looked envious I'd dreamt of her. But if my brother did not sleep, how could he dream?

"Tonight you must rest," I said. "There is sickness yet beyond Cadzow's walls."

Lail's face only darkened.

"Lailoken." I caught his sleeve. "Sooner or later you will have to speak."

He ignored me, reaching instead for the door's iron latch.

"You cannot force her to come to you," I said. "After all, the Wisdom Keepers say—"

Lail turned on his heel, his narrowed eyes unmistakable.

Don't be stupid—you're going to wake Crowan.

I bit my tongue. I didn't want to wake our nursemaid any more than he; Crowan would never allow us to go down to the river this time of morning. And though neither Lailoken nor I could explain it, we knew the beast waiting in the shallows waited for us alone. As though it were ours alone to see.

I followed Lailoken down the dark corridor, softening my footfalls as we crept past the entryway to the great room with its sleeping warriors and softly dying embers.

Yes, Mother was dead. Now our rambling timber hall felt like a husk without her.

I swallowed the stinging that rose in my throat and followed Lailoken out the heavy oaken door and into the milky morning light.

In the courtyard, mist swathed the late winter grasses. Past the fallow kitchen garden, Brant stood watch on the platform of the inner rampart, breath clouding beneath his hood. At the sound of our footsteps, his grip tightened on his spear before he caught sight of us and smiled.

"Ho, there, little cousins. And where do you suppose you're off to?"

"We're only going down to the river," I said.

Brant looked at Lailoken. "Still no good morning from you, eh, Lailoken?"

"He isn't speaking to anyone." I shifted my weight, and Brant's brown eyes softened.

"Right, then. Down to the river." He gestured us through. "But you two had better mind each other. The cliff trail is slick as a snake's belly."

"We'll be careful," I swore, but as we hurried through the gate, I made certain Lailoken felt my eyes on the back of his head. It was hurtful and foolish, his vigil of silence.

"Do you imagine you miss her more than I do?" I said. "You are not the only one who lost her, Lailoken. Mother's gone and we cannot bring her back."

My brother stiffened as he ducked beneath a low-hanging bough, but at the sound of hurt in my voice he glanced back, reaching for my hand.

An offering, an apology.

I joined my fingers with his and we wound our way along the forest path to the place where the towering outer rampart ended. At the cliff's edge, a deer trail stretched down hundreds of feet to the gorge below. A thick sponge of moss lined the narrow trail where the first tender shoots of fern budded from their peaty winter beds. We edged down the steep path toward the river, mud caking the leather lacing of our boots, and I breathed in the earthy smell that always brought relief. My mother had spent endless days in the forest with us, plucking mushrooms from fallen tree trunks, gathering blackberries and marshmallow and nettle, using the knife she kept at her belt to strip the bark from hazel and birch. Mother was the wife of a king. But she had also been a Wisdom Keeper, trained in the art of healing. It was the lady Idell our tenants visited for a tonic to ease their child's cough, a salve to slather on their horse's foot, or a remedy to ease the aches of old age. And it was by her side, in the woods, under our great roof of trees, that I felt most at home.

The river Avon glinted like liquid glass as we emerged at the cliff bottom. Stooping low, we moved softly through the underbrush until we neared the bank of the river and Lailoken squeezed my hand. We crouched at the water's edge, just out of sight, as I struggled to quiet my breathing.

The red stag was magnificent—nine points on each of his antlers. We watched the river course round his black hooves as he drank in the shallows, the graceful muscle working in his throat. It was strange to spot deer this late in winter, and stranger still to find one so close to our fort; most had been hunted into the deepest glades beyond Cadzow by now. Surely such a beast was wise to the ways of men. And yet, each morning since our mother's death, we had descended the steep banks of the gorge to find him standing in the current as if he, too, were keeping vigil.

Now the only sound was the soft gurgle of water over rock. Fog pillowed over the dark sheen of river and I opened my ears to the sounds of the stream, longing to hear the sweet strains of the melody my mother so often hummed while walking the woods.

Then, a movement flickered in the corner of my vision. I turned instinctually, looking upriver. At first I could make no sense of the shadowy form that appeared where nothing had stood a moment before. I blinked to clear my eyes. But there, in the water, rising out of the mist, stood a figure, her dark hair flowing over her simple green dress. If my fingers hadn't been stinging with cold, I would have been certain I was still dreaming.

Mother.

Her skin was no longer flushed by fever or marred by the blisters that had come. Her face was smooth and her lips wore a smile, but her gaze was unsettling; her eyes were wild and dark in the river's dim. I opened my mouth to cry out her name, but the stag bolted upright, nostrils flaring. I glanced back upriver, and my heart sank. My mother had vanished as quickly as she had come.

Or had she been there at all?

I balled my fists until my nails bit into the flesh of my palms. How could my eyes play such cruel tricks? There was nothing now but the soft wash of water. Only the great stag stood regarding us, his tawny pelt shimmering in the growing light of morning.

Of course I hadn't seen her. We had scattered her ashes high in the hills. But next to me Lailoken let out a puff of breath.

"It *was* her, wasn't it?" I turned to him. "You saw her, Lail, tell me! She was just there . . ."

Lailoken gave a tight nod. Because he was my twin, I could feel his tears before they began. I sank down onto the pebbled bank. My brother sank down beside me. And together we poured our grief into the slowly waking world.

We sat at the river's edge until our bodies grew stiff from cold and our sobs gave way to the sound of birds in the forest behind us. All the while the stag moved softly in the shallows. Perhaps tomorrow the beast would come no more—after all, it had been nine days. Cathan the Wisdom Keeper said nine was the most magical of numbers.

I was wiping my face with the corner of my cloak when Lail stiffened.

"What is it?" I asked.

He lifted a finger and gestured to the edge of the nearby thicket, where a brown hare was hunched beyond the brambles, its head tilted as if it were listening. Lail watched as it shivered its whiskers and scampered into the forest, his gaze following its trail. Then he turned to me, eyes rimmed red, and spoke the first words he'd uttered in days.

"A rider is coming. He brings news from the east."

A "Knowing," or so the Wisdom Keepers called them. At night, and even in waking, Lail told me, he dreamt of such things: salmon circling the bottom of a forest pool, or the speckled eggs of a faraway falcon's nest. It had been Lail who had woken from sleep that first morning after Mother died and heeded the call to the river. There he'd found the red stag standing in the shallows as if it were waiting. My brother had a gift for reading such signs from the Gods. We were only ten winters—Lailoken was young to have such skill. Yet Lail could not make sense of why the great deer had come. Even so, I could sense now that my brother's gift was growing. Messengers came often to Cadzow with news for our father, but never before had Lailoken foreseen one.

I shifted on the stones, straining to hear the sound of hoofbeats I knew were not yet approaching. A rider was coming—it was only a matter of when—and soon our nursemaid Crowan would wake to find our beds empty. I knew we should hurry, yet I could not take my eyes from the water.

"Was that truly Mother we saw?" I asked. "Is that what it's like when you see someone from Spirit?"

"Don't know." Lailoken squinted. "I've never seen a spirit before."

"She looked just as real as anyone. Do you think if we stayed . . . we might see her again?"

Lail's blue eyes trailed to the water almost hopefully. But then he shook his head and wiped his nose on the back of his hand. I felt the small stab as he shut me out again and looked to the cliff top, where a yolky sun was filtering through the forest. The spell of dawn had broken. In the current, the stag shifted and meandered toward the opposite bank. I wanted to rest my head on his smooth flanks, make my mother reappear so she could chase away the emptiness. But we moved instead to climb the trail, turning our backs on the water.

As we reached the little gully where our mother had so often sat by our side, I heard the echo of her voice rising up from the depths of my longing. She had called out my name in the darkness of my dream. But her voice had not been tender or full of love.

Her voice had been full of warning.

CHAPTER 2

W e'd lingered too long by the river, and our nursemaid Crowan had worked herself into a state over the sight of our empty beds.

"Just where have you been? And in your cloaks, I see! On such a cold morning as this, with marauding men about? Haven't you a care for old Crowan's heart? In with you now, lest your father catch sight of you."

She ushered us into the warmth of the hall and toward our chambers, all the while mumbling, "*Keep 'em safe, Crowan, and let no harm come to 'em.* Hmph. Not so easy with these two rascals roaming the wilds."

Lail regarded her mutely. Even in the depths of his grief I knew Crowan's ceaseless ministrations rankled him no end. But what was Crowan to do? She'd tended us since we were babes, and our father before us. I looked at her as she planted her small feet, arms crossed over her bony chest.

"And well? Will you tell me where you've been, or don't I deserve an answer at all?" Her tidy gray hair had escaped in wiry strands from her plait, and her little hazel eyes were clouded with worry.

"Don't be cross," I said. "We were only down at the river, Crowan. Nine mornings in a row we've spotted him—a great stag—and he doesn't flee at all!"

Lail shot me a look for betraying our secret.

"Nine mornings you've been down to the river, sneaking from bed without me waking?" Crowan threw up her hands, but the rebuke faded from her tongue.

"I suppose your mother loved them woods, didn't she?" She softened and gathered us close. I inhaled the smell of peat smoke and pine that always clung to her rough woolen smock.

"Gods know, the beauty left this house when she took her last breath," she said. "But you must be careful. There's talk of evil men roaming this land. Things aren't what they once was. Swear to me you'll not sneak away again. I couldn'a bear it if something ill were to happen to you. Swear it, now."

Lailoken leaned into her but did not reply.

"We swear it, Crowan," I said. Better me than Lailoken. If my brother didn't speak it, it couldn't hold him, and who knew where his wanderings might lead?

Lail gave me a nod of thanks as Crowan hurried us down the corridor to ready us for breakfast.

In my chamber before the bronze mirror, I watched as Crowan worked to comb and re-plait my long, wavy hair. Father swore she would outlive us all, but her wrinkled face looked worn now, her skin as thin as parchment.

"Crowan." I stilled her hands.

"Yes, dove?"

"Do you believe that when we die, we truly go to the Summerlands?"

Her eyes searched mine in the reflection. "Aye. Don't you believe it?"

I glanced away. There was a time when our warriors boasted of the bottomless horns of ale they'd drink in the land of the Gods, the fair women they'd bed, the riches they'd have. Once we were a people who held no fear of death. But that was before the Romans came. Before our warriors were cut down and our fields watered with blood.

Cathan—Father's counsellor—had taught us the histories. How the Romans had slain entire villages, entire tribes, men, women, and children alike falling to the sword. They outlawed our Wisdom Keepers and put them to slaughter. Those who survived were sent to work in the mines. They set fire to our fields and then sowed them with salt.

They created a wasteland and called it peace, Cathan had said.

Now our warriors watched warily from our high hills and fortresses.

Did I believe in Summerlands when such things could happen? Did I dare believe a world of spirits and Gods could be real at all?

"I want to believe," I said at last.

"Well. I'll tell you what I know." Crowan smiled. "The Ancestors keep their vigil at the edge of the worlds, waitin' to bring their children home. It was them that taught us the plants that heal, the fire that burns, how to work our metal, and how to keep our stories. It was them that could shift their shapes to any animal of the forest in the blink of an eye." She sighed and pressed her face beside mine in the mirror.

"Such times are hard on all of us, and on none harder than the young. But you're the lady of this hall now. Gods be true, you'll make your mother proud." Crowan straightened, and her hands resumed their work.

"I'll tell you what else I know. Your mother lived well on this land. She was kind and generous, always tending to the people. The Ancestors wouldn'a miss guiding her home. The lady Idell suffers no more. I can promise you that."

I nodded, but I couldn't keep my eyes from welling at the mention of my mother.

Nor at the memory of her standing knee-deep in the half-frozen river, pale and silent, like a stranger.

Like a ghost.

• • •

Father's chair sat empty at breakfast. The servants had set out plates with salt pork and cheese, warm bread and fresh-churned butter. Lail and I ate dutifully before pushing back our chairs to find Cathan beyond the courtyard. The Wisdom Keeper's hut sat just inside the inner rampart, beside a thorn tree and a small stand of crab apple. When Cathan and my father weren't traveling to collect the food rents or summoned to the capital by the high king, Tutgual, we visited Cathan daily for instruction. Smoke emanated from the thatching of the little hut, telling me he'd just thrown a fresh block of peat on the hearth. I pushed open the door to find the coverlet pulled neatly over his bed, the usual clutter of fossils and parchment cleared from the table in anticipation of our visit. Cathan was seated on the floor in silence, his white sleeves pushed up past his elbows and hands clasped in his lap.

I'd been frightened of Cathan as a babe, difficult as it might be to remember now. He was a sturdy man, tall, and must have seemed towering as a standing stone in his billowy white robe and stormy wilderness of hair. His blue eyes were clear as a forest pool and as chilly, too, until some fair humor struck him—for as stern as he might appear, Cathan the Wisdom Keeper was quick to laugh.

The floor creaked beneath our feet and Cathan opened his eyes. Standing slowly on stiff legs, he assessed us.

"No sleep, I see. At least, not for you," he said, gesturing at Lail. Lail shrugged as we took our seats on the little bench beside the hearth.

"And you, Languoreth? How do you fare?"

The tenderness in his voice summoned the swift sting of tears, and I bit my lip against the wave that threatened to drown me.

"Eh, now?" Cathan bent, clasping his weathered hand in mine. "There, there. No sense in battling tears. We all weep. Sometimes it's best to let them fall."

I blinked their hotness onto my cheeks, and Cathan sighed and straightened, looking at the two of us.

"It is good we are here." He bowed his head. "The lady Idell would not want you to miss any more instruction." The Wisdom Keeper's eyes trailed out the unshuttered window, where our shaggy white cattle were roaming the bleak winter pastures of Cadzow, the fields sprawling hay-colored against a smoky morning sky.

"Death is no easy thing," Cathan said. "There is always the missing. But the dead never leave us. Lady Idell watches over us all. Someday you shall understand the truth of what I mean."

I wanted to tell Cathan what we'd seen, to ask him why Mother had looked as she did and what she might have to do with the great stag; but Lailoken was watching, and he fixed me with a hard look. Why didn't Lail wish me to speak of it? It was Cathan who was teaching Lailoken all he knew of augury. Signs and omens in nature, messages that came from the spirits of the woods.

Besides, no good ever came from keeping secrets from Cathan.

Cathan, unnoticing, only flexed his fingers, clearing his throat.

"So. Today we shall learn about the laws that govern our people. Why must we have laws?"

I fought to still my racing mind as his instruction began.

"Why must we have laws?" he echoed. "It is a rhetorical question. To attempt any organized society without them would be an exercise in futility. Laws do not simply dictate right from wrong. They provide measures of balance. In this way, laws are not only laws, they are Spirit. Laws become our guardians. They help men and women keep the course between right and wrong when they cannot do so themselves. A law broken results in a punishment, most often payment—the aim of which is to encourage correct action in the future."

"But what about raiding?" Lailoken asked. "If raiding cattle is stealing from others, why are no fines paid by warriors or kings?" My brother thrived on instruction, and it cheered me a little to hear him sounding more like himself.

"Because when raiding's done right, it's all in good sport. Proper kings don't go to war over stolen cattle!" Cathan grinned. "They learn instead to guard them better the next time. It is when the laws built to protect men and women are broken that raiding turns to war. Lords and chieftains take their revenge. Blood feuds begin. Always a messy business." He waved his hand dismissively.

"But how can laws be Spirit, you may wonder?" he continued. "Well. Our laws were divined by the Wisdom Keepers from the earliest of days. In keeping to the law, we are obeying instructions on how people should walk the earth, sent from the highest authority—that of the All Knowing, the forces we call Gods. Laws prevent bloodshed. They provide care for the sick. They bind a warrior to his king. And they keep a king close to his gods."

A gust of frosty air blew in through the open window, meant to keep us alert, but I leaned closer to the hearth as it crackled and spit, warming my back. Cathan's deep voice soothed as he went on about the fines owed—for land disputes, failure to contribute goods for rents, mistreatment of a tenant farmer or a wife, and, worst of all, murder. Perhaps Cathan was right. Even in the pit of our sadness, there was room for instruction. Some thought it tedious, but Lailoken and I had a mind for it. After all, our father was a petty king, one of the thirteen kings in the north. As his children, we were expected to commit such laws to memory.

The overseeing of our laws fell to our council of jurists: Wisdom Keepers, the most respected of whom were chosen to uphold them. Cathan, in our kingdom, was such a man, though he was an expert, too, in philosophy, augury, star knowledge, and the wonders of the earth. It was Cathan who'd noticed the pair of sparrows beating their wings outside my mother's window in the days before our birth. It was he who foretold the twins that shared her womb.

"The Gods are watching," he'd said. "There will be two, and there is magic in them."

Magic . . .

There were tales of Wisdom Keepers from long ago who could call forth a tempest from the bluest of skies, or lay a curse upon a man with a murmur of breath. But this was the stuff of Midwinter tales. If there was any magic in us, it dwelled in my brother. This was why he'd been chosen by Cathan to train as a Keeper. When I dreamt, I dreamt only of the forest. It was the place I loved best, so why should I question it? I could not shift the weather or foresee events. I was no message taker between our land and the land of our gods, and I was thankful for it.

Until now. There was a gnawing in my chest I'd never felt before. First the dream, and then the shock of seeing my mother, no longer living and yet so real I could almost touch the strands of her dark, silky hair. If I had rushed into the wintry freeze of the river, could I have wrapped my arms around her and tethered her to the earth?

Over and over I heard her voice, and her warning.

Suddenly a rap on the door sounded, and Cathan looked up, smoothing his robes in annoyance. "Why is it they *insist* on interrupting?"

My cheeks flushed as I realized I hadn't been listening for quite some time.

"Enter," Cathan sighed.

"Your pardon, Master Cathan"—my father's man bowed—"but a rider has come."

Lailoken's eyes caught mine.

"Yes, yes. We all heard the horn, didn't we?" Cathan said. Truth be told, Cathan became so enraptured in lessons that he would scarcely have noticed if the building caught flame. But he nodded to our guard nonetheless, motioning for us to follow.

"Come on, then. I suppose we shall have to continue our lesson later." He bent to collect his leather satchel, grumbling somewhat mockingly, "A *rider has come*."

Lailoken ducked through the door, but not before Cathan fixed him with a shrewd gaze, giving his head a playful swat.

"Couldn't have warned me, eh, Lailoken?"

Father stood in the courtyard in the same woolen tunic he'd been wearing for days, his beard sprouting down his neck and his wavy auburn hair hanging about his shoulders. My father was a warrior first and a king second, but my mother had always minded he dress in the robes befitting a lord. Now he was beginning to look as wild as a Pict. Still, his brown eyes brightened at the sight of us. The weak afternoon sun did little to warm the air, and I leaned into the bulk of him as he drew me close, hungry for his warmth. The Song Keepers sang that my father's clan was descended from giants. He stood a full three heads taller than most men, and broader, too, which had only made my mother—slight and small-boned—appear more like a bird. Would that I were half as graceful as she was. Instead, my limbs had grown lanky alongside my brother's. I had taken to slouching so I might not appear so tall. Now as the sound of hoofbeats came closer, I stood straight—for her—as the guards shouted something I could not hear.

Father scanned the courtyard and realized someone was missing.

"Gwenddolau!" he called.

A moment passed and my foster brother appeared in the courtyard, out of breath and running with sweat, his beloved falcon still tethered to his arm. Our cousin Brodyn, Brant's younger brother, jogged easily by Gwenddolau's side.

"She nearly caught an otter," Gwenddolau said, stroking his bird, but where there might have been joy his voice fell flat. He pushed his golden hair from his face. "Apologies, Father. We came as soon as we heard the horn."

"And just in time," Father said, but not unkindly.

Gwenddolau and Brodyn had been falconing again. It seemed all Gwenddolau did these days was hunt with his falcon or swing his sword, as if he could beat back Mother's death with the quarries of his bird or the hacking of his blade.

I'd heard Mother tell Gwenddolau that he, too, was her own. Fostering might be a tradition meant to strengthen alliances between families, but Gwenddolau was as much a brother to me as Lailoken was. He taught me to catch and carry his bird; he taught Lail to grip his first sword. He pointed out wolf tracks in the forest and the best fishing holes for trout. Even though he was fourteen winters, he still took time to play with us. Gwenddolau's falcon shifted her wings, smoothing her brown feathers, and he came to stand at my side, his eyes fixed anxiously on the tall courtyard gate. I hadn't even thought of it. What if this rider bore ill news of Gwenddolau's father? After all, Ceidio was at war. Ceidio had been rightful king in the eastern lands of Ebruac before he was betrayed by his brother and forced into exile.

Now Gwenddolau's uncle ruled, and Father said his name as if it had a bitter taste.

Eliffer.

The timber gate groaned on its hinges and issued a rider into the courtyard, his cloak caked in dirt and the flanks of his horse frothing with sweat. He swung easily from the saddle, passing his horse off to our groom, and a fragment of light caught the brooch pinned at his chest. A noble stag gleamed from a thicket of silver interlace. Brant and Brodyn wore the same: a mark of fealty sworn to my father, a talisman that gave proof of King Morken's protection.

Father strode forward to clasp the messenger's arm.

"Oren, you are most welcome. Come. Dust yourself off and come into the warm."

"Morken, King," Oren gripped his arm in return. "I was sorry to hear news of our lady Idell."

"I thank you," Father said, glancing away. "Please. Come inside."

Oren bowed to Cathan and unfastened his muddy cloak to follow us through the courtyard.

Even if Oren bore no ill news of Gwenddolau's father on this day, it would be only a matter of time before Gwenddolau left us. He'd been sent to my father to be raised up out of harm's way, and next summer he would turn fifteen—when a boy became a man. Though Gwenddolau loved us, he was the rightful heir to a fiefdom and his father had been wronged. When the time came, Gwenddolau would ride off to make war. He had many reasons, it seemed, to hack with his sword.

Inside Cadzow Fortress the oil lamps had been lit and the high beams and dark timber walls flickered with light. Lailoken and I took our seats at the end of the sprawling table, where we were meant to watch but not speak, as Father raised his hand, signaling for ale to be brought. Oren drank deeply, but there was an air of impatience about him that left my stomach twisting beneath my ribs. Cathan drummed the pads of his fingers on the table, his blue eyes dark.

"What news, then?" Father asked. "You arrived in much haste."

"Yes, my king. I rode out as soon as I heard. There has been an uprising. Ida the Angle has taken Vortigern's kingdom."

Father slammed his fist on his chair, and I jumped. "Vortigern, the fool! To invite them behind his ramparts, give them silver to protect his kingdom. To bed that bastard Ida's daughter. Brutish men. Landless," he shouted. "Happy to settle on even the most unfit plot of soil and so gain a foothold in our country."

"And so it would seem they have gained much more than a foothold now," Cathan stood. "Had we not foretold this? Consumed by greed, controlled by fear. It was a deafened ear Vortigern turned to our warning."

"I fear no amount of prophecy will aid us now," Father said. "The old ways are lost to him. He cares only for women, riches, and his own sallow hide." He turned to the messenger. "Tell me, Oren. What is the state of things?"

"Vortigern has left Bryneich and retreated to his fortification on the Liddel Water that lies heavily guarded. His people were left to fend for themselves. Angle warriors swarmed the land, burning houses and watchtowers, rendering villages to ash. Vortigern's lords have fled from their lands—some go to Gaul, others seek shelter in Partick, or King Tutgual's fortress at Clyde Rock. In their wake these Angles leave nothing but fire. Pooled blood and body parts. Women and young children are cut down by the sword. Babies, even, are dashed against rocks."

I shrank in my seat and Father stiffened, inclining his head toward us.

"Apologies"—Oren dipped his head—"but I mean to say they do not spare a single innocent. People flee. Some, being taken in the mountains, are murdered in great numbers. Those seeking shelter at Vortigern's fortress are turned away. Without warmth or livestock, they are left to freeze. To starve."

"Vortigern hides behind his walls whilst his countrymen are slaughtered," Father said. His gaze flicked to Gwenddolau and back. "Tell me. What path have the Angles sought?"

"From Vortigern's fortress at Bryneich straight through the Borderlands, 'til they wet their boots in the western sea," Oren said.

A shadow fell across Gwenddolau's face. His father, Ceidio, had taken refuge in the Borders.

"Our countryside is yet filled with fierce men who are ready to fight." Father cast Gwenddolau a steadying look. "My friend Ceidio is such a one."

"It seems that is so," Oren said, his voice taking on a new tone, one of excitement, perhaps even belief. "Even now, I hear tales of such brave men who have gathered in the wild places. They wait in the glades, caves, and by the coast, eating no more than sea kelp and shivering in the damp. They wait for a worthier man to lead them."

My heart skittered in my chest to hear it. Lailoken stood.

"Can we not ride out to challenge them, Father?"

"Do not be in such a rush to claim your glory, Lailoken." Father turned to him, tapped a finger upon the thick white scar that marked him from temple to chin. "Such scars of war may come. But for now a king of the north cowers in hiding. His son and lords have fled. The Angles raid the countryside in much greater numbers than our own. This is not yet our war. You will have many battles yet to fight without luring the enemy to our door."

Lail sank back in his chair with a frown.

"And what of King Ceidio?" Father asked. "Is there any news of our friend?"

Oren looked to my foster brother. "I am sorry. I have heard nothing of your father's whereabouts."

"We will have news; give it time." Father gripped Gwenddolau's shoulder. "Ceidio is a sound warrior with good men yet by his side."

"Tutgual will call a Gathering. We must prepare our belongings," Cathan said, then turned to Oren. "You say there are yet men who lie in wait for a leader. Is there talk of such a man?"

"There is talk of a man called Emrys," Oren said. "They say he is a shrewd man, and battle hard. His people are Sarmatian; they came with the Romans. For five generations since, his family has guarded the Wall. Warriors all."

"A Dragon Warrior," Cathan observed. "If any can hope to press back the Angles, it is he."

Dragon Warrior. I mouthed the words at Lailoken, my eyes wide. Cathan had told us of the Sarmatians. They fought in scaled armor and hailed from the far East, the frostbitten lands of grass. Their standard was that of a great dragon that made furious shrieking sounds when it met with the wind, causing their enemies to pee in their britches.

They, too, had once fought the Romans. When they, too, were defeated, they were shipped over the broad sea to guard the Wall built by the wicked emperor Hadrian. The Sarmatians were paid handsomely to keep us wild Britons, Picts, and Westmen at bay.

"His forefathers may be Sarmatian," Oren said, "But he is a Briton, a man of the Wall through and through. They call him *Pen Dragon*."

"Head Dragon, indeed." Cathan looked pleased.

"But he is lowborn." Father turned to his counsellor. "You know as well as I the lords and high chieftains will never follow him."

Cathan smoothed his white sleeves and strode to the hearth, his gaze settling on the crackling flames.

"We shall see, Morken, my old friend. In times such as these, when the people need a hero, so are such heroes made."

CHAPTER 3

I woke to the nicker of horses in the courtyard, Father's voice coming muffled through the thick timber walls.

"Aye, Herrick. Load it on the cart."

I heard the unmistakable scrape and thunk of Father's heavy wooden trunk and bolted upright. Yanking my boots over bare feet, I wrapped my cloak over my shift and rushed out into the dull gray morning. A gloomy gust of wind assailed me as I rubbed my eyes to take in the flurry of activity. Beside the naked branches of the apple tree, Father's chestnut stallion stood sleepily next to Cathan's mottled gray. Macon, our groom, was leading Gwenddolau's mount along the narrow dirt path that led from the stables.

"My lady." Our servant Herrick gave me a nod, the corded muscles of his back straining as he worked to angle my father's trunk past two others in the cart and secure them with rope.

At the sight of me Father straightened, dropping his hands from the girth buckle. "Languoreth."

He'd trimmed the wiry cinnamon hairs of his beard and was clad in his fur-lined traveling cloak. His thick golden torque gleamed heavy at the hollow of his throat.

"Where are you going?" I asked, my boots clomping as I crossed the wet grass.

"Tutgual King has called for a Gathering of the kings and lords of Strathclyde. It is as we thought. I must leave this very morning for Partick," he said.

Days ago I'd lost my mother. Now my father was being called away?

Father shook his head. "You look at me as if I were going to leave without saying farewell! Come now. It'll be a fortnight, maybe less."

I stared at him, gutless, and he bent, leveling his brown eyes on mine.

"Daughter. What would you have me do? Ignore the summons of our high king in the capital? You know I must go."

I looked frantically round the courtyard. "Then you must leave Cathan with us, or Gwenddolau!"

"Cathan is not only my counsellor and your tutor, Languoreth. He is also head Wisdom Keeper of Strathclyde and lord of the White Isle. He can no more ignore such a summons than I. And Gwenddolau is nearly a man. He will soon need to make his own way among these courts. You will be in trusted care. Brant and Brodyn will stay."

"No. I want to go with you," I said. "Take me to Partick."

"Languoreth. You are far too young, and the roads now are far too dangerous."

I didn't believe him: there could be nothing so dangerous between here and such a place. Partick was shining and ripe, a capital full of sweet orchards where all the nobles kept residences. Gwenddolau had told me of shops there laden with pottery from Gaul, the vendors selling herbed olives and exotic spices, their carts full to bursting with creamy cheeses, perfumes, and incense that had journeyed all the way across the ocean, up the glittering expanse of the river Clyde. I longed for Partick and yet I did not know which I wanted: to travel with Father or to keep him from leaving.

Foundering, I searched until I found it, the thing I knew would stay him.

"But Mother is dead. It has only been days! Would you so soon forget her?"

As soon as I said the words, I wanted to swallow them.

"Still your mouth, child." Father's dark eyes pinned me, his hands curled involuntarily into fists. He had never struck me, but if he did now, I might have earned it.

"With every fiber of my body I grieve for your mother," he said. "But I am a king, chief of Goddeu. Even now, Picts and Westmen creep their boats up our stretch of river in search of weakness. They lurk round my borders eyeing my cattle and grain, the very wealth we depend on. Even now, the Angles march, burning and slaying as they make their way back toward Bryneich. The blood of my father and all four of my brothers has soaked this land. I will not forsake them. You think I am the only man to lose a wife? Death is no excuse for any man. Least of all a king."

I flushed. A long moment passed before Father straightened and sighed, rubbing the bridge of his nose.

"Languoreth, I assure you. You will have plenty of time in Partick once you're fully grown."

Father moved to take my hand but I yanked it from reach, narrowing my eyes instead. "Gods know where you got your temper." He glowered as he bent to yank his horse's girth.

"Likely the same place she got her fiery hair." Cathan appeared from the kitchens clasping a hunk of bread stuffed with strips of beef that he used to gesture vaguely in Father's direction. A send-off from our cook, Agnes, no doubt. She was forever stuffing Cathan with food.

Father shot him a grim look and smoothed a hand over his head, where thick strands of auburn yet battled the gray.

"You must be easy on her," Cathan said, striding across the courtyard. "It takes practice to get used to farewells, but with leadership comes obligation." He turned to me. "Languoreth knows this. Do you not?"

My nod was reluctant.

Father bent to me once more, his eyes searching mine. "I will return, you have nothing to fear. I've got ten men-at-arms accompanying me to Partick. I swear to you, all will be well."

He pulled his cloak more closely about his shoulders and extended his heavy silver brooch to me. "Here. Be a kind daughter and help your father fasten his cloak."

I took the metal halfheartedly, pushing the thick pin through the fabric to secure it at his breast, and he smiled. "I nearly forgot. I've got something for you. A gift."

Reaching into the folds of his cloak he pulled out a leather packet with a flourish like a traveling magician. It was heavy and wrapped in buttery calfskin. A weapon, I was sure of it. Too small to be a sword. And yet the weight of it felt substantial in my hands. I touched the cord that bound it.

"Go ahead. Open it."

Slowly, I tugged the cord, and the folded leather fell open to reveal the thick golden handle of a knife. I drew the weapon from its intricately tooled leather sheath to examine it more fully. How could something so beautiful be functional? The handle was decorated with delicate threads of interlacing. Amber, amethysts, and rubies were fashioned into the glittering scales of a fierce and magnificent serpent. His tail curled around the handle's tip and the strong iron blade emerged from his gaping mouth, a cold and slicing sort of fire.

The sight of it left me speechless.

"I have seen you watching your brother and Gwenddolau train at their weapons," Father said. "There is no reason you shouldn't learn the skill of it. You are, after all, the daughter of a warrior."

Cathan leaned in to admire the knife. "A strong and beautiful weapon," he said. "Fit for a queen."

A weapon of my own. Despite my sadness, my heart became a feathered thing, testing its wings in the cage of my chest. I had been

wanting this—oh, how I'd been wanting this. It had been decades—
no, centuries—since women were privileged to train in weapons.
Now, at last, I had my chance. I traced my fingers over the glittering
scales in disbelief.

"This is mine?"

"Yes."

"And I may learn how to wield it?"

"Well, that was my hope. It's otherwise a rather dangerous gift to
give a child, wouldn't you agree?" Father's smiled broadened. "Your
brother's gone off with Brant and Brodyn to do their weapon work. If
you hurry, you might begin right now."

"Truly?"

"Truly."

I folded the knife into the pocket of my cloak and reached to place
my hands on either side of his bearded face. "Thank you, Father."

The corners of his eyes crinkled in the way they did when he was
truly happy. "Wield it well, little one. I'll soon be home to see your use
of it. May the Gods keep you."

"May the Gods keep you," I echoed, praying it might be true.

He hoisted me up and kissed me, then handed me to Cathan.
"Cathan. Say good-bye to our warrior princess."

Cathan groaned at the weight of me. I breathed in the deep scent
of incense as he held me against his cloak. "Tell your brother to mind
what you say, eh? We all know who's the wiser."

Voices sounded from the direction of the stables, and as Cathan
set me down, I looked up to see Gwenddolau coming through the
courtyard, my father's men close behind. His heavy green cloak made
him look like a forest spirit, but his eyes were shadows. No news yet
of his father.

I reached for him and he ducked beneath the haggard fingers of the
apple tree to embrace me.

"Hey now, little one. Don't be so sad. We'll be home before you know it." He gave a small smile and swung onto his horse. "I'm leaving my bird in your care. Take good care of her, will you?"

I looked up at him, so handsome and noble upon his mare. "I want to go with you," I said, my voice small.

Gwenddolau rested his callused hand on my head.

"Your place is here at Cadzow just now. Do not be in such a hurry to grow up, Languoreth. Before you know it, you'll be fifteen, and these times will be like a gust of wind. One moment through the trees, and the next, forever gone."

His light eyes were sad. I wasn't sure how to answer, or if I was even meant to. I climbed the rain-slick ladder of the guard tower instead and watched as they rode out, until the far gate was bolted behind them. In the quiet that descended I let out a breath. But the sinking feeling was buoyed by the weight of the new gift in my pocket. Scrambling back down the ladder, I found Crowan waiting in the courtyard, a heavy shawl wrapped tight round her little frame.

"I'll not be the one to say it, not me, but it don't seem fitting, giving a young lady a knife."

I gripped the cold metal protectively, the way a sillier girl might hold a doll.

"Oh, go ahead, then," she said. "Go and find your brother. But mind you don't run with that evil blade unsheathed! And, for the sake of the Gods, put some clothes on you first! Is that a shift I spy under that cloak?"

"I'll dress," I promised, and ran from the courtyard before she could change her mind.

I found the men by the stables. Brodyn was leaning against the barn with an easy grace, his long brown hair tied back and legs clad in training leathers, watching his older brother, Brant, parry the swift clash of Lail's sword. Brant was short and slightly stocky, whereas Brodyn was lean. But what my cousin Brant lacked in height, he'd gained in brawn and in his sense of command. Brant was serious, while Brodyn was forever jesting. Both brothers—with their dark hair and acorn-colored eyes—were as gifted with weaponry as they were in their looks, as the young maids of Cadzow would readily agree.

I watched Lailoken's feet move in their rhythm of attack like the steps of a dance, his sandy brows knit in concentration. My brother moved with such ease now. I'd tugged on a tunic and a pair of Lailoken's trousers, the ones I always borrowed for tromping the woods and mucking round by the river—the ones I wore when I most wished I belonged in the world of men.

I observed them sparring until Brant sensed me standing behind him and lifted his hands in surrender. "Peace, Lailoken, peace. Your sister has arrived."

Lail lowered his blade and turned to me. "Father's given you the knife!"

Brant smiled. "I thought he might."

"It was *I* who thought he might." Brodyn unfolded his arms and pushed his tall frame from the barn wall. "I told you it would be this morning."

Brant swung at his brother as Lail jogged to greet me. "You must be happy, sister. May I see it?"

My face burned with pride as I extended the knife and Lail drew it from the sheath.

"It belonged to a Westman king." Brant leaned in to admire it. "He made a run last summer at Clyde Rock. Do you remember, Languoreth? He met with Morken's sword. Bad luck, really, raiding during a feast."

"Bad luck raiding when *we* were there, I say," Brodyn scoffed. "Eight boats of hairy Westmen against the likes of us? We made such quick work of them; old Tutgual's soldiers had scarcely made it down to the water by the time we were through."

Brant looked wearily at his brother. "There's a braggart, and there's you. Did our father teach you nothing about humility?"

"Did our father teach you nothing about pride in one's accomplishments?" Brodyn countered. "We've still got it around here somewhere if you want to see it. The Westman's head, I mean." Brodyn grinned. "Cedar oil. It's an age-old trick. Does a beautiful job preserving."

"No, thank you," I said too quickly.

"Ah, no matter." Brodyn clapped me on the shoulder. "We'll build a warrior's stomach in you yet."

"Come on then," Brant said, a smile playing at his lips. "Our little cousin is wanting to wield her weapon, no doubt."

"Right. Our wee Languoreth. Let's see what you can do." Brodyn yanked Lail down beside him in the dead winter grass. I took a breath and tucked my thick braid into the collar of Lail's tunic.

"Firstly," Brant said, "do not stand front-wise to me. Turn your body like this."

He angled his torso and staggered his legs. "You leave your enemy too many opportunities. That's better. And keep your weapon out of my reach." Before I could blink, Brant's ironlike grip had locked on my wrist and squeezed, causing me to cry out in pain and drop my knife.

Shocked, I rubbed my wrist and waited for an apology that did not come. Instead he tucked his toe under the fallen blade and, with a flick of his foot, lofted it, catching it swiftly in hand.

"If you think a Westman or a Pict would be any kinder, you are mistaken. Now try again," he said, returning the knife.

The next time Brant made a grab for my wrist, I shrank away just in time. He nearly stumbled forward in surprise.

"And never let your guard down with a girl of ten winters, eh, brother?" Brodyn called out.

"I'll thank you to shut your trap whilst we're training," Brant said, fixing his eyes on me. "Now attack."

My cousins had fashioned a thick wax covering for the tip of my blade so I'd be able to parry and thrust with no risk of injury. I think they'd intended I not cut myself, but after a few close encounters with the hollow of his neck, Brant's dark eyes lit, surprised.

"How about that: she knows to go for the neck! Brodyn?" he called.

"Yes, brother?"

"I'm glad you cast the wax so thickly."

I beamed in the warmth of their praise. *This is what I was built for,* I thought, as I reveled in the chill of the winter air on my face and the stretch and spring of my limbs as they moved in the foreign rhythms of defense and attack.

After some time had passed, Brodyn stood, stretching. "Come, brother, give way. She's clearly got talent. Let the girl benefit from a more experienced instructor."

Brant shook his head but sank down beside Lail in the grass while Brodyn showed me how to jab, how to slice, and the places on the body most impacted by a wound from a smaller blade: the neck, the thigh, the stomach. All the while Lail watched, a distinctly proud look on his face.

I could have stayed practicing all day had the rain not begun to come down, soaking us to the bone in a matter of moments, the wet causing the knife to go slick in my hand.

"That's enough now," Brant said as he shielded his eyes from the onslaught of water. "Come, Languoreth. It's time for midday." The shivering overtook me and I let them draw me away.

Brodyn draped his arm over my shoulder as we made our way back to the hall. "It seems, Lailoken, that you are not the only one gifted with the warrior's way."

But my brother did not return his smile. "I would be proud to have my sister battle at my side. I think, someday, she shall, in whatever way she can."

• • •

The brothers shook rain from their heads and leaned their weapons against the wall in the great room, oblivious to the weight of Crowan's disapproving glare as she nudged Lail and me onto the wooden bench and tucked a thick wool blanket round each of us. The fire blazed hot as the summer sun, and I breathed in the bright smell of rosemary rising in wisps of steam from the heaping bowl of mutton before me. The four of us fell upon our midday meal as if we hadn't eaten in weeks.

I had just devoured my second helping of stew and was sopping the extra gravy with a hunk of bread when shouting erupted over the steady pounding of the rain.

Brodyn shot up, nearly knocking over our bench. "Someone's at the gate."

"Go," Brant said. "I'll stay with the children."

"*Children?*" Lail scoffed.

"You *are* children," Brant said. "And you'll mind what I say."

In one swift motion, Brodyn lifted his spear from the wall and took off running into the rain. I watched a shift come over Brant. I'd seen it before, when Father gathered his men in the courtyard before riding off to raid. The sparkle in Brant's dark eyes drained away and his body tensed, as if something inside him had coiled like a snake. He positioned himself between us and the door, hand on the hilt of his sword, ready to strike.

"It might be the Angles," Lail said without a trace of fear in his voice.

My mouth went dry. It was winter. My father could raise an army of two hundred, but the bulk of them were tenant farmers, home now with their families. Of the small retinue we kept on through winter, ten had traveled with my father to Partick. That left ten guarding the storehouses down by the river and only ten who remained here.

If the Angles had come, there would be no saving any of us.

As if reading my thoughts, Lail stood and yanked his sword from its baldric. "I can fight."

"Stay back, Lailoken," Brant said, his voice low.

"I can fight," he insisted.

"You will not."

"Sweet Gods, Lail, do as he says!" I shouted.

"Let them come," Lail said. "I *will* protect you."

Brant's jaw clenched, but he let my brother stay.

I gripped the handle of my new knife, struggling to calm myself. Moments stretched. The tension in the room pulled taut as an archer's string. I strained my ears, listening until I could hear my own blood racing. And then a series of shouts sounded from the courtyard. The heavy slap of footsteps came thundering down the corridor. Brant lifted his sword, his eyes set on the door; but when it thrust open, only Brodyn appeared, his dark hair wet as an otter's pelt.

"Sweet Gods, brother, I nearly took off your head!" Brant cursed.

Brodyn made no apology, rushing forward to murmur something low in his brother's ear.

"What?" Lail demanded. "Who is it?"

Whatever Brodyn had said, it made Brant's face fall. He blinked a moment, then nodded to his brother. "Let them in."

Brodyn retreated quickly into the damp and I heard his deep voice call for the gates to open.

Our cousin swept his dark eyes over us, deciding something.

"Come, Lailoken, Languoreth," Brant said. "We will need your help. You must come right away."

CHAPTER 4

At first it seemed as though the rain must have turned to waves and we were now lost in an ocean. How else could I explain the swarm of bodies that washed through our gates, tumbling into the courtyard like piles of rotting fish? Rotting, for that was the smell that assaulted our noses, causing Brant, Brodyn, and the rest of my father's men to clamp their wet wool to their faces even as they ran to help the wounded through the yawning timber doors. Men, women, children, victims of the Angles. How far they had traveled, I could not say, but they looked half-starved, their travel-worn clothing stuck like paste to rain-drenched limbs.

They rushed toward the hall with hollow eyes and jerking movements, like corpses brought back from the dead. They rushed toward the hall until the courtyard became a waking nightmare, with wounds that glistened dark and slick like eels in the pelting storm.

I heard someone cry out, "Merciful Gods!"

And then Crowan and our man Herrick ran from the kitchens, blinking against the streams of rain coming from the sky. "Quickly! Get them into the stables; get them into the warm!" Crowan shouted.

Brant nodded at Lail. Did he want to take command? Lailoken reached out a hand as if to steady himself before gesturing to Herrick.

"Herrick. Help Macon bed clean straw in the barn. We'll treat the wounded there. Any remaining will take refuge in the hall."

How could my twin be so clearheaded when my vision was coming in flashes?

The weeping split of a stomach wound. The pearly white gleam of leg bone bursting through skin. Hair glossy, clumped with blood, staining faces crimson in the rain. Everywhere the putrid smell of wound rot and the stink of wet bandages.

I felt my eyes water from the stench and my stomach spasm in revolt. I don't know how long I would have stood there, paralyzed by the horror before me, if I hadn't felt the sharp sting of fingernails rake my arm. My gaze fell to the ground, where a boy my age had stumbled, his hand outstretched.

"Please," he said. "Please . . ."

Wintry mud seeped into my trousers as I dropped down beside him. "Where . . . where are you hurt?"

My eyes found the wound on his chest before he could answer. His face was white with pain. Biting my lip, I reached a trembling hand to tease back the soggy fabric of his bandage and gasped.

The boy's eyes widened as he watched me, and he shifted with fear. "It's soured, hasn't it?"

I had seen infection before, but never like this. It stank of death.

"My sister told me it wasn't so bad," the boy said. "But it hurts—it hurts so much." Drained of what little strength he had, he sank back onto the puddled earth.

"Where is your sister now?" I asked.

"They took her." His voice was a whisper in the rain.

What would Angle men want with a girl my age? I swallowed. The question sickened me. The boy lifted his head and I noticed his eyes were blue like my brother's. They held mine as if I were an anchor.

"Come. We must get you to the barn." I tried to lift him, but my feet slipped helplessly in the mud. Sweet Gods, his body was a boulder.

I braced my hands under the pits of his arms and tried again to raise him, but he screamed in pain.

"Stop, please, stop! I can't. It hurts."

"It's all right"—my voice came in a rush—"it's going to be all right." I looked frantically round the courtyard. "Please, somebody . . ."

"My lady." Herrick caught sight of me across the yard and raced to scoop the boy into his arms. "I'll take 'im."

The boy cried out over Herrick's shoulder, his chest heaving now, his eyes wild, hysterical.

"You'll be all right," I called after him, but my voice was thick with panic. "I promise, you'll be all right."

My head was spinning and I blinked, commanding myself to think. Mother's healing hut. There would be bandages, salves, and ointments. There was no time to waste.

I dodged through the chaos of the courtyard as fast as I could, past the stables and the rampart and into the woods. Lail's soggy woolen trousers clung to my legs. My lungs burned. I forced my feet to pound faster, down the narrow forest trail that skirted the pasture. Here the towering trees sheltered the path from rain, and my feet could gain purchase on the soggy ground. At last I came to the thatched hut that stood abandoned in the forest of gnarled oaks. Chest heaving, I yanked the wooden latch. The door swung open.

There was no welcoming fire in the hearth. No shaft of light to illuminate the dim and forgotten room. Everything was just as my mother had left it. Poplar twigs hung from the ceiling alongside thick bundles of hyssop, sage, and lavender that filled the air with a moldy, verdant smell. Ceramic pots filled with bloodroot, velvet dock, elderberry, and crushed meadowsweet blossom lined the sturdy set of wooden shelves beside the glass vials that held Mother's herbal elixirs. Her mortar and pestle sat on the table, a cluster of sunny, half-ground pods resting in its hollow.

The rain on the roof whispered, *hush, hush.* I balled my hands into fists and forced myself over the threshold. Moving past the sturdy oak table, I searched blindly in the twilight room for the basket that held clean strips of linen. When the wicker met my fingers, I let out a sigh of relief. Snatching the basket, I moved to the shelves. That was where I foundered. Here was the elder, but that was for coughs and winter sickness. I knew the blue jar contained nettle, but the brown one . . .

Frustration swelled, and I battled the urge to scream.

Think, think. The scores of bottles and jars stood silent, taunting me. My mother had known each herb and root by heart. I was no healer.

Curses! Why had I not paid better attention? The boy was going to die and it was my stupid fault.

Oh, Mother, please help me. I squeezed my eyes shut, praying with every ounce of my will. Let her appear once more. I would even give her back, let her return, if only this once she could appear and help me, help me treat these people, save this boy.

For a heartbeat, I waited. The only sounds were the wash of rain and the rattle of wind through leafless trees. Biting back tears, I clutched the basket to my chest. Never had I felt so alone.

And then a soft creak came from the doorway. I spun, nearly startled from my skin, to see a hooded figure in a blue cloak standing on the threshold.

A woman. My breath caught in my throat.

She looked as though she'd been standing there for some time, watching me.

She must have heard my gasp, because she reached a slender hand to shift the hood from her face. Her hair was dark, wet from rain. But she was far younger than my mother had been. Hers was the face of a stranger.

My disappointment turned brittle. "You frightened me."

"Apologies," she said. Her voice was as low and smooth as water. "I was told I would find medicine here."

She was willowy, her hair the color of nighttime and her skin so translucent, it reminded me of moonlight. There was something about her, some flashing curiosity behind her eyes, that struck me as strange, almost otherworldly. Sensing my scrutiny, she ducked her head and entered the room.

"It appears to be well stocked," she said. Her eyes were a luminous sort of blue, like a pot of cerulean ink. She brushed past me and her fingers traced the ceramic pots as if they were telling her their secrets.

"My mother built her collection over a number of years," I said.

"A number of years?" She turned in alarm. "Then I should hope their properties will not be diminished."

The look on her face ignited my anger.

"My mother knew the property of every plant this side of the sea. She stitched our warriors after battle. She birthed babies. She treated the frail. She tended our village children. She was a Wisdom Keeper and a healer of great renown. You will not find these herbs depleted."

"Good," the woman said. "Then grab as many as you can carry. And hurry. We must get to work."

Who was this woman to barge into my mother's healing hut and command me as if I were a common tenant? I stood still, my eyes a challenge.

She looked at me, unfazed. "You've lost your mother. I'm sorry for you. If you continue to stand here and do nothing, other children shall lose their mothers, too."

Suddenly I hated her. "How dare you speak of my mother?" I demanded.

The woman sighed with impatience and snatched the basket from my arms. I watched as she began pulling bottles and jars from the shelves, stacking them hastily on top of the linens. "You're a child at play in a healer's workshop. Let me help you. We have no time to waste. Even now, people die in your courtyard! We'll need another basket. Can you fetch one?"

My cheeks flushed. She was right. I snatched the basket near the hearth, the tinder clattering onto the floor as I upended it. In a few moments we were racing back along the forest trail, our arms laden with tinctures, salves, and remedies, an uncomfortable silence between us. The rain had ceased, leaving behind rivulets of water that coursed their way over the path and down toward the river. I studied the strange woman out of the corner of my eye until my curiosity got the better of me and I broke my stubborn silence.

"Will you not tell me your name?" I asked.

"My name is Ariane. I am a Wisdom Keeper. Healing is my trade. And you are Languoreth," she said, before I could speak, "daughter of Morken. And a twin."

I was accustomed to meeting strangers who knew of my family. But this woman seemed different. I glanced at her, wary. "If you are a Wisdom Keeper, then where are your robes?"

"I have no robes."

"All Wisdom Keepers wear robes," I insisted. "How else do you travel as a woman without being accosted? How else do the nobles know you are exempt from paying taxes?"

She seemed to think this was funny. "I do not worry about danger. Nor about taxes."

I narrowed my eyes. "You have a funny way of speaking."

"Perhaps it is you who has the funny way of speaking."

I frowned. Cathan praised me for my impeccable diction. I spoke Latin and perfect Brythonic. Whoever she was, this Ariane was certainly not a Briton.

"Where is it you hail from?"

"You ask a lot of questions." She hefted her basket to keep it from slipping. "I treated many on the road best I could, but I have no more supplies. Hurry now." She gestured with her chin. "We are nearly there. Tell your man to let us in."

The rampart gate had been secured, but only a single warrior manned it: Arwel, our messenger's brother. As he ushered us in, clanging the heavy bolt behind us, I saw his hands were slick with blood. The courtyard was empty now save for Father's hounds, who had somehow gotten loose from their kennel. Their noses were bent to the earth, eager snouts darkened from lapping pools of rainwater and gore.

"Go on! Shoo!" I cried. They lifted their heads and slunk off toward the Hall. We reached the stable to find the double doors thrust open, a deafening muddle of voices echoing from within. Inside, rows of the wounded were bedded on piles of fresh straw, and our horses were gathered in the corner, quartered off by thick bales of hay. Steam rose from piping hot buckets scattered round the room, where my father's warriors were tending the injured as best they could, cleaning wounds with flasks of liquor and tying fresh tourniquets around arms and legs.

A plump woman propped on one elbow caught sight of us and her eyes sharpened in need. "Look! They've brought medicines!" she shouted. I turned my gaze from the weeping wound on her pale, doughy stomach. "Help me, little girl! Please, I beg you . . ."

In an instant the whine of voices rose to a clamor, men and women clutching at Ariane, shouting at her to tend them first. I shrank back, the feeling of fingernails still fresh on my skin. Crowan hurried forward and touched my cheek before snatching away a stack of clean linens. I searched the rows of the injured until I caught sight of the boy. He was lying as if thrown on a mound of straw not far from the horses, his breath coming fast and shallow as a bird's.

"Ariane, please. That boy."

She assessed the room in a practiced sweep.

"Yes. We'll tend to him first." She rushed to kneel beside him, her fingers gently probing his chest. "Languoreth. Fetch me a clean linen soaked in hot water."

I clenched my jaw against the heat as I plunged the linen into a bucket and passed it to her. Drawing a small knife from her belt Ariane cut away the soiled bandage to reveal the wound. Infection. Her eyes betrayed the damage. And now I saw the gash to the boy's sternum had exposed the white of his breastbone.

"An axe." Anger flashed before Ariane blinked again and her face became a mask. "Hold him down," she said. "The shoulders. Pin the shoulders."

"But he isn't moving," I protested, not wanting to hurt him.

"He will be."

Bird bones. The boy's shoulders were hollow beneath my hands. I took a breath and forced myself to watch as Ariane doused the steaming cloth with liquor and pressed it to the wound. The boy thrashed with a scream.

"Hold him down!" Ariane commanded. Tears sprang to my eyes. I forced the weight of my body down upon his shoulders, pinning him to the straw.

"You're all right," I said again and again. "Lie still, lie still."

The boy let out a strangled sob. Ariane was moving quickly now, her slender fingers packing the wound with a pulpy mixture of ointment and herbs, and I turned away, my breath coming in short puffs. My face was close to his ear. With the stench of the wound gone, I could smell the earthy scent of his scalp. It smelled of birch bark and winter leaves.

"I'm going to stitch him now." Ariane unrolled a leather kit with varying sizes of bone needles tucked beside neat spools of horsehair thread. But then her eyes flickered to his face and she turned to me. "Languoreth. I need you to fetch more hot water."

The boy clutched at my tunic. "No. No! Don't leave me," he begged, but his voice sounded thick now, muted and unnatural.

"Languoreth," Ariane said, "I need more water before I begin. Go now. Quickly!"

I scrambled from my knees and dashed across the courtyard into the kitchens. I was gone for a heartbeat—just long enough for Agnes to fill the wooden bucket from the vast iron cauldron over the fire and for me to race back to the barn, the bucket sloshing against the sides, scalding my legs through my already sodden trousers.

But Ariane was no longer beside the boy.

She was bent now at the side of a graying old man, dressing a wound to his head. Her blue eyes met mine. I looked to the place where the boy's body lay. She had covered him with a flour sack. His twiggy legs stuck out from beneath it like a broken puppet's, his shoes still caked in mud from the rain.

There was a thudding between my ears that drowned out the din. For a moment everything stood still. I leaned my face against the splintered wood of the barn and closed my eyes. I might have stayed there had I not felt a warm whoosh of breath and the velvety wet nudge of a nose against my neck.

"Fallah." I turned to bury my face in my horse's soft white neck and she leaned into me. "Oh, Fallah." My voice broke, and I let her thick winter fur soak up my tears.

"He was my friend," I heard a small voice say.

I blinked and turned from my horse to find a brown-haired girl sitting against the stable wall, her knees drawn to her chest. Her up-turned nose was streaked with dirt. She smelled rancid, as if she hadn't bathed in days.

She fiddled with a loose thread on her dress, and I noticed a soiled cloth doll in her lap. "His name was Drustan."

"Drustan," I echoed. Her dark eyes were hollow. I took a step closer. "Which town have you come from?"

"Bryneich. Our village lies just beyond its gates."

"But Bryneich is where the Angles began their assault," I said. "How ever did you escape?"

The girl just stared at me, her chin thrust in a defiant way that made me sorry I'd asked.

"You've come an awfully long way," I said. "Was there no other refuge you happened upon before ours?"

"None far enough." Her small eyes studied me. "Are you the lady of this hall?"

I thought a moment. "Yes."

"You look terrible young to be the lady."

"My mother has died."

"Oh." She screwed up her face. "I'm sorry."

"Thank you." My face felt suddenly hot with guilt, accepting condolences from a girl whose parents were obviously dead. "I'm called Languoreth."

"Languoreth." She echoed my name almost with a sense of wonder.

"What's your name?" I asked.

"Desdemona," she said.

My gaze traveled to her feet, where welted sores puffed over the heels of her rough leather shoes. "Are . . . are you hurt?"

She shook her head.

"You must be hungry. There'll be food in the great room, and a warm fire there. You must get something to eat. And perhaps get some rest." I offered. "My brother is there. He'll welcome you."

"No." Desdemona shook her head. "I'm waitin' for my mum. She fell behind in the wood. She'd an injured leg is all," she said. "She made me swear to keep goin'. She did swear she'd find me here." Her dark eyes were wide, hopeful.

"The Caledonian Wood?" I bit my lip. I'd never seen it, but I knew of the vast forest that bordered the Wall. They said the trees grew so thick that noon was dark as night. There were packs of wolves the size of bears, wild boars with tusks like spears. People said the wood had been cast under a dark enchantment long ago, and if you strayed from the path, the trees themselves could twist round your body and swallow you whole.

Desdemona looked at me impatiently, widening her eyes as if to make me understand. Her mother was coming. Couldn't I see? I fumbled for the right thing to say.

"Of course. Please. Head inside to the warm. If your mother arrives, I'll send her straight to you. *When* your mother arrives," I amended.

This seemed to satisfy Desdemona, and she nodded. I let out a shaky sigh as she stood with slumped shoulders and headed out into the chill.

She had no sooner departed than Ariane called to me. "Languoreth, come. I need your help."

She'd finished with the snowy-haired man and was scrubbing her hands with a bar of lard soap. She gestured. "Rinse, please."

I tilted clean water onto her pale, soapy skin. "You didn't save him," I said. "You knew the boy was going to die and you sent me away."

She bowed her head as if she hadn't heard. "You must clean your hands often when caring for the injured. It prevents wounds from going sour. Surely your mother taught you that."

Of course my mother had taught me that. But it hadn't saved her, either. I stared at Ariane, unmoving, and she let out an exasperated sigh.

"Everyone dies, Languoreth. Mothers. Fathers. Lovers. Even little boys." Her blue eyes were piercing. "Did you wish to watch that little boy die?"

My face went hot with tears, but Ariane only straightened, wiping her hands on her dress.

"I can tend to the others. Wounds that need stitching or sealing with fire, some broken bones. Mostly they need nourishment—more than they've gotten. Have the old woman in the kitchen make a heartier batch of stew. We need more wine and ale also, or we'll be in danger of draining your well. Most have sour stomachs. It gives them a terrible thirst."

"Agnes. Our lady in the kitchens is Agnes," I said.

"Have Agnes make a heartier batch of stew," she said patiently.

"Would you have anything else, or would you dismiss me now?" I could not keep the edge from my voice.

"Yes, wait." She lifted a slender finger. "There is something we must discuss. Compensation."

I looked at her in astonishment. "You wish to talk of payment?" There were men and women yet bleeding before us.

"My father is not at home," I said coldly, "and I am but a child. I do not deal in such matters."

"It appears your family has need of my skills," she said. "I have heard of your father, Morken, and of course Cathan the White. I have no need for jewels or cattle or other such trifles given to Keepers who take up employ. I ask only food, lodging, and whatever clothing I like for as long as I should stay. Most important, I shall need the freedom to come and go as I please, without question. Do you accept my terms?" She folded her slim arms over her chest. "I believe they are more than fair."

Keepers were lavished with feasts and gifts wherever they traveled. After all, they carried the Gods' good favor, and it was ill luck to turn away someone who could bend the ear of the Gods. She might not wear robes, but her training as a healer was evident. Still, Father would be angry if I accepted Ariane into the household without consulting him first.

"I . . . I cannot make such decisions," I said. "I must consult my father."

"Your father is not here. And are you not, at present, the lady of the house?"

"I am."

"Well, then. I shall pledge my services to you. Surely your father would find no harm in that."

Pledge her services to me? I frowned. I didn't even like her. In fact, until only moments ago, I was certain I despised her. But the buckets of water surrounding me had gone cool, and Ariane was right. I was a child at play in a healer's workshop. We had a responsibility to the people. Isn't that what Father always said? Surely he would not begrudge us a healer when one was so greatly needed.

Ariane waited, her blue eyes unwavering.

"All right. Yes."

"Yes, you shall have me?"

"Yes."

"Well, then. I have found a new home. Now, if you please. Go and see about the stew. And spirits. We'll all have need of drink, I imagine, by the time this day is through."

I made my way across the stable yard and through the courtyard into the kitchens, all the while wondering just who was now serving whom.

CHAPTER 5

Brant's deep voice broke the silence. "They carry with them the darkness of war."

We were gathered in the small chamber immediately beyond the Hall's entryway, Lail, Brant, Brodyn, the hounds and I, having settled the great room for the newcomers. In the corner Crowan dozed in a fleece-lined chair, her little gray head wedged uncomfortably against the wall. Lail eyed her in the flickering lamplight.

"Shouldn't we help her to bed?"

"I shouldn't wake her if I were you," I said.

Beyond our door the oil lamps had been snuffed out, and in the great room the firelight cast slanting shadows that wavered like specters in the dark. If we were quiet enough, we could hear the sounds of muttering and sleep talk, of chests rising and falling in a soft chorus of sighs.

"Aye, the darkness of war," Brodyn agreed. He moved his spear-hardened fingers listlessly over one of the gaming pieces on the board that rested between him and my brother. Neither had any heart for playing. The rain had moved off toward the coast, and a deep black night crushed in around us. Two cauldrons of stew had been emptied, and we had gone through no fewer than three barrels of mead.

"How many are dead?" I asked.

My cousins exchanged a look.

"Tell her," Lail said. "My sister is not an infant."

"Of the thirty-five who discovered us, so far more than twenty have perished." Brant's voice betrayed little emotion.

"When do you think Father will return?" Lail wondered.

"Not for some time yet." Brodyn grimaced, rubbing his neck. "We sent word, of course. But he's needed now in the capital. And besides, all is well here now. No one is in danger."

All did not seem well. I closed my eyes, wishing I could find the peace in it my cousins had. I knew that death was a part of life. Even in the cycle of the seasons, death reminded us of her presence. In the dark half of the year, when the crops shrank and withered to the ground and the sun rose late and sank too early, when the great oaks in the forest bowed their branches and dropped their burning leaves, casting a chill in our bones not easily warmed by fire. We were raised celebrating the coming of the light at the winter festival Imbolc. And at autumn's end, on Samhain, we gathered to usher in the coming darkness at the end of the harvest. Our Wisdom Keepers taught of everlasting life, while my father's warriors rode off to battle only to return draped over their horses' backs, their lifeless bodies wrapped in blood-soaked cloaks.

When my mother died, I thought, *So this is how it happens*.

You burn young and bright. Death comes to steal your breath, your eyes go sightless, and you are snuffed out, a candle burned to its wick. They tell those who loved you, *This is the way of the Gods*.

I thought of Desdemona, and what dangers might have befallen her mother in the thick of the Caledonian Wood.

"Will more survivors come?" I wondered.

"No, little cousin. I fear no more will come if they've not made it by now." Brant's voice trailed off and I followed his gaze. Ariane had appeared. She didn't look at any of us, just unfastened her blue cloak, tossing it on the iron hook by the door.

Brodyn looked up from his gaming, his eyes sweeping over her. "Hey-ho. You're the healer."

She looked at him, her blue eyes expressionless over her angular cheeks.

"You did fine work today," he went on.

Ariane did not answer, only lifted the slender amphora of wine that sat on the cracked wooden table and poured herself a brimming cup. We watched as she tilted her head back and drained it, filling another before sitting and leaning her head against the wall. Her lashes fluttered against her cheeks as she closed her eyes.

"Her name is Ariane," I said.

Brodyn looked at her approvingly. "I like how she drinks."

Brant shot his younger brother a look, and a soft snore rattled from Crowan in the corner. Lailoken set down his gaming piece, clearing his throat.

"We are fortunate you arrived today, Ariane. Thank you for aiding us."

At the sound of my brother's voice, Ariane opened one eye to regard him. "Then you'll feel fortunate I've decided to stay, Lailoken."

"So you'll answer the boy, is that it?" Brodyn asked.

"Him, I like," Ariane said.

Brant smiled, but leaned back in his chair beside the oil lamp, considering her. "You are most welcome to Cadzow, Ariane. But you must understand that, you being a stranger, we are curious to know what's brought you here. They say the Angles have blazed a trail of fire from the east. How is it that you alone seem to have escaped any injury?"

I could tell by the way Brant watched her that he thought her quite pretty, but he wouldn't be lured from his wits by a pretty face.

"I do not come from the east; I come from the north," Ariane said, her eyes yet closed. "I happened upon these people on the road."

"Traveling alone, were you?" Brant asked, but beneath his friendly tone I heard the warrior's edge.

"She is a Wisdom Keeper." I surprised myself by defending her. I didn't even like her. Did I?

Brodyn spoke up. "If she is a Wisdom Keeper, then where are her robes?"

Ariane opened her eyes to regard him frankly. "I wear no robes."

"How unusual." Brodyn leaned forward to rest his elbows on his knees. "No robes. And you must know the penalty among the Britons for impersonating a Keeper?"

I stiffened in my chair, looking between the two of them. Death. The penalty was death.

Ariane stretched and stood, reaching to refill her cup. "Are you prepared, then, to question me, warrior? For only a Keeper may question a Keeper. Are you a Keeper, then? Do you know the words we must say?" She turned, her eyes lit with humor. "I am certain you know the penalty for impersonating a Keeper."

Brodyn laughed. "I like her more and more! So we shall wait until Cathan returns, eh? We shall see what he has to say."

"Leave her." Brant stood and pushed back his chair. "The woman has had a long day. As have we all."

The hounds roused, too, shaking the sleep from their shaggy gray fur to follow the man they liked best after my father. I wondered if Ariane noticed Brant's muscled chest beneath his tunic as he stretched, straightening his shoulders. The village girls certainly did. Ariane looked away. From his seat at the gaming table, Brodyn rolled his eyes at his brother's display.

"Ariane can bed this night in Languoreth's chamber," Brant said. "We'll lay out our bedrolls on Lailoken's floor."

My chamber? I concentrated on the pool of burning lamp oil, refusing to let Ariane see my frown. I did not want to see her harmed. But to share my bed with her?

I had not imagined this day could have gotten any worse.

• • •

The next morning we resumed our duties, but Ariane insisted we work from Mother's healing hut.

"I will not be carting supplies to and fro like some sort of mule," she said. "We'll tend to those in the hall who cannot rise, but the others must seek us here. It will do them good to move, to walk."

I had worried she would crowd me in my bed, but Ariane slept with her hands knit beneath her breast as if she had been laid to rest and was awaiting the pyre. She didn't stir until morning, when she went to check upon the injured in the great room.

Over the next several days, Ariane and I fell into a strangely easy rhythm as we moved about the little hut where I'd spent so much time with my mother. We spent early mornings walking the forest, collecting what early springtime medicines we could, sometimes talking but mostly in silence, Ariane breaking the spell only to pull a wild root here or a budding plant there. She tested me on the contents of the jars and glass bottles. Soon she tasked me with bringing her the plants and roots she called out for.

In stolen moments, I studied this strange young woman who'd so suddenly appeared among us. Her skin was as translucent as the underbelly of a leaf. I supposed there could be a place where Keepers did not wear robes, though the thought was puzzling. I watched her mix poultices and salves to soothe torn feet. I stood behind her as she pounded roots I'd never seen my mother use into a fine powder, which she steeped in boiling water to make a pungent, bitter tea to help treat dysentery.

Ariane spoke little, but when she did, it was with that strange accent I could not place. Though I probed her with questions, she would tell me nothing of her home, nor anything at all about her training. Nonetheless, she treated the ill with great care, and her knowledge was vast for so young a Keeper, for she couldn't be older than twenty winters.

Before I realized, a fortnight had passed and I had grown accustomed to her presence. Soon I realized I'd even begun to welcome it.

It was the first mild day we'd had since the snows of winter had ceased, and outside the oaks were feathering, green-tipped, in the meadow. Rare shafts of sunlight poured in, turning my mother's glass tincture jars into glittering green jewels as we took stock of our remedies. The shutters of the little window were cast wide and Ariane had propped the door open with a bucket.

"More woundwort," I said, my fingers scraping the last flakes of dried plant from its vessel into the cup of my hand.

"Mmm."

Ariane reached to take the empty jar and I moved to the next. Elderberry. The sweet, earthy scent only deepened as it dried. A swift wind swept in through the unfettered window, and I drew it deep into my lungs. It carried the first viridescent smell of spring, and played with the wisps of hair at my neck that had escaped my thick plait. Ariane's hands stopped their work and she closed her eyes as if listening.

"Your father is coming," she said.

I looked about, confused. "My father? Now? However do you know?"

"*Listen to the wind, let it whistle through the valley . . .*" She looked at me in surprise. "Have you not heard those words before?"

"No."

"It is an old *kenning*. Your mother was a Keeper, was she not? And she did not teach you the kennings? The old wisdom hidden within the lines of our stories?"

"I have learnt such kennings as Cathan has taught me," I informed her. "I know that *wound-wasp* means arrow. A *forest-walker* is a bear. *Wind's brother* is fire."

"Any child knows such things," Ariane said. "I am speaking of the teachings that lie beneath. The kennings that are kept safe by the Keepers. *Listen to the wind, let it whistle through the valley.* This kenning is a reminder that, in its travels, the wind touches all places. It carries with it sights, sounds, and remembrances. The wind is always speaking. But if you cannot allow it to whistle within, you will never be able to hear. Did your mother not speak of such things?"

"She would have," I lied, even as I blinked at the memory. I had begged for such knowledge in the woods with my mother that day. She had been speaking of mayweed and Aaron's rod, wood ear and dock.

I want to be a Keeper, Mama . . .

It was the way my mother's eyes had been shining before the light was so suddenly snuffed out. When she spoke, it was with the hardness of remembering what she had bargained for in bearing the children of a king.

You cannot become a Keeper. Your father is king, and you our only girl. You must marry someone of rank and keep safe our family. Daughters of kings are married to kings.

The words had fallen like ashes between us. In that moment I understood I would never belong to myself.

I studied the fine lines that whorled over my knuckles.

"Well, I will teach you the kennings," Ariane said simply. "And you must remember them. Someday you will teach them to your daughter."

I looked up. "But such kennings are only for Keepers."

"Not where I come from." She pursed her lips. "Where I come from, kennings are meant for those bound to carry them. And you are such a one."

I studied her a moment. "Ariane?"

"Mmm." She jotted a note in the ledger.

"How does the wind speak?"

She looked up as if she'd never considered this before. "It catches my attention, I suppose. Though it went first to you"—she gestured—"blowing about your neck. And then I saw it. An image of a man with hair like your own. He was sitting astride a dun-colored horse, approaching the gate." She reached a delicate finger to tap her own heart. "I saw this, and I knew that this man was your father."

"Are you a Seer, then? Can you see everything?"

"No," she laughed. "I am no Seer. I hear only what the wind chooses to tell me. Now, go and greet your father. He has missed you, I am certain."

A hollow blow of the horn sounded from the guardhouse, announcing the return of our king. I set down my jar and took off running.

In the courtyard our hounds lifted their black noses to the breeze, their tails thumping expectantly. Our man Arwel called out and the gates were thrust wide as Lailoken and the others came to join me. My heart took flight at the sight of Father, Gwenddolau, and Cathan trotting in astride their mounts. They were home. Safe. I felt as though I would nearly burst. Father dismounted on stiff legs and I raced to wrap my arms round his waist, breathing in the leather of his padded vest and the mud from the road.

"Languoreth." He pressed me to him as the hounds circled round, barking. "I should have been here, eh? I came as soon as I was able." His horse shifted its weight beside him, eager to find bed and grain in the barn. He ruffled Lailoken's hair.

"Come, let us go inside and wash the road from our faces," he said. "Then there will be time enough to tell our tales."

Later that evening, Father addressed the people of Bryneich from his chair in the great room. "It is with a solemn heart I greet you and welcome you to Cadzow. Many of you have suffered the loss of loved ones and a harrowing journey to find sanctuary among us. We have sheltered you this past fortnight. Now any who wish to bide under my protection may present themselves. Any who wish to return and rebuild their homes may share in our feast on this night, and tomorrow we shall bid you farewell."

At the long pine table the warriors' conversation resumed in a respectful hum to allow the newcomers to seek my father's audience in private. Father smoothed the thick purple tunic that set off the burned copper threads of his hair, and the first woman in line approached, head bowed, and began to speak.

"I'm a weaver," she said in her east-country lilt. "I made wall hangings for warmth and rugs for the king himself. I can help with the shearing and dyeing—spinning, too. Vortigern's queen always praised my work."

Ariane stood next to me, waiting her turn. She wore the same blue cloak she wore each day, regardless of weather, her black hair coiled neatly at the nape of her neck. She would come forth last, as Cathan must question her, and at present he was needed to bear witness to the oaths sworn by those who wished to come under Father's care. One by one the people of Bryneich approached, some proud, some with tremors in their voices. In the end, oaths were taken by the weaver, two new grooms—brothers—a blacksmith's apprentice, and a cowherd.

I searched the room until my eyes fell upon the girl named Desdemona, who was not so much standing beside the wall as being held up by it. She'd combed her brown hair and washed her face. Her knuckles pearled white where they gripped her soiled doll. She looked to be my age, old enough to know that you should not bring your doll when you speak with a king. But as I looked at the stitched mouth of the doll with its straggles of yarn hair, it occurred to me it must have been made by her mother. A mother who would never come. Father would not turn her away, but when her time came, I spoke for her. We agreed to make a place for her with Agnes in the kitchens.

At last Ariane stepped forward, and the room fell silent. She nodded to Father, but it was to Cathan she spoke.

"Question me. I am a Keeper."

These were the old words spoken by any Wisdom Keepers seeking entry into a faraway court. Just as a smithy must dazzle with a sampling of his work, or a Song Keeper must impress with his or her knowledge of the epics, Wisdom Keepers must submit themselves to questioning and so prove their station. Cathan had turned away musicians who faltered at their strings. He had turned away inexperienced smiths who professed to be masters at their craft. But if Ariane could not prove her claim, she would not receive the mercy of being turned away. She would lose her life. Cathan looked Ariane over now with curiosity.

"You come forth to pledge your oath to Morken?" he asked.

"No. I come forth to pledge my oath to the king's daughter, Languoreth."

Cathan and my father exchanged a glance.

"Languoreth? The lady Languoreth has many protectors, of which I am only one," Cathan said. "What benefit do you propose to bring to her service?"

"I will act as her counsel," Ariane answered. "And I will act as healer for the people of Morken until another can be sought."

"Languoreth is but a child, and I am her tutor. She has no need of counsel." Cathan frowned. "Surely you must see the unconvention in this."

Ariane drew herself up, her willowy frame growing regal. "You may believe this to be unconventional. But I am a Keeper. Am I not free to pledge my services to whomever I please?"

"You say you are a Keeper, yet you wear no robes." Cathan's voice held a note of warning. "You do not speak as if you hail from our lands. Here among the Britons, to pretend the title of Keeper is a crime punishable by death."

I broke my silence. "She wears no robes, but Ariane is as skilled a healer as Mother ever was. She knows the kennings and—"

"Languoreth." Father held up his hand to silence me. "If she is indeed proven to be a Keeper, would you accept this Ariane's service?"

Ariane looked at me without expectation, as if the fact she might stay or go was of little consequence. I envied her the freedom I would never have. I had already learned much from her in only a fortnight's time. And she had promised to teach me the kennings.

"Yes," I said. "I would accept her service, Father."

Cathan's face was grim. "Very well. Then we will see. Ariane, you will follow me."

They were absent for what seemed like hours. At last, when they returned, Ariane gave me a reassuring look as Cathan strode to speak with my father, murmuring something low in his ear.

"My counsellor Cathan has questioned this Keeper and found her claim to be true," Father said. "I would no more begrudge my people a healer than I would begrudge my daughter an advocate all her own. I trust you and my daughter have settled the terms?"

Ariane looked to me.

"Yes," I said.

"Then it is settled. Whatever the terms may be, I will pay them. Welcome, Ariane, Wisdom Keeper. To my household and my chiefdom."

Father stood and reached to clasp Ariane's arm as he would do a man's.

Ariane came to sit beside me. "It is done, then," she said. "I am to be your counsellor."

"Are you to be like Cathan, then?" I asked.

"No, not like Cathan." She frowned. "I am always myself."

"I mean," I said, "what will we *do* together? What will you teach me?"

She studied me. "I will be your companion. I will talk, and you will listen. And it will go on like this until I decide that you are ready, that you need my service no longer."

"But when will that be?"

"I cannot say." Ariane gave a little smile as she looked to the shuttered window. "Perhaps we must ask the wind."

CHAPTER 6

Spring came in earnest, and with it lambing season.

It was late afternoon, coming on evening, and the sweet char of roasted meat drifted from the kitchens high above the cliffs as Gwenddolau, Lailoken, and I squatted at the river's edge below, cleaning our catch from the day.

"Languoreth caught the biggest brown. Well done, little sister." Gwenddolau grinned at me. "Where's your knife? Shall we see how it fares when put to a task?"

I drew my blade from my hip. The leatherworker had stitched the tooled leather sheath to a soft belt stained to match. Fastening the buckles round my waist had become as natural as breathing.

The trout's eyes were lifeless, but Gwenddolau still drew it gently from the pail. "Have you thanked it?" he asked, as he always did.

"Before I struck it," I said. But now the sun shimmered off the yellow belly of the fish as if it had been dipped in gold, and I wished I could plunge it back into the river, where it could retreat under the shadow of a rock.

Gwenddolau must have noticed my hesitation, because he asked, "Do you want me to clean it?"

"No," I said. "It's my catch. I'll clean it. That's what we say."

"Yes." He smiled. "That's what we say."

I took the fish and slit its belly from tail to lip, the knife slicing as if through butter. As I scraped my finger along the slippery innards, Lail came to stand next to me.

"I'll wager you're the only daughter of a chieftain who knows how to gut a fish," Lail said, looking proud. But then, as he gazed at the trout, something shifted in his eyes and he blinked.

"What is it?" Gwenddolau asked. "Is something wrong?"

"It's nothing." Lail looked up. "I'm hungry is all."

"Hurry up, then, Languoreth. Let's make quick work of it. It's nearly time for supper," Gwenddolau said.

I rinsed the fish in the river and placed it back in the pail. Gwenddolau stood and stretched, and Lailoken, eyeing him, did the same. I shook my head. If Lailoken had his choice, he'd be Gwenddolau's very shadow.

"Right. Get you up, then." Gwenddolau gestured and I hopped onto his back, dangling my legs through the crooks of his arms. We had already neared the top of the cliff trail, when Father's voice came, hollering for our return.

"There you are," he said as we emerged from the trees. He didn't pause to admire our catch, and there was a grim set to his mouth. "I would speak with you. All of you."

We looked at one another as Gwenddolau eased me from his back, but followed Father obediently into the Hall. Once in the great room, Father exhaled. "Come. Sit."

I settled beside Lail on the pine bench that lined the table, my legs still wet from wading the river.

"There is good news," Father began. "Ceidio has sent word at last that he is alive and well."

"My father is well!" Gwenddolau's face lit. "But where is he?"

"He has joined his forces with Emrys Pendragon in the Border-lands." Father's voice grew thick and he cleared his throat. "He sends word now that his son and his sword are needed."

Across the table Gwenddolau bowed his head, his blue eyes fixed on the table. "If he wishes for me to join him, I must go."

"Yes. He is your father, after all. This is a day you've been hungry for," Father said, as if to remind him.

Gwenddolau looked up. "Do you think I am ready?"

Never before had he looked so vulnerable. Gwenddolau was never afraid.

Father settled his brown eyes on Gwenddolau. "I do. As much as I would have you stay. You may be fifteen winters at Beltane, but to me you are already a man. I have raised you as my flesh and blood these past seven years, and I have come to see a man whose character is beyond reproach. You are a fierce fighter with unbendable honor. You will grow to become as fine a warrior as Brant or Brodyn, I have no doubt in that. Ceidio would be fortunate to have you fight at his side." It was a trick of the light, or Father's eyes glistened with tears.

"You have been more of a father to me than I had ever expected." Gwenddolau reached to clasp Father's hand upon the table. "I am grateful to you, Morken. I will be bonded to this family until the end of my days."

"You will always be a son to me," Father said. "And a brother to my children."

I fixed my eyes on the pine whorls of the table, determined not to cry.

"Gwenddolau must leave us," Father continued. "And we will soon depart on a journey of our own. I must return to Partick and I'll not leave the two of you behind. It was your mother's wish that I keep you from the capital until you were grown, but that was a wish made in less troubled times. I will keep you close now. I have decided."

I blinked, waiting for a thrill, but the long-awaited visit to Partick went soggy beneath the weight of Gwenddolau's leaving. Lailoken tilted his chin at Father, defiant.

"I will not go to Partick," Lail said. "I will travel with Gwenddolau to join Ceidio and Emrys Pendragon. I wish to fight."

"Lailoken . . ." Father drew himself up in warning.

"No." Lail set his jaw. "You travel to Partick to lift your cup before the high king, safe behind Strathclyde's borders, whilst our brother rides to fight for our land, the land of the Britons! You say Vortigern hides behind his walls whilst his countrymen are slaughtered, but you are no different!"

Father pushed up, his chair clattering to the floor. "And what do you, a ten-year-old boy, know of war? War is not a game!" he shouted. "When Ceidio calls for my aid, I shall grant it. If Gwenddolau should call, I will ride out to war. Until that day, I will lay neither my life, nor the lives of my men, at the foot of the Gods for land that is not my own!"

They stood, father and son, chests heaving and eyes locked, until Father blinked, his voice softened by disappointment.

"A true king must know the weight of a human life, Lailoken. It is a lesson I fear you have not yet learnt."

Lail's face reddened with the rebuke before he turned on his heel and ran out the door.

Gwenddolau stood. "Shall I go after him?"

"No," Father said. "Let him go."

The fire in the hearth felt suddenly stifling, scalding the breath in my lungs. "I'll go," I said, and shoved my bench back hastily before Father could tell me otherwise.

I found Lailoken pacing beside the apple tree in the courtyard, his nostrils flaring like a horse's.

"Lail . . ." My fingers went to his sleeve but he shook me off.

"Leave me be!"

I recoiled. The bitterness and self-pity in his voice twisted something inside me, and my blood ran hot with anger. How could he be so selfish? He would go off and get himself killed, leave me, and all because of his stupid pride!

"Father is right," I said. "This is not our battle. We must let Gwenddolau go." At this my voice broke, but Lail could not hear me. His face tightened. Letting out a roar that made me jump, he ran at the apple tree, kicking the knotted trunk again and again.

"Stop," I shouted. "Stop—the apple! You mustn't!"

The apple tree was sacred, a symbol of the Summerlands. To harm it was a crime punishable by beating, and my brother would not be spared a whipping.

"I don't care!" he shouted. His breath came short, his chest rising in small heaves. "I *hate* kings and their summonings. When I am old enough, I swear it, I will ride to the Borderlands where men fight for freedom! When our warriors are mine to command, I will ride out to join my brother. I swear it on this day. Do you hear me? Do you hear?"

I heard the dull crack of bone against wood and he cried out, clutching his foot. I watched as he sank to the ground, his eyes lit with a fury that shrank me to tears.

"You are so pigheaded, Lailoken. You are so selfish!" I shouted. We had all lost. Mother was dead, and now Gwenddolau was leaving. Father and Lailoken were fighting. My vision blurred as I turned from him, feet pounding along the path beyond the inner rampart.

I sprinted along the forest trail until I reached the trickling, muddy stream where Mother and I would sit beneath the thin shelter of birch trees. The damp wool of my trousers made me shiver, and I pulled my knees to my chest.

What was the sense in loving if all those you cared for were taken away?

A chill wind stirred, gusting over the nearby pastures, turning my face clammy where tears yet clung. A feathery fern brushed against my forearm, and I reached to yank it from the ground, the uproot-

ing of the tender shoot somehow nourishing the darkness that consumed me.

That was where Cathan found me after some time, sitting on a
half-rotten log by the trickling stream, a mound of tattered ferns at
my feet.

"You're clogging up my head, child." His knees creaked as he
crouched beside me. His coarse gray hair had come loose from his
braid, making him look more like a wildwood recluse than the lord of
the White Isle.

I can feel you thinking of me as surely as you are in the room, he'd once
told me. And yet I could never sense it when Cathan thought of me.

I looked up. "I think Lailoken has broken his foot."

"If he did, then he likely deserved it."

I bent once more to the streambed, my dirt-crusted fingers searching for more shoots to unearth. "Gwenddolau is going off to the
Borderlands, where babies are dashed against rocks and whole villages
are reduced to cinders."

Cathan eased down next to me, wrapping his long arms about his
knees. He paused a moment before speaking.

"Languoreth, the earth is very old. Tragedies will occur on nearly
every patch of land, given enough time. But given enough time, miracles will unfold on every hillock and valley, too. Who are you to say
a disastrous fate awaits your foster brother? Gwenddolau's future is his
own, and he has much to accomplish before the Ancestors call him
home."

I stared at the soil, saying nothing.

Cathan turned to me, his blue eyes calm. "I do not think it is only
Gwenddolau's leaving that troubles you."

He waited, but I could not find words for the shadows that had
stirred since I'd woken from my dream. My mother's voice. Her ghostly
apparition standing in the winter river. The glistening wounds. The
mud-caked boots of the little boy. And so I told him of the stag.

Cathan listened keenly, the tips of his fingers pressed together until at last I fell silent.

"You and your brother have been visited by the stag, the spirit of your ancestors," he said. "This is a mighty thing."

"But what does it mean?"

"The antlers of the stag arch into worlds unseen. This is why he is seen as a messenger. Perhaps he came to offer comfort. Perhaps he came to show you he is a power that may be relied upon. Perhaps he was only looking for a quiet drink." His eyes sparkled with humor. When he did not find the same reflected in mine, he bowed his head. "This message has come unto you. You and your brother. But I can tell you one thing of importance. Spirit does not choose to show itself lightly. Spirit cannot be commanded. It comes to those in need, when it is needed, and, most important, in its own time. I can promise you that should you desire to know the stag's true message, you will discover it when the time is right, and not a moment before."

I let out a sigh.

"Do not sigh like a servant who's burnt the pudding," he said. "I have not finished, you know." He lifted a finger. "Most important, the stag comes to tell you of a journey that is about to unfold."

"What sort of journey?" I asked.

"Oh, an epic sort, always. Filled with dashing heroes, a wicked villain, battles, enchantment, and lionhearted feats of bravery. This is the stuff of stories told round the fire." But as Cathan looked at me, his smile waned.

"It's the living of it that's the hard part," he said. "There may well be shadowed days. The stag comes to signal the beginning of a new journey you must take. And so the path of this adventure has been laid at your feet. Yours and your brother's. Soon, I think, you will be asked to walk it."

The journey to Partick. The Wisdom Keeper's words had taken

something once enthralling and hung it with a cloud of doom. I shook my head, eyes stinging with a fresh swell of tears.

"Eh, now," Cathan said. "Have I not been at your side, all these years? I who foretold your and your brother's coming? I have bent my life to the task of your learning, Languoreth, and not only from the tenderness that grows for two young babes. I have seen the shadows of the times that lie ahead. You and your brother have roles to play in the events that must unfold. And I mean to arm you to the teeth for battle in ways perhaps only a man such as I am able."

"Lailoken may have a role, but what role have I?" I challenged. "I was not chosen to become a Keeper like Lailoken. And I was born a girl. Neither will I be allowed to fight!"

My role was to marry and someday bear children, but I could not say those words because they sickened me.

"Do not envy your brother, Languoreth. It is true, the Gods have not chosen you for Keeper. And, as a young woman, neither can you become a warrior like Gwenddolau. But you will have your own influence, as is your fate. You will come to understand that each of us has the power to fight."

He meant to encourage, but Cathan's words nearly sank me. I did not choose to live in such shadowed days. For generations our land had been torn by violence. Now Cathan spoke of more battles to come, of the roles I and my brother must play, as though we were little more than game pieces on a wooden board.

And to what end?

Because there were men in the world with black hearts who brought pain and gore to this place of clouds and trees and swift-moving rivers. Who brought slaughter and death to our timeworn mountains and the people working to carve their abundance from the hardened earth of our fields. A shiver coursed through me and Cathan draped his thick white cloak about my shoulders, engulfing me in warmth. We sat that way for a while, the Wisdom Keeper's strong arm about me and our eyes fixed upon the hills that slumbered in the north. Twilight was falling. The lowing of a cow sounded in the faded grasses and against the purpling sky, while a hawk circled beyond our ramparts. Cathan watched it keenly before turning to me.

"If you are afraid, then you are wise," he said softly. "But you have nothing to fear, for I will be with you. Now come with me, Languoreth, daughter of Morken. There are trunks to be packed and provisions to be seen to. Your journey awaits."

CHAPTER 7

G wenddolau had gone.

I sat numb as Crowan pressed me onto the stool to rake through my tangles, setting to work on what she muttered was the "disgraceful, fiery lark's nest" that had become my hair. Around us, servants bustled, folding the last of my belongings into my trunks as Crowan plaited my hair into delicate strands, pinning them into a coil at the nape of my neck. The shine of Partick was a faded thing. I wanted nothing more than for Crowan to finish with her fussing so that I might slip away to the stables to be with Fallah, to lean my face against the smoothness of her neck. I hadn't had time to ride since the coming of the people of Bryneich and Father's return, and I longed for the comfort of her dark, soulful eyes and creamy white lashes. Crowan must have sensed this, for she sent to the kitchens for a bannock and tucked it firmly into my hand.

"Off with you, then. I can't do more with you now." But her hazel eyes were full of understanding.

The grass along the stable trail was spiked with frost. Spring, it seemed, was a fickle thing, but with any luck the mist and chill would burn away by late morning. Ariane had gone to the healing hut to pack the leather satchel she wore at her waist with a fresh supply of remedies. We would be leaving soon: Partick was a half day's ride at a good pace, and far slower with the carts. The barn was heady and sweet with fresh-lain straw, the clean scent of pine planks mingling with the earthy musk of horses. Fallah turned her head as I slid back the bolt on her stall, nickering softly in greeting as I ran my hand along her velvety white flank.

"Hello, beauty."

Father believed a horse chose its rider as much as a rider did their horse. Fallah had been no more than a shaky-legged foal when she appeared one afternoon beside the stables to nudge the baby girl my father held in his arms. Now, in no hurry to reach for her saddle blanket, I wrapped my arms round her neck and she bent her soft muzzle to my ear, letting out a hot, wet breath that sent shivers down my back.

"You know that tickles!" I ducked away, but she'd succeeded in making me laugh and she tossed her head lightly.

"No more snorting," I scolded, checking my hair and my woad-dyed dress for horse drool. "We're traveling to Partick today."

Fallah blinked her long lashes impassively and I brushed a strand of her mane from her face, reaching to lay the thick saddlecloth over her back. The rhythm of tacking her always soothed me, and I liked to do it myself rather than leave it to Macon—whose hands I knew were becoming arthritic and pained him—or submit Fallah to the overly boisterous new grooms. Saddle skin, saddle, girth, and bit. Unlike Lailoken's horse, a stubborn brute precisely deserving of my brother, Fallah's girth never needed tightening. She bore my work patiently and never distended her belly like other horses in hopes of making it looser round her middle.

I looked at her lovingly. "Crowan would find you a better lady than me, I'm afraid."

I heard a laugh and turned to see Macon smiling, his flaxen hair pasted to his forehead with sweat.

"My pardon, m'lady. I only meant to tell you your father and brother wait in the courtyard."

"Of course," I said.

"For what it's worth," the groom said, helping me walk Fallah out, "I think you're a fine wee lady just as you are."

I bowed my head as we led Fallah along the stable path. "Thank you, Macon. You're a kind friend."

In the courtyard Father and Lailoken stood in their riding cloaks and stout leather boots, waiting beside their mounts in what seemed a fragile peace. Father's face was grim and Lailoken's yet stubborn. But as Lail shifted his weight to avoid his injured foot, his eyes softened and he said, by way of apology, "You look like a lady, yet we stand here waiting for my sister."

"Oh, do be quiet," I said, forgiving him. Gripping the saddle, I pulled myself astride.

"Let's be under way," Father said, "for I know Cathan will insist on stopping within moments for his midday meal."

Cathan sputtered something about an unjust accusation—which I could not understand, given his mouth was stuffed full of bannock. As Ariane drew her horse up behind Fallah and the rest of Father's retinue eased onto their mounts, I urged my horse forward with a squeeze of my calves. Already the mist was causing loose strands of hair to curl waywardly about my face, and I reached to flatten them, self-conscious.

"You do look pretty," Lail said in earnest, guiding his horse beside mine. I glanced at his stirrup where his boot was laced loosely, his foot resting unnaturally on the iron rung.

"How is your foot?"

"Broken. My toe, anyway."

I knew his toe was fractured because my own had been swollen and throbbing since the evening before. Damn being his twin. I wanted to say it served him right, but Lail looked so tender then, his lanky form dwarfed by his monstrous gray horse, even with his jaw thrust out like a strutting cockerel's. Beneath it all we swam in currents of the same ocean. His uncertainty and fear sloshed within me, mingling with my own.

"I'm sorry," I said.

The gate closed behind us and we rode in silence, Fallah's easy walk and the rich smell of earth soothing my jittery stomach as I sank deeper into the sway of my saddle.

The road to Partick was a muddy ribbon that wound west, high above the Avon Water as it passed beneath towering oaks and shady pine forests. Alder, ash, and birch found light closer to the pastures as we turned north, where the trees gave way to fields and open wind. In the distance the pastures rose with the mounds of my father's ancestors, the sleeping dead. We joined the main road and looked out over the great river Clyde, where flat-bottomed boats floated downriver toward the capital carrying stout barrels of ale or swaths of timber for the shipyards of Partick or for Clyde Rock, the fortress of the high king at the mouth of two rivers. Much of our wealth came from the taxes my father levied on these boats as they passed through our checkpoint on the upper reaches of the Clyde. The river and our cattle were the staples of our power.

A few miles passed beneath our horses and the mist burned off. Shafts of spring sun struck the roadside grasses with slivers of gold, and I stripped off my cloak, draping it over Fallah's pommel, my eyes traveling to the front of our caravan where Father and Cathan rode side by side, deep in conversation. Brodyn and Brant rode ahead, scanning the way with watchful eyes.

To be a king of the north was to be ever on guard. Picts could at any moment raid Strathclyde over their steep mountains in the north, or take to their boats, sweeping like a fiery tongue from the western sea. There were many who might seek to usurp my father's claim on his fertile lands nestled southeast of Partick and north of the Roman Wall. Our lands had belonged to my father's kin as far back as any Keeper could remember, before the Romans came, back to the earliest memory, when my ancestors had come and tamed the white cattle that were now chief among our fortune.

Fallah's gray-flecked ears bent back and I straightened suddenly, listening. Someone was approaching on the road. I heard our men call out an alarm as three warriors left their places in our caravan to circle back, spears lifted and shields gripped at their sides.

"Keep on, Fallah," I soothed her. Craning my neck, I spotted two cloaked riders approaching on sluggish horses from behind. Our warriors halted them and, upon recognition, parted the wall they'd made with their mounts. The men wore the brown woven hoods of Christian monks. These were not the full sorts of robes our Keepers wore; rather, their hoods were knit and pulled over their heads, so that they wore simple cloaks or tunics of their own choosing. One man rode farther ahead, and as the stranger drew closer, he gave a broad wave.

"Brother Telleyr!" I called out.

The monk slowed his horse to walk beside mine. "Young Lady Languoreth! You and your kin are a sight to be seen."

It had been many seasons since Brother Telleyr had last paid us a visit at Cadzow, but he and my family had always enjoyed the most spirited conversations. Before he'd become a devotee to the Desert God, Christ, Telleyr had been a Wisdom Keeper. His dark eyes swept our company in anticipation.

"And where is your mother, the lady Idell?" he asked.

The stab was swift at the sound of her name. "She died this past winter," I said.

"Died?" The monk's face fell. "Oh, no. Oh, Languoreth. I am so very sorry."

Brother Telleyr's sorrow was so evident, I wanted to stop my horse right there and speak of everything: about how the sickness had come back to Cadzow so unexpectedly, decades after the last family had perished from the boils; how I had helped her that very morning, folding hot baked bread into the basket to take to the miller and his wife, whose little girl had fallen sick. And yet I knew I could not bear it.

"You're coming from the wrong direction," I said instead. "South rather than from the north. Are you coming from the Wall?"

Telleyr's eyes softened with the realization I did not wish to speak of my mother, and he nodded, wiping the sweat from his brow.

"Aye. I'm returning to Partick," he said. "We heard news of the Angle attack. Britons along the Wall have much need of help in rebuilding their homes. My brothers and I have spent some time in the Borderlands. In fact, four of my brethren have stayed behind."

"But you did not wish to stay?"

"I dare not keep too long from my duties," Telleyr said. "My work at the monastery is consuming. We have only just cleared some swaths of land and built a few wattle huts. We have plans for a stout church made of timber and stone, and in my absence there is no one yet equipped to aid in giving sermons."

"There are no other monks who can speak to your people as you do?"

Telleyr thought on this. "We do have one man, recently come from Culenross. His passion is unmatched. But he is undergoing a period of silence just now. When he emerges from his seeking, he may prove himself a charismatic priest indeed."

Telleyr glanced behind him. "In any case, I am glad to have come upon you. I've had a long journey home with my fellow Brother, Fergus, and my patience is worn thin as a mare's hair. He's ill, you see, and quite cross. I'm afraid you shall meet him all too shortly."

I flashed what I hoped was a sympathetic smile. Telleyr was forever making light of difficult situations. He was tall and strong, only a few years younger than my father, and he'd been busy clearing land for a new monastery on the outskirts of Partick for many seasons now. "Monks," he once said, "are as well equipped for tilling soil as they are for wielding a sword."

We'd been wary of Telleyr when he first appeared at our hall, a middle-aged Wisdom Keeper who'd traded his white robes for the earthy-brown hood of the Christian faith. But he delighted in discussing healing and tending the land with Mother, and Cathan held a measured respect for the teachings of the man called Jesus. I'd always taken great pleasure in the news he brought, for he often kept company with King Tutgual and his retinue both at Clyde Rock and at the high king's hall in Partick.

Telleyr looked at me now, his dark eyes bright. "I gather you and your brother are bound for your father's hall in the capital?"

I nodded.

"Well, I must say it'll be refreshing to have you and your brother in residence. Partick is overfull these days with great hordes of puffed-up chieftains and their retinues who are too preoccupied with toasting one another and getting drunk on barrels of ale to discuss anything of meaning—save your father, of course," he added. "I suppose talk of war draws to it a certain sort."

"Have you any news from the Wall? Have you heard anything at all about a man called Pendragon?"

"Indeed I have. I've heard in fact that Emrys—the one they call Pendragon—will be arriving to Partick any day now. He brings with him no fewer than forty of his armed guard for his meeting with the high king. There were many I met in the Borderlands who spoke of his bravery."

Tutgual had summoned Pendragon to Partick? I could hardly believe my luck. Perhaps at last we would catch sight of him.

"He is a hero, and Lailoken and I would be quite happy to meet him," I said, unable to keep the excitement from my voice. "Do you think we might?"

"To be certain," Telleyr smiled. "Partick may be the capital, but it is not so large as all that." He shifted in his saddle as someone called out from behind.

"Brother Telleyr!"

At the sound of desperation in the other man's voice, Telleyr squinted as if he'd been suddenly struck with a headache. I turned to see a heavyset man with shifty eyes trotting toward us on a sad, arthritic pony.

"Christ grant me patience," Telleyr murmured, then turned to me in earnest. "I must warn you, Brother Fergus is a bit of a zealot. He may well say something foolish."

Fergus, who'd caught up to us, overheard this and shook his jowls, indignant.

"I am no zealot, Brother! I am a devoted servant of God. And I would say to *you* that in the very least it is not *I* who spends my time pandering to wolfish lords and chieftains. For the day will come—"

"Oh, Brother Fergus, I beg you . . ." Telleyr dipped his head. "Don't take offense, Lady Languoreth. It's likely one of the more complimentary things Brother Fergus has said of your father."

Fergus's eyes grew wide as gourds as he realized who he'd come upon, and I stifled a laugh.

"Brother Fergus, meet Languoreth, daughter of that wolfish chieftain I pander to. Morken's clan has long been a family that keeps the counsel of many gods."

"Greetings," Fergus said loudly, as if we did not speak the same tongue. His several chins waggled in his cowl.

"Fergus is a seventh son," Telleyr said. "And so we at the monastery have the obsequious good fortune of hearing Brother Fergus prophesize on a daily basis." He leaned closer. "He fancies himself a visionary."

Fergus, who'd been eyeing me with a discomforting amount of interest, shuddered in offense. Apparently he had very keen hearing.

"*Fancy* myself? Such words are false and . . . untrue! Did I not foresee, just the other day, that a fox would find his way into the chicken coop?" He was overtaken then by a fit of coughing, and Telleyr reached to clap him on the back.

"We all foresaw it, if you recall, when we noticed the gap in our fence, Brother. And still no one has gotten round to fixing it." He turned to me. "The good Lord takes all kinds."

"May he reign everlasting!" Fergus cried, but was taken by another spasm of coughing.

"Brother Fergus, you must try not to excite yourself. It's not good for your condition."

"What condition has he?" I asked.

"There's no need to speak of me as if I weren't here, young lady," Fergus said. "I've been ill for some time now. A disease of the lung, or so they think. There is no treatment for my malady."

"Oh. I am sorry."

Fergus let out a snort. "Nothing an apology can address. My Lord will keep me."

"Well," Telleyr said, "I think I'll ride ahead and give my regards to your father."

Brother Fergus squinted as if he could not imagine which would be worse—staying here with me or riding forward to meet my father.

"It's been lovely to make your acquaintance," I offered.

Fergus tipped his head like an overstuffed bird and kicked his poor pony into a turn, heading back to the end of our company.

CHAPTER 8

Across the expanse of the river, the walls of Partick were dark and forbidding, the ramparts encircling the town like a dragon curled round its treasure. Dusk cast the clouds in a purple glow as Tutgual's men looked down from lofted platforms and guard towers along the wall, shadow people holding spears that sent shivers down my spine in the coming dark.

"Is it as you imagined?" Ariane asked, pulling her horse to walk beside mine.

"I did not imagine it to look so . . . imposing," I said. "Have you visited Partick before?"

"Only once," she answered. "A long time ago."

She met my eyes in the way that told me she would say no more.

"You and your mysteries," I mumbled.

Ariane bowed her head with a little smile as we crossed the wide Roman bridge that led to the town, the hooves of our horses rumbling over stone. Beneath Partick's walls, the salty river slapped against the hulls of merchant vessels docked in the shipyard, and gulls hovered, their wings flashing white against the darkening sky. Brodyn called out to a sentry and the massive gates were unbolted with a heavy clank. I smelled the sharp tang of seaweed before the gates swung open and the sights and sounds of the capital engulfed me.

Even in early evening the streets were crowded with merchants and makeshift stalls. A group of musicians spun and twisted, stomping their feet in time to the beat of the bodhran while townspeople haggled over hunks of fresh goat's cheese, crocks of butter, and end-of-day prices on butchered pigs. The sights and sounds of Partick assailed my senses like a herd of stampeding cattle. Suddenly I missed the rushing water and gently creaking trees of Cadzow's forests. Here the people were so accustomed to caravans of kings, they hardly glanced up from their conversations as we passed.

"Look to the water," Father called over his shoulder. "Do you see those granaries there? Those hold the bulk of our grain stores."

I followed his gaze to three squat buildings perched on the riverbank and recognized two of my father's flat-bottomed vessels tethered in the slips beside.

"We'll visit them whilst in Partick. It's good that you both learn the running of things. Ten men guard them at all times," he said, a touch of pride in his voice. "So my children needn't worry about our wealth slipping into the river."

We followed Father down the flint-topped thoroughfare, my eyes not quite large enough to take it all in. A copper-haired slave moved a broom listlessly over the threshold of a shop piled with swaths of fabric. We passed another shop brimming with blue-glazed pottery, and beside it a shop stacked with shelves upon shelves of delicately tooled leather booties and shoes. We followed the road until it terminated at a grand hall in the center of town.

"The Gathering Place," Ariane said as I examined the ornately carved wooden doors—such skill! Craning my neck, I looked to where the towering thatched roof peaked high above the nearby hickory trees.

"It must hold over a hundred people," I said. "However do they repair all that thatching?"

Ariane looked at me sidelong. "They must be very good climbers."

Roads struck out from the Gathering Place like the spokes of a wheel. We took the road to the right, following it until it narrowed under the shelter of pine trees. The hum of merchants and mothers and packs of shouting children faded into the dim. We were scarcely beyond the center of town, but the air smelled sweeter here. Crab apples were in blossom. The last birds of daylight called from their roosts as we reached two large hitching posts at the head of a path.

"We're here at last," Father said. "Welcome to Buckthorn."

How sophisticated and ordered Buckthorn was compared with our wooden country fortress of Cadzow. Grasses lined the path where medicinal plant beds were dug in neatly ordered patches, bordered in white quartz that glowed like moonlight—my mother's work, I knew. But the hall itself seemed to glow, the timber coated with daub and a smooth covering of whitewash, stretching into the treetops. Light blazed in preparation for our arrival. The thatching of the roof was tight, as though recently redone, and oil lamps flickered on either side of the double-set wooden doors, each as heavy as an ox and reinforced with iron banding.

Beyond the main building sat the kitchen house, and just past that I could make out the stables tucked against a small, rolling orchard of fruit trees. Thick hedges of buckthorn bramble enclosed the pastures, where I sensed animals breathing in the growing dark.

"Come, children, come," Father said. "We must greet the servants."

Father eased from his mount to greet the servants who had issued from the house and stood now, heads bowed. I dropped from Fallah's back, suddenly shy, and handed her reins to Macon, who was already giving directions to the two young grooms from Bryneich.

There were too many new faces, but the faces were kind; I could tell they loved my father well. Desdemona, who'd ridden the long journey in the back of one of the heavy-wheeled carts, hovered behind Agnes, and I hoped our cook would help her find a warm welcome within.

A young man stepped forward, a creamy fold of parchment in his hand. "This came for you, Morken. I would not wish to trouble you upon your arrival, but the messenger asked that I deliver it right away."

I squinted, trying to make out the seal, but Father slipped his thick finger too quickly beneath the wax, bending the message toward the dim yellow light. I watched his dark eyes move over the Latin script, his brows lift. He passed the missive to Cathan, who scanned it quickly, unable to hide his delight.

"Emrys Pendragon has requested an audience. He arrives two days hence."

The mere mention of his name was enough to charge the air with enchantment. That we might see the leader of the fierce Dragon Warriors, the man who'd inspired the bravest of the Britons to rally beneath a new banner?

"The Pendragon—here!" I exclaimed. Lailoken's eyes had gone wide as soup bowls. Father held out a hand to silence us.

"He comes to me first. Before Tutgual, it would seem. I do not know if I should consent to such a meeting."

Cathan gave a shake of his head as if to dismiss the question altogether. "So he is not a man who answers to high kings. You think this makes him unwise. I think this makes him all the more interesting. Play the fool with Tutgual if you must, but I see no danger here. Throw him a feast. I should like to know what this Emrys Pendragon wants with the likes of Morken the King."

"And will you attend?" Father asked Cathan.

"Nay, though I regret it. I must travel on the morrow to White Isle. But you will do well enough on your own."

Concern etched Father's face as he nodded, looking to Agnes and Crowan. "If we are to meet, we must be ready to host Pendragon the day after tomorrow."

"Give me a real test," Crowan answered, but in the half-light her face blanched at the thought of it.

"Young Languoreth can help," Cathan said. "She is the lady of the hall now, is she not?"

"She is," Father looked to me.

"Of course I will help," I said, trying to sound braver than I felt. Plan a feast for Pendragon and his famed Dragon Warriors? Lailoken's blue eyes found mine, full of sympathy.

"Ale for the warriors," he whispered. "Just make sure there's plenty of ale."

"Up you get, beauty." Crowan planted her hands on her bony hips, her cheeks already flushed with the morning's activity. "We've got the feasting to plan, and we'll need to gather supplies yet. Well? Aren't you eager to explore the town?"

I looked at her, bleary-eyed.

"Splash some water on your face—that'll do the trick." She hummed as she moved about the room, unhinging the shutters to usher in fresh air that smelled like rain. "A bit o' sun and now more rain. Let's hope it doesn'a muck with our guests and their travel."

The thought of Pendragon's arrival at Buckthorn sent a flood of excitement through me, and I swung my feet over the edge of my bed.

Crowan swept aside my plait as I plunged my cupped hands into the icy water of the washbasin, splashing the sleep from my face.

"Just think: the Pendragon, dining in our hall," she said. "He may not be a king, but he's as brave a man as any Song Keeper might celebrate."

"Far braver than that coward Vortigern," I said.

They said Pendragon could cut down scores of men with a single stroke of his sword; that he could hide in plain sight; that he could leap from horse to horse at full gallop with nary a falter. I could hardly imagine that at sundown tomorrow he would arrive at our hall to feast.

"Well, if he's a soldier used to life on the Wall, he'll be thankful to have some good meat," Crowan said.

She chattered on as she helped me dress. From my small window on the upper floor of Buckthorn I could see the rounded huts and stately wooden lodges that lined the road to town beyond our tall trees.

Ariane had gone off to the markets already, and outside Desdemona waited by the stables, her dark hair pulled from her face but her brown eyes expressionless. I offered a smile.

"Good morning, Desdemona. Are you eager to see the market?"

She fixed her eyes on the grass. "I suppose so, m'lady."

Crowan saw my frown and cleared her throat. "Go ahead, now, Desdemona. Macon will be ready with the cart."

She leaned in with a touch of her hand. "Don't fret yourself, dove. Some people don't know when a stroke of good luck's found them is all."

"Do you think she's unhappy with us?" I asked.

"The poor child's only just lost her parents and is making a new home among strangers," Crowan said. "She'll settle in. Give it time."

Macon drove us to town. It all felt like a grand adventure. In the market, bottles of oil in green glass glittered in daylight like liquid emerald. Boisterous olive-skinned merchants with wax-tipped mustaches called out their wares against the sizzling intoxication of meat pies, and the hollow clang of the shipbuilders' mallets echoed from the river's edge below. We passed from stall to stall, Crowan testing the firmness of leeks or tasting a crab-apple preserve. I felt the townspeople's eyes upon me, heard one of the merchant wives whisper, "Is that Morken's little daughter? Isn't she lovely!"

By the time we were through, Crowan had arranged for twelve legs of lamb, four barrels of wine, cheeses, herbs, three heads of cabbage, and six ceramic jars of honey. I was passing a bushel of carrots back to Desdemona, when I realized she was no longer there. Crowan turned, ready to scold her, but the rebuke dried upon her tongue. Desdemona stood several paces behind, her way blocked by the arm of a nobleman.

"Whatever is he doing?" I said, alarmed.

That he was a royal was clear; his torque was a thick twist of gold, worth more cattle than I could count. He was short and wiry, with close-cropped black hair that would have made him appear nearly boyish were it not for the fact that he was surely a few winters older than Brant and Brodyn. Desdemona must have stopped to admire the little pen of young chickens, I realized, for her fingers yet gripped the top of the wicker fencing even as the nobleman leaned casually toward her, his eyes strangely lit at the look of fear upon Desdemona's face.

My hackles rose, and before Crowan could stop me I called out, "Step away from my servant!"

Beside me Crowan cursed as the nobleman turned his wide-set eyes upon me.

"If this be your servant, you should have a care to teach her better manners," he said. "She was staring at me like a witless boar from across the marketplace. 'Surely the child must wish to meet me,' I said to myself, 'for why else would she stare at me so?' "

There was giddiness to his voice, as if he were directing a game to which only he knew the rules. My eyes fell to the gleaming silver brooch upon his chest bearing the emblem of a raptor.

"Perhaps she stares because she recognizes you as a lord of Ebrauc," I said, unable to keep the disdain from my voice. That very emblem had been Gwenddolau's to claim as a boy prince, before his uncle, Eliffer, turned traitor and usurped Ceidio's throne. Given the size of his torque, this could be none other than Gwrgi or Peredur, one of Eliffer's sons.

"No, no," the nobleman said, and moved toward Desdemona as if to conspire. "I think she stares because she knows how very fond I am of chickens."

He turned to the poultry keeper standing nearby and held out his hands, nearly beseeching. "May I?"

By now the people of Partick had stopped their business in the market, sensing a strangeness. The poultry keeper reached hesitantly into the pen to select a chicken. The halt of activity in the market heightened the swell of tension, but the addition of an audience seemed to only further delight the man. As the poultry keeper handed over her livestock, I saw her dirt-streaked fingers were trembling. She'd gathered a brown-speckled hen with a beak the color of yolks and two peacefully blinking eyes.

The face of Eliffer's son lit with delight as he took the bird and drew it close to his chest. "Ah. Do you see what I mean? Yes. This is truly a fat and magnificent bird." He bent his dark head to bury his nose deep within her feathers. "Oh!" He breathed. "The smell of her."

"Very well, then, Desdemona." I summoned my authority and called to her, beckoning. "Let's be on our way."

"No, no, you mustn't go!" he exclaimed, his face seeming suddenly kind. "Your servant girl—look! She is afraid of me. I would not part knowing I had frightened the girl." He extended the bird to Desdemona with a smile. "I saw you admiring her. You like chickens, too, don't you, little girl? Would you like to stroke her?"

Desdemona swallowed, dark eyes wide, and shook her head. She startled as Eliffer's son threw back his head with a laugh.

"Well enough, then, because truly I do not like to share, and I am powerfully hungry."

It happened so fast—the flash of his teeth like a hunting dog, the wild look of abandon on his face as he suddenly bent his head to the bird. And then there was a ripping and a horrible, garbled squawk. I screamed as the bird's eyes went wild, her wings and claws thrashing as a spray of blood erupted from the severed artery of the chicken's neck, spattering Desdemona's pale face even as she stumbled forward, swiping the blood from her eyes blindly, trying to escape.

I rushed at him. "You're mad! A mad and vile man! My father shall hear of this and you shall be sorry!"

My fury only fueled his lunacy, and the man fixed his eyes upon me, bearing his bloodstained teeth in delight.

The bird had fallen to the ground, where it jerked and flapped its tawny wings in the dirt. I burst into tears at the sight of it, covering my face with my hands as he tossed his head back with a howl. Then there was a flash of metal and the bird went still. A voice came.

"That's enough, Gwrgi." But where the voice should have been stern, it sounded merely put out.

I turned to see a tall man with long black hair disdainfully wiping the blood from his sword. Crowan rushed to help Desdemona to her feet, and I stepped over the severed head of the bird to stand between Gwrgi and Desdemona.

"This man accosted my servant." I pinned my eyes on Eliffer's son. Gwrgi only glanced at the taller man and shrugged, wiping his mouth with the back of his hand.

"Brother, why must you insist upon spoiling my fun?" Gwrgi said. "Did I not tell you I was famished? 'Let us settle the horses and have some ale,' you said. But I have such hunger! And this woman has such lovely chickens."

His brother hushed him as one might a child and turned to me. His black hair was so thin that, as he bent to offer me a bow, I saw the pearly white of his scalp peeking through the heavily oiled shine.

"You have the apologies of Peredur and Gwrgi, sons of Eliffer. My little brother should not have trifled with you, nor your servant. I can see you are the child of a nobleman yourself, are you not? I assure you Gwrgi meant no harm. We have only just arrived to the capital, you see." He gestured to the horses standing before the inn across the lane. "I am afraid all the travel has put my brother out of sorts."

There was a blade's edge to his voice, but where I should have felt fear, there was only fury. I regarded him a moment. "The price of harming another's servant is two silver pieces."

Peredur's dark brows shot up with his laugh. "So it's money you want? Whose child are you? I must know."

"It isn't your silver I want, it is justice. I know the laws. I am Languoreth, daughter of Morken. And the cost of harming another's servant is two silver pieces—that is what you must pay. Unless you would have me take this matter to the Council, of course. Though I am certain they would award me the same."

Peredur's dark eyes shifted at the mention of my father's name, and his smile faded. But beside him Gwrgi clapped his hands with glee. "She is Gwenddolau's foster sister!" he exclaimed. "Brother, I can hardly believe our luck."

Peredur turned to Gwrgi, and this time his voice sliced as it should. "Pay her; pay her and be done with it."

Gwrgi's eyes were upon me, dark and slippery. But he reached into the leather pouch at his waist and counted out two silver pieces. He watched my eyes as he placed the coins into my outstretched hand, his fingers departing with a tickle against my palm that made my stomach pitch. I yanked my hand away, the coins balled tightly in my fist.

"Now you have our apology and our reparation, my lady," Peredur said. "I would not hear of this again. Tell your father we have no quarrel with Morken."

Behind me Crowan pulled at my dress. Poor Desdemona; poor old Crowan and her heart!

"Very well," I said. "The matter is settled."

No sooner had I spoken than Crowan wrapped her bony arms around me and hurried me toward the cart, Desdemona following close behind.

"Oh, why did you vex them, dove? And I no more than a servant myself, who could do nothin' to protect you? Oh!" she exclaimed, pulling me to her. "Noble or not, you mustn'a risk yourself ever again, do you hear me? I saw that Gwrgi's eyes. His heart's black as a shadow—a danger, I say!"

"It's done now, Crowan," I assured her, even as I shivered. It had pained her, being unable to protect me, and from the way her eyes now darted I could see it had shamed her, too.

"You cared for Desdemona," I said. "It's over and done. There was nothing more you could do."

Macon's face tightened in alarm at the sight of blood-spattered Desdemona as we drew near the cart.

"What's happened?" he demanded. Crowan told him all as he hoisted me up and we pulled away from the market with all haste. Desdemona at last began to cry.

I turned from my seat at the front of the wagon and reached for her hand. The chicken's blood had clumped her dark hair, and her up-turned nose was red with weeping. She looked up at me from her place among the carrots and lamb shanks.

"Here," I said, uncurling her palm. Her brown eyes widened as I placed the silver pieces in her hand. "These belong to you."

"Nay, m'lady," she stammered. "You mustn't . . ."

Two silver pieces was more than any servant expected to see in their lifetime. They were not paid in coin; they were paid in food and shelter. In protection.

"I never meant them for myself," I said. "That Gwrgi is a horrid man. You must take his money and do with it what you will."

Desdemona looked at the coins a long moment before folding her fingers around them and tucking them into the pocket of her dress.

"Thank you, m'lady," she said. "I didn'a mean to stare, m'lady. It's only we heard such tales about them, Drustan and me."

"I do not doubt it, Bryneich being just north of Ebruac," I said, be-cause I did not want to hear Desdemona's tales. I had just seen a man tear the feathered throat from a chicken with his bare teeth in the marketplace, and my heart was yet racing as though it were I who'd been yanked from my wicker pen. Some said Peredur was older. Some said Gwrgi was a bastard. Some said they were twins. But I had always known that Gwenddolau's cousins were his most deadly of enemies. Now I had seen just how evil they were.

"Would that Gwenddolau had killed them when he still had the chance," I said.

Crowan reached to cover my knee with her thin hand. "Gods hear us, he yet will."

Back at Buckthorn, the hounds startled at the sound of Father's roar when I told him what had taken place.

"Some dark god must shelter Gwrgi, for had he touched a strand of hair upon your head, I would have routed him from that inn and gutted him where he stood," he growled. He drew me to him, and I lay my head against his chest. I could hear his heart beating against his ribs. Lailoken stood nearby, his face red with anger.

"Are you certain you're hale, Languoreth? Are you certain he did not frighten you?" he asked.

"No, Lail, I wasn't frightened," I lied. But Father drew back to look at me, reading the truth.

"Gwrgi will pay."

"What would you have us do, Father?" Lailoken waited, his jaw set.

"We will satiate his hunger," Father said. "Lailoken, you will go with Brant and Brodyn. My nephews know my mind, I think?"

My cousins hovered nearby, hungry for retribution. "Aye," Brant said.

"Very good," Father nodded. "See that it is done."

"I'm proud to call you my daughter." He turned to me. "You may be yet a girl, but this day you acted every bit of a queen."

I did not have to wait long to learn the breadth of Gwrgi's lesson. By the following morning news had spread throughout the capital about the rage Gwrgi had thrown at the inn at day's end; he'd thrust back his covers only to find his bedding soaked in blood and cluttered with entrails, the heads of a dozen chickens resting companionably on his pillows.

"You'll be sorrowful for the chickens," Father sighed when he saw me. "Don't worry, my love. The birds were due for slaughter, and I've kept the choice parts; I wouldn't waste a butchering on those two if the Gods themselves decreed it."

The next afternoon saw the great room swept and the tables decked with spring flowers. There were amphorae for wine and platters waiting to be piled with food. Dane the Song Keeper, one of Strathclyde's finest poets, had been sought to entertain, and I'd helped arrange it all. My encounter with Gwrgi and Peredur had emboldened me. I stood straighter now, and the men of my family eyed me with greater respect. Now the meat was roasting and the servants were busy chopping cabbage in the kitchen house as Crowan appeared to replait my hair, twining it with delicate seeds of freshwater pearl. She helped me into my moss-colored dress embroidered in gold and eased me into my best pair of exquisite leather shoes.

As I moved to the doorway, a fumbling and cursing from Lail's chamber drew an exasperated sigh from Crowan. She threw up her hands and shuffled down the corridor.

"This is what befalls when you don't let old Crowan help pack your *things*," I heard her scold.

I followed only to catch a glimpse of my brother knee-deep in trunks, his robes and tunics spread about the floor.

"I can manage myself, Crowan," Lail insisted, though the state of his chamber said otherwise.

I left them to it and found Father in the great room, feet propped on an old wooden stool and a vellum-bound book in his grasp. Two small braids had been threaded through his shoulder-length hair to keep it from his face, and the brilliant blue of his tunic made the cinnamon streaks in his hair gleam boldly. Pinned to his breast was his most extravagant brooch, a gift from my mother. Two fierce-toothed hunting dogs joined openmouthed, their amethyst eyes glittering amid an intricate gold interlacing designed by the smith to ward off harm.

Sensing my stare, he glanced up and lowered the little book down upon his lap.

"What's that volume you're reading?" I asked. "I've not seen it before."

"This?" He shifted his feet so I could perch upon his stool. "Brother Telleyr has lent it upon my request. It is a collection of Christian texts. *The Holy Books*."

"*The Holy Books*," I repeated. "Are they in Latin?"

"Latin, yes. Taken from Greek."

"And what do they say?"

He studied me. "This interests you? Christianity?"

"I only wonder why a Wisdom Keeper would become a priest of Christ as Telleyr has."

"I suppose Brother Telleyr believes Christ is the god above all other gods, the great high king."

I considered this. "Is not our god Belenus rather a high king?"

"Nay; Belenus may be great, but I cannot place one god above another. Christianity is a foreign religion begat in a foreign land," Father said. "Where is the many-faced Anu, the mother who sustains us all? Where are the countless spirits of rivers, mountains, and seas? I have stood at the bank of the Clyde and felt the power of Clota call to me. I have given my body over to Morrígu in battle and felt her might overtake me. These gods belong to no other gods but themselves. No, this religion is not the way of thinking for me."

"Then why do you read it?"

"A leader must understand the new thoughts that may take hold among his people."

"But aside from Telleyr, we know none who are Christians."

"In our lands, perhaps. But in King Tutgual's domain they grow in number. Even now there are lords and chieftains of the Old North who send their children off to the tutelage of monks rather than Wisdom Keepers. They hope to keep their heads above water in what they believe will be a turning tide." He looked almost sad as he moved the book from his lap, but then he seemed to remember himself and he smiled.

"Tell me, daughter, do you look forward to the festivities this night? The smell of lamb pervades, and it has set my stout stomach to grumbling."

"I cannot help but wonder if Pendragon will be fierce or full of wile. Will he come wearing his armor, do you think?"

"You speak of him as though he may sprout wings and fly." Father chuckled. "As for armor, I would think he'd wear a leather plate when using the chamber pot. There are lords here who are none too keen with his presence."

"Is this why he has been summoned to Partick?"

"Pendragon has been summoned to Partick because he is seen as a threat," Lailoken said from the doorway.

Father swept a scrutinizing glance over Lail's wrinkled tunic as he came to join us, but nodded. "Aye, that's right."

"And because he draws warriors to him like flies are drawn to honey," I added.

"Aye. But there is greater reason he is seen as a threat." Father shifted and rose, moving to stare into the great fire at the center of the room.

"Pendragon rides from Vortigern's fortress above the river Esk," he said.

"The fortress Vortigern retreated to?" Lail asked.

"The same. There, Pendragon sought an audience with the king, beseeching him to return to Bryneich to join him in taking up arms against the Angles, and so shake the grip they had gained on Vortigern's kingdom. But Vortigern refused. That very night, Pendragon returned. His men mounted the walls. They barred the doors." Father's voice grew quiet, his eyes locked on the flames. "They burnt Vortigern's fortress to the ground, with the king yet inside."

My hand flew to my mouth but Lailoken shushed me, his blue eyes lit.

"The thick black smoke and ember glow were seen all the way from the kingdom of Rheged," Father continued. "A signal, a warning. A message to all of what consequence may come from turning in cowardice from this new Angle terror."

I blinked in disbelief. Heroes did not slay kings; they fought to protect them.

Emrys Pendragon would dine at our table this night with the ashes of a king on his fingertips.

"I heard Pendragon himself bolted Vortigern inside," Lail said excitedly. "That even neighboring villages could hear the sound of his screams as he burnt alive."

I looked at my father as if to say, *And this is whom you have brought to dinner?*

Father waved a hand. "Vortigern was a coward. I do not begrudge Pendragon this victory. I will decide for myself what to believe and whether or not I admire him." He drew himself from the fire and his dark eyes settled upon us. "Emrys should have sought an audience with Tutgual to discuss the proper manner of dealing with a king like Vortigern. Instead he has made it clear that he will act first and seek reparations after. Do you see why some think him dangerous?"

I understood now why Father had been so hesitant upon receiving Pendragon's request. And the fact that Pendragon wished an audience with my father before meeting the high king who had summoned him was not respectful conduct.

"Why did you not refuse his request?" I asked.

"Because whilst I pay due respect to our high king, I do not fear him. If Lord Emrys would meet, I would see what he's made of. I am intrigued by this man, who only a season ago was captain of the guard. In slaying Vortigern, Emrys has claimed his kingdom. Now we will see if he and his Dragon Warriors can hold it."

"The act is rebellious!" My brother's voice was tinged with excitement. Father looked at him with concern.

"It is indeed. And there are many who would see Emrys deliver Vortigern's land to a more rightful owner. Like Pascent, Vortigern's son. Vortigern's lords, too, were driven from their lands."

"Fled, you mean," Lailoken said.

"Aye, they fled. And some have taken refuge with King Tutgual himself."

"They want land they are not willing to fight for," I said. "They are cowardly!"

"Every man wants land, Languoreth." Father moved to close the shutters as a soft rush of droplets came against the thatching overhead. Outside, indigo swaths of clouds had built without my noticing. Our guests would arrive in the rain.

"Here on this island, we battle for every measure of land we own," Father said. "Land, crops, cattle. This is our wealth. None in our federation—whether they be Pendragon or one of Vortigern's lords— would be fool enough not to lay claim. Vortigern's fortress on the Esk controls all the trade coming into our kingdoms from the south, and any traveling south from the north as well. Pendragon saw a failed standard and burnt it to oblivion. It's what he chooses to do with his power that remains to be seen."

Just then, as if summoned by our talk, our watchmen called out and the heavy hooves of horses sounded from the road beyond: Pendragon and his men. Lail's eyes found mine, offering me strength.

Father turned to me. "Our Lady of the Hall, our guests approach. Be certain all is ready. We will be seated shortly."

CHAPTER 9

I called to the servants to stoke the central hearth to spitting, and soon cracks and pops were sending red-hot embers onto the flagstone floor. Oil lamps flickered from their wrought-iron hooks like fireflies as Crowan passed me like a feathered thing on her way to the kitchen house. I skimmed the three long wooden tables decked with ruby-filled wine amphorae and rich ocher earthenware from Gaul. I'd helped arrange the pine boughs that spilled from the centers of the tables, tucked wildflowers and tufts of rosemary among their emerald branches, and they gave off a sweet scent. I felt a small surge of pride as Father and Lail smiled approvingly at the sight of it. But no sooner had they entered than the thudding of boots came, their echo tracing a shiver up my arms.

In the burning torchlight his shadow preceded him, stretching broad as a giant. And then I saw him, Lord Emrys, the man they called Pendragon.

Though he was thickly muscled, he was the height of any man, not tall, yet not slight, his dark hair clipped close in Roman fashion, and his skin yet bearing the olive tone of his Sarmatian ancestors. His face, which might have been handsome, was made rougher by the presence of an oddly beaked nose, but it was his eyes that pierced like a dragon's: deeply set and so azure that they were nearly hypnotizing. He scanned the room, rain dripping from his cloak into little puddles at his feet. Where I'd expected forty, only ten men rode in his retinue, all soaked to the bone in their thick leather armor.

"Emrys Pendragon. Your bold deeds precede you." Father strode forward to greet him.

This sparked humor in Pendragon's eyes and he bowed his head, a smile tugging at his lips. " 'Bold deeds,' " he echoed. "My friend Ceidio did warn me you did not play at words."

At the mention of Ceidio's name, Father stiffened. "I have heard you and my friend Ceidio have formed an allegiance. Have you any news?"

"Ceidio is well. When last we met he was awaiting the arrival of his son. We lodged with him some nights ago on our way north. I know he is indebted for your care."

Father nodded, and Lord Emrys looked upon me with a smile. I stepped forward, remembering my role.

"Please, cast off your wet cloaks. Come warm yourselves by the fire."

If he was surprised to be met by so young a lady, he had the good graces not to show it.

"This must be your daughter."

"Aye. Lord Emrys, meet my children: Lailoken and Languoreth of Cadzow."

"Lady Languoreth. Thank you for welcoming me and my men."

"I am pleased to meet you." I bowed my head as my mother had taught and moved to stand beside my brother.

"Come," Father said. "You've traveled far and you must be hungry. Sit. Let us dine. Wine, ale! Whatever you please."

At my father's gesture the servants poured drink. I took my seat between Lail and my father, watching my brother's eyes kindle with pleasure as the steward poured him unwatered wine. The toasting was boisterous enough, but as my father reached once more for his cup, his voice grew somber.

"As Ceidio has said, I prefer to speak plainly. I am certain you know there are some in Partick who are not pleased that you are here, Lord Emrys."

Emrys raised a brow. "None, I hope, who are seated at this table."

"You'll come to no harm whilst under my roof," Father assured him. "But you seem no fool. You knew you would make enemies of a powerful few when you set fire to the hall of a king."

Silence fell over the revelry, and Lailoken lifted his eyes to mine. Only the soft strains of the cruit could be heard as all in the room shifted their eyes to Pendragon.

"Yes," Emrys replied. "Though it seems stranger that lords who fled their own lands, abandoning their people, could find cause to quarrel with me, Morken."

"I hold no admiration for men too spineless to stand and fight. But you've murdered one of the Thirteen and risen to take his place. I wonder now what it is you would do."

"I do not seek to claim any crown. The man I deposed was a coward; he was no king. I have only risen to protect the forgotten people of his realm." Pendragon took a deep draught from his cup. "Do you think it was my choice to slaughter my fellow Britons?" He did not wait for my father's reply, his azure eyes flashing. "I and my men battle in the fields and the forests as it is, each time astonished to have escaped with our lives at all. No"—he shook his head—"Vortigern left me no choice."

My father considered him. "And what did you make of Pascent, his son?"

"Did you not hear? I offered him some gain. The ashes of a fortress with the ghost of his father residing within." Pendragon's voice rose to emphasize the breadth of the boon, and one of the Dragon Warriors bit back a laugh.

"Pascent refused the land," Pendragon continued. "He has no men brave enough to hold it. We spotted him riding toward Bryneich. He means to make some plot with the Angles, no doubt. It would seem he learnt no lesson from his father."

"And is this what you will tell Tutgual King?"

"I will not stand by whilst the innocent suffer," Pendragon said. "I laid claim to those lands because it is my men and I who can protect them. I will tell Tutgual that it is not I who is his enemy. The enemy comes from across the sea, from Angleland, and they arrive in wave upon wave, like locusts. They mean to consume the Britons in totality. They would see the blood of our children make fertile the fields their own progeny will sow. I mean to stop it."

My chest swelled with admiration. Emrys Pendragon was no murderer. He was a hero; there was no denying it. I glanced at Lail and saw his eyes burning with zeal.

Father leaned across the table. "If this is so, I commend you. And it seems your methods of warfare have taken the enemy much by surprise."

"Aye, we're suited to the woods and wild places, eh?" The smile that came was fierce and cunning, like the dragon he was named for. Across the table Lail moved closer to the edge of his seat, and Pendragon, noticing, gave him a wink.

"We meet the enemy wherever we can engage them. The Angles play now at letting a man or woman run, only to track them and string them gutted from trees. And so we want them to know fear. We want them to know pain. We wait, sometimes for days, hungry and wet. Eaten by insects and wallowing in our own stink. We wait for them to send a scout or a raiding party." He downed his drink. "They will soon come to know that death is a far better fate than to be taken in irons by the Dragon Warriors."

His men raised their cups in a shout and Father smiled. "We are a strong people," Father said. "This is not the first time we have faced this sort of warfare and survived."

"You speak of the Romans," Pendragon observed.

"Aye. Though in the kingdom of Strathclyde we survived thanks to our cunning in negotiation, our height on the map, and the din made by our neighbors."

At this, Emrys chuckled and the mood round the table lifted.

"They say you are Sarmatian, Lord Emrys," Lailoken ventured.

"Aye," Pendragon smiled. "My ancestors were born on horseback, our cavalry among the best in the world. We fought the blight of Rome until it consumed us. When the Sarmatians were offered a living wage within the empire, my father's people came across the wild sea to build the Wall. When Rome retreated, we held it still. When Vortigern fled to his fort above the Esk, we held it still. Then the Angles attacked, and my brothers laid their broken bodies at the foot of that Wall. We held it still . . ." His voice fell away, his eyes dim with memory.

I knew what had happened next—I'd heard the vendors in the market. Some thought Emrys quite mad. Others thought him a hero. He'd used the blood-soaked cloth from the tunics of the dead to sew a new standard. Little by little, men caught word on the wind that there was such a man as he. They rallied to the Dragon.

"Lord Emrys, I am ashamed to say I possessed some doubt as to the nature of your character," Father said. "You do not disappoint me. You fight on behalf of the truest cause: the preservation of our people. And so you have found a friend in Morken. What do you seek from me?"

"Men." Emrys did not hesitate. "There will come a time when I need an army. We need seasoned warriors, and whilst your clan may be smaller in number, your men are among the best. It won't be long before we are forced into the open."

"When you call for men, you shall have them."

I drew in a breath as Father's brown eyes locked with the steady blue gaze of the Dragon. The deal had been made.

But I couldn't help but wonder what this would mean for Brant, for Brodyn, for Lail, for each of us. My father took the wine amphora and refilled Pendragon's cup along with his own. I watched as King Morken drank, swallowing the weight of his vow.

CHAPTER 10

Lailoken and I could scarcely believe our luck when Cathan returned to Buckthorn and announced he was taking us to visit Bright Hill.

I'd only ever seen the distant glitter of torches on the hilltop during our springtime festival of Beltane, when we gathered to bid Belenus, the shining one, ruler of light, health, and livestock, come back to the land. His blazes were lit on mountains and hilltops across our kingdom to celebrate his return in spring. The slopes of Bright Hill were the domain of our Wisdom Keepers: it was a sacred hill where rites were worked to bring prosperity and seek the favor of Belenus in spring planting and the safety of our animals. The villagers of Cadzow said the veil between the worlds was spun so thin on Bright Hill, you could hear the Gods breathing.

The salty smell of the Clyde blew in gusts off the water far below as we entered a thick forest of elm, river ash, and oak. Flashes of sunlight lit Cathan's silvery hair as he led his horse on until at last he stopped beside a giant old yew. Here a sturdy wooden bridge arced over a swift-moving stream where tiny white stars of pearlwort blossomed over the moss-covered rocks. We dismounted to let the horses drink before tethering them beside the great old tree.

"There it is!" I exclaimed, pointing over the bridge to the steep rise of Bright Hill.

"Come on"—Lail jabbed me—"I'll race you."

"Halt!" Cathan's strong arm barred the way. "Lailoken, you wish to become a Keeper? Surely I have taught you better than this. You are about to enter a sacred place. For when you step off this bridge, you step out of our world and into another. You must always seek permission."

Lail bowed his head, duly chastened, but for me the Wisdom Keeper's rebuke stung more deeply. I knew Cathan had not intended it, but his words were a reminder that the path both my brother and I so coveted was barred from me. Cathan and Lailoken often broke from our lessons to continue discussions in private, for the teachings of Keepers were sacred. Secret. I wondered if my brother had any idea of the pain it caused. But now Cathan's eyes had drifted closed, his lips moving in a whispered prayer. I could catch no more than the rhythm of it, swift and reverent, until he abruptly ceased his mumbling and tilted his head, waiting. For a long moment there was no sound, not even the rustle of a red squirrel in the tree overhead. And then came a small breath of wind. It rose as if from the earth, gently rustling the buds on their springtime branches. At last Cathan opened his eyes.

"We are welcome here. We may cross now, children. Hurry up, then: this way."

Even the grass seemed to sprout more lushly on the opposite bank, brushing the hem of my dress as we left the bridge and followed a narrow footpath upstream. Cathan moved ahead, humming something low and mirthful until, a short distance away, we arrived at a clear forest pool. A narrow spout of water issued from a tiny split in the rock where the hill had broken open, like a woman who could not hold back her tears.

"The White Spring," Cathan said. An ancient thorn had dug its roots into the slope above the spring, gnarled arms outstretched as if to shelter it.

"The water is so clear," I said, but waited this time as the joints of Cathan's knees gave sharp cracks and he squatted at the water's edge, swaying softly with a blessing for the Lady of the Spring.

"Come, Lail, Languoreth." He smiled. "You may settle beside me now."

Sunlight rippled the surface of the water in playful, light-footed patterns, and Lail's eyes had already drifted, soft and unfocused. Glancing at him, Cathan nodded to himself and reached into the leather pouch at his waist, withdrawing two delicate chunks of amber. They flashed in the filtered sun as he pressed one into my palm, giving the other to my brother.

"Go ahead. Tell her your wish," he said, and stood. "And do take your time. I'll be waiting just there." He departed in a soft rustle of grass, leaving me and Lailoken alone at the pool.

A wish?

I wasn't prepared for a wish. The delicate piece of amber felt leaden in my palm. I glanced at Lailoken, but his eyes were already closed. He was just the sort to always know what to wish for. With an uncertain sigh, I let my eyelids drop as I'd seen Cathan do. I willed my mind to go still, listening to the clean trickle of water.

A moment passed, and soon the silvery whisper of the spring became the only sound I could hear. I sank into it, like swimming underwater. Slowly, I felt my body begin to sway, although I was not quite certain I was moving at all. But I *was* moving. I was swaying so softly, awash with the feeling of being rocked in my mother's arms. I was embraced. Enfolded. So safe, so at peace. The sensation pulsed through me in waves as gentle as the roll of the sea, and I tilted my head as if to capture its rhythm. Within me I could almost feel a rivulet of light rise and spill, filling the darkened cracks of my heart.

I do not know how long we sat there, my brother and I.

It was as if time stood still, or perhaps there was no time at all.

Gradually the pulsing within me grew fainter and fainter, fading like thunder on a hill in the distance.

I made my wish.

With heavy lids I opened my eyes to watch the tiny piece of amber sink to the bottom of the pool. Lail's eyes were yet closed, his lashes a sandy fringe against his cheek and his brow creased in concentration. When at last he looked up, he did not so much cast his pebble of amber as he let it slip from his fingers.

"Did you see her?" he asked, his light eyes shining.

"Of course I didn't see her." My voice was clipped, but Lailoken didn't notice.

"She was beautiful," he said. "Like a mild summer day, or the sound of the ocean as it laps on the shore." He turned to me. "I think she quite liked you."

"Liked me?" I shook my head. But I had felt something, hadn't I? I searched but found no words to describe it.

"What did you wish for?" Lail asked, standing to brush off his trousers.

"Goodness, no," Cathan called out from his seat upon a moss-covered log. "Don't tell each other. That's terrible luck! A wish is to be kept between yourself and the lady."

Lailoken gave a slight nod, and Cathan hoisted himself up to join us, squinting in the sun.

"Well, then? What did you make of the White Spring?"

"It was lovely," I said. Words felt empty as I sought to describe it.

Lailoken thought a moment. "I felt as though she wanted to heal us."

"Yes." Cathan stretched his arms over our shoulders, guiding us along the forest trail. "She is a good spring for healing. She has such a very large heart."

Young fern curled their heads along the trail, and fat red-capped mushrooms squatted round tree trunks. The hill wasn't tremendously large, but the incline was steep, and as the path meandered in switch-backs we lingered, moving slowly, as if the sound of our footsteps might shatter the stillness.

I remembered what Father had said about our river. Never before had I felt the magic of our gods. But I felt their nearness now. The green canopy folded overhead like the roof of a cave, and there was a quality to the air, as if another, more shimmering world had enfolded itself over this one. We moved through it slowly, observed by hidden eyes.

A soft gust rose through the forest, causing me to shiver. And then I heard the deep-throated caw of a bird. A crow. Cathan heard it, too, and lifted his head, seeking out the direction from which it had come.

"I will confess I was not paying attention," Cathan said. "Shall we test your skills as an augur, Lailoken?"

"It came from just there." Lail gestured to an elm below. "From the south."

Cathan had been instructing Lailoken in the ancient art of augury, and in stolen moments I watched them observe the way an animal skittered or soared, noting the time of day, the place it was seen, the direction in which it was traveling. It was a knowledge given only to Keepers, the meanings of such signs having been divined by our ancestors, their deciphering passed on since time out of memory. Someday, when Lailoken stood as counsellor at the shoulder of his own king, it would be his responsibility to decode such omens for the safety of a kingdom.

But now Cathan's face was clouded. His beard twitched as he looked to my brother. "The south, you say. Lailoken, are you quite certain?"

"Quite certain." Lail frowned. "Though I can't remember what it might mean."

"That is only because we have not yet learnt it," Cathan said with a sniff. "Rain. I do think the crow means to warn us that rain may be coming."

Lailoken hesitated, as if he did not agree.

I was still puzzling over it when the forest opened up and we arrived on the summit of the hill. Now I could see how high we had climbed. There was the little bridge we'd crossed below, and the canopy of trees that sheltered the spring. In the distance, the wide ribbon of the river rippled like serpent scales in the sun. Cathan gave a satisfied sigh at the sight of it, pointing to a gently sloped mountain in the distance.

"We wait for the signal from that mountain when we light the great fire. And so on and so forth, until a jeweled stream of fire blazes across the entire land. The Beltane fire wakes the land from slumber, blessing the herds as they travel to summertime pastures. Blessing our hearths as we carry its embers into our homes."

I could almost imagine how it might look from the clouds, a blazing strand of stars glittering from hilltop to hilltop from here to the ocean, and even across the western sea to the burning mountaintops of Scotia, the land of the Westmen, uniting all of our people whether at war or at peace.

Gray wisps of clouds raced overhead, momentarily darkening the sun, and my pulse quickened with the feeling of weather. Of course, Cathan had been right. It was going to rain. The Wisdom Keeper turned from the view to acknowledge the ancient grove of trees that commanded Bright Hill's summit. Tucking a wayward strand of silver hair from his face, he cleared his throat, turning tutor once more.

"As for the oaks, the generation of Keepers who propagated this grove has been lost beyond memory. Yet the trees still remain."

The oaks were fat-footed giants, their trunks tumorous with age. But they were beautiful, like a grandmother, their gnarled fingers tapering into delicate branches bursting with new leaves of spring.

"These oaks are the children of the first tree, the children of Bile," Cathan said. "The very memory of creation has been forged in their rings. This is why we come to the groves to work our rites—because oaks remember the old magic, the song the earth was singing when it first came into being."

Lailoken's eyes trailed the grove in reverence. He'd been waiting for this, I knew, to stand upon this hill among these majestic old trees.

"Go ahead," Cathan urged us. "Wander. Greet them! See what messages you might hear rustling through their leaves."

I moved toward an oak with a deep hollow and extended my fingers, exploring its burls. I did not have much hope for messages in leaves. That was the domain of my brother. Instead, I wandered the peaceful grove for a time before I grew restless, and decided to trace our footsteps back down the hill to get a better look at the red-capped mushrooms I'd seen clustered at the foot of a tree.

I had to hunt for a while before I finally found them, and with a hum of delight I crouched to pry a rounded bulb from the earth. Delicate white warts dotted the red cap. Poisonous, I was fairly certain. But I would bring one for Cathan to see.

I had reached to tuck the mushroom into the small leather satchel at my belt when suddenly the very air around me prickled, the fine hair of my arms bristling like the hackles of our hounds.

I was not alone.

I straightened swiftly, my eyes scouring the underbrush. It was nothing, I told myself. A squirrel or possibly a fox. But then I heard the sharp snap of a twig.

I spun on my heel, the mushroom bulb falling from my fingers.

A skeletal man with piercing blue eyes stood not ten paces behind me, paused midmovement. A blond mustache drooped over the beard that covered much of his thin face, and in my terror I wondered for a moment if he might not be human at all but a spirit sent to haunt me from some dark place between the worlds.

Danger. The forest around me pulsed as if in warning. And yet I couldn't cry out; I could scarcely swallow. I could only stand as his eyes pinned me, surveying my fine-spun garments and the slender golden torque I wore. An understanding kindled as he realized I was royalty, and the way his face shifted made me reach instinctively for the handle of my knife.

This man was no Wisdom Keeper.

"Who are you?" I demanded. "What is your purpose here?" But my voice sounded meek in the expanse of forest. Where had Lail and Cathan gone? How quickly might they come if I could even muster air enough in my lungs to scream? The blue-eyed man did not answer; he only dropped his hands to his sides a moment as if wondering what to do with me. A little girl, alone in the wood.

"Who are you?" I demanded again, louder this time. He raised his brows, looking at me the way I'd once seen a cat eye a wounded robin. The thought that this encounter was some sort of game to him, that I was something weak to be preyed upon heated the blood in my veins, and my fury boiled over, shattering his spell.

"I am Languoreth, daughter of Morken, and you trespass on a sacred hill. State your purpose or leave here at once! I will not ask you again."

I whipped my knife from its sheath and sliced it in the air between us. But the threat of my blade turned the amusement in his eyes to shadow. He took a step toward me, and my instincts took hold. I rushed at him like a shrieking banshee. I meant to startle him, to chase him away, but the man only slipped aside as if he were made of water. I felt a sharp crack upon my wrist and cried out in pain as he knocked the blade from my grasp as if it were a plaything. It fell to the earth with a thud that left me queasy.

"That knife belongs to me! Give it back!"

The man bent slowly to pick it up, his eyes admiring the jewel work adorning the handle. He passed the knife from hand to hand, testing its weight. Sensing my chance, I billowed my lungs to scream, but he closed the distance in an instant, clamping a rough hand over my mouth and knocking me off balance. He crouched over me now, so close I could smell the sour musk of his sweat. I struggled to force the breath through my nose, my heart thudding as he shook me in his grip, forcing me to go limp, to submit to his will.

As he raised his free hand I braced myself to claw out, to fight whatever he may do. But he only brought an earth-stained finger to his lips, his hard stare silencing me.

Quiet.

Slowly he eased the pressure on my mouth and stood.

His eyes bored into mine as he backed slowly away, until a safe distance lay once more between us. And then, as if he were flicking a fly from a banquet table, he tossed my knife to the ground.

I scrambled to my feet as the man turned and fled downhill, into the forest. Lurching for my knife, I brandished it, fingers trembling, eyes fixed on his back as he retreated into the undergrowth. This time I would not miss my mark.

"Languoreth!"

I heard the panic in Lailoken's voice as he careered down the trail, his face tight with worry.

"What's happened?" he asked. "I heard you cry out."

His eyes raked my body in search of cuts or bruises.

"I—I'm all right . . . There was a man . . ."

"What man?" Lail's hand flew to his sword. "Did he harm you? Did he touch you?"

"No," I insisted. "Not in that way. He—he twisted my wrist." I rubbed the place where it was sore and swelling. "He was right there," I gestured to the trail. "He was right *there* when you came upon me. Did you not see him?"

Lailoken scanned the tree line, wary. But the only sound was the wind through the trees and the high-pitched tittering of the forest birds.

"I'm sorry, sister. What did he look like? Was he a Keeper?"

"This man was no Keeper!" My words came as a shout and Lailo-ken stopped.

"How do you know this man was not a Keeper?" His voice was keen.

I took a breath. There was the memory of the stranger's skeletal frame, his drooping mustache and wiry beard, the amphibious chill in his eyes. Never had I been looked at with such loathing.

But it was something far simpler that had given him away.

"This man was not a Keeper," I insisted. "He wore the brown hood of a monk."

CHAPTER 11

"Tell me precisely what happened," Cathan said. He tugged at the thick hair of his beard as I related my story.

"It was only my wrist," I said. "But . . ." I searched the ground, feeling rather foolish now to have been so shaken by a chance encounter in the wood.

"Go on," Cathan urged.

"The forest changed. And he looked at me with such loathing. As if I were little more than a grain rat."

"A grain rat." Cathan paced the trail, his eyes bright with anger. It seemed for a moment that he would leave us and strike out in search of the man, but he could not abandon us with no escort, no guard. He raked a hand through his hair and turned.

"Languoreth. Are you quite certain this man wore the hood of a monk?"

I hesitated, wondering if I dared repeat the truth. Brother Telleyr was our friend. We had always lived in peace with Christians, what few we had met. But there was no mistaking the man I had seen, the brown cowl he'd worn. Nor the feeling of danger that yet pooled in the pit of my stomach.

I nodded. Cathan closed his eyes a moment.

"That man had no right to trespass on this sacred hill. Worse, I do not think his intention was to tread it lightly."

"We must ride out," Lail said. "We must find him and bring him before the Council!"

"You and your riding out," Cathan said. "You would wage war with the world! This is now a matter for the Keepers, Lailoken. I will thank you to ponder it no further." The Wisdom Keeper reached to smooth the hair from my face, and the edge dropped from his voice.

"No harm has come to you. This is what matters. Come, now, let's get you home. I'll thank the Gods that no more adventures should find us on the road."

Cathan rode ahead, his body stiff as he surveyed the fields for any sign of danger. But even as I eased into the soothing rhythm of Fallah's gait and Bright Hill receded into the distance, my mind returned to the forest.

What was a Christian monk doing walking the slopes of Bright Hill? The Wisdom Keepers and Telleyr's monks had always lived peaceably. Partick was Cathan's domain. The Christians had their monastery and grounds on the outskirts of town. And White Isle, Strathclyde's center for training young Keepers, was only a small stretch downriver from the hill.

When we arrived at Buckthorn, we told Father of all that had taken place. He gestured for me to come and cradled my wrist, turning it gently in his weathered hands.

"Not broken," he said.

"I will tend to it." Ariane came swiftly with a salve to ease the swelling and wrapped my wrist in cloth, her eyes dark with anger.

"I should have been with you," she said. "It will not happen again."

There were warriors among Father's retinue who had earned their keep by skill in their stealth. Men like Arwel, Oren's brother, who had been at Cadzow the day the people of Bryneich came. His smile was easy, his voice even. But his eyes were keen. It was he Father sent to inquire about the monk I had seen in the woods.

We waited, and tried to forget.

No news came, and as Beltane drew closer, more merchants arrived, the hulls of their boats filled with salt, wine, and succulent sweets like raisins, figs, and dates.

On the morning of Beltane eve, Buckthorn bustled with activity. Father had been called to the hunt by the high king and had ridden off that morning. We would host a feast on the morrow, and Wisdom Keepers had been arriving from all corners of the kingdom to join in the lighting of Bel's Fire on the summit of Bright Hill. Children mobbed them in the streets in hopes of a cloutie or a charm, a blessing or a glimpse of otherworldly magic.

Now I sat in the little chamber beside the door in a rare moment of peace, quill in hand, practicing my lettering. Crowan had thrown herself into preparations weeks ago, and I'd busied myself in observing how she managed the servants, in stitching garlands, and in visiting the market with Desdemona to fetch the necessary ingredients.

With all the preparations for the feast, I hadn't time to forage with Ariane that morning, but now my work was done and she'd promised to fetch me when she returned.

"When I get back, I will teach you a kenning," she'd promised in an effort to cheer. At last, when I heard her voice call out to the guard, I sprang from my seat.

Lail looked up from his seat beside the oil lamp, where his head had been buried in a Greek text on geometry. "Who is it?"

"It's only Ariane."

He nodded and turned back to his reading. Ariane had lifted her hand to knock when I thrust the door open.

"I thought you would never arrive—" I began, but stopped when I saw her. Her dark hair was windblown, hanging in pieces from her plait. When she lifted her head, I saw her pale face was streaked in dirt, her eyes wet with tears.

"Languoreth, is your father returned from the hunt? I would speak with him right away."

I stood for a moment, dumbstruck. I had not imagined Ariane could weep. "What's happened?" I asked.

"Your father," she demanded. "I must speak with him right away!"

I shrank from the bark in her voice. "He's not yet returned."

"On all the days!" Ariane threw up her hands with a curse. Rushing past me into the corridor, she shouted for my cousin. "Brant!"

Brant materialized drowsy-eyed from the great room, where he'd been dozing, but at the sight of her he came awake as if someone had doused him with snowmelt.

"What is it?"

Ariane's eyes flicked between the two of us as if she would spare me but hadn't the time. "There has been . . . a terrible act on Bright Hill," she said. "You must come right away."

A terrible act.

Panic rose in my throat. Cathan had traveled there only this morning to make offerings and to pray.

"What's happened?" I demanded. "Ariane, you must tell us. Is Cathan all right?"

Upon hearing, Crowan and Lail rushed over, but Ariane gave no answer. "We must go now, Brant." She yanked at his tunic. "There is no time to waste."

He slung his baldric over his shoulder and hurried toward the door. "I'm ready."

"I'm coming," Lail said, snatching up his cloak.

"And me," I said, doing the same.

Crowan stepped forward, her little frame growing impossibly large as she blocked our way. "Nay, I think not! You'll stay here where it's safe!"

Brant was moving through the door. Lail clutched Crowan's frock like a caged animal. "Crowan, please."

I leaned in close so she could not mistake me. "If something has happened to Cathan and you do not let us go, Crowan, I shall never forgive you."

She looked between us, frowning, her thin mouth pursed.

"I'll look out for them, I swear it," Brant called from the courtyard, then turned to the warrior at the gate. "Send word to Morken. He must know of this right away."

Crowan followed us into the courtyard, shaking her fist at him. "So be it, Brant. But the Gods hear my oath. If any harm should come to them, I'll nail your parts to—"

Her words were lost in the wind as we raced toward the stable, calling out for our horses.

We had scarcely arrived at the edge of town when we heard the shouts. Tutgual's soldiers were mounted on horseback, yelling for order as people streaked from the shops and huts of Partick, their anguished cries filling the streets. Brant jerked the reins of his mount and skittered to a halt, nearly trampling a dark-haired woman who had rushed at him with a babe on her hip.

She looked up at Brant, clutching at his calf. "The Hill," she wailed.

"We are headed there now. Make way," Brant shouted. "Stay back!"

The scarlet capes of Tutgual's men flashed amid the masses. "Stand back!" one commanded. "Let Morken's man through."

With the road clear, I leaned into Fallah. "Faster, girl. Go faster."

We sped onward, out of town and through the fields, my heart thudding in time with Fallah's hooves as we dodged the twisting procession of townspeople making their way to Bright Hill. I saw them in flashes as we passed, their tear-streaked faces tilted to the sky or buried in disbelief in the fabric of their tunics.

Fallah's coat was near frothing by the time we reached the towering yew at the foot of the bridge. White-robed Keepers were pacing the foot of the hill, eyes wild with grief, arguing, shouting, or keening, all of them thrusting their arms toward the mount of Bright Hill.

It was the fear of what we might find that pushed me to drop from Fallah's back, Lailoken close on my heels, as I brushed past Brant and Ariane, up the trail I'd climbed only a fortnight before.

I heard Ariane calling after me, but I had left them behind now, lungs burning, until at last I breached the summit of the hill.

A lone white-robed figure stood as if stunned in the center of the ancient grove of oaks.

What had once been a grove.

Now ragged stumps protruded from the earth like bones burst through skin. It was difficult to see amid the mangle of fallen trees the number of oaks that had been felled. I reached a timid hand to touch a jagged stump. Some had been more cleanly cleaved with an axe, while others lay splintered, hacked by something duller that possessed less mercy. Whoever had done it had not taken them all; perhaps because the trunks were so thick, they found themselves unable. But those that remained looked battered, too, as if the very life had been sucked out of them. Tears stung and I blinked them onto my cheeks, staring at the man who stood motionless in the wreckage. Beside me Lailoken made a sound as though the wind had been knocked out of him.

"Cathan?" I called.

His head tilted at the sound of my voice but did not turn. He moved instead like a feeble old man to sink down beside a fallen tree. The sound of his humming came, drifting and achy with grief as he laid his hands tenderly upon the splintered wood.

As we closed the distance between us, I thought I heard him mur-mur something.

"When the trees were enchanted, there was hope for the trees."

But then his breath hitched and his shoulders began to shake.

Cathan the Wisdom Keeper was weeping.

I knelt beside Cathan, leaned my head against his shoulder. Lailoken came and swiped gently at Cathan's face with the edge of his sleeve. The Wisdom Keeper looked at us then. Took a breath as if relearning the habit.

"They were the watchers in the wood, carriers of hopes and dreams. Their hollows were the keepers of secrets. Every knot and whorl marked the memory of a story so ancient, the echoes faded eons ago. And yet those stories lived on, kept safe in the circles of their rings. This is why we come to their groves, why we sing to them. Because the oaks help us to remember: who we are, who we were, where we once came from."

I looked across the hilltop, a battlefield where none had come to claim the dead. At first I was too stunned to feel any anger. But as the destruction seeped in, a heat began to smolder somewhere deep inside me like an ember in the belly of a dragon.

That was when I saw it, some distance off. A solitary mound of earth.

"What is that?"

Cathan inclined his head, willing me to look. Lailoken and I rose and approached with mounting dread. It was a grave—a mound of freshly dug dirt pierced by a rudimentary wooden cross. I squinted at the Latin inscription it bore.

Hic depositum est corpus Fergi
pius servus Dei

Here lies the body of Fergus.
Devoted Servant of God.

CHAPTER 12

Grief clung to the great room as if it were smothered in soot. Father, Cathan, Lailoken, Ariane, Telleyr, and I sat in silence, each of us feeling the rage and splinters of the grove in our own way. Our anger was like a sickness.

"I am confounded." Telleyr's broad shoulders slumped. "I cannot make sense of how this did happen."

"Confounded, are you?" Cathan fixed the monk with a stare. "This is an act of war. A sacred hill defiled, marked with a Christian burial like the piss of a cat. The wrath of the Keepers will be swift, I can promise you that."

Across the room, Father was hunched in his great oaken chair. "Telleyr. Long winters have passed since I first called you a friend. But this Fergus was a monk of your order. Was he not in your private company when we met on the road on our way to the capital? And yet you insist this devastation has been wrought without your knowledge."

"Morken. Christ may be my God, but I am your friend and a former Keeper. Never before has religion come between us. Let it not divide us now," Telleyr said. "Can you think it does not grieve me to see such a sacred place laid to ruin? Do you imagine that Christians cannot also hear the cries of the trees?"

Father shifted in his seat. "I do not wish to insult you. Yet I cannot understand how a plotting of this magnitude escaped your notice."

Telleyr tugged his cowl from his head as if it itched him. His hair beneath was disheveled. "My people do not plot," he said firmly. "There are none among my community, whether they be worshipper or Brother, who could conceive of such a hateful and violent act."

Cathan slammed a fist to his knee. "Dead men do not work alone! There is a monk of your order buried upon Bright Hill in a Christian grave!"

This sickness would turn to madness. Any could see Telleyr's innocence. I opened my mouth to speak, but Ariane reached out a hand and pressed me deeper into my seat.

This is not your place, her stern look said.

"Perhaps Brother Telleyr might start from the beginning," Father said.

"Of course."

Father rubbed a hand over his bearded face as Telleyr stood. "I have gone over and over the events in my mind," the monk began. "Since our return from the Borderlands, Fergus's health began fading by the day. When he was absent for first vespers yesterday morning, I found him abed. His suffering had been long, but he'd passed during the night. Prayers were said. He was cleansed and dressed, readied for burial. I laid his body out yesterday evening in the church myself; we were to bury him this morning, once we had consecrated the ground.

"Brother Anguen had gone to light the candles for this morning's service when he noticed—with some alarm—that the body of Brother Fergus had vanished. We did not know what to think! Had some wild animal come and somehow carried him off? Was this some cruel prank brought upon us by village tricksters? Some even spoke of divine resurrection."

Cathan snorted at the ridiculousness of this and was preparing to say something further, when a pounding sounded at the door.

Father looked up in annoyance. "Come," he called out.

The doors of the great room swung open and a scarlet-cloaked soldier from Tutgual's guard swept in, his black hair clipped as short as the cap of a jackdaw.

The warrior stepped forward, bowing his head in greeting. "Morken. I realize the hour is late."

"It is no matter, Breg. There will be little sleep this night." Father lifted his cup, an offer of drink, but Tutgual's man gave a curt shake of his head.

"The high king would like to extend his sympathies to Cathan of the White Isle for the horrific act that was carried out on Bright Hill this day. He has convened a meeting of the Council first thing on the morrow. Until then, sentries have been posted at the foot of Bright Hill for the safety of all concerned."

Cathan tilted his head like a hawk. "And just who are these sentries there to protect?"

"The sentries have been ordered to keep the peace," Breg said. "To that end, the king has requested both the hilltop and the grave lie undisturbed this night."

"Let the grave lie undisturbed?" Cathan balked. "Just whom does the king think he commands? The land of Bright Hill is under our divine jurisdiction."

Tutgual's man stiffened. "The land of Bright Hill is also under the jurisdiction of the Kingdom of Strathclyde."

Cathan stood with an agility I didn't know he possessed. In his white robes, his silver hair lit amber by hearth light, he was transformed into something formidable, almost otherworldly. His eyes darkened like a storm on the sea.

"Do you wish to debate the law with me, warrior? I could tell you the history of the land grants of this kingdom with an accuracy that stretches back to its roots in the beginning of time out of memory. Or, if it please me, I could rattle such a curse that would leave your ballocks shrunken in the seat of your pants."

Breg shifted ever so slightly, and Cathan shook his head in disgust. "Tell your king his sympathies are wasted."

Father bowed his head. He was no less angered, but, unlike Keepers, who could say whatever they pleased, my father was beholden to Tutgual, the high king. Breg looked to him. "And, Morken. What say you?"

I held my breath. Father stood. "Tell your king I will attend the meeting of the Council on the morrow. Until then, Gods keep you."

"And you." Breg turned on his heel, eager, it seemed, to leave. Our servant closed the doors behind him and retreated to his station at the edge of the room.

Ariane thrummed her fingers absently against her collarbone as she did when she was thinking. "It would be foolish not to consider the involvement of Tutgual himself, or, in the very least, people from his court. I have heard he is a man who likes to bolster his wagers. After all, was it not he who drew Morken away for the hunt?" she said.

"I confess I do not know Tutgual's mind," Father said. "He does not profess to be a Christian, but he welcomes Christian families into his lands and his courts. One does not become high king by refusing to bend in a powerful wind. Long has his family courted the protection of Rome."

Cathan motioned for a cup. "We will discover the culprits and the desecration will be removed."

Telleyr ceased his pacing. "You cannot mean to remove the body."

"You cannot think I would allow it to stay."

"Lord Cathan. You place me in a difficult situation. Can we not seek a peaceful resolution?"

"Peace?" Cathan said. "You ask for peace? This may be no act of yours, but there can be no mistake. The burial of this body on sacred soil was designed to ignite a war. My people will riot should I let that body stand."

"I do not argue your point," Telleyr said. "But the fact remains that Fergus was a consecrated monk of my order and a man of the church. My people will riot to see his body removed. Can you not see what a predicament we are in?" He looked at the Wisdom Keeper, his kind face imploring. "I would humbly request that you allow the body of Brother Fergus to rest."

"What you ask is impossible," Cathan said. "A human body, and moreover the body of a Christian zealot, now rots in one of the most sacred sites to the Britons north of the Wall. Oaks that have stood sentinel for nearly one thousand years have been most abhorrently hacked down. You know too well the punishment for felling such a tree. And you ask me to let this lie?"

"Cathan is right," Father said. "This cannot stand. This night is Beltane eve, and the fires were extinguished by this act before they could even be lit. The rites for the land were not conducted. Our people are enraged! They worry for the crops. They worry that famine will return. Listen! Even now, at this distance, you can hear them on the streets."

Telleyr turned to Father, defeated. "What would you have me do?"

"Get some sleep," Father sighed. "We will attend the Gathering on the morrow. We will discuss this act and decide what shall be done. It is late, and you have a long ride home in the dark. You may bed here if you like."

"Thank you, my friend. But I have already accepted King Tutgual's offer to bed in his hall in Partick this night. It is an invitation I cannot refuse."

"So be it." Father nodded. Telleyr moved to the doors but then turned back, his dark eyes beseeching.

"Morken. You are a just and considerate king. Before I depart, I would ask for your word that Fergus's body will rest undisturbed this night."

Father stroked his beard, regarding the monk. At last he bowed his head. "You have my word. I will not remove his body."

"I thank you." Telleyr's shoulders sank in relief.

"Travel in safety, Brother."

"Until tomorrow."

Father nodded. "Tomorrow."

The monk's dark eyes touched on mine in parting, and I read sorrow in their depths. As the doors to the great room closed behind him, Father turned to us.

"To bed, children. You have heard enough talk for one day."

I was too bruised to argue, though when I closed my eyes, I could only see Cathan on his knees, weeping in a field of splintered giants. I gathered my sewing from my lap and rose. "Good night, Father."

"But, Father," Lail said, "what of—"

"Lailoken. Do you question me?" Father's wick had burned short.

I stared at my brother, begging him to be silent. At last Lail rose reluctantly but followed me all the same.

"Good night, then," Father said, and we closed the doors to the great room behind us.

I sighed. "I wonder if there has ever before been a Beltane eve on which the fires were not lit."

Lail did not answer, and I looked back to see him kneeling with his face pressed to the slender gap between the doors.

"Lailoken!"

"Shhh!" he hissed.

"Lailoken," I whispered, "one of these days you are going to get caught. And you will be deserving of your beating." I narrowed my eyes but then lowered myself down beside him all the same, just in time to hear the soft scrape of a chair against the floor. The doors could not muffle the gloom in Father's voice.

"Brother Telleyr asked for my word. I cannot go with you."

"I would not ask it of you," Cathan said.

"What of Tutgual's men?" Ariane's voice sounded as clear as a bell, as if she stood just on the other side of the doors, and I tugged at Lail's sleeve, but he swatted me away.

Cathan scoffed. "I will not wait for a king's permission to cleanse my own land. It is Beltane eve. The presence of soldiers will be no trouble for me."

My brother's eyes lit with pride. I looked at him as if to say, *You do realize someone could get terribly hurt.*

"We share this outrage. I should be with you." Father's voice was solemn. "Who would you take? Brant and Brodyn can follow. They'll stay out of sight."

"No," Cathan said. "I may be able to cloak myself in shadow, but I cannot cloak another. Let alone two. There will be men on the road. And this is the business of a Keeper. I will have your iron at my back should I need it."

I heard the scrape of another chair and Father's sigh. "Yes. If it comes to that, you know well that you do."

Lail frowned as if to say something, but at the shuffling sound of feet we scrambled from the doors, disappearing up the stairs just as the doors swung open below.

I stood on my toes to peer over the high wooden rail. Down below, Cathan loomed in the gloom of the doorway, a dark riding cloak cast over his sleeve. Ariane's slender shadow stretched on the floor before him.

"Perhaps I am new among you," she said. "But one man against so many . . ."

"There is no other way," Cathan said. "March my Keepers up Bright

Hill and it is as Telleyr says: we would beget a war. I will not be goaded into such action."

"And what if war were inevitable?" she said. "What would you do then?"

"You speak as though you have seen something I cannot," Cathan said.

"I have only seen the hearts of men."

"Ariane." Cathan bowed his head. "I hear your warning."

Lailoken and I ducked from the railing, our footfalls masked by the heavy groan of the iron latch on the main door before it closed behind Cathan with a clang. Lailoken motioned me into his chamber.

"He's going to Bright Hill." I leaned against the welcome solidity of Lailoken's door.

"Cathan is lord of the White Isle, sister. He has no choice." Lail seemed uneasy, as if his skin itched from the inside out. He moved to the small pine table that sat beneath his window, letting his fingers roam restlessly over the clutter of objects on the tabletop: a chunk of mica, a silver brooch, a tablet of slate on which he'd been practicing his Ogham alphabet, a thick wooden comb.

"But the guards," I said. "How will he not be seen?"

"You think guards will keep Cathan from Bright Hill?" Lail asked. "Wisdom Keepers have their ways. Just as the sea god Manannan can veil himself in mist as if it were a cloak. Cathan keeps counsel with many gods. Surely they will come to his aid."

"Just as the Gods came to the aid of our trees?" I asked.

Lail looked up, angry. "You have no faith in what the Gods can do."

"And what if I do not? The Gods did not protect Mother. The Gods did not protect Bright Hill. Yet they will come to Cathan's aid?"

Lailoken turned away. Like all men, Cathan had fought battles in his time, but he was older than Father. The hands that had once tossed a spear now held only a staff. I tried to summon once more the magic of walking Bright Hill—unseen eyes—but nothing came. Worse was the way Lailoken's gaze kept shifting toward the door. The moment I left, he would do something foolish.

"I'm frightened for Cathan is all," I tried. "I know I will not sleep. Stay with me, like when we were little."

Lail leveled his gaze at me as if, in a different light, he'd find my attempt amusing.

"Languoreth, you are not my keeper. I can look after myself."

"Can you? And what exactly is your plan?" I said, hands on my hips. "Father will have men posted not only at the gate but also at the outside doors. If you think Brant and Brodyn will look the other way, you're mistaken. Truly, Lail. Causing trouble with all that's happened today? It's the middle of the night! Bright Hill is guarded by a score of Tutgual's men or more. You'd be found out in an instant. And what do you think will happen when the son of a king of the Old Way is caught meddling with a Christian body on Bright Hill? Father will be to blame, that's what."

"Keep your voice down." Lail's blue eyes were stony.

"You're as stubborn as an ox and as foolish, too!" I whispered.

"A fool, am I?" Lail tipped his chin. "I have begun my training, Languoreth. I should be there. I should be there with my teacher."

The haughtiness in his voice broke the dam of my anger. "I need no further reminders that you have begun your training, Lailoken."

"You're only jealous."

"Yes, I *am* jealous!" I exclaimed. "And why should I not be? Did it never occur to you that I might wish to train as a Wisdom Keeper, too? Do you not imagine how it pains me to be excluded from your lessons—that I shall never have the freedom to become a healer like Mother, to be the master of my own fate? For me these are impossible dreams. For me there is no other destiny than to become the wife of a stranger!"

Lail stood as if he'd been struck. A shadow of guilt passed over his face.

"You're right. I have been selfish," he said. "I did not think of how you might feel."

"It doesn't matter." I looked down at my hands. "You are too hasty, Lailoken. You cannot ride out into the night as if you weren't made of skin and bone. Can't you see? You are my twin. We are made of each other. If anything should happen to you . . ." My voice broke. At the sight of my tears, Lailoken's face fell as if he might cry, too.

"Don't cry, Languoreth. I will stay, all right? I will stay."

"It isn't enough," I said, searching for what might be. First my brother had wished to ride out and fight the Angles. And now . . . What if Lailoken *had* somehow managed to sneak away, only to be mistaken as an interloper by Tutgual's men? I'd seen enough to know Tutgual's warriors were not kindly. Perhaps they would have returned him to Father. More likely they would have sought to teach my brother a lesson he would not soon forget.

I sank onto his bed. "You must promise not to do such things without first confiding in me, Lailoken. We must look after each other."

He looked at me for a long moment. "You're right. After all, you are my twin. Your blood is my blood, and my blood is yours. If we cannot trust each other, who can we trust?"

"Swear it, then," I said, reaching for his hand. "Swear that from this day forth we shall always look after each other."

"All right," Lail said. "I swear it."

"No. Not like that."

I could not explain it, but I sensed a moonless danger lurking in the shadows of our path, one that could be satisfied only by blood. Something loomed this night, with Cathan riding into the dark, with the wind rattling against the shutters as if the Gods themselves were wailing.

Lailoken came to sit with me and offered up his hand. The blade of my knife glinted vermillion in the light of the oil lamps. A crimson bead sprung up as I pressed its point to the padded whorl of his finger like a jewel we might toss into a pool. The sting of the knife on my own finger was my lot to cast. Solemnly we pressed our fingers together.

And we told ourselves our bond would never be broken.

CHAPTER 13

There were no buttery wreaths of May Day broom decking the doors of the huts the next morning as we rode into Partick. Absent was the earthy smell of woodsmoke from the Beltane fires that lingered so long after they'd burned out. Shops were shuttered, market stalls empty. The royal town of Partick was in mourning. People thronged the square outside the Gathering Place, scarcely moving aside for the warriors and chieftains trotting in with their retinues to attend the Gathering called by the high king.

Cathan had not yet returned, but I refused to believe any ill had befallen him. Still, I shivered in the rush of wind that bent the trees. High on the thatched roof of the Gathering Place, a murder of crows stood, their bodies gleaming like ink pots in the morning sun. Ariane loosened her grip on her reins and lifted her eyes to the dark flapping birds.

"Look at the crows," she said. "Do you see how they hop? They wait for something. The Gods. They are watching."

I pushed back the hood of my riding cloak, shielding my eyes. "Perhaps they wait for Cathan," I said.

"They wait for justice," Ariane said.

Brant and Brodyn rode up ahead with Father, edgy as a pair of falcons who'd been tethered overlong. We led our horses to a stand of hickories and dismounted, leaving them for our grooms to tend.

I scoured the crowd in search of Gwrgi and Peredur, despite the news they had returned to Ebruac some days earlier. Never had I seen so many noblemen in one place. Father's torque winked in the dappled light as he strode to greet the other chieftains. They looked to me like living myths, wild-haired and bearded, with their magnificent brooches and finely woven plaids. They were fierce-faced and straight-backed, some of them marred by war, though none bore a scar like my father's. As they spoke to one another, I sought to read the stories upon their faces. This one was a friend to Father. That one he did not trust. When their sights rested on me, on my brother, my heart hammered small and fast, and I wanted to cling to Father's cloak or hide in my mother's skirts as I'd done as a babe. Sensing my nerves, Father turned to me and clasped my hand, his undereyes bruised with purple from last night's vigil.

"All will be well, Languoreth. Don't forget, you must stand behind your brother. Do you remember what I've told you?"

"Do not speak unless I am bidden."

"And?"

"Do not laugh."

"Do not laugh? I doubt there will be much occasion for laughter this day."

I frowned. "It's only that Brant and Brodyn said there are many who endeavor to make them laugh at King Tutgual's court."

"I see." Father shot my cousins a grim look. "What your cousins mean to say is that there are many at court they find amusing. It would be a very good idea, Languoreth, to try not to laugh."

I nodded and slipped into place behind Lailoken. It wasn't just the birds that made me anxious. It was as if the air itself were alive and breathing. Waiting. Ariane eyed my coiled plaits and deep purple frock and reached to give my arm an awkward pat.

"Lift your chin, now, Languoreth," she said, nudging me into the throng. "Let them see the daughter of a king."

The people parted for Morken and his retinue like water skirts a boulder. I fixed my gaze on Father's amber hair as he moved toward the immense timber building, his bulk towering above the crowd. I blinked as we entered the dizzying inner sanctum of the Gathering Place, trying to adjust my eyes to the dimmer light.

So this was court. The lords and petty kings of the north were plumed in plaids like rare birds, proud-chested and preening in clusters round the perimeter of the grand hall, their voices like the deep hum of a hive. Wives stood in the shadows of their lords, their cheeks bright with berry stain, their eyes lined with kohl, their hair coiffed and coiled, their slender bodies wrapped in jewel-toned robes tipped with delicate handwork of the finest embroidery.

As we followed Father to our places, Ariane gagged, coughing as if to clear her throat.

"Ugh. This *perfume*. It is as if they would drown me."

A green-eyed woman in a clinging scarlet robe fixed Ariane with a stare, and I tugged her along, giving the noblewoman a small bow of apology.

Members of the Council, some white-robed Keepers, some clad in royal garb, stood huddled, heads bent, already discussing the matter at hand. But all of the room, Council and court alike, leaned, as poppies toward the sun, toward the man who sat at the head of the open arena in an ornately carved oaken throne.

Tutgual, the high king of Strathclyde.

I attempted to read him, as I had so readily divined the natures of the other nobles, but his blue eyes were serene as a cloudless sky, devoid of feeling. His face was thin and bearded, framed by wavy graying hair that might once have been brown, and the sharp angles of his cheeks gave him the appearance of a ravenous eagle. He was tall but built with fading muscle. The heavy ocher fabric of his cloak was clasped at the shoulder by the most exquisite brooch I had ever seen.

A beautiful woman stood behind him, her slender fingers resting casually on the arm of Tutgual's throne.

"Look." I prodded Lailoken. "That must be Elufed, his queen."

She was slightly younger than my mother had been, but where my mother had been all forest and earth, Elufed was a winter river, thick with ice. Her pale yellow hair was swept from her face by two jeweled combs, left to cascade in luxuriant waves over her shoulders. She wore a deep-sapphire robe that made her eyes appear impossibly crystalline. Not blue, but gray and elemental, like glaciers or shadows on snow. She looked languidly about the room, and then my breath caught as her eyes locked on mine, frank with curiosity. She tilted her head to say something low in her husband's ear.

"She's a Pict," Lail whispered. "One of the First People. I heard Tutgual wed her when she was little more than a girl. She couldn't have been much older than you are now." Looking at me, he winced. "I'm sorry, sister. It was a stupid thing to say."

"Forget it. I don't mind," I lied, and craned my neck instead in search of Brother Telleyr. I spotted him standing just beyond where the Council members were gathered, his ruddy face solemn. Behind him stood a cluster of monks from his order, brothers in brown hoods, but the edges of the Gathering Place were lit by shafts of sunlight and pockets of shadow, and I couldn't quite make out their faces.

A whisper rose from the crowd. How much longer would Tutgual delay the proceedings? Still there was no sign of Cathan. Quite suddenly the high king's captain stepped forward and addressed the crowd.

"Tutgual, son of Cedic, high king of the kingdom of Strathclyde and Clyde Rock, the ancient rock of the Britons, welcomes you to the Gathering convened on this day."

Tutgual's eyes rested on my father and he gestured, the sleeve of his tunic flapping like a bird.

"Morken. Come."

A hush traveled through the room until it was so silent I could hear the soft slapping of my father's boots as he crossed the expanse to clasp the arm of the king.

"Morken," Tutgual repeated, looking about the crowded room. "Such news as befell us upon yesterday's hunt has never before darkened the hills or hollows of Strathclyde. You have answered the summons so that the Council might decide the due course of justice. But it appears Lord Cathan has chosen not to appear."

"It appears that is so, my king."

"Perhaps you will tell me why."

Father inclined his head. "Would that I knew, my king. But I am afraid I cannot say. Though Lord Cathan acts as my chief counsellor, he keeps counsel only with himself, as any Wisdom Keeper has the right."

Tutgual narrowed his eyes and lifted a finger to his lips as if considering what he might do. "Then we must conduct our Gathering without him," he said. "You will stand in his stead."

Father's grimace was so slight that any who didn't know him might not have noticed.

"Aye. It is only fair we should begin."

Lail and I looked at each other. Our father was a king, not an orator. A warrior, not an arbitrator. He was neither trained nor comfortable fulfilling Cathan's role. But it appeared the king would see this matter concluded whether or not the Wisdom Keeper was here to speak. Father had little choice.

"Then let us turn to the matter at hand," Tutgual began. "The desecration of Bright Hill, undertaken by unknown men. We shall ask Brother Telleyr be first to speak."

Telleyr bowed his head in a gesture of respect to Father, the Council, and the high king before striding into the center of the room.

"For many years now, good Christians have called Partick their home," he began. "We have lived peaceably despite any difference in belief, as has long been the way of the Britons. We are shopkeepers and shield makers, farmers and bakers, just like you. Our God may be Christ, but we are not separate. We are all of us Britons. It is only together that believers of the one God and the many can make a prosperous kingdom."

A murmuring of approval came from the crowd, and Telleyr let it drift before he continued.

"Who carried the body of Brother Fergus up the sacred slopes of Bright Hill? Whose axes and blades felled our ancient grove of oaks? These are questions I cannot answer. I only know that none among my community are capable of such acts. Many Christians who worship with me now were not long ago worshippers of that same hill. What has taken place is unconscionable. The hearts of our community bleed alongside those of our neighbors."

"We are thankful for your compassion, Brother Telleyr," the king said. "It does much to mend the spirit. Does it not, Morken? What say you?"

Father bowed his head.

"I am a warrior and a king, not a jurist or Wisdom Keeper. But I am learned in the law as befitting my station. My people have worshipped the Gods of our ancestors since time out of memory. And since time out of memory, it has been law that to fell any sacred tree is an act punishable by death." His brown eyes swept the room. "Therefore I would say that the body of Fergus must be removed. And I must demand that those who undertook this violence be sought out. They must be brought to the sort of justice only a sword can relay."

Cries rang from the throng, and Tutgual lifted his hand, demanding silence.

"Brother Telleyr"—the high king gestured—"what is your reply?"

"We cannot even guess which man might be guilty of this crime. An agreement can be achieved, I am sure of it. Allow the body of Fergus to rest, and in turn, the Christian community will repair the damage done. Hauling away wood, repopulating the trees. Whatever we may do to be of use, let it be done in the name of kinship. This divisive situation can yet serve as a monument to peace if we can only see beyond this grievance and let this body lie."

At this, Father snorted like a bull. "You ask us to look beyond this grievance?"

"It was an egregious act." Telleyr looked guilty, as if he did not wish to say what he was about to. "However, I would remind King Morken that to remove a Christian body from its resting place is an equally criminal act, punishable by pain of death."

I clutched at Lailoken's shirt.

"By whose law?" Father scoffed.

"By law of the Holy Roman Empire. The burial place of a person, regardless of faith, constitutes a *locus religiosus*, and as such, it is as inviolable as any temple or church," Telleyr said. "The body of one who has been laid to rest may not be removed from its place of burial under penalty of injury and even death. The law applies to all citizens and lands under the canopy of Rome."

Father laughed. "It is fortunate, then, that we are no longer governed by the laws of Rome. I am certain I need not remind the Council that we have not been subject to the laws of a foreign empire for more than one hundred and fifty years."

Disquiet swelled in the Gathering Place, and I looked anxiously to Telleyr.

"That may be so," Telleyr said. "But by Roman law, any Christian in Britain yet falls beneath its protection. The body of Fergus has been entombed. The laws of Rome yet protect the rights of the Christian people and make sacrosanct their final resting place."

"If we are to be governed by Roman law, the sanctity of the site— the *locus religiosus*, as you say—would also refer to the sanctity of Bright Hill on behalf of the Old Way," Father said. "For it is a sacred place with far more ancient a history than the hastily dug grave of this man called Fergus. The Beltane fires have not been lit. There could not have been a more foolish time to toy with the affection of the Gods. The citizens of this kingdom depend on our harvests. If a blight comes to Strathclyde, you and the men of your church will be to blame."

Shouts erupted from the crowd, and I shrank back as the towns-people began to push and rattle the wooden barrier that separated the peasant and merchant caste from the nobles.

"A curse on the Christians!" someone called out.

"What of our children?" a woman shouted. "The fires have not been lit! Our children will starve!"

The warriors posted round the wooden barrier stiffened, gripping their spears, and Brodyn's fingers edged toward his sword. Tutgual stood, his voice booming over the tumult of the crowd.

"Silence! I will have silence!"

Tutgual's warriors turned in one swift movement to face the dis-senters, their shields clattering to form a shield wall. It stayed the people, though some yet glared, their eyes lit by a fire I did not think would soon be extinguished.

The room went still, and the high king eased back into his throne and steepled his fingers, his face placid with reflection.

"It would appear that we are at an impasse," Tutgual said. Furrow-ing his brow, he surveyed the room, reveling in the great silence, the power he commanded. The vast importance of what he prepared to say next.

A shame, then, that he never had the opportunity to say it. For at that very moment, another voice sounded from the farthest corner of the Gathering Place, deep as a boom of thunder.

"You say we are at an impasse."

Nobles and peasants alike turned to behold Cathan the Wisdom Keeper, lord of the White Isle, standing on the threshold of the Gath-ering Place, and a cheer rose up from the people. His white robes were lit in a swath of morning sun. Before him he balanced a sturdy three-wheeled cart. I saw something disguised in stiff folds of burlap sticking up from the cart as Cathan waited for acknowledgment from the king. But he did not bow. Wisdom Keepers bowed to no one.

Tutgual eyed the cart a moment before beckoning. "Lord Cathan. Come."

Cathan did as he was bidden. "You say we are at an impasse, Tutgual King," Cathan repeated, "but I cannot agree." There was no mistaking the glimmer in his eyes when he lifted his head, his gaze piercing Tutgual's like a pike.

"Then it would please the Council to hear your argument." Tutgual's face belied his words; it would not please him at all.

"Ah. My argument." Cathan tilted his head. "The Council will thank me, as there is no need for argument. The offending body has been removed."

With a thrust of his arms, Cathan upended the wooden cart.

A shower of loose soil rained over the smooth slate floor. Something heavy tumbled from the cart. The burlap unraveled itself with a flourish.

The waxy and distended corpse of Brother Fergus fell at Tutgual's feet with a deep and sickening thud.

CHAPTER 14

For a moment there was no sound, like the silence I imagined in the time before the Gods took a breath and the new world was born. The eyes of the room were upon the body of Fergus, his thick, discolored limbs splayed like a butchered hog's upon the floor. And then it was as if a sudden snap of wind woke the crowd from their stupor as a dissonant army of voices rose in a fury, echoing wildly off the stones.

Ariane reached to grab me. Across the room Father's dark eyes found us and he moved toward us, alert, the way he looked when he swung upon his horse to ride off to battle. Brant and Brodyn moved to shield the three of us as Father's hand closed about my wrist.

"Quickly, children," he said, low. "We must go now."

"What's happening?" I asked.

"We must go *now*." His voice held a warning I'd not heard before.

"A riot," Lail said. "Father's worried they'll riot."

The nobles were scattering now, trying to maintain their dignity as they moved toward the same grand entryway, but their fear smelled sour. The peasants behind the barrier began to pulse, to push, and Tutgual's warriors bristled, their iron-tipped spears baring like teeth—a warning to the crowd. Brodyn reached back roughly for my hand and hooked my fingers firmly round his belt.

"Hang on to me, Languoreth," he commanded. "Do not let go."

I gripped Brodyn's belt as the shouting grew to a fevered pitch. Ariane pressed close. "Do not be afraid," she said.

Just beyond the muscled tower of Brodyn, I caught sight of a young man, the son of one of our own tenants, as he ducked beneath the barrier and ran with a cry at one of Tutgual's warriors.

It happened too quickly—the thrust of the spear. And I watched as the young man's face shifted from fury to surprise as the spear gored his chest, blood issuing in a crimson and clotted geyser, soaking the leather armor of the warrior who had impaled him, igniting the outrage of the crowd. I screamed. The young man fell back like a scarecrow, gurgling onto the floor. Tutgual's soldier yanked the spear from his body with a satisfied smirk, and the Gathering Place exploded into chaos. The crush of bodies thrust me off balance and I bit my own tongue as my chin collided with the hilt of Brodyn's sword.

"Languoreth." Brodyn steadied me. "Do not let go!"

I gripped his belt once more as men in rough tunics launched themselves over the barrier in a torrential rain, beating against the shields of Tutgual's warriors with bare fists.

"There!" Father pointed, and Brodyn changed our course from the main entryway—where chieftains, warriors, and kings had now drawn their blades—to lead us instead straight into the crushing mob.

"Keep your head down, Languoreth," Father called. In one smooth motion he bent to retrieve a discarded shield. Gripping it to his chest, he leaned into the clash of bodies, forging a path toward a little gap in the barrier just wide enough to pass through.

The crowd had turned upon itself. I caught sight of a shopkeeper I knew to be a Christian leading a cluster of men into the seething mob, rocks and sticks gripped in their hands. In the blindness of their fury, the people no longer recognized my father. As a thickly muscled peasant collided with Brodyn, his elbow came crashing through the momentary gap between us, slamming against my ribs. I gasped in pain as the blow sent me stumbling beneath the swift and deadly churning of feet. Brodyn turned, eyes wide, and yanked me up by my cloak.

Behind me Ariane pressed her body against mine to shield me and shouted, "She cannot pass, Brodyn. You must lift her up!"

"I need both arms to protect her!" he shouted. "We haven't enough men."

Ariane cursed and lifted me from my feet, stumbling for a moment beneath the weight of me until she foisted me up, my gangly legs dangling over the crook of her arm. Father ducked and plowed forward like an ox, bracing himself against the barrier, his body a human rampart against the seething crowd. Tears blurred my vision.

"Quickly, now." He grimaced. "I cannot hold them."

"Uncle," Brant yelled, "you cannot stay!"

"Go!" Father lifted his shield to block a blow. "I'll find you at the horses!"

"Father!" I shouted.

Brodyn snatched me from Ariane's arms and tossed me over one shoulder, ducking beneath Father's shield arm. Flung like a doll, I lifted my head in panic and caught sight of Cathan.

His arms at his sides, he was a fixed point in the storm of thrusting spears and clanging swords. His eyes were lifted solemnly to the heavens. He looked like an oak on a hill, or a man of ancient magic who might still control the weather. And then I felt the jolting shock of bone colliding with bone. Someone struck my skull, shattering my vision into a flurry of sparks. A blinding, searing pain surged through me.

The world went dark.

I was rocking from side to side. The rumbling of a cart drowned out all other sound, lulling me back into the blackness from which I was struggling to surface.

Cathan's robes, lit by sun. A three-wheeled cart and the flick of a wrist. A corpse on the ground.

I fought to open my eyes only to be met by a white-hot pulsing at my temple that caused me to cry out.

"It's all right now. You're all right." My father's voice came low and gentle.

Through the fog of my pain I felt the firm pillow of his leg supporting my head. I was so very sleepy. But the sound of wheels over road grew louder. We were moving. I opened my eyes to find it was twilight. Hours had passed.

"You have been in and out of sleep all day," Father said. His bearded face looked almost ghoulish by the light of a lantern. His shadow flickered against the tautly stretched cowhide canopy of the cart. Somehow I knew he was bringing us home. Back to Cadzow.

I reached my fingers to the swollen egg upon my temple and winced.

"It hurts, does it?" Father reached gingerly to stroke my hair. "Aye. I should think it does. You took a stout blow to your noggin."

Scenes from the riot flooded back unbidden. Remembering Cathan standing alone in the clashing crowd, I struggled to sit, but a spinning overtook me. All I could do was say his name.

"You worry for Cathan," Father chuckled. "That's a task I surrendered long ago. Cathan is safe enough. He rides not far behind."

"You left him," I said. I would not let Father laugh it away.

"Cathan desired to be left. More important, your mother bade me keep you safe," Father said. "Your mother, she had no love for Partick. She desired nothing more than to keep you and your brother at Cadzow until you were fully grown. I betrayed her in bringing you, but after the Angle massacre of Bryneich, I could not leave you behind. I see now that Partick is no place for children. Forgive me, Languoreth."

It came back now: the crush of bodies, the thrusting of spears, the spraying of blood. Warm and viscous.

"We are going home," Father said. "We will send for our things. It was not safe to linger at Buckthorn. By the time we reached the gates of town, hundreds had taken up arms to fight. Such bloodshed has not been seen on the streets of Partick as long as I have lived."

"It was as if your own people did not know you."

"Such is the nature of a riot. It is madness. Madness that seeks only blood. You cannot reason with a mob."

"I cannot help but wonder how Cathan did it."

"What?" Father raised a brow. "How he evaded a king's guard to unearth the body of Fergus? Why, magic, of course." He gave a small smile, but his answer did not satisfy.

"If the Gods could aid Cathan in unearthing the body of Fergus, why could they not prevent the felling of the trees in the first place?"

Father considered this a moment. "Just as there are laws of our world, I believe there are laws that govern the world of the Gods, the world of the dead. Perhaps the Gods cannot stay the blow of an axe. But who is to say they did not try to warn us in their way?"

I remembered the shifting of the forest when I'd encountered the monk on Bright Hill. The gathering of the crows on the roof.

"I will never forget the face of the man I saw on Bright Hill," I vowed. "If ever I should see him again, I will know him. I will see he is brought to justice."

"Aye. You must only say the word." Father squeezed my hand. "Shall we try to sit now?"

I nodded and, with his help, rose slowly.

"King Tutgual seems a horrible man," I said. I risked a glimpse from the corner of my eye, but Father's face was not angry.

"Tutgual is a warlord and a king," he answered.

"As are you. But I do not think you horrible."

"Perhaps you would if you knew of the things I must do in raiding and war." His voice was grave. "You think me a hero, but I lust for blood as every man does. There are things I have done in battle that visit me still in the quiet of the dark. But, no, Tutgual is not like me, Languoreth.

"He is a man of far greater power. He controls the trade from the rivers to the sea. The Westmen of Dalriada pay him tribute. Every lord and chieftain of Strathclyde pays him tribute. It is either pay him or be slain by him—for the high king and I both know I do not have men enough to challenge him. And so we must play the game our family has bested now for centuries."

Father covered my hand with his. It was as tanned and tough as a turtle shell, hardened by years of sun and wind and weaponry. I did not want to think of the things my father might have done that continued to haunt him in the dark, and yet, even though I was still a child, I felt shame in avoiding it.

Did I not live under his roof and benefit from his profits?

Did I not have the finest spun wool for my dresses and even silks? Did we not have two properties and more land and livestock than any other kings or high chieftains in Strathclyde save Tutgual himself?

Such things, I knew, came at a price. Someday, too, I knew, I would be expected to play this game and so protect the legacy of our family.

The thought of it turned my mind back to those I loved, and I asked Father to help me peer beyond the domed roof of the cart. I could just make out their forms in the dusk: Lailoken and Crowan. Brant and Brodyn and Ariane following in silence on their horses. I leaned back against the taut covering of the wagon as Father passed me his skin of water.

"You see? We are all safe, and thank the Gods it should be so," he said. "Drink now, then rest. We have some distance yet to travel."

I hadn't realized what a desert my body had become until I closed my eyes and drained the bladder, the water soothing a course down my throat. As I passed the empty bladder back to Father I reached to cradle my tender ribs.

"Father?"

"Yes?"

"I still cannot understand why anyone would do such a thing when we have lived in peace for so long."

"It is for the same reason men do all things, daughter. For power. They mean to challenge our tradition and, in doing so, claim possession of Bright Hill."

"But Cathan has unearthed the body. He has claimed Bright Hill for the Old Way once more."

"Nay," Father said. "Cathan claimed nothing he intended to keep. Bright Hill has been fouled by that body. It cannot be remade. There's little to stop Bright Hill from becoming a burial ground now." Father rubbed his face. "Our Wisdom Keepers will move their rites to an unspoiled site. Let the Christians do with it what they will."

I thought of the sparkling waters of the White Spring. Who would come to cup their hands and drink her healing waters now? Who would bend their knee at her banks and remember her? The thought of the spring lying solitary and forgotten 'til her waters ran dry and she faded into earth was enough to brim my eyes with tears.

"So it was all for nothing," I said bitterly. "We have lost Bright Hill and this is the end."

"Nay, this is not the end, Languoreth." Father leaned back, resting his auburn head against the dome of the cart.

"Nay, little one, this is not the end," he repeated with a sigh. "In fact, I fear this is only the beginning."

II.

I am a falcon above the cliff . . .
I am a wonder among flowers.
–"Song of Amergin," translated by Robert Graves,
The White Goddess

II

CHAPTER 15

Cadzow Fortress, Strathclyde
Midsummer, AD 554

It had been more than four years since my shining dreams of the capital had been churned to dust beneath the retreating wheels of our cart, and I was happier for it. My home was amid the towering shelter of Cadzow's trees, where the shallow gurgle of the Avon lulled me to sleep each night and happenings at court felt far, far away.

Necessity still summoned Father to Partick for months at a time, but now he traveled with Lailoken, just as he'd once taken Gwenddolau. They'd come home bearing gifts: ivory combs for my hair and perfumes from the Mediterranean; an embroidered dress from the seamstress who lived on the outskirts of the market. My brother would tell such tales: of a troupe of brown-skinned Arabian dancers, of a Song Keeper from Gaul who wore a cloak made of feathers so that he might fly to other worlds when he sang, and who could recall from memory more than one thousand songs. Lail's eyes were bright as he related such tales, but my memories of Partick were stained by blood. I did not long to return.

And while the men were at Partick, I was never too long alone. Ariane and Crowan made good company. Besides, there was much to learn at Cadzow. I had no brothers save Lail, and, as a Wisdom Keeper, Lailoken could not lawfully own land. When the time came and Father passed, Cadzow and Buckthorn would fall to me.

Or to my future husband, Ariane was too quick to remind me. Not because she wished me to marry, but rather because she wished for me to take the project more firmly in hand.

"Nothing can be taken from you that you do not freely give," she said. "If it is you who knows the tenants and the mill keepers, if it is you who hears disputes, who collects the rents and runs the harvests, it will be you the people demand. It will be you who holds their loyalty."

So, in Father's absence, I received the merchants winding their way up or down our stretch of the Clyde. There was always news from a tenant bringing a gift of flour, cheese, carrots, or livestock, or from the herdsmen who wandered the wild summer pastures minding our cattle and sheep. It was they who brought news from the Borders: that Gwenddolau had grown to be a noble and warlike lord. That Ceidio and Pendragon yet kept the Angles at bay. Battles were lost but mostly won, and I gathered news like a squirrel hoarded acorns, eager to hear of my foster brother's safety but saddened that the fighting had made Gwenddolau a stranger, keeping him so long from our door.

Now another summer had blessed the soft green fields of Cadzow and found me lazing beneath the oaks, gazing up at a sky as blue as a dunnock's egg. The deep calls of our cattle sounded from the nearby pasture—mothers moaning to their little ones—and the thought of the snowy-white calves was enough to stir me from my daydreaming and send me meandering along the forest path in search of their velvety noses.

The air was thick with the honeyed smell of wych elm, and as I moved through the trees, the starry white blossoms scattered, catching in my hair like snowflakes. As I neared the pasture, two calves who'd been racing clumsy-legged through the tall grass stopped and studied me, their dark eyes curious. I drew in a deep breath of loamy earth and smiled at the cowherd, a strong, fair-haired boy a few winters older than I. Though he leaned against an oak whittling at a stick,

I couldn't help but notice his eyes lingered uncomfortably long on me, and I reached to shake the blossoms from my hair, fanning it over my chest to hide the rising curve of my bosom.

My dresses were suddenly tight across my back and shoulders. How had this happened, seemingly overnight? Crowan must have noticed, though she hadn't said a word. Hadn't I always known it would come to this? It did not matter how much Father loved me. As soon as I reached marrying age . . . The thought brought a swell of sickness, and I chased it away. I slipped behind a copse of trees to evade the prying eyes of the cowherd, stretching out my hand to the calves.

"Come, little ones. Come and see me."

The calves pricked their ears, wary. At last a brave youngster rose uncertainly from the shadow of the hedge, inching closer until his curiosity got the better of him. I smiled at the tickle of wet breath as he sniffed the air above my fingers.

"Yes, you remember me, don't you?"

I stroked the downy tuft of white hair between his black-tipped ears and he blinked his long lashes in pleasure. I'd been stroking his forehead for some time when he suddenly jerked upright and bolted from my side, startling me half to death as he tore away toward the shelter of his mother.

I turned to see Cathan skirting the edge of the pasture, his thick gray hair braided back from his face and staff in hand. He lifted it triumphantly in greeting when he caught sight of me, the worn lines round his eyes creasing in little branches.

"A wise beast to skitter from you," I called out and gestured to the calf, now sitting resolutely in the shadow of his mother. "It seems he knows who selects the bulls for sacrifice."

"At least we know where to look when you do not meet us at the gate," he replied.

I grinned, rushing to embrace him. "You're back! I didn't hear the watchman's call."

"We've only just arrived."

"And how did you find your visit to Partick?"

Cathan hesitated. "Troubling," he said at last.

"Troubling? Why?"

"It seems a new settlement has taken root across the shore from the White Isle. Christians. They come to hear the proselytizing of a monk they call 'Mungo.' "

"*Dear One*. And what do you know of him?"

"I sent men to seek his history. He is of noble birth. His mother is Taneu, daughter to Lot, king of the Lothians. She fled to a monastery at the Firth of Forth to evade marriage to a son of Rheged, and Mungo was birthed there. He makes no claims to his grandfather's power now, of course, but he is of noble blood, and it draws the people."

"But how is it he came to Partick? The Firth of Forth is leagues away."

"He arrived to Brother Telleyr with a letter of endorsement from a priest called Serf some years ago now."

"How strange we have not met him."

"The monk had taken a vow of silence these past five years, or so Telleyr has related, a vow which he has only just concluded. Now the two men have parted ways. This Mungo speaks, and pilgrims travel vast distances in search of his wisdom and miracles. They build hovels on the bank of the river near the White Isle. They launder, bathe, and defecate in the waters sacred to Clota."

I drew a breath. "It cannot be! That stretch of water has been a place of sacrifice since time out of memory. The broken swords of their very own ancestors must lie sleeping in the silt of that river."

"It would seem they seek to atone for the misgivings of their fore-fathers." Cathan laughed without humor.

"Misgivings," I said. "Despite the destruction of Bright Hill on Beltane eve, we have not seen famine, flood, or disaster. Despite raids and the presence of the Angles, the Gods have kept us close to their breasts."

"So one might say. But there are Christians in Partick who believe it is the Christ god who shines his favor upon us now, so pleased was he with the sacrifice of Bright Hill. In these past days the Council has even sanctioned the building of a new monastery beside the burn at the bottom of the hill."

"A monastery? Beside the burn that flows near the White Spring! However could you sanction this?"

"Come now, I? I sanction nothing. I may yet be head of the Council, but I cannot control its ruling. You know as much. The monastery will be home to Telleyr and his monks, not this Mungo. At least I could see to that." Cathan rubbed his brow.

"And what of Tutgual? Does he yet keep counsel with Brother Telleyr?"

"You have not heard." Cathan's brows arched in surprise. "Nay, Telleyr has fallen from the king's favor. And whilst we were in Partick, Tutgual decreed all female Wisdom Keepers banned from his court."

I nearly staggered. "Tutgual has banned female Keepers from his court? How can he do such a thing? What of the female Song Keepers? Would he banish them, too?"

"Nay. Never the Song Keepers. The winter is far too long, and the old king wrings far too much enjoyment from their stories."

"Well, then certainly our female Song Keepers should refuse to visit the court of the king."

"They will not," Cathan said. "The Song Keepers know well the wisdom that lives in our stories. There are many in the capital—and even in Tutgual's own court—who yet cling to the Old Way. The Keepers will not abandon their people, nor the hope that the stories will work magic on even the most taciturn of ears. Besides, Tutgual is not truly a Christian. He only wishes to appear as such when it serves him."

"Whatever do you mean?"

"Tutgual trades with Gaul and with Rome. He looks across the water, and what does he see? Wisdom Keepers long since stripped of their power, and kingdoms gathered under the rule of rulers like Chlothar, with wealthy churches backing their reigns. Here in our lands, the power of a Wisdom Keeper nearly outranks that of a king, whilst Christian kings answer to no other but their god. Tutgual yearns for such power, yet does not know which way the tide will turn in the land of the Britons. So he must play both sides. This may yet be to our benefit."

"How can you say so?"

Cathan's eyes roamed the pasture, fogged by something troubling before he shook the thought and turned to me.

"All this gloom. Come. Let's talk no more of this. Your father and brother await." Cathan straightened and dug into the folds of his robes. "But whilst we are undisturbed . . . I've brought you a gift."

"Cathan, you needn't have brought me anything."

"Stuff and nonsense. It is yours already, in a way." With that, he lay a simple cloth packet in my hands. I tested its weight. Too light to be a weapon. Confounded, I unfolded the cloth to reveal a carved leather mask and drew a breath. There was no mistaking it. This was one of the masks the maidens wore at Midsummer.

The leather tooling was delicate yet ferocious, an intricate map of whorls and symbols carved onto its surface. The stiff skin of the mask had been tanned a fiery shade of orange, and I traced my fingers along the edges that rose and fell in a semblance of flames.

"It belonged to your mother," Cathan said. "She wore it when she danced as a Torch Bearer at the Midsummer fires. Now it has come to you."

A Torch Bearer. My pulse skittered. With all the talk of Partick, I'd nearly forgotten this would be my first year taking part in the Midsummer rites. So many summers I'd watched the young women of our village race with burning torches to ignite the Midsummer fire; watched as they moved to the rattles and drums, twisting and spinning in the dizzying chase between darkness and light. Now I was finally of age. I could almost feel my mother there with me as I caressed the fine leather—could almost summon the scent of her—but then the memory was lost.

"I can scarcely remember what she looked like," I said. "If I close my eyes, I can see only her dark hair twirling about her as she spun."

Cathan smiled. "Your mother danced with the grace of a roe deer. There was hardly a man who could catch her."

"Yet I dance with the grace of a sow," I said.

"A sow?" he laughed. "Oh, no, we can't have that. After all, we'll have very important guests for the celebration this year."

The tease in his voice made me narrow my eyes. "Tell me."

"Why, Emrys Pendragon," Cathan said, his smile broadening at the sight of my gaping mouth. "Indeed, it's true. Emrys and his retinue are to join us for Midsummer. Better yet, he travels with Gwenddolau."

I rushed at Cathan with a shriek. But then the weight of it struck me and I threw up my hands. "Sweet Gods! My first summer as Torch Bearer and the Dragon Warriors for an audience." As if the eyes of the entire village weren't enough.

"Oh, come, now, Languoreth. You worry over much." Looking over my shoulder, he nodded at the forest path. "Eh, is that Ariane?"

I turned to see her emerging from the forest path across the field, her dark hair loose about her shoulders and her blue cloak catching on the tall grass. At the sight of her basket, heavy with greenery, I realized I'd forgotten to string up the plants for drying as she had bade. As she took in my proximity to the cows, she raised her brows amusedly as if to say, *So this is what you've done with your day?*

I offered a weak smile as Cathan turned.

"Ariane, well met!"

"Lord Cathan." She nodded.

"Will you walk to the courtyard with us? We were speaking of the

Midsummer rites. Our Languoreth is worried she'll trip over her own two feet and wind up face-first in the fire."

"That is not *precisely* what I said."

"Silliness," Ariane said as we moved together along the forest path. "The earth is always singing, and every creature upon it engaged in dance. So many forget. This is why we do ceremony. This is what raises our power. When we dance, we are one with everything, seen and unseen. In these moments the Gods are breathing through our bodies." Her eyes were the color of salt water in the afternoon sun, and she poked a finger at me playfully. "So you see? You are not *truly* the one who is dancing."

The Gods are breathing... her words transported me back to the forests of Bright Hill, and I thought of the monastery soon to be built at its foot. The people who were fouling the river. But as we neared the courtyard, the sight of Lailoken standing there, grinning, banished my melancholy and I ran to him.

He let out a grunt as I collided with him, folding me into his newly muscled embrace. "Some welcome you've given us. We had to send the old Wisdom Keeper off to find you. Harassing the livestock again, I'll wager." He held me at arm's length. "They haven't yet made you into a cowherd, have they?"

"I would happily become a cowherd if any could succeed at the substantial task of making you into a proper lord."

I ducked to avoid the swat of his hand, but, truth be told, my brother was growing into a fine lord indeed. Muscle had appeared seemingly overnight on his once lanky frame, leaving him nearly as tall as Father, with broad shoulders and a tapering waist. His voice had developed a richness that was pleasing to the ear, his sandy hair darkened into a golden-streaked brown. He wore it longer now, like Brodyn, bound from his face with a length of leather cord. His blue eyes were striking. There was no denying it: my brother had become a handsome young man.

A handsome young man who stank of horses and sweat and riding dust.

I wrinkled my nose. "In truth, I delayed my arrival in hopes you might bathe before I saw you," I laughed, then glanced around the courtyard. "Where's Father?"

"He's gone to his chamber."

"At this hour? Is it the swellings again?"

"You'd do well to lower your voice," Lailoken said. "He doesn't want the servants to know. Father doesn't like to speak of it, but the pain is back. This morning as we departed, his foot was so enlarged, he could scarcely put on his shoe."

I'd seen the swellings on his feet, shiny and scarlet, bulbous at the base of his big toes. It was a type of arthritis, a sort not uncommon among kings. I had seen it once catch him unawares, watched it nearly double him before he clamped his jaw and straightened with a laugh—an effort to hide his weakness.

"I'll make him a poultice," I said.

"He'll be glad for it."

The shutters were drawn and Father's chamber was dark, his face pale against his pillow.

"Languoreth." I heard the pain as he struggled to rise.

"Don't sit up, Father. Rest."

He sank back against the bedding with a heavy breath. "It was the feasting, that's all," he said. "And then the journey. I'm only taking a wee respite."

I looked about the dark chamber. "But has nobody lit an oil lamp for you? Shall I unfetter the window?" He'd sent the servants away, no doubt.

"No, no windows," he said. "Light the lamp on the table if you will."

I set down the poultice and a jug of fresh water on the table and moved to draw a dry reed from the earthenware vase stocked beside the hearth. Kneeling, I held it to the dying embers until it caught and brought it with cupped fingers to the wick of the lamp, casting the chamber in a world of darkness and light.

"It is good to have you home," I said.

"Aye, and it's better to be back," Father said. "My heart is here at Cadzow with my cattle and my daughter." His amber hair glowed in the lamplight, and I smiled, drawing back the coverlet. Father eased back onto his pillows, watching me bind the poultice to the pulsating swell on his foot. My touch likely seared like hot iron, but Father did not so much as wince: warriors were students of pain. Still, I searched for something to distract him.

"It seems Brant and Brodyn endeavor to cast Lailoken in their image." I smiled. "They will make him a vain young cad."

"He is already a vain young cad," Father scoffed. "Do you see how the village girls gawk after him? With his golden-brown hair that blows in the wind. And now that he is bronzed by the sun, he fancies himself a vision of the Gods themselves.

"But you . . ." Father looked to me. "This will someday be your land, eh, daughter? Tell me the state of things."

I told him of the taxes I'd collected in tribute from the merchants traveling our stretch of the river and of the goings-on at the mill.

"All grown-up, you are," he said, smiling. "Better you than your brother." He brandished an imaginary sword. "Nearly fifteen winters and Lailoken wishes to fight! Your brother is consumed with comely maids. With philosophy and rhetoric and weaponry! He has his beasts to battle . . . though I've yet to meet a specter that will succumb to a sword." Father dropped his arm to his side.

I swallowed. "I suppose some are less bound than others when it comes to pursuing their passions."

He fell quiet a moment, his dark eyes sad.

"I have watched you these past years, your head bent over that table, drying this and crushing that. You have your mother's gift," he said tenderly. "Do not think I cannot read your heart, Languoreth. You long to be a Wisdom Keeper, too, and well I know. But the Gods have chosen Lailoken to walk the path of the Keeper. And I am learned enough to understand the Gods will have their way. Just as the Gods have chosen you for a life of leading the people, as the head of another household. You will be safe by the side of a powerful king or chieftain. And when I die, I will rest well in the Summerlands knowing that all this has come to you."

He must have seen the tears in my eyes, because his voice brightened and he nodded to the swollen weal on his foot. "Right, then. What magical remedies have you blended there?"

"Yarrow. Among other things." I smiled as I tightened the wrappings.

"I trust you've heard news of our Midsummer guests?" His voice strained as I secured the knot.

"Yes. It will do us all good to see our Gwenddolau again. In truth, I can hardly wait. It will no doubt be a celebration to remember."

Father nodded and sank back, his thick lashes lowering to his cheeks: the poultice was easing the pain. At last he might sleep.

"Enough chatter now, Father. I'll leave you to rest." I doubled the sheepskin under his foot to raise it.

"Yes, rest," he said gratefully.

As I turned to leave, I looked back at the peaceful rise and fall of his chest, and my heart filled with the elusive satisfaction only a healer could know.

Life is not only filled with the pain and longing of the things that cannot be, I reminded myself. There was the ease of my father's suffering; his restful breathing. There was Gwenddolau's homecoming and the excitement of hosting Pendragon and his Dragon Warriors alongside Cadzow village for the Midsummer rites.

And yet the sadness of my destiny still loomed like a shadow.

As the head of another household, Father had said. To be wed, for allegiance, to a faraway stranger. A stranger who would someday own my home.

Darkness and light.

CHAPTER 16

Five days before the Midsummer celebration, I woke to find my bed linens streaked with blood. My cry sent Crowan rushing into my chamber as I threw back the covers searching wildly for the cause of my injury. As she glanced at the linens, her eyes kindled with understanding.

"Your moontime, my dove. 'Tis only your moontime."

Of course. How silly. I must have known it would come, but no one had spoken of the pain. My belly felt so tender, seizing in dull knots, that I would have spent the day curled up in the sheets if Crowan hadn't stripped the bed and sent orders for a hot bath to be drawn. I was submerged to my chin, eyes closed in relief, when Ariane came through the door, a vial in her hand.

"I'm not clothed!" I cried, splashing water over the edges of the wooden tub as I covered my parts.

She perched on the wooden stool at the edge of the tub looking at me unabashedly. "Tincture of nettle. A few drops should do."

I nodded my head as I accepted the slender glass vial and tilted a few bittersweet drops onto my tongue. Naked bodies were as nothing to Ariane. It was all the talking—for her, that was the difficult part.

"It will help ease the cramping. It is a great honor, you know. To become a woman." Her attempt to discuss it made her shift in discomfort.

"It hurts."

"Yes, and so will bringing life into the world. Why should its messenger be any different? Where I come from, this is a time that we celebrate."

I laid the soaking cloth over my shoulders and peered at her from beneath lowered lashes. "Ariane?"

"Yes?"

"Why is it you will never speak of where you come from?"

Something flickered across her face, but when she answered, her voice was pleasant enough. "I come from the north. This much I have told you. There, when a young woman first gets her moontime, the women gather to celebrate." Her eyes softened with memory. "They come to you at first light, to bring you to the forest and wash you in rosewater. They towel you with thick linen and drape your body in a glorious gold-threaded cloth. They braid ribbons into your hair until you become a shining thing, sacred as a goddess. You spend the day in the shelter of the forest . . ."

"And then what? What happens in the forest?"

"You understand that you have become a woman," she said simply. She cleared her throat and looked at me. "You are sad that your mother is not here to mark this moment."

The truth stabbed in tender places. "Truth be told, I haven't any idea what my mother might do if she were."

"Surely as a Wisdom Keeper she would have wished you to undergo a ritual." She studied me. "Perhaps I could lend some small working of my people's moontime celebration into your Midsummer rites. That is, if you would wish it."

My heart swelled at the thought of it. I dared not speak for fear I would burst into tears, so I nodded instead, more brusquely than I intended.

"Then so be it." Ariane stood, smoothing her skirts. "Ah. I nearly forgot. I also brought some water elder. Crowan will steep you some tea, but for now it'll ease you to chew on the bark."

"Thank you."

Ariane gave a small smile and turned to go. But she paused at the door, as if she would say something more.

"It is bitter," she warned.

"That's all right," I assured her.

Obediently, I put the cramp bark in my mouth and bit down. It was indeed bitter, sickeningly so. But I couldn't help but think it was womanhood, not the bark, that Ariane had been speaking of.

The following days were mad with preparations for Midsummer and the impending arrival of our guests. The nettle and water elder relaxed my seizing womb, so I was able to spend my days in supervising the preparations: Cathan's blessing and the slaughtering of the cattle for the feeding of nearly three hundred people, the decorations, the re-stuffing of the mattresses, and the acquisition of new platters. I heard Crowan grumble more than once that she was thankful we hosted such events at Cadzow only twice a year.

A new field was cleared and fire pits dug and edged in thick slabs of stone. Lail threw himself into the preparations with new vigor; he would be taking part in the ceremony with the men for the first time, a moment he'd been awaiting since before he could crawl.

When my bleeding ceased the morning our guests were slated to arrive, I was certain it was some sort of blessing. All morning my stomach had been a host of butterflies, as though something exciting or wonderful were about to happen. If only I knew what.

Already the strains of a cruit sounded from the great room where Father, Lail, and the others sat drinking as they idly awaited our guests. Unable to sit still, I slipped from the hall and through the empty courtyard to the practice field beyond the stables where the warriors' targets sat, my fingers itching to grip my knife.

The weight of the blade in my hand was satisfying after days upon end of women's work. I sank into the rhythm of throwing and retrieving until the bold heat of the sun raised a dewy sheen of sweat that had my dress clinging to my back and itching uncomfortably at the neckline. I had just sent my knife hurtling with a triumphant thunk into the heart of the closest target, when the hollow blow of the watchman's horn sounded. Sweet Gods. They were not meant to arrive until midday. And such a state I was in!

I wrenched my blade free and sheathed it hastily at my waist. Across the field I could see Father's men on the lofted platforms of the outer rampart, readying to open the outer gate. I brushed furiously at the bits of hay clinging to the emerald folds of my new gown and cursed the disemboweled targets, my pace quickening at the ominous rumble of hooves in the distance. They were riding at great speed. I would never make it to the courtyard in time to greet them beside Father, that much was clear. I prayed that, for this one impropriety, he would forgive me.

And so it was that I was only midway through the field when I heard the bone-chilling chorus of baying and yips, saw the Dragon Warriors streaking through the timber gate, and felt for the first time the fear they must incite in their enemies.

Their mounts were warhorses, meanly muscled and masked in leather guards. But it was the men themselves who were most fearsome. Battle-hard and fierce-faced, at a distance they seemed more like beasts than men in their scaled leather armor. Their shouts and whoops were deep and unbridled, their spear points thrust to the sky as they charged into the pasture.

It was fortunate that the guards had flung the doors wide, for our guests were yet at a canter, pressed over the necks of their horses as if the unbridled joy of speed was a god demanding complete and utter sacrifice. Heart hammering, I scoured their lines for Gwenddolau, squinting into the sun. So mesmerized was I by the graceful stretch of their horses in full run, the way the late morning sun streamed round them in halos of gold, that I had to wrench myself—at the very last moment—out of harm's way, lest I be trampled where I stood, dumbstruck at the edge of the road.

Could that be Gwenddolau leading the way? The man who approached had hair streaming past his shoulders, braided back from his face, bleached nearly bone-white by the light of the sun, but his figure was unmistakable. My brother! Beaming, I lifted my arm in greeting, but he blew by giving only the swiftest of nods, as if he did not know me at all.

I dropped my arm to my side and lifted my chin in an attempt to appear regal as one by one they sped past, the earth trembling beneath the beat of their horses' hooves. They rode light on their mounts, as if more at home on horseback than on foot. Brightly colored beads and silver clouties flashed in the sun, dangling from saddles or braided into their horses' manes for luck: talismans from wives or lovers to bring their men safe home from war. These men, however, unlike Gwenddolau, paid me no notice at all. And I, their hostess! Just who did they imagine I was, a swineherd? Well, they would see, wouldn't they? I scoffed and had nearly turned away, when the last rider came into view. He was a black-haired man on a magnificent brown and white stallion, his hands wound into his horse's mane. He rode with no bridle. I looked up at his face and his eyes locked on mine.

They were as green as forest leaves and flecked with amber, set into a strong, olive-skinned face beneath a sturdy set of brows. It was the way he regarded me, his gaze so penetrating it might have pinned me to a target board. A heat rushed through me so suddenly that it uprooted me, leaving me nearly stumbling over my own two feet. We stopped, each of us seemingly startled by the look that passed between us, before he bowed his head in greeting and rode on. I stood, swirling as if struck, until my wits returned.

Who was he? I could not understand what I'd felt, but knew I should dare not seek to. Warriors were beguiling, overproud, and pig-headed, my brother and my cousins chief among them. Hadn't I seen for myself the way they rendered the village girls dumb and witless, as if winning their affections were nothing but sport? The way they loved and abandoned for the next pretty thing?

I tossed my head and straightened my shoulders, remembering: *I am Languoreth, daughter of Morken.* Perhaps it was a boon that I would never suffer the trials of love with a fickle-hearted warrior. Sacrifice or no, I would be wed to a prince if not a king. There was much pride in that. Smoothing my hair and lifting the hem of my dress, I followed the fading din of Pendragon's retinue into the courtyard.

The men had already dismounted and begun their greetings by the time I arrived, but the Dragon Warriors swiveled as I crossed the expanse. Suddenly I was too aware of the attention my emerald gown was garnering, with its low-cut neckline that offered the high curve of my breasts. *Curses on you, Crowan.* I felt like a lamb trussed for a feast before a table of lions. But Ariane had held a place for me. I moved quickly to stand beside her as Gwenddolau came forward, his hand-some face split into a smile.

"Languoreth! I am shamed to say I did not know you. It seems only yesterday I carried you upon my back as a little girl, yet I see now that you are grown into a woman. Tall and graceful as a swan."

Color heated my cheeks, but I accepted his embrace. "And yet I could never mistake you, brother. Welcome to Cadzow. Welcome home."

I glanced over his shoulder at the men who stood behind him. They wore thick leather padding under their breastplates, even in the heat, and the massive swords slung at their shoulders looked more Pictish than our Cymric blades, so broad were they. Gwenddolau released me and reached to clasp the shoulder of the man who stood beside him.

"You have met Lord Emrys, of course."

Met him, yes, but I scarcely recognized him. His eyes were the same azure, but where his hair had been dark not four years before, it had gone white as fresh-fallen snow. I'd heard it said that the strain of kingship could drain a man's hair of its hue, but never before had I seen it.

"You are most welcome, my lord," I said, bowing my head. "Only you travel in such modest numbers. We prepared for many more. I hope you did not curtail your retinue on our behalf. We can host quite a number at Cadzow."

"We travel fast and we travel light," Pendragon said. "Should I have none others than these men at my back from here to the ends of the earth, I would sleep soundly the rest of my days." Then a smile creased his face, and I could not help but think his white hair suited him. With his beak-like nose and long eyelashes, it lent him the appearance of a great, snowy dragon.

"Fine men, the lot of you," Father said. "This shall be an evening of stories! Come in, come in, and we will chase away the weariness of your travels."

Cathan and Father led Gwenddolau and Pendragon past me into the fort, but the Dragon Warriors did not follow. I stood there frowning until the black-haired warrior with the green eyes shifted his weight ever so slightly, reminding me they awaited an invitation from the lady of the Hall.

"Come in, please, and join us. You must be thirsty," I said quickly.

"Thank you, Lady Languoreth," the black-haired man said, stepping forward. He looked to be twenty winters, the same age as Brodyn, and I saw the war band was looking to him, though whether it was out of authority or respect, I could not tell, for he had not introduced himself.

"I'm sorry, I do not know your name," I said pointedly.

"Maelgwn," he replied, but offered nothing else. His emerald eyes sparkled with humor, like those of a cat toying with a sparrow.

"You are most welcome to Cadzow, Maelgwn." I spoke politely, my blinking the only betrayal of my annoyance as I led them through the courtyard. This man Maelgwn was good-looking, perhaps, but clearly he was as vain as any warrior, and every bit as irritating, too.

In Cadzow's great room, Father and Cathan were already seated at the center of the table, their heads bowed in conversation with Gwenddolau and Pendragon. I nodded to Brodyn and he guided the Dragon Warriors to the fleece-lined couches that sat along our walls. Maelgwn took a seat beside Gwenddolau at our table, adjusting his sword in its baldric before sitting. If he'd earned a place at the table, he would be a proper general, then, not just a warrior. Gwenddolau glanced up and slid him a cup of wine. There was an ease between them that spoke of brotherhood, and it occurred to me just how little I knew of Gwenddolau's life since he had left Cadzow.

"Before we begin . . ." At the sound of Pendragon's voice, the conversation in the room dropped, and I took my seat hastily beside my brother.

". . . though we are joyful to celebrate the Midsummer at Cadzow, we come to your festivities bearing grave news," Pendragon continued. His eyes flicked to Gwenddolau. "Perhaps it is best that Gwenddolau speak, if he is willing."

Gwenddolau gave a curt nod. His tanned fingers moved to his cup before retreating again. At last he spoke. "My father, Ceidio, is dead."

The warriors bent their heads in a gesture of respect. My heart twisted as I looked at my foster brother. Gwenddolau had only been reunited with his father for four winters. Now King Ceidio was no more.

"Ceidio is gone? But I received no word." Father sounded baffled.

"I hope you will forgive me for not sending a messenger. I wished to tell you myself," Gwenddolau said. "I know he was not only a father to me but also like a brother to you, Morken."

Father blinked. "Tell me how."

"All had been quiet for weeks on end—which didn't suit my father, as well you might know."

"He was a battler to the core," Father said. "A caged bear in times of peace."

"Yes." Gwenddolau gave a small smile. "We were traveling east on patrol, when Ceidio mounted to ride with us. It was quiet. Deceivingly so. We were readying to make camp for the night, when we were set upon by a band of Angles. They hadn't many men. Four took spears to their guts before they fled. We should have known something was afoot, but we had grown too comfortable in our victories, pride deafening our reason." Gwenddolau's face darkened. "Light was fading, and yet we gave chase. We crested the hill and were descending into a valley, when their party split off."

Cathan spoke up: "A trap."

"A tactic we ourselves are known to use," Pendragon said. "No small coincidence in that. Over the rise came an army of Hengist's men."

"We were forty men against one hundred," Gwenddolau said. "I do not know when my father fell."

Across the table Maelgwn spoke up. "It was four to one, brother. You cannot lay blame upon yourself."

"Had you carried on, it would have been foolish," Pendragon agreed. Gwenddolau glanced at the men on the couches. A few of them sat with eyes locked on the flickering of the fire.

"Go on, then," Gwenddolau said to Pendragon.

Pendragon inclined his head to his young protégé. "It was a slaughter. Thirty of our band had fallen when our men were forced to flee," Pendragon said. "They knew Ceidio's face—knew his son would come back for him. And so they left Gwenddolau his body but took with them Ceidio's head."

Father's grip tightened on his cup. The head was where the soul resided; the barbarians could have shown no greater disrespect. So long as the head of Ceidio was held captive, his spirit could never enter the Summerlands. Gwenddolau's father could never go home.

No one spoke. Then at last Father broke the silence, pushing away his cup.

"Now all my brothers are truly dead. I should have been with Ceidio to fight by his side. Your father was the last of the men who came up with me. All sons of Mor: we were wild and fearsome then, just like our ancestors. Now all but one of us rot in the earth. Ceidio and myself—we were the last of our kind."

Gwenddolau looked at Father, his eyes bright. "Morken, you are many days' ride from us. Even if you and your men had whipped your mounts to their bones, you would have arrived only to bury him."

"This was no pitched battle in a field," Pendragon said. "I and the greater bulk of my army were spread throughout our lands between the Liddel Water and the coast. Spies have infiltrated our kingdom. That is the only answer. They knew of our patrol; they killed my scouts at the borders and entered unseen. The gathering strike was quick as lightning. The days of Ida the Angle are over. It would seem his son Hengist is cleverer than his father and more studied in our ways."

"Why have you not yet hunted this Hengist down?" The words fled my mouth before I could trap them. Pendragon turned, appearing surprised.

"A worthy question, Lady Languoreth. But it would be foolhardy to launch any attack on Hengist's fortress with fewer than one thousand men. We would need a confederation, and Tutgual will never consent. It is not his battle to fight, or so he says."

I nodded, my face gone scarlet.

"So the Angle bear has sired a fox," Pendragon went on. "Now we lose too many good men to lightning raids, to torture."

"He sends fingernails, followed by hands," Gwenddolau said. "If he is generous, he may yet send a horse over the border with my father's head in a sack. But he would be certain to put out his eyes first."

A curse to wander the afterlife blind.

Gwenddolau bowed in my direction. "Your pardon, Languoreth."

I waved it away, indicating no offense, but as I looked at them, my heart sank with the weight of these men and their thousand sorrows.

Damn those Angle hounds bent on destruction. And damn the foolish kings who led them to our shores. The full beards and long hair of the Dragon Warriors could not conceal the scars their bodies bore. I felt shamed to have passed judgment and found them wanting. Truly these men who fought with Pendragon were heroes, and my heart thudded with a new pride simply sitting in their company.

Cathan stood, raising his cup in a blessing. "To Ceidio. A great warrior and rightful king. Long may his name echo in the halls of his descendants. I pray he will soon find the peace he deserves among his kin in the Summerlands."

Deep voices rose in a toast as my eyes caught Maelgwn's. His gaze was curious and he gave a small smile, but I shrank from his scrutiny, my face growing hot. The doors to the great room swung open and the serving began. It took two servants to carry the platter of roasted pork. And as the smell of toasted hazelnuts and creamy goat cheese caught the noses of the Dragon Warriors, they rose to take their seats at the surrounding tables. Stewed barley with figs. Rosemary beef and fresh bread with golden hunks of fresh-churned butter were laid out before us. The Dragon Warriors fell to eating as if they hadn't seen food in a week.

After a while, Pendragon turned to me. "Languoreth. It is true what Gwenddolau has said. You and your brother have grown mightily since last we met. I hear Lailoken has entered the folds of the Wisdom Keepers. What will your path be?"

How could he ask a woman such a thing? The question seemed almost cruel, and the pain was not lessened by the interest etched on Pendragon's face.

"I am the daughter of a king, am I not?" I did not look at Emrys, but rather leveled my eyes upon Father. "As such, my life's dedication will be to make an advantageous marriage and so secure the well-being and way of life of my family and our people."

A momentary silence descended upon the table.

"Yes, well," Emrys said. "Then you are a dutiful daughter indeed."

Dutiful. The men returned to feasting, but I found I had little appetite. Looking round the table, I saw that Maelgwn, too, seemed poorly matched for his plate. I was insulted in spite of myself.

"Is the food we have provided not to your liking?" I asked.

"I could ask the same of you," he said, gesturing to my plate.

"Talk of war turns my stomach."

"As it should." His green eyes settled on mine. I wasn't prepared for the spark that burned through me.

"And what of you? Have you no appetite?" My voice was softer.

Maelgwn looked at his plate. "Did you have a hand in planning this feast?"

"I did."

He lifted his knife almost gingerly. "Then I shall do my best to enjoy it."

I looked away as Gwenddolau stood and lifted his cup. "To Morken, one of the great kings of the north. Though I have lost one father, I am thankful to be welcomed into the hall of another who yet lives."

"To Morken," the echo came.

Father bowed his head and the men raised their cups, faces lit by the glow of the fire. But as I lifted my goblet, I noticed there was another who was not smiling.

Maelgwn sat, his broad back straight in his chair, cup lifted, regarding me. His lips echoed the chorus of voices. But his gaze pierced right through me, to a place where I held no secrets.

CHAPTER 17

I lay awake that night, mind racing. The hall had been quiet for hours and still sleep would not come. Restless, I rose from bed to open the shuttered window. A cool wind rushed up the walls of the gorge and I breathed in the fresh smell of silt carried on swiftly moving waters. Overhead the moon rose full and round, like a glittering brooch on a swath of black silk. I gazed into the pure white of her orb until I grew dizzy. They said if you slept beneath a full moon you would either wake with the gift of prophecy or rise to find you'd gone mad. Perhaps, then, the moon was to blame for these traitorous pulsings threatening to overtake me.

When I closed my eyes I saw the sweep of Maelgwn's black hair, the dark fringe of lashes that lined his startling green eyes—things I hadn't thought I'd noticed until alone in the dark.

Maelgwn's good night at the end of the evening had been cordial, exceptionally so. I'd lingered long past the music, until the heat of the fire and the warmth of the drink had made my eyes heavy with sleep.

And now I found I could hardly wait until morning. Surely this was moon madness. Or else I had drunk far too much wine. I wasn't accustomed to keeping company with men, and they'd kept their glasses full even while I laced mine with water. I hugged my linen shift to my body, shivering a little in the night air as my thoughts wandered back over the evening.

News of Ceidio's death had only strengthened my father's commitment to Emrys's cause. He had not called upon us yet, but how long until my father and his men were needed? Brant and Brodyn might soon be wielding their swords against some of the most deadly men our country had seen since the Romans: the Angle warriors. Would it be Brant or Brodyn to arrive home next, draped lifeless and bloodied over the back of his horse? And what of Lailoken, now grown to a man? He was as adept with his sword and spear as he was versed in the epics. He would not only be a counsellor; he would also fight beside his king, just as Cathan had. My heart could not survive the loss of him should his shield be shattered by an Angle sword. Would I feel each hack and blow? Would I feel the scorch of flames as we burned him, lifeless, on the pyre?

Then there was Father, who'd survived more battles than most, but his health was not his to command anymore. The arthritis crippled him. How many times had I watched him set his jaw against the pain, stubbornly refusing to keep to his bed? If it wasn't the mill that needed checking, it was the granaries in the capital. He would never rest while there was a tenant's dispute to be settled, a widow who'd been left without compensation, or the food rents to collect.

I wrapped my arms around my body and looked up at the moon. The sight of her glowing full and round reminded me that the morrow was Midsummer, and a welcome anticipation swept away my fear.

Tomorrow I would become a Torch Bearer at last. Soon, Ariane would arrive to wake me. I shuttered the window and climbed back into bed, pulling the coverlet over me. This time my head had scarcely hit the pillow before I drifted away to a place of dreaming, where I could blessedly think no more.

• • •

Ariane came to gather me in silence, wearing her blue cloak. As we moved through the morning calm she didn't speak, as if a word passed between us might shatter the spell. It was an earlier dawn than I was accustomed to; the endless cups of wine and lack of sleep made my head feel as if I were floating. The sun had just leveled the horizon. Dew clung to my boots as we left the main path and I followed Ariane deeper into the woods. Here the light had not yet penetrated the canopy. We walked in ghostly twilight, shadowed by the thick trunks of elms. Birds overhead still roosted in the boughs, heads tucked to their breasts, and I wondered if Lail, too, had been woken and what ritual of his own he might undergo. In the semidarkness Ariane's skin glowed like starlight.

A while passed. Soon we were moving through unfamiliar forest, land of my father's even I had not yet explored. The woods this far from Cadzow felt different: I was used to my towering stands of oak, pine, ash, and elm, but this was a forest of birch, their papery trunks bright in the dim. At last the forest opened up and we stood before a clearing. Ariane stopped. The sky overhead was streaked with shocks of orange and pink that beat back the gloom, gilding the tips of a thousand wildflower petals that had been strewn throughout the grass of the clearing. It would have taken dozens of hands countless hours.

Or perhaps this was some sort of Ariane's magic.

Her blue eyes were shadowed in forest light as she gave a sweep of her arm, bidding me enter.

I stepped into the grove and a wet morning breeze rustled through the trees overhead, causing the petals to shiver and shift, scattering crystallized droplets of dew. I turned to her, my face a question. She lifted her eyes as if to say, *Look*.

Overhead, the slender birches bowed in the breeze like willowy maidens, their leaves rustling against the painted morning sky. She guided me to lie on my back amid the glittering bed of flowers. The chill of the dew soaked my dress as if I were lying on a bed of ice. I fought to keep my body from shaking from the wet, the cold. And suddenly the breeze dropped. The trees went still.

It was so quiet, I could hear the soft rise of Ariane's breath, as if the wood itself were listening. And then her voice came, soft and clear through the forest, as haunting and mysterious as a selkie's song. The words must have been in her native tongue; they were undulating and sweet, ethereal, as though the language were that from which all other languages sprang. In the space between her breaths I felt an eerie sense of gathering.

We were alone, weren't we?

I risked a glance beyond the grove to find only Ariane standing, the hood of her cloak cast back to reveal the gleam of her dark hair, her arms lifted to the sky. I relaxed then, as her song began to come faster, a drumbeat, a chant, a consecration in a tongue so very foreign from my own, in words that sounded like music.

Did it matter that I did not know them? Though the words were strange, their meaning was not lost. They echoed in my core—a claiming, an invocation.

Time became a slippery thing. I lay in that sea of grass and wildflowers gazing up at the sky for a moment.

For hours.

What magic had she woven when she let those flowers fall?

It was only when I felt Ariane's cool fingers on my shoulder that I realized I was drifting someplace beyond myself, reluctant to return.

I blinked as she knit her slender fingers in mine, pulling me upright on heavy limbs.

"You must come away now; it is time to come away. There are dangers that come from lingering too long in a grove."

"What dangers?" I wondered, my head yet floating.

"The Gods," she warned, her eyes full of mischief. "They might decide to keep you."

Then Ariane dug into the deerskin bag slung round her waist and withdrew a wide strip of blue cloth.

"Don't be afraid," she said, knotting the cloth to cover my eyes. "This part is not for seeing."

She looped her arm through mine and guided me from the birch grove, deeper into the forest. Tree roots caught my toes as Ariane led me in what felt like a circle, guiding me this way and that, as if the path we walked were not man-made but serpentine. At last we stopped.

A *hut*, I thought, though I knew of no dwellings in these far fringes of Father's wood. The earthy smell of peat smoke filled the air as Ariane helped me through a creaking door. Inside I felt the heat of a fire, which warmed my clothes, still soaked in dew.

Ariane lowered me to sit atop something soft—a sheepskin—that had been laid on the floor. I heard the trickle of liquid before the steam and heat of a full cup was lifted to my lips. The brew smelled of soil, the unmistakable woodiness of mushroom. Ariane's voice came low by my ear.

"Drink now, daughter. Receive what wisdom She'll grant you."

There were mushrooms believed to grant a gateway into other worlds, I knew. Visions and mysterious happenings were the gifts they could bring—messages from the Gods. But such brews were forbidden to any but the Keepers who knew how to wield them, they who could travel between this world and that one at will. I might have known fear, but I trusted Ariane—she would not place me in danger. I parted my lips and took a deep draft, the warmth tracing a route down into my stomach.

Several moments passed with nothing but the quiet crackle of the fire. And then out of the quiet came a soft scrape, the shuffle of footsteps. From beyond the walls of the hut, I thought I heard the approaching murmur of women's voices. And then, to my surprise, the door of the hut moaned on its hinges. I swallowed the emotion that rose in my throat as I realized Ariane must have summoned the women from the village to join in my initiation. I listened to the sweep of leather slippers over the floor as they moved without speaking around the hut. Soon the intoxicating scents of lavender and cedar enveloped me as hands with nimble fingers urged me to stand. Stripped away my damp clothing. Dried me with linens and massaged the soft oils into my skin.

Never, even as the daughter of a king, had I felt so tended to. Never had I felt more treasured.

As they combed the tangles from my hair, the women began to hum. Soft and low, their voices joined the fingers that deftly sought my thick hair as if working a loom, weaving and tugging it into delicate braids that they dropped like miniature ropes to mingle with the strands falling in waves below my shoulders. Last came the cloth: thick and soft and impossibly light, it cascaded over my raised arms like foam on water, hugging my breasts before falling loosely about my waist and hips. It fit as though it had been made for me. Made for this night.

And then I felt fingers working the knot of the blindfold at the back of my head. The cloth fell away from my eyes and I blinked, struggling to adjust my eyes to the light. I looked round the little hut in confusion. A fire, a sheepskin, a rough wooden table. A ceramic bowl and, beside it, a simple earthen cup.

"Where have they gone?" I asked.

Only Ariane stood before me, her blue eyes bright in the firelight.

"They?" She asked. "Of whom are you speaking?"

"The women." I hadn't heard the creak of the door, hadn't gotten the chance to thank those who had so kindly tended me. Now they were nowhere to be seen.

Ariane smiled. "There were no women, Languoreth. None other than me."

"But . . ."

Ariane put her finger to her lips and produced a small bronze mirror from her cloak.

"Look, Languoreth of Cadzow. See what you have become."

I gazed at the woman before me, wondering what unearthly realm she had risen from. Her skin was too pure, pearly as a water sprite's. Her auburn hair twisted like living flame in the firelight. Her breasts were too full, her eyes too wild. Could this truly be me?

A proud and feral beauty rose to fill the space within me where the little girl had once been. My heart slowed. A calm came over me.

"Yes," Ariane said, stepping forward, her eyes taking my measure. "Now you are a woman. A Torch Bearer, unlike any other."

I let my eyelids drift closed, then opened them, looking once more. In my own eyes I saw the shimmering reflection of the Gods. The woman who stood before me was untamable. Timeless. She was mother, crone, maiden, and beauty.

Ariane nodded and gave a little smile. She took the mirror gently from my fingers and tucked it back into the folds of her cloak.

"Now you are a woman," she repeated. "Now you are ready."

CHAPTER 18

The women of Cadzow gathered in the wood beyond the pasture just before sunset, greeting one another as the torches were passed, one to each maiden. Their eyes widened when they saw me, but my transformation was fitting: we were the Torch Bearers, the endless power of life that thrummed from the sun, from beneath the soil. Now was the time for women in vibrant twists of cloth that clung to their bodies, torches in hand. The fires were lit. We moved through the forest in a line of flickering light, not yet within earshot of the murmuring crowd.

This was the time before we were seen, when none knew of our presence save the spirits of the wood in their sunset kingdom. A stream trickled, giving voice to the wild as the vibrant pulse of Ariane's tea still coursed through my body, igniting my senses. Leaves rustled in thickets as we passed. As we walked, I found that I could slip into their thin-veined bodies to watch our jeweled procession pass by. I could even become that crow, a smear of ink in the sky, winging my way toward the Midsummer pyre awaiting our torches in the middle of the field.

We arrived at the tree line, my heart fluttering against my ribs like a cage full of moths. Hundreds from our village and the surrounding countryside had gathered. In the crowd I spotted Forgal and his wife, the caretakers of our mill, standing with their children. Rogan the horse trader and Waylon the wool merchant were already jostling each other in good cheer, ale slapping over the brims of their drinking horns. And there, circling like hunters, stood the Men of Winter, waiting to block our attempt to light the Midsummer pyre. With their unbridled hair and soot-caked faces, they were no longer brothers or cousins, warriors of noble bearing, though I knew Lailoken and Gwenddolau stood somewhere among them. These men were a daunting human rampart rooted with their backs to the pyre, the rippling muscles of their stomachs bared to the setting Midsummer sun. The whites of their eyes were bright against the soot that disguised their faces; they had become something other: doom and decay. Destruction and blight. Seventeen maidens against seventeen men, pitted in a contest of darkness against light.

I took a shaky breath, reminding myself what I must do.

Race past the men and cast my torch on the pyre.

I brought my mother's mask to my face and tied a knot over my tumble of hair. Keela, the horse trader's daughter, stood before me, her fingers trembling as she fumbled to tie her own.

I closed my hand over hers. "Let me."

Taking up her leathers, I secured the knot against her fair hair. "They look so fearsome, my lady," she said.

"They may seem frightening," I said, "but where they are fearsome, Keela, we will be fast."

Her lips curved into a smile and she turned, eyeing the grassy expanse before us. As we watched, the rhythmic hiss of rattles came like snakes through grass. The sound drifted over the field, prickling the hairs at the back of my neck. I looked to where Cathan stood on a wooden dais, his gray hair whipped by an eager gust of wind. He lifted his white-robed arms to the slowly sinking sun. I swallowed the thickness in my throat as a rumble sounded.

Dum, ta-dum.

The drums kicked in like the footfalls of giants. We watched the sun sink slowly below the horizon.

I took a breath and gripped my torch, praying it would not fail me.

And then Cathan's arms swept down in the signal, and we were off, streaming from the forest like a band of savage beauties. A shout rose from the crowd as they spotted us, and I urged my legs to pump faster, until the gauze of my dress whipped wildly about my thighs, the drums thundering in my head. I was a deer, a fast-footed rabbit, my bare feet pounding against the hardened soil of the field, closer to the pyre where the warriors were now shifting, eyes hungry, their bodies hunched like wolves tracing the paths of their prey.

The game was afoot. If it was a hunt they were after, we would give them a chase.

The drums were deafening; the drums demanded. We were still a distance from the pyre when I tore away from the other Torch Bearers so any man would be forced to catch me out beyond the fringes of the circle. Even as we scattered, the Men of Winter sprang into motion and I ducked as a skulking figure lunged at me, my heart hammering its own frantic measure.

Was it Brant? Brodyn?

It did not matter. He was a streak, a blur as I spun, surefooted on the thick grass, racing and dodging the tussle of bodies. Screams pierced the night as Torch Bearers were snatched into the steely arms of their captors. I stood, singled out for a moment, frozen in a trembling game of cat and mouse with a Man of Winter as we both eyed the pyre. He rushed me and I twisted, rewarded by his curse and the scrape of fingernails against my arm. And then, eyeing the circle, I saw it: a space between the pairs that grappled on the outskirts of the pyre. Only a few paces more. Mother's mask and my flame would not fail me. Taking a breath, I pivoted on my heel and raced toward the waiting tinder just as a shadow flickered from the corner of my vision.

It must be now.

Stretching my body long, I launched myself in an arc, thrusting my torch into the heart of the pyre. I felt the bone-clattering jolt of my body colliding with another as the flames licked and caught, igniting in a crackling gust of kindling.

An iron grip closed about my middle as the bonfire roared to life. He was too late! I threw back my head with a triumphant laugh.

"I've won." I struggled against his grip. "You must release me."

The crowd roared my victory even as I was dragged from the fire.

My captor's breath was warm on my neck, and I was suddenly too conscious of the hard muscles of his thighs against the soft curve of my bottom. He tensed as if realizing it, too, before releasing me slowly, setting me before him.

"Fair enough, Torch Bearer."

I turned, ready to lord my victory over him, but found myself breathless as my eyes met his.

Maelgwn.

The strong planes of his face were handsome even covered in soot, his green eyes flickering in the firelight with something primal that quickened my pulse in response.

He bowed as if about to speak, but just then, above the thundering beat of the drums, a chorus of voices rose. The Call to Summer had begun. As the singing swelled and picked up pace, the Men of Winter drew the Torch Bearers into the heart of the circle. Our dance. I had somehow forgotten.

Maelgwn hesitated, questioning. I bowed my head in consent and felt the rough skin of his hand against the sheer fabric of my dress as he guided me into the circle, his hand at the small of my back.

The sweat on my skin had cooled, and suddenly I felt clammy in the heat of the fire. I stood still with the other maidens as Maelgwn dropped his hand from my back and took his place at the edge of the fire. As the Men of Winter began to circle us in the fading light, their brawny legs shifting, rocking their bodies, I searched their soot-

darkened faces. There was Gwenddolau, and Lord Emrys, his bare
chest inked, I saw now, with a fierce and twisting dragon. The mark
of Pendragon. There was Lailoken, eyes lit with mischief as the drums
stormed, their vibration thrumming through my body.

Dum, ta-dum dum. The drums demanded and the warriors answered, pounding their feet against the earth as if they could stamp
their memories into the crust of her body.

And then a shift came in the singing. Our turn.

I closed my eyes. Their keening was the heart of every song, a blaze
that crackled and churned like the fire at the center of the earth. I felt
my body give over as my sisters shifted and began to sway, soft against
the insistent stomping of the warriors and their primal thunder. The
drums asked and we answered, hips swaying, arms reaching, backs arching as we moved on the balls of our feet, twirling and spinning in the
blazing heat before the molten and ancient spirit that lived in fire. I ran
my fingers through my hair as the drums picked up tempo and a cheer
rose from the crowd as they moved to join us, bodies that had been separate melding into one, faces lifted in abandon to the Midsummer sky.

When Maelgwn's arms circled my waist, I knew him. I tilted my
head back and leaned boldly into the hard plane of his torso, letting
the breath of the Gods move through me. His hands slid possessively
over the curves of my hips. Wrapping his corded arms more tightly
about me, we knit our bodies to the wild pound of the music, mirroring each other's movements instinctively. My blood raced through my
veins like liquid fire as I came into my power. I turned to face him, my
lips brushing close to the olive skin of his neck, where he smelled of
pine needles and leather. I breathed him in, heady from Ariane's brew
and the chase, the thrill of my victory, and this new animal instinct
that had awoken inside of me. For the first time, I wanted with a ferocity that would not be denied. It was Midsummer, a night of dark
corners and passionate shadows. We were fulfilling our duty to honor
the Gods, nothing more, I told myself from within my haze. He was

intoxicated by me; I could feel it. We were two bodies buried in a throng that heaved in dance. Surely no one would notice if I let him kiss me?

I lifted my chin to meet Maelgwn's eyes, then faltered. Only a moment ago I had felt his searing gaze, but now his eyes were trained over my shoulder. I watched a shuttered look come over him as he stilled our movement. It was as if he'd been entranced and were suddenly startled awake.

"Perhaps we should rest," he said.

I stopped, but my head felt as though I were still swaying. I did not want to rest. I wanted to dance through the night. With him. Searching his face in confusion, I followed his gaze across the bonfire. Father stood at a distance, arms crossed over his broad chest, staring in our direction. Beside him, Crowan's little face glowered.

My cheeks burned. I wanted to fly at them. We were doing nothing wrong!

But I had wanted Maelgwn to kiss me, hadn't I?

I stiffened my spine against the weight of Father's gaze as Maelgwn led me from the frenzied circle of dancers. Behind me the Torch Bearers and their partners wheeled round the blaze like moths in moonlight, their bodies locked in spirals that would last until they spun themselves out. Other couples wandered breathlessly from the fire, laughing and whooping in clusters as they followed the welcoming light of torches across the field toward the feasting tables beyond.

"You must be thirsty." Maelgwn's tone was chivalrous, but I nodded wordlessly, setting my jaw. I was shamed by my own desire and disappointed by his cowardice.

What warrior would dare defy a chieftain? a small voice asked.

But I withdrew my hand from the crook of his arm nonetheless, reaching to untie my mask. An uncomfortable silence hung between us as we moved across the grass until finally Maelgwn cleared his throat.

"This was your first festival as Torch Bearer?"

"Yes." I followed him to a sturdy table where heavy jugs of wine were lined up tidily beside double-stacked barrels of ale.

"You run fast. And you dance . . . well." His mouth twitched as if he had been about to say more but thought better of it. I turned my head away in a gesture he mistook for thirst.

He remembered himself. "A drink—of course. What will you have? Ale? Wine?"

"Wine, thank you."

He turned to fetch a jug but looked perplexed. "I'm afraid there are no drinking vessels."

"No, you won't find vessels here at Cadzow." I couldn't help but smile. "At least, not to serve hundreds. You're meant to use your horn." I nodded at the cattle horn slung at his belt. "I'll drink from yours."

Maelgwn lifted a brow as though surprised a lady would suggest such a thing.

"It is no great trespass, if that's what you fear." I rolled my eyes. "I drink from Brant's and Brodyn's often, I assure you."

"But Brant and Brodyn are your kin, are they not? And I am a stranger."

"There could be no stranger Gwenddolau would trust. And I, in turn, trust the judgment of my foster brother."

"As you like." Maelgwn's dark hair fell across his face as he nodded and sat on a nearby bench with a warrior's ease. He gestured to a place beside him, but I felt the watchful eyes of the village upon me and moved to sit at a distance.

He studied me in the torchlight, lifting the cumbersome jug as if it weighed nothing. "You are unlike most noblewomen I have met."

"Why do you say so?"

His gaze was like the heat of a candle. I focused on the stream of wine as it spilled into the black pearl of the cattle horn, suddenly self-conscious.

"You train with some sort of weapon, foremost."

I looked up in surprise. "How do you know?"

"Your dress in the courtyard. It was covered in target hay. Any man would notice." A smile tugged at his lips.

"I train with a knife. It was a gift from my father."

"I know many kings who would not allow such a thing, much less encourage it."

"My father is a learned man of history. It was not long ago that all women trained in weapons," I said. "Or have you forgotten our own stories?"

"That was many hundreds of years ago, before the Romans." Maelgwn took a sip from the horn. "Then the legions came, and men discovered they did not much like to see their women cut down beside them."

"Well, I believe men have lost much since the presence of women has been forced from the battlefield."

"And what do you know of battle?" Suddenly his voice had an edge.

I wanted to tell him I had seen bodies thrown over horses. That I had tended wounds inflicted by Angle axes and swords when I was little more than a girl. But these were not things I liked to speak of.

Instead I said, "I know the great queen Boudicca raised an army of one hundred thousand, and in doing so nearly brought the might of the Roman Empire to its knees—something no king in the history of battle has done. I know Cartimandua led a nation of thousands, defending her ancestral lands from the clutches of greedy, warring men who wished to tame her."

"Cartimandua was a traitor and Boudicca's army murdered hundreds upon thousands of innocents before succumbing to famine," Maelgwn said evenly. "You speak of warrior queens whose deeds have become legend. But just like warrior kings, not all warrior queens who wear golden torques are fit to rule."

I stiffened, and Maelgwn's gaze swept my face. He extended the horn—a peace offering.

"I did not mean to offend. I speak of kings like Vortigern, not men like your father."

"Then we are in agreement on one thing," I said. "Let us drink to men like my father."

The horn was heavy enough that I needed to grip it with both hands, but I tipped my head back and drained it just as I'd seen my cousins do. Maelgwn's eyes sparked in amusement as I reached to wipe the corner of my lip and set down the horn.

"Seeing you are such an expert in war," I said, "what do you imagine will happen with the Angles? Do you think they might truly overcome us?"

Maelgwn considered this. "Unification has always been our greatest challenge. As a people, we prize the individual: Who is the greatest warrior? Who is the greatest king? Who out of the dozens is the greatest of our gods? We are a people of choices, and in these choices we find our freedom. I choose for whom I fight. Cathan chooses to whom he gifts his counsel. A farmer chooses to which chieftain or king he pledges his spear.

"Yet I fear our love of freedom is also our greatest weakness," he continued. "Perhaps we, the Dragon Warriors, can hold off the incursion for the time being. It could be months or even years that we might manage it. But I have seen the swarm of Angle ships that come. They have long since settled the eastern shore. They arrive in such numbers, you cannot imagine."

He reached for the wine and refilled the horn. "For now, they meet us in skirmishes; they raid and squabble among themselves as one of their kings claws to overcome another. But if the time comes and Emrys cannot rally the entire confederation to join our cause, then yes." Maelgwn turned to me. "I believe we may be entirely overcome."

My throat tightened at the thought of it. "Then we should toast not only to men like my father but also to men like Pendragon."

"To Pendragon." He drank deeply. I watched him, curious.

"How is it you came to ride with Pendragon?"

Maelgwn looked at me sidelong. It was a look Fallah gave when I forced her to ride in the rain.

"Surely mine is not an unusual query?" I laughed, but Maelgwn only fixed his eyes on his empty vessel.

"Perhaps that's an answer for another time. This is a night for cel-ebration."

"But—"

"There they are!"

I startled at the gleeful shout that interrupted us and looked up to find Gwenddolau and Lailoken lumbering toward our bench, their eyes bright from women, drink, and dance.

"Sit." Maelgwn gestured. "Join us."

"Join the victor, more like it." My brother, beaming, took my arm and forced it aloft.

"Oh, hush," I pulled away, unable to hide my smile.

"What came over you, Maelgwn, to let young Languoreth win?" Gwenddolau jabbed an elbow at Maelgwn and gave me a wink. "He's woefully competitive, you know."

"Don't tell me you let me get away," I accused him.

"I was too late," Maelgwn answered. "You said so yourself." His face betrayed nothing, but it made me wonder if he couldn't have caught me more quickly had he wanted to.

"And you?" I looked to Lail. "You wouldn't do such a thing."

Lail scoffed. "What, let you win and light the pyre? Never. I'd have knocked you flat and well you know it." He grinned.

"Ale—more ale," Gwenddolau announced. "Or are we drinking wine?" He peered in the horn and looked at Maelgwn. It looked for a moment as if Maelgwn flushed beneath his covering of soot. He reached to twist the wooden spout of the ale barrel so that Gwenddolau and my brother could refill their horns.

"So tell me: What were you and my little sister speaking of?" My foster brother sat, his blue eyes slightly bleary.

"I asked Maelgwn how he came to join Pendragon," I said, "but he would not answer."

Gwenddolau's eyes met Maelgwn's. He was supposed to poke fun, to tell me the tale. Instead he only shrugged.

"There's not much to tell," Gwenddolau said. "Though I *will* say— since he won't say himself—that my brother Maelgwn can take five men to my one. If there's ever been such a warrior as he, I have not encountered him."

Maelgwn's smile revealed a disarming dimple as he lifted his horn, but something behind his eyes was brittle. I knew I had spent too much time in Maelgwn's company already; I could tell by the way the other revelers shifted their eyes toward us as they stood swilling drink and laughing round the benches. Men and women, loyal to my father, all. Protective of me. And they were watching.

"Well, then"—I nodded—"I should go back to the fire."

I expected Lailoken, at least, to protest, but he was already enraptured, sitting with his hand balled against his cheek as Gwenddolau began to recount a story. The men nodded as I rose. I wandered back toward the fire, feeling unsettled. Whatever scar bound Maelgwn to Pendragon and the cause of the Britons, it was still etched deep.

I should not have prodded it.

Hours later, when wine jugs lay shattered and barrels of ale began to dwindle, there was bodhran and cruit by the fire. Dane the Song Keeper sang of Cerridwyn, and babies slept on their mothers' breasts, dreaming of feathered things. Ariane's brew and unwatered wine had left me heavy with sleep, and as embers flitted into the night, I watched them trail like spirits into the sky.

Wanting was a weary thing, I decided, better suited to Wisdom

Keepers and warriors, who could travel at whim, and to kings who answered to few but themselves and could bed any woman they wished in the privacy of their chambers.

It is bitter, Ariane had warned. Bodies moved in shadows round the fire, and I looked up to see Ariane leading Brant away from the tangle of people, off into the woods.

I sighed into the dark and tucked my knees to my chest. Would I never be able to follow my heart?

Maelgwn spoke of freedom being our very foundation but also our greatest weakness. But I saw no weakness in freedom, only strength. To travel from court to court, practicing the trade of healing and loving whomever I wished. And yet that dream wasn't meant for me. My mother had known it. How had she suffered to think her own daughter would not benefit from the same freedoms she had enjoyed?

No, wanting was wearying, and love made one do foolish things. In marrying a king, my mother had sacrificed the freedom of her daughter.

Still. How was my mother to know she would bear only one girl? Had I a sister, or even more brothers, my fate might have been different. They could be matched, married to this family and that. But there were only Lailoken and me. He had his role to play, and I would have mine.

At the thought of it a sudden anger flashed through me. Who was this green-eyed warrior to stir my longings?

No.

I settled my head on my arms and stared at the fire. At last I was a woman. Who was to say how many more days of freedom stretched before me? How long would it be before Father decided it was time for me to marry? Already I could feel my time spinning thin. I wanted all of me for myself only, for as long as I could savor it.

I would not while away another moment pining for the love of a stranger.

CHAPTER 19

The Dragon Warriors had only just arrived, and now they were off. A messenger had come in the early hours of morning with news of a raid on Pendragon's eastern borders. Angles, no mistaking it. Lord Emrys could have sent a force after them, especially given he'd left the bulk of his men behind. But Gwenddolau and Emrys would answer themselves; they would be the ones to thrust their spears and punish with their blades.

Pendragon's men were pallid and bleary-eyed as they packed up their saddlebags. Others appeared like raggedy crows in the hard summer light; having slept in the grass where they'd fallen, they'd not yet scrubbed the soot from their faces. I watched them, standing beneath the apple tree in the courtyard. Pendragon and his men were meant to stay; we'd planned a hunt and a horse race in the coming days, when I knew the weariness from the Midsummer celebration would have eased. I had arranged provisions enough to entertain them for at least one more week. And I'd had so little time with Gwenddolau, he still felt like a stranger. I felt so hollow, and who would not?

But as I took in the activity in the courtyard, it was not Gwenddolau my eyes were drawn to; they fell upon Maelgwn as if by habit. As he stroked the sleek neck of his horse in greeting; as he bent efficiently to tighten the girth. He glanced up as if sensing my eyes upon him, but I looked quickly away, smoothing my features with a woman's composure.

The maids of Cadzow had gathered. They stood moony-eyed in the courtyard, watching the men who'd lured them into the forest with such honey and charm only hours ago now slap saddles on their horses and set their hardened sights on the horizon beyond. Midsummer enchantment had been cast as thick as pine pollen the night before. I thanked the Gods my conversation with Maelgwn had been cut short before I, too, had become ensnared.

The warriors were packed all too soon. I bowed to Pendragon and kissed Gwenddolau on the cheek and then they were off, shifting easily into their saddles and racing toward the outer gate as if the very tide were licking at their heels.

Climbing the ladder to the watchmen's mount, I looked out over the pastures as they kicked their horses into a gallop, envying the calluses that leathered their hearts. Pendragon's men were most proficient with good-byes. Of course they were. Above all warriors, it was they who lived most in danger; perhaps it was they who, in loving, had the most to lose.

I shielded my eyes against the sun as they sped through the outer gate, never looking back. Only Maelgwn's form stiffened as if hearing a voice carried on the wind. Words I had not spoken. If he had turned to look over his shoulder, he would have seen me standing there, my emotion etched plainly on my face, my mask of composure fallen away. But he only shook his head as if to clear it.

Then, leaning into his mount, he disappeared into the distance.

A few lazy days passed. The fire pits were cleared and covered over, and I was harvesting nettles beside the pasture, when a shadow fell across the grassy bank. I turned to see Cathan watching me. The firm line of his mouth told me all I needed to know.

"You've come to tell me you're returning to Partick." I lowered my knife to study the plant before me. "I do not wish to go."

Wrapping a thick stretch of linen round my hand to keep the sting of the nettles at bay, I bent to make a clean cut of the stems with my knife.

Cathan folded his arms, leaning his towering frame against the trunk of a nearby ash.

"Well, we can't very well leave you here this time."

"Whyever not?"

"You have reached the age where you require a different sort of chaperone."

"You mean since I've had my moontime." I flashed him a look as I yanked the linen rag tighter. "I have a perfectly fine chaperone in Ariane, I can assure you."

"Ha! Ariane?" Cathan touched his ribs as if they ached. "Oh, that is amusing. Come, please. Tell me more tales."

"Very well," I sighed. "Then trust that you have known me the whole of my life. I would never do anything unbefitting of my position."

"What you would or would not do is of no consequence. The fact of the matter is that it is time you joined your father at court. Lailoken has been attending these past two years. I'm certain there are some who think you to be little more than a ghost." Cathan leaned in. "I have even heard some say that the young Lady Languoreth has become monstrously disfigured."

"I beg your pardon?"

He shrugged. "You know how some delight in such tales."

I gritted my teeth, and Cathan pushed off from the tree to come stand next to me. "Languoreth, you are grown. A woman of your age and bearing is to be kept close. Have you no idea what troubles could befall you—or your father, for that matter—should some rival chieftain or son of a lord decide to come and snatch you away for cattle or grain, or to force some unwanted political alliance? The blood that would be spilt? Come now. This is no lighthearted matter."

I straightened. "This is Cadzow. There is no danger here. Even so, I am never without a weapon when I walk the wood. And if Father so wishes for me to join him in Partick, he should tell me himself."

"Command you to do something he knows is against your will?" Cathan raised a brow. "Your father would sooner drink watered wine."

"How can you make light?" I stopped my work and looked at him. "You know what you truly ask of me. You mean to put me before the men of Partick. Find me a suitable match.

"Well, the thought of it sickens me. To be paraded like some prize cow, destined for the highest bidder! And what of my work here? Who will treat the calves of their ringworm? Who else knows where the whortleberry grows, or how to properly strip the willow bark?"

Cathan studied me. "Languoreth, child. You have long known of your duty as daughter to Morken King. Surely you knew this day must come."

I sheathed my knife at my belt and turned to him, beseeching.

"Leave me, only this once, and I swear I will attend on the next visit. Please, Cathan. I give you my word."

"Do you think, then, you might be any more ready?" Cathan asked tenderly. "The days of youthful freedom are passed, Languoreth. You have danced in the Midsummer circle." His eyes told me he, too, had seen me dance with Maelgwn. "You are a woman now. You have hidden yourself from Partick long enough. You cannot creep off to the wood and make believe your obligations will disappear." He caught my eyes so his meaning would not be lost.

Was that truly what he thought of me? I turned my head, blinking away the sudden swell of tears.

"You needn't compare me to Vortigern," I snapped.

Silence fell. A sheep in the pasture moaned and the bank of nettles trembled in the breeze. If I did not go willingly, they would have no choice but to force me. And I refused to be slung over a horse and dragged to Partick kicking and wailing like an infant for all to see.

"I will need some time to prepare my things," I said tightly.

"Of course," Cathan nodded. "We leave three days hence."

His blue eyes were solemn as he bowed, and then he was gone, the grass rustling as he made his way back to the Hall.

My throat felt stuffed with coarse wool. Sinking to my knees, I blinked as the nettle bank before me became a watery haze of green. The sobs rose, choking me, and I put my fist to my mouth to stifle them.

This is it, then, I thought, even as my ribs shook with fury. *My time has come.*

I was no fool. I knew I had beauty. I read it in the faces of the men who surrounded me, even if I could not grasp it myself when gazing at my reflection in bronze. It was a matter of months or days now until I was promised—of that I was certain. Now I felt the tug of the land like never before. It had been these trees that had sheltered me, this river that had bathed my body on a hot summer's day. It was this wood that knew me, better than any living thing. I may be forced to leave, to live for a time at the hall of another family, but Cadzow would be mine. Someday I would return. Cadzow was my heart. Nothing could take it from me.

I sat there until my harvest of nettle went limp in the sun. I wished I could commit to memory every scent and sensation, each blade of grass.

It wasn't until evening, when I was alone in my chamber reflecting upon what Cathan had said, that it returned to me. What Cathan had done. It was a monumental act that had marked my entry into adulthood. My entry into service.

Through the cloud of my tears, I almost hadn't seen it, the sign of respect that acknowledged my sacrifice. Wisdom Keepers bowed to no one.

Yet Cathan the Wisdom Keeper had bowed to me.

CHAPTER 20

Rain was falling by the time our retinue reached the towering walls of the town, rushing in rivulets off the hood of my traveling cloak. It sent townspeople scurrying for the thatched shelter of their huts while merchants hovered over their goods like dragons, wet cloaks outstretched like leathery wings.

I'd watched the purple clouds billow in from the west, mounding over the ramparts of Partick until the air had grown heavy and tasted of metal, until it prickled with the promise of lightning.

Good.

Send them scuttling away, the gawking flocks of men and women who cluttered the roadside, so eager to catch a glimpse of Lady Languoreth, the reclusive daughter of the king. Send them off to the isolation of their houses where their greedy eyes could not pry beneath the hood of my cloak. I lifted my face to the sky and willed the storm to rage on, as though I could thrust my anger into the churning summer clouds and watch with satisfaction as the storm punished the landscape.

I had not spoken to anyone since I'd received my summons. Not even my brother. He glanced back at me now as our horses slopped through the muddied streets of town, that same small wrinkle creasing his brow.

Lailoken did not understand. I was not angry with him. Nor with Cathan or my father. It was only that there was nothing to say. At least Crowan and Ariane understood as much. They followed close, but did not press me. They left me to myself.

Now Partick appeared as empty as a plundered town. When at last we reached Buckthorn, hearth smoke rose in a plume of mist through the thatching as if it were some great monster breathing.

Perhaps, if I bid it to, it would swallow me whole.

A knock at my door roused me some hours later. I sat up in bed as a doughy young woman with dark hair entered, a wooden bowl cupped in her hands. The rich steam that rose from it stirred my hunger and I swung my legs over the bed, suddenly ravenous.

"You missed your supper," she said. "Your father bade us let you sleep."

"Thank you." I rubbed my forehead and gestured toward the table near the window.

"Stewed beef w' herbs and barley." Her brown eyes lingered on mine a moment as she moved my mirror aside and set the bowl down gingerly.

"Thank you. It will do me good after a long day's ride, I am sure." I nodded, waiting for her to take her leave. Instead she turned to me, expectant.

"Pardon, m'lady. But do you na' remember me?"

Remember her? The faces waiting in the courtyard earlier had been a blur of unfamiliarity, and truly I'd been too numb to care. But now as I took in her rounded face and upturned nose, I felt a rush of shame. My mother had raised me better.

"Desdemona." I blinked. "Of course I remember you. But you're a woman now. Could that truly be you?"

She nodded with a slight flush and bent to retrieve the frock I'd draped over my traveling trunk.

"I didn't greet you earlier," I said. "You must think me awful. It was the journey; it has me overtired."

"Nay. It's been many winters since we met, but I won't forget what you done that day. You've been at Cadzow—of course you mightn't know me straightaway. And all the while I've been here."

"Well, I am grateful to see a familiar face." I rose from my bed to take a seat in the simple pine chair. "Do you like your work in the kitchens?"

"Well enough, m'lady. In fact, it was me what made your soup."

I breathed in the stock, rich with the roast of marrow and thyme. It tasted like the round days of autumn.

"It's very good," I offered, trying to separate her from the memories she summoned: a dying, rain-drenched boy in Cadzow's courtyard, a chicken twitching on the blood-slicked street of Partick's market.

"And the other servants—do they treat you well?" I asked.

"Well enough," she said again. Silence fell. From the edge of my vision I could see her standing by the door, still watching me.

"I am glad we shall have a chance to get to know each other at last," I said. "Thank you for supper. I will finish up on my own."

I did not wish to be unkind, but could she not see I yearned for solitude? But Desdemona only swallowed, twisting her fingers.

I turned, somewhat exasperated. "Unless there is something else?"

"I donna ken if I should say," she began. "It's only . . . there's talk. The folks a' town have been sayin' such things!"

This damnable place. "I suppose that should not surprise me," I said evenly. "If there is talk, I'd rather hear it."

Desdemona was eyeing the door now, as if she could slink back through it.

"Nay, I were wrong. I shoudn'a spoken . . ."

"No," I said. "If there is gossip, you are right to speak. It is not our habit in Morken's clan to punish those who watch out for our family."

"As you like." She took a breath. "It's just the folks a' town have been whisperin' such things! That you'd sooner be a Keeper than the wife o' a king. That you're wild and willful, more likely ta spear a man with that knife you wear than . . . let 'im spear you." Desdemona flushed full scarlet, and I managed a laugh.

"Is that all?"

"Would it were, m'lady." She dropped her gaze.

"Oh, go on, then." I smiled. "I'm sturdier than I look."

She hesitated, then the words came rushing like a geyser. "They've been sayin' your mother was a woods witch. That she died o' the boils, an' you were struck by 'em, too. She used her magic, else ne'er you nor your brother would ha' lived. They say that's wha' cost her her life."

I set down my spoon.

"My mother was no common wood witch," I said tightly. "She was a Wisdom Keeper and a healer of great renown."

Mother. Even as I spoke, the memory took me. Our tenant's wife had fallen ill. Mother had hurried to their hut and bid us stay home. Inside, the air must have been close. It must have smelled sweet, like rot and sickness. We'd heard tell of how it had traveled in years before like the curse of a vengeful god through Rheged and farther south, laying entire kingdoms to waste. Mother must have known when she saw the pustules that the sickness had returned to Cadzow. But by then it was too late. I hadn't fallen sick, and neither had Lailoken, but it wasn't due to magic—it was due to common sense. My mother had come home and ordered us sequestered. Even as she was dying, she kept herself away. It haunted me still.

Desdemona looked away. And yet something behind her eyes told me this was not all.

"Could there be more?" I said bitterly. "What more could the comely residents of Partick have to say on the private matters of our family? Come, Desdemona. Tell me. I would hear it all."

Desdemona studied the floor. "Well, m'lady, they been sayin' the pox marks you still, under your clothes. That's the reason you've been hid away. 'Til now, that is. Now that your da saw fit to have you wed."

I blinked, momentarily blinded by rage. But it would not suit to let Desdemona discover where my scars truly lay. It was then that an idea came to me.

So the people of Partick thought me freakish and scarred. Unweddable.

Desdemona had risked my fury in relaying Partick's slander, which meant she was most likely loyal. But if she'd heard such gossip, perhaps she was not so far above the carrying of it. I swiveled in my chair, considering her. Her small brown eyes were skittish, fearful. It was almost too easy. Allowing a tremor to come to my voice, I turned my chair and began to speak in earnest.

Just let Father try to match me now.

CHAPTER 21

For some days after, I refused to leave my chamber at Buckthorn. In turn Father forbade any visitors, hoping to flush me from my room like a pheasant. Still I kept to my bed, my protest sustaining me like a vigil. Meals came and went, but no one came to see me— not Ariane, not Crowan, not even my brother. Only Desdemona appeared, her thick hair plaited neatly from her face as she carried in wine and slices of brown bread alongside whatever food the others had enjoyed for supper. I studied what vellum tomes I had packed in my trunks and even practiced my stitching, wondering if Desdemona had carried the rumors round Partick as I had intended.

At last, on my fifth gloomy morning in the capital, just as my revolt was beginning to taste like ash in my mouth, Ariane blew through the door with a stout wicker basket under her arm.

"At last, you've come!" I thrust down my reading. "How ever did you sneak past Father?"

I stood to embrace her, but Ariane slapped her palm against my breastbone, sending me careening back into my chair.

"You *fool* of a girl," she said. "What have you done?"

I scowled, rubbing my elbow. "Whatever do you—"

"Never mind. Say nothing. Not a word."

She eyed my state of undress and muttered something unintelligible in her native tongue. Striding to my window, she thrust open the shutter.

"Get dressed. You will smile and greet your father. You will tell him you need some air and we are going to gather saltweed." She turned, her blue eyes piercing mine. "Do you understand?"

I nodded, and for the first time felt afraid. Could the slander I'd plied on an unknowing servant have traveled so fast? I felt the first creepings of regret.

Moving to the wardrobe, I fumbled with a clean shift as Ariane opened my wooden jewel chest, her fingers sifting through my possessions.

"Wear these," she commanded, lifting a pair of silver and green amber earrings that had belonged to my mother. "They will complement your hair. And your torque," she added, tossing it to me. "You are royalty, after all."

I pulled the shift over my head and Ariane gave an impatient sigh. "Where is your servant?"

"Crowan has not come these past four days."

"Crowan's eyes are failing; she can no longer tell amber from lapis. You are a woman now, and the daughter of a king. You must have your own servant to help you dress, not some aging nurse-mother."

"Don't speak of Crowan so," I said. "I can ready myself."

"Then make ready. Later I will speak to your father."

I plucked a rust-colored dress from the trunk and pulled it over my head, yanking to loosen the lacing. "Why have you not come to see me until today?" I asked, looking away as I secured the lacings and reached for my torque. It felt leaden about my neck, and my wavy hair caught painfully in the twisted metal as I struggled to tame it.

Watching my struggle, Ariane softened. "I have been on White Isle," she said.

"White Isle? What for?"

"To listen to old men talk too long over simple things. Here, let me." She tilted my head back and gathered the heft of my hair in her slender hands, twisting it into a loop at the nape of my neck. "Hand me that strip of leather."

I did as she bade, and she wound the leather round the nest of my hair, securing it with a knot.

"There." She stepped back swiftly to assess her work, then bent to retrieve her basket from the side of the bed. "Come now—we must go. I have already asked Macon to ready the horses."

I followed Ariane down the corridor, my heart banging in my chest. But in the great room Father scarcely looked up from his gaming. He was still sore with me.

"Brant," he said gruffly. "Follow them."

I kept close behind Ariane's chestnut mare until we turned downhill and the narrow lane widened, leading us past the Gathering Place and through the market, where the townspeople of Partick stopped to stare wide-eyed like fish.

Brant urged his mount to walk beside mine, but I could still feel their eyes prying as if they might peel off my very clothing. At last we reached the banks of the river, where ships breezed in on the prevailing tide. Salt water slapped at the quay as merchants directed the servants unloading their cargo, and warriors in bright tartans strode the docks with spears in hand, minding the shipments bound for their chieftains and kings. Overhead, the seabirds disappeared into thick banks of clouds gathering from the east.

Ariane nodded in greeting to those we passed and spoke idly to me.

"Partick. One day sunny and the next spitting rain. The wind, at least, is constant. Like the pull of the tides."

I nodded, ill at ease. Whatever it was, it seemed she would not speak of it 'til we were truly alone. At last Ariane dismounted beneath a sturdy stand of oaks and handed her reins to Brant.

"Leave us, please. Languoreth and I must speak in private."

Brant lowered his dark brows with a frown. Warriors were not accustomed to taking orders from women, even their lovers. He planted his feet as if to make a point, but a hard look from Ariane made him lift his arms in surrender.

"Fine. Have it your way. But I'll not be far."

Ignoring him, she turned to me, pointing to the sandy banks of the riverbed. "Here. Do you see where the water has drawn away? Come down and help me gather these piles of weed into the basket."

I edged down the slippery bank of rock and sand.

"Shoo the flies away," Ariane said. "We'll rinse it later."

I grabbed a handful of the slick green weed; it smelled of the bottom of the sea. Shaking it, I tossed it into the wicker, eyeing her expectantly. "You're angry with me."

"Yes, I am angry. And you know why."

"You cannot tell me you wouldn't have done the same," I said.

"What I would do is not for you!" She turned sharply. "You are the daughter of a king. You must be wed. I travel to White Isle to parlay with the Keepers, to ensure that your sacrifice of marriage will not be in vain, and what do you do? You spread lies and gossip, trying to ruin any chance of an advantageous match." Her jaw tightened as she bent to thrust a bundle of weed into her basket, then straightened, regarding me.

"Have you any idea what sort of man wants a woman he thinks must be broken? Oh, your bride price will be paid, and doubly. With bruises and welts. With a life of misery and rape, of unimaginable torture. There are plenty of chieftains who would pay for a pretty young wife they can beat like a dog. And what choice would your father have then, when you have ruined any better opportunity for yourself? Is this what you desired when you opened your mouth and so sabotaged your future?"

Ariane's words knocked the breath from me.

I thought I had been so clever. Never had I been so foolish. I sank onto the sandy bank, my head in my hands. "What have I done?"

Ariane took a breath and let it out, calming herself before sitting down at my side.

"Lucky for you, there are whisperings. Whisperings in the trees. Word has come to the Keepers that Lord Rhydderch wishes to meet you."

"Lord Rhydderch . . ." I lifted my head. I had never even laid eyes on Tutgual's son.

"He wishes to meet you. And he will like what he sees." Ariane's gaze was steady.

I shook my head, wishing I could send the words back into her mouth. Surely Tutgual's son had his pick of child brides. Young and green and blissfully unwillful. Given the damage I had done to my own reputation, I could not imagine why he would even agree to such a meeting.

"They will ask your father to arrange it," Ariane continued.

"But Tutgual is a tyrant!" I said. "A supplicant to Rome. Surely his son is no better than he! You present this as if it were a better option. This is no option at all."

Tears blurred my vision. I knew I should not have come to Partick. And yet, what choice had I?

"Languoreth." Ariane's voice was stern. "For a moment, think not only of yourself. Have you heard nothing of the goings-on around Partick?"

My eyes flashed. "Think not of myself! Say you, a woman who is free to do whatever she might wish! I will thank you not to tell me what I should think."

"You have accepted me as your counsellor, and as such, it is precisely my duty to tell you what you should think," she shot back. Then she sighed. "Even as the hero Pendragon rides off to fight his war, Lord Rhydderch's popularity rises. Should you marry Rhydderch—and should he someday become king—you would become queen of all of Strathclyde. Wife to the high king. Your father cannot refuse such an alliance, nor, do I think, would he. But more than this"—she bent her head, forcing me to meet her gaze—"if you succeed in winning Rhydderch, you could provide security for your people. For the ancient ways of your people."

"Tell me what you mean."

The depths of Ariane's eyes were troubled. "There are those among Telleyr's community who are no longer content to live side by side with men and women who do not follow the Christian way. Their resentment festers. It begins to grow something dark and ungodly. I have seen what will transpire. They will draw something to them to accomplish their ends. Blood will run through the streets of Partick and beyond. I warn you, Languoreth: the Britons cannot sustain a war from the Angles as well as this war that will rise up from within. It could bring about the ruin of your people. The end of the Old Way. Do you understand?"

Ariane's words came like the rush of a river, rising until I felt I might drown.

"But how am I to effect these coming events?" I asked. "I am only a woman. And I have never even been to court."

"Only a woman." Ariane frowned. "Languoreth, your family has long been followers of the Old Way. Your father is a much-beloved king; your own mother was a Keeper. If you think you are powerless, you are mistaken. Tutgual is like a reed in the wind, one day bowing to the Gods of old and the next day to the new. Who is to say which way he will ultimately bend?

"Should Tutgual and the men of his banner baptize themselves to the Christ god, the people of the Old Way may be punished; they will need our protection. Even should Rhydderch never rise to the kingship, as his wife you would be placed advantageously within the high king's court. You will hear things—observe things—before they come to pass. In you, the people of the Old Way will yet have a leader. It will not be an easy task. But I, and others, believe that you alone are suited for it."

I wanted to sink into the murky ebb of the river. It seemed so long ago that I had sat on another bank beside Lailoken, a girl of only ten, watching a great red stag drink in the shallows.

How long had it been since I'd dreamt of the forest?

My childhood was gone.

"Even now, there is talk at Clyde Rock of installing a *bishop*." The distaste in Ariane's voice brought me back to myself.

"Languoreth, you are courageous," she said, "and I have seen how you tend to the villagers of Cadzow. You love the people. The people of Cadzow have come to love you. You must ask yourself what you would sacrifice for them; for your Father may well decide it and decree it to be so, but it is not he who must win Rhydderch's heart. That task belongs only to you. Rhydderch is a man, not a boy. It is said he possesses wit beyond measure. It will take more than a pretty face to win his affection. This is not a gamble you or your people can afford to lose. Without the heart of Tutgual's son, you will hold no influence. This is why I have come to you. Because we may not always have the choice we would like. But we always have a choice."

Ariane shifted her eyes from me and fixed them on the water, allowing me the time I so desperately needed to make sense of my boiling emotions.

In the ripple of the river, visions from the bloody riot in the Gathering Place reflected back unbidden. The oaks of Bright Hill had been felled. The White Spring was now home to a monastery. Christian zealots had desecrated the sanctity of Clota's waters in the very sight of White Isle. Such things could not be undone, and they warned of more danger to come. What kind of woman would I be to turn my gaze from this?

I could not become a Wisdom Keeper. But I was being given the opportunity to become a leader. If Ariane and the other Keepers were right—if I alone was suited for this task—could I regard myself with any honor in refusing?

The choice was mine alone. I could attempt to win Rhydderch's affections, or I could sabotage his heart against me. The sharp cry of a gull sounded overhead, and a shiver traced my arms as I watched the bird dive for a fish; its call summoned a memory of standing on Bright Hill the moment Lailoken had heard the call of the crow. Cathan had once said a path was being laid at my feet. *Soon*, he said, *I think you will be asked to walk it.*

A salt breeze blew off the water, whipping at my cloak. I blinked and turned to Ariane as if stirring from a dream. The crow's call. Though it was years ago, it quite suddenly seemed of great importance.

"What does it mean when a crow calls from the south?" I asked.

Ariane frowned, taken aback. "Whatever are you speaking of? A crow?"

"Yes. I once heard a crow call out on Bright Hill, just beyond the White Spring. It came to me now, the memory of it, as if on the wind. It was before the oaks were felled, before the body of Fergus was buried on the hill. What does it mean?"

Ariane studied me a long moment. "Death," she said at last. "When a crow calls from the south, there will be death."

Death. So this was why Cathan had seemed so keen to protect us from the truth. He hadn't wanted to frighten us. But whose death might the crow's call portend? Was it merely the death of Fergus and his entombment in our sacred grove? Or was one of us yet in danger? Me or Lailoken. Or Cathan himself.

Ariane angled her head as if reading my thoughts. "The birdcall you speak of. I do not think this event has yet come to pass."

"Perhaps not." I twisted my fingers in my lap. The mere thought of it struck me with dread. The tides were shifting. I would be a fool not to see it. And now I was being given a chance to protect the balance between the Old Way and the new.

If by winning Rhydderch's favor I could somehow prevent this death and at once protect an ancient way of life for my people, how could I not act?

I must only say the words. I took a steadying breath and turned to Ariane.

"It's done, then," I said. "I have made my choice. Now tell me what I must do."

CHAPTER 22

A fortnight passed before the summons arrived from Clyde Rock. In that time I set about repairing the devastation I'd wrought to my own reputation. I rose early and dressed in my finest robes despite the timid assistance of Desdemona, my new dressing girl.

"Keep Crowan by your side as a companion," Ariane said. "But you are no longer a child, and Crowan is aged, burdened by too many duties. You need a chamber girl who can travel, not one whose bones will crack with each jolt of a pony. You need a young girl who will keep up with the latest preenings from abroad. This is what women of court will expect."

"But Desdemona has no skill in dressing. She is a servant in the kitchens! And it was she who spread the slanderous—"

"The slanderous stories you intended?" Ariane raised her brows.

"It only proves that she cannot be trusted."

"You knew you could not trust this girl. You used her to spread your lies, and now you owe her a kindness."

"But—"

"Enough." She held up a hand. "You think you are clever. You are not yet nearly clever enough. You are soon to be surrounded by those you cannot trust. It is a lesson you would do well to learn before you enter Tutgual's court. I prefer you learn it here. Desdemona will stay. And you will make it your work to be ready."

Ariane was right: I was yet ill-matched for court. And Ariane, being a female Keeper, could not accompany me. She was forbidden from entering the high king's court.

In the fortnight before the summons, I visited the market daily with Desdemona and Crowan, chatting with the merchants of Partick's finest shops. I nodded and smiled at the other noble families as they passed in their carts. I attended feasts with Father and Lail, matching wits with war-mangled chieftains, smiling coyly at their boastful sons and even laughing at the tales of their bloodthirsty warriors.

But on the morning we were due to depart to Clyde Rock, I woke before dawn, my throat so tight I could scarcely breathe. Outside, night was giving way to a dusky pearl morning. I tugged on the old tunic and breeches Lail had given me, belted my knife round my waist, and crept outside to the stables.

I could not see the horses, but I could hear them gently breathing. The soft snores of Macon and the grooms sounded from the loft overhead as I moved silently along the planking. Only the moonlike glow of Fallah's coat was visible in the stable's dim, the lamplight long extinguished. She turned to blink her lashes at me as I bent my head to her flank, tacking her in darkness. I had just led her beyond the stable door when a razor-sharp sting jabbed at my breastbone. I dropped her reins with a gasp and froze.

"Who's there?" A deep voice demanded.

"Languoreth," I said quickly.

Brodyn stepped from the shadows, casting his hood back to reveal his scowling face.

"Gods save me, cousin, I nearly impaled you," he said, lowering his spear.

"All's well. Not a scratch."

He eyed my riding clothes warily. "And where is it you're going?"

"I'm just taking the path that runs above the river," I whispered. "I swear I will come back."

The crease of his brow eased but he nodded to the man posted by the gate. "Then Arwel and I will accompany you."

"No need. I'll be back for breakfast."

"Languoreth. You cannot ride alone."

"I will answer to Father."

"It is not yet morning. If anything should happen, it is *I* who will answer to your father."

"Brodyn"—I met my cousin's eyes—"in just a few hours we must leave for Clyde Rock."

Brodyn's dark eyes softened and he bowed his head. "Very well. As you wish. But I beg you to take care. And should they notice you're gone, you'll find I'll be quite quick to tell them where you've run off to."

"Of course. I'll be careful, I swear it."

Brodyn took Fallah's reins in hand and saw me to the gate. The previous night's rain had left the lane muddy but not dangerously slick. I slid my hands along Fallah's neck as we trotted beyond the fields of Buckthorn and away from town, turning onto a grassy path that opened onto a windswept plain scattered with towering oaks. The last breath of summer gusted over the fields, ruffling my hair, and I inhaled, letting the fresh smell of rain and wet grass fill my lungs. Fallah tossed her head, her smooth muscles tense beneath me; she wanted to run as much as I did. Leaning forward in my saddle, I gave her ribs a quick squeeze.

"Go, Fallah."

In an instant we were off in a gallop. We raced over the field as if the ground smoldered beneath us, away from Father and Lail and the Wisdom Keepers, away from obligations of highborn daughters.

Away from Lord Rhydderch.

Ahead of me the eastern sky burned crimson. The shadows of night were retreating to their secret world, the world of the Summerlands, the world of the dead. I took a breath and let myself sink into the relentless drumming of Fallah's hooves, wanting, willing. Emptying myself again and again, until there were only me and my horse, streaking like a pair of furies across the lands of the north. The fields and forests became a wash of green around us. The wind lashed at my face, ripping hungry hands against my clothing. We were nowhere now; we were in between. Dropping the reins, I thrust my arms wide, lifting my face to the rising blaze of the sun, my eyes closed in surrender.

As though the sheer starkness of my longing had summoned her, the ancient and wild goddess of Midsummer, her hair coils of living fire, her heart a molten flame, peered from the east. A keening built from deep within me, a wail born of resignation, of acceptance, and, finally, of purpose. Lifting my head to the brightening sky, I let this brazen new song rip through the break of morning like the cry of a hound.

We raced for what seemed like an eternity, the waters of the Clyde burning orange and pink with the rising sun. Fallah showed no signs of slowing. It was as if she knew that after today we would never be the same. I felt as though we could keep on racing, riding until we hit the kingdom of Gododdin, which bordered the edge of the eastern sea.

In the end, we rode as far as the gates of the city, where I saw the soldiers stiffen atop their high wooden watchtowers. Spotted, I pulled back on Fallah's reins and she slowed to a trot.

We turned reluctantly and headed for home.

In the courtyard, mist swirled in shafts of light. My eyes met Brodyn's with a grateful nod as I entered Buckthorn's gate, my backbone as strong as iron.

Sliding from the saddle, I led Fallah to her stall and returned a moment later with a bucket of sweet-smelling grain. She chomped contentedly as I worked her coat with a hog's-hair brush, coaxing the salt and sweat from her pearly flanks.

"So you're off to Clyde Rock."

I spun to see Maelgwn leaning against the rough planks of the stable wall, his thick, dark hair free of its usual leather binding. He wore his padded leather armor open at the neck, a lightweight linen shirt peeking from beneath it. My hand went self-consciously to my hair. What a sight I must be with a head full of tangles, dressed in Lail's clothing.

"Sweet Gods, you frightened me!" I blinked in disbelief, as if he were a trick of the light.

He eyed the knife at my belt, lifting his hands in surrender. "Apologies. I didn't mean to startle you. I suppose I've gotten too accustomed to stealing about quietly. Lucky for me I'm wearing my leathers." His smile was easy but his green eyes were troubled, as if heavier matters weighed on his mind.

I set Fallah's brush aside. "Whatever brings you to Buckthorn?" My voice was sharper than I intended, but I couldn't reconcile his standing before me, the way his green eyes roamed the length of me, recalling the memory of his hands round my waist, his lips at my ear.

"I've come bearing messages," he said. "One for a chieftain in the west, another for your father." He straightened and gave his shoulders a slight roll as if his back were stiff from riding. "I arrived here not long after first light. Your father was kind enough to see me."

"Bearing messages?" I asked. "Surely you are more valuable to Emrys Pendragon than a common carrier bird."

Maelgwn shifted uncomfortably. "Some messages require a more personal delivery. This was not one suited for a henchman."

"Please do not say Gwenddolau is unwell."

"Nay, Gwenddolau is well—well as can be," he said. "In recent days there's been raiding; Picts, we think. Since we doubled our patrols, sleep has become a precious commodity." Fine lines around his eyes spoke of exhaustion.

"I am sorry to hear it. Though I must say I'm relieved to hear lack of sleep is the greatest danger on hand at present. Far better that than the threat of Angle swords."

"Ah. Angle swords." Maelgwn grinned. "Shoddy pieces of work, really. Dull as the men who carry them. You needn't worry 'bout that."

I allowed a smile, but I couldn't evade the feeling there was something Maelgwn was not speaking of.

"I suppose you consider matters of state beyond my understanding," I ventured.

"No. In fact I do not." His eyes lingered on my face. "It's only that the issue has resolved itself. And I'm afraid that now I must be leaving."

"Leaving? But you've only just arrived."

"You wish me to stay, then?" Maelgwn seemed pleasantly surprised.

"Any proper hostess would wish a tired rider the comfort of her hall," I said, trying to conceal my attraction, to make my invitation perfunctory.

"Of course." He straightened. "No, I'm afraid I must go. I've lingered too long already, I'm sure."

"At least let me summon the grooms," I said, heart sinking. "They'll fetch you your mount."

"No, don't trouble yourself. I like to tend to him myself." He gestured to a handsome brown-and-white horse waiting patiently on a tether, and a look of consternation flashed across his face. "With good reason," he added. "It seems they've braided his hair."

I laughed at the sight of it. "Ah, well. I think he looks beatific. I hope you'll forgive them a harmless prank. I'm afraid our stable hands are young and too quick-witted. Last week I came to ride only to find Fallah wreathed in flowers."

"It would appear you have more than an average woman's share of admirers," he said.

"It's nothing like that. They're grateful is all. They came to us as boys. Their parents were slain during the Angle incursion and Father gave them shelter. They've been with us ever since."

"Your father is a good man," he said sincerely. "He wears the purple well."

"Yes, I believe so." A silence fell and I swallowed the tightness gathering in my throat. From her stall Fallah regarded Maelgwn beneath sooty lashes and he reached to stroke her.

"She's a fine horse." He patted her flank. "White as winter's snow."

"Yes. I suppose Fallah's middle-aged by now, but she can still run." I brightened. "My father delights in recounting the day she first wandered up to me in the fields, a foal on trembling legs. I was little more than a babe myself. He has always said the best horses choose their masters."

Maelgwn's eyes found mine. "It is a lucky horse that can choose its master. Many do not have the luxury of choice."

His meaning was unmistakable. But it was the tenderness in his voice that threatened to undo me.

"Please don't pity me," I said. "I have long known that when the time came I would be given away to a stranger. It was a dream to believe I might be afforded the right to choose."

"Did you?" he asked, suddenly intent. "Did you dream?"

Alone in the stables, Maelgwn's nearness was dizzying.

"What young woman doesn't dream?" I looked away. Feigning a lightness I didn't feel, I gave Fallah a pat and tried to brush past Maelgwn, but he reached out to catch my fingers.

"Languoreth."

I turned and wished I hadn't. Maelgwn's eyes blazed green, flecked with gold like fallen leaves, and in that moment I was terrified I might drown in them completely. His hand touching mine sent a gentle buzz down the length of my body, and I steeled myself against it, summoning my strength even as he drew me gently closer.

"Languoreth, I—"

He was so close I could smell the clean scent of leather and soap mingling with the dust of the road on his skin.

"Please," I begged, not knowing what I was asking for. I could not bear for him to move away yet could not stand for him to stay so close. He reached a callused hand to gently trace the curve of my cheek as if I might shatter. I closed my eyes, my pulse pounding in the hollow of my throat.

" 'Tis a funny thing." He shook his head.

"Whatever could be funny?" I whispered, lifting my eyes to his.

"Talk of your beauty does not prepare one for the thing itself."

"Come, now," I said. "I may be an innocent, but I am wise to the ways of warriors."

Maelgwn drew back suddenly as if struck, and the spell was broken. "You think I have come here for sport?"

"I would not flatter myself," I sputtered. "But you happened upon me, here, in the barn—"

"*Happened* upon you?" His jaw clenched. "Is this what you think?"

"What am I to think?" I shot back. "I've heard the way my father's men speak of their conquests. And you, one of the great warriors of Pendragon? I cannot imagine your bed goes cold."

Maelgwn's face reddened. "I can see now you have formed an opinion of me."

"Do correct me if you feel it unjustified."

He turned away with a curse before swiveling back, raking a hand through his dark hair. "This is not how I hoped our conversation might fare."

I took a breath in regret. I was baring thorns because I had to, because a charlatan was what I needed him to be. But Maelgwn's eyes were stormy, as if my words had pained him. And my fingers still hummed from the heat of his touch.

"I'm sorry," I said. "I did not expect to see you again. And certainly not here. I'm afraid you've caught me unawares, and with matters weighing heavy on my mind."

"Indeed." His green eyes softened. "You travel today to win the heart of a prince, I hear. I've no doubt you'll have it."

"I cannot thank you for such a compliment. Winning his heart would bring me no joy."

Maelgwn paused. When he glanced up, his voice was softly accusing. "I have only just met you, and now you are bound to another."

I searched for the iron-sided resolve that had flooded my veins only moments before.

"I am not yet bound, but I must be. This is what I must do—what is best for my people."

Maelgwn's eyes pinned mine. "You ask me to believe you have reconciled yourself so easily to this? You of all people?"

I opened my mouth but no words would come. Maelgwn shook his head and turned on his heel, beginning to pace.

"So be it. If you will not speak, I will," he said. "Since Midsummer night, my head has been full of nothing but you. From the first moment I saw you, I felt I had at long last found my match. And that evening, when we danced beside the blaze of the fire . . ." He trailed off with a swallow. "It cannot be right that we should encounter each other now only to be driven apart. Forgive me if I cannot accept this so easily. Languoreth, you are unlike any other woman I have known. You intoxicate my very senses—"

"Stop. Please," I threw up my hands. If he said one word more, I was certain my heart would burst. "I beg you."

"Very well." He looked away, his handsome face setting into stone.

I despaired, thinking he meant to leave, but he rubbed a hand over the dark stubble of his cheek instead.

"Very well," he repeated, his deep voice measured. "I realize it is true—we have not had long to become acquainted. But tell me you do not feel as I do and I will leave you," he said. "Tell me you do not know me as I feel I know you, and I will leave you this day and you will never see me again. I swear it."

The thought seized me with panic. Why did I feel as if we were smelted of the same ore, split between two molds? *You do not know him*, I told myself. *You do not know him at all.* And yet, from the first moment I'd set eyes upon him, I'd felt a dizzying kind of relief. As if I had been treading in fathomless waters only to be suddenly washed ashore.

Maelgwn stood motionless before me, the chiseled lines of his face illuminated by a shaft of light streaming through the stable window. I wanted nothing more than to collapse into his arms, to bury my face against his strong chest and press my eyes closed, willing the world away. In that moment it felt almost possible.

But it was selfish.

Selfish.

I could not wish the world away, and this—he—was not for me. I bit my lip as a hot swell of tears rose and forced the words from my mouth.

"I am sorry if I misled you. Surely such feelings will pass."

I lifted my chin as if to dismiss him, but my breath hitched in my throat, giving me away.

It was nothing. It was everything.

Surprise flickered in his eyes before it was replaced by something fiercer. He reached to take my face in his hands, but this time his touch was strong, possessive. And then Maelgwn's lips molded to mine.

I had never kissed a man before, and yet it seemed as though my mouth were meant to fit against his—hungry and biting, soft and demanding. I hadn't known my body had been sleeping until his fingers roamed me and it came so hotly alive. I swayed beneath the force of this wanting, head spinning, finding mooring in the hard planes of his body as his hands swept the low curve of my back, drawing me closer, pushing me almost roughly against the slatted timber wall. I wrapped my slender legs around his, our breath coming in quiet gasps as he threaded his fingers through my hair, claiming.

I could not touch enough of him.

The strong curve of his jaw, his powerfully muscled arms, the buttery leather armor that padded his chest. Unable to stop them, I traced my hands along his torso, down to the place where the lacing of his trousers met his linen shirt, until he suddenly went still, letting out a low growl against my mouth. His chest rising hard, Maelgwn pulled away, resting his forehead against mine with his hands firm on my shoulders as if to keep me at bay. I blinked up at him, confused and nearly groggy, as if I had been jerked upright from dreaming.

Maelgwn bent his head down, so close I could feel his lips brush behind my ear, sending a hot shiver through my body, his voice low and slightly strained.

"If you are going to wed a man like Rhydderch, you are going to have to learn better how to lie."

CHAPTER 23

ootsteps sounded from beyond the stable doors, and I struggled to catch my breath, my head still spinning as Maelgwn moved away, the gap between us widening like a chasm. He held my eyes as Lail called out from the entrance.

"Languoreth?"

"Here. I'm here," I managed.

Lail rounded the corner, his brows arching in surprise at the sight of us.

"Maelgwn," he bowed. "We assumed you had departed." My brother's voice was warm but his face protective. I sent him a reassuring look, but his shoulders relaxed only slightly.

"I've overstayed my welcome." Maelgwn dipped his head in return. "It was not my intent."

"It's only that we found Languoreth gone from her bed." Lail's clear blue eyes flickered to mine, missing nothing. "Father sent me to find you."

And lucky it was I who found you, not someone else, his look implied.

"I went for a ride."

"Brodyn said as much," Lail said. "But there is food on the table and a long day ahead. Come, you must eat."

"I thank you, brother, but I'm not hungry just now."

"No food, then." Lail shifted uncertainly. "Still, you must have time to ready yourself. To dress."

"Of course," I said. "I'll be only a moment."

A look passed between me and my brother, but he shook his head ever so slightly, planting his feet like a stubborn old mule.

I turned to Maelgwn. "Well, then."

A shadow of vulnerability flickered in his eyes as he waited for me to say something more, but I could only stand there dumbly, lost for words. I watched as Maelgwn's gaze became hooded.

"My apologies, Lady Languoreth. It seems we've stolen time that is not our own. You must be on your way."

The stiffness chaffed at me, but what choice had he?

"It seems I must." It was not how I wanted to say good-bye, with so much left unspoken.

"I—I do hope to see you again," I offered. Lail's eyes widened imperceptibly and he reached for my arm.

"Yes, of course," Maelgwn said. "Perhaps our paths will cross again."

"Good-bye, then. May the Gods keep you safe on your journey home."

He dipped his head. "Good-bye, my lady. May the Gods keep you."

I watched as Maelgwn swung himself astride his horse. Weaving his fingers into the horse's braided mane, he gave a polite nod to my brother and fixed his eyes on me one last time.

"I wish you a safe journey to Clyde Rock."

I nodded and turned away, unable to watch him go.

"Come, let's go in," Lail said, breaking the silence and offering his arm. Outside, Macon and the grooms had pulled the cart from the stables and were busy preparing for our journey to the quay, where one of Tutgual's ships was waiting to carry us to the fortress on the rock.

Lail turned to me expectantly. *"I'll be only a moment?"*

"It was nothing," I rubbed my forehead and accepted his out-stretched arm. "We were speaking is all."

"Speaking." His eyes flickered to my lips as if they still bore bruises.

"Don't look at me so," I said, my cheeks aflame. "I cannot imagine that you, of all people, would begrudge me a moment's happiness."

"You mistake me, sister. I do not begrudge you. It is only difficult to see you traveling a road that can only bring you heartbreak."

My breath came in a huff. "Brother, I thank you, but I do not need your warning. Am I not doing precisely what has been asked of me? Am I not trussing myself up to seduce a man who might someday be king? I will go to my chamber and I will ready myself for Clyde Rock. I will keep my word, no matter the cost."

Lail pulled me aside, his voice a low whisper.

"Languoreth. Do you not think I would rather see you wed to a man like Maelgwn than the likes of Rhydderch? That my sister could be kept close, married under the banner of Pendragon . . ." For a moment his eyes looked almost dreamy, but then he shook his head.

"The Borderlands are no place for you. They are not safe. And whatever Maelgwn desires, he knows this, too. You are the daughter of a king. He is a soldier. What station can he offer you as the wife of a warrior? That he is one of Pendragon's generals is no comfort. He is a target on the battlefield, and there is certainly no protection in that—neither for him nor for you."

"The wife of a warrior? Don't be foolish," I said. "I told you, we were only speaking. Besides, every man must fight. Rhydderch is no different. You cannot tell me the son of the high king is less of a beacon. Surely his head is a prize to be won on any field of battle."

Lail shook his head. "When Rhydderch rides off to war, it will be at the helm of a host of thousands, all charged to protect that precious neck of his bearing the golden torque. Your soldier Maelgwn rides headfirst into battle with an army of fewer than two hundred. The

Brothers Pendragon do what they can, but they live in a world where each man must survive by looking after himself."

I lifted my chin, my eyes trailing to the courtyard gate.

My brother sighed. "I know you better than anyone. Believe me when I tell you: you were not built with the right sort of heart to fall in love with a warrior."

"I do not think we can choose whom we love with any more freedom than we can choose whom we might marry," I said.

"You mustn't say such things. You have not yet met the man. Besides"—he straightened—"if Rhydderch has any sense, he may not even *like* you, much less love you."

He meant to elicit a smile, but my heart was yet a pool in the cavity of my chest. Still, as much to cheer myself as my brother, I indulged him.

"How fine that would be. And tell me, brother, what do you know of love?"

"What do I know of love?" Lailoken took my arm once more, guiding me toward the servants' door. "I hope to know nothing of love for a very long time, except that which fair maidens may give me readily. And often, I hope."

"Shame!" I muttered, swatting at him.

"You see?" He grinned. "I can cheer you yet."

But I wasn't cheered. I was still reeling, struggling to make sense of this traitorous racing of my pulse, this heavy pit lodged in the center of my stomach. Maelgwn's appearance out of the mists seemed a cruel and untimely joke. I closed my eyes a moment, wondering aloud.

"Why should he appear on this of all mornings when I had so freshly cleaved myself from any desire of my own?" I pressed. "And what was this message from Pendragon? It must have been of some import for Maelgwn to travel all this way, and yet he would not say."

Lail turned. "Pendragon? There was no message from Pendragon."

"Whatever can you mean?"

My brother stopped. "I assumed Maelgwn had told you. I assumed back there in the stables—"

"Told me? Told me what?"

"You don't know." His face went grim. "Fine, then. I'll say it. For we both know Father would spare you." He took a breath. "Maelgwn rode to Buckthorn to ask Father for your bride price."

I rocked back on my heels as if struck. "Pardon?"

Lailoken winced. "I'm sorry, sister. I thought surely he told you. Why else would I be speaking of marriage? Maelgwn came to Father in search of your hand. Of course, Maelgwn is no prince, and you are bound for Clyde Rock. You should know that Father was kind in his refusal."

My fingers flew to my mouth. I was going to be sick. I was going to break apart.

"Speak," Lail begged softly. "Say something."

I shook my head, swaying a little as Lailoken glanced about.

"Come, we cannot let the servants see you. Desdemona will be searching you out within the hour to dress you."

Lail gathered me beneath his arm, ushering me through the servants' door and out of sight of Agnes, who was tidying up the morning's breakfast. Easing me up the stairs, he helped me into the solitude of my chamber. As the door closed behind us, emotion overtook me. Maelgwn had ridden from the Borderlands in search of my hand. He'd wanted to pay my bride price. And I had been so cold, when there was nothing I had wanted more in the world. I clutched blindly for my coverlet, yanking it to my face to stifle the sound of my sobs.

"I sent him away! I sent him away . . . ," I cried. So much was left unsaid. And now I might never see him again.

"Languoreth . . ." Lail rushed to sit with me. The pain was searing, sickening.

"I cannot overcome this. I cannot . . ." My voice broke.

"Tell me what to do," Lailoken said. He reached to stroke my hair. "I cannot stand to see you weep."

"Leave me; there's nothing for it." I brushed away his hand. "Bid them stay away. I need them to stay away . . ."

"I will not leave you. I—"

"Leave me! Lailoken, please." I balled my fists against my stomach, curling inward like a salted snail.

Lailoken was silent a long moment. I felt the bedding shift as he stood.

"Very well. I will go. But in two hours' time we will board that boat together. I will be with you," he said, his voice steady as the sea.

"You are my twin, Languoreth. Remember our vow. I will always be with you."

CHAPTER 24

"I suppose it would have been impolite to refuse an escort," I said tightly.

Father gave a solemn nod to the soldiers lining the gangway. "You suppose correctly."

I eyed the alabaster sails of Tutgual's vessel as they flapped restlessly against the mast. "Impatient as the king who owns them, no doubt."

Father turned to me. "Would you say as much to the high king himself?"

I did not answer.

"No? Then you would be wise not to say it here." He leaned in, voice low. "I will warn you of this only once, daughter. Nothing you say from this moment forward shall go without regard."

I looked away. A lone black-capped gull soared overhead, casting its winged shadow against the ship's ornately carved prow. Father followed my gaze with a measure of disdain.

"Gods and heroes of a foreign land," he muttered. He held out his hand, a peace offering. I did not take it. The scene painted on the prow left little doubt where Tutgual's allegiance lay. Jupiter in the form of a white bull chased a bare-breasted Europa through a forest. A crimson-haired Diana stood, muscled legs planted firmly apart, bowstring pulled taut against the curve of her cheek. At the bow's crest, a frothy-haired Neptune rose from cerulean waves, the barbs of his trident gilded in gold. The dark-eyed figures left me cold. Tutgual yet suckled from the pap of Rome.

"Desdemona, girl," Father called. "Make haste with that trunk."

I shivered in the wind off the water, the aubergine silk of the robe I wore beneath my cloak fluttering at my feet. It came from the Far East, and I knew my father had acquired it at great expense, but it draped and clung to every curve, making me feel as naked as a sylph. I felt the absence of my blade and sturdy leather belt at my waist like a phantom limb and tugged my cloak more tightly about me.

Father bowed his head as he led me to a bench on the vessel's leeward side. "I do not wish to speak so harshly. I cannot imagine this to be easy."

"Now you would speak of it?" I gave a laugh. "When these many days past you have behaved as if nothing at all were the matter?"

"Whatever you may think, Languoreth, I do not enter into this arrangement lightly," he said. "No man wishes to give away his only daughter."

I squinted as Brant and Brodyn strode on board behind my brother, stern-faced in the bright summer light.

"You have spoken with Ariane." Father's eyes were fixed on me. "What else would you have me say? That we need this allegiance? You know this. That I am not immortal? You know this, too. When I am gone, who will protect you? Who will protect your impetuous brother? It falls to you, Languoreth. You know what you must do. You are no longer a child. It does more harm than good to coddle you any longer."

His words might have stung, but he spoke to himself more than to me. I had wept until I was nothing but a husk. I was tired of fighting. I swallowed the burn in my throat, tracing the delicate cording of my torque.

"Let it lie." I met his eyes. "The time for talking is over."

Father's smile was sad. "You are more like your father than you know." He reached across my lap to cover my hand with his. This time I took comfort in the strength of it. He was a man of so few weaknesses. I could not be angry that I accounted for one.

The captain on the quay barked his orders and the vessel's sails were loosed to the breeze, billowing with a firm snap of sheeting. The oarsmen took their seats and we eased into the wide saltwater channel of the river Clyde that led all the way to the western sea. Lailoken came to stand next to me, his thick green tunic flapping in the wind.

"The tide is yet high. Sailing will be swift today," he said.

I nodded and we fell into silence. We passed low-bellied fishing boats where dead-eyed salmon were heaped, their scales flashing like a hoard of jewels. A woman with a face like creased parchment set down her washing, squinting into the sun as we passed. Soon a thick tapestry of forest stretched into shadow on either side of the river, dotted here and there by clusters of reed-roofed huts where pigs, cattle, and chickens roamed in rough-hewn enclosures. As I watched Partick fall away I realized this was the farthest I had ever been from home.

And then, at last, I saw it up ahead, rising from the water like a hunchbacked behemoth. From deep within its watchful black crags, the solemn bellow of a horn sounded our arrival.

"Welcome to Alt Clut, the Rock of the Clyde," Father said. "The iron fist of the Britons since time out of memory."

The pride that filled his eyes told me his allegiance to Tutgual was not the only reason he'd fought to defend it. Two massive dark mounds of rock rose from the water, making the trees that pricked their craggy skin look like river moss on a boulder rather than the forest they were. The seaward mound was steeper, a pointed pap hosting a solitary hut—a barracks and lookout, no doubt—while its eastern twin was more gently rising, the hunch of its spine home to a cluster of dwellings. Beyond the uppermost rampart I could make out a grand hall of timber and stone with gabled windows, a scattering of several huts surrounding it.

Four stone ramparts circled the island, each more formidable than the last. Nearly twenty guards patrolled the platform of the first wall alone, their helmets visible above a rampart topped with sharpened stakes. Father gave me a reassuring nod as Tutgual's men lowered the sails, guiding the boat toward the quay. Soldiers in padded vests and scarlet regalia reached for her ropes, and I accepted Lailoken's outstretched hand, stepping onto the sturdy planking.

Lail attempted to distract me. "There's a freshwater well and even a granary at the base of that peak." He gestured to the uppermost slope, populated with dwellings. "Even if the bottom levels of the fortress are breached, Tutgual and his kin can stay safely entrenched for a season or more."

"Has it ever been breached?" I asked.

"No. Not for generations," Lail said. "Though I'm certain your knife remembers the most recent attempt."

It had been on these very shores that my father had claimed it from a Westman king. Now that I stood at the watery feet of Clyde Rock, I could see for myself: any man would be a fool to mount an assault on this fortress. My fingers slipped absently beneath my cloak to trace the hilt of my knife in search of comfort and came up wanting.

The sound of footsteps heralded a warrior striding along the quay, his graying black hair clipped short, his garnet cloak fluttering in the breeze.

"Morken." His silver brooch gleamed as he gripped Father's arm. "You and your retinue are most welcome."

I recognized his face: he was the soldier who'd come to Buckthorn the day Bright Hill had been ravaged. He was yet captain of Tutgual's guard.

"Breg." Father's acknowledgment was perfunctory.

"Please. Follow me." The captain gave an abrupt signal and the warriors opened the outermost gate. Its doors were hundred-year-old oak and reinforced with iron, and as the great bolt clanged shut behind us I chased away a shiver. A prison, then, not a home.

But beyond the sharpened stakes and towering wall, the scene was surprisingly pastoral.

Servants poured out slop beside a set of neatly ordered barns, where spotted pigs and several head of brown cattle stood sleepy-eyed behind a reed-fence enclosure. On the pasture that sloped uphill, black-faced sheep with snowy fleeces chomped thick summer grass, looking out contentedly over the deadly rampart to the tidal waters below.

Father gestured to the steep stone pathway leading uphill. "Now we climb."

I fought to keep my breath even as we followed the path up, deeper into the belly of the fortress. A firm knock from Breg at the second rampart gained us entrance through a narrow door, after which the peace of the pasture disappeared behind us. Here, stairs had been carved into a chasm between two cliffs, no wider than four men across. Ivy tumbled over the sheer cliff walls, and small rivulets of water trickled down through thick tufts of fern. It felt hidden. Almost enchanting. But to any raiding party, I knew the chute was a dead man's trap. Warriors from above could rain down arrows or drop vats of burning oil. They could spear invaders here like salmon in a pool.

Behind me Father winced ever so slightly. "Forgot about the stairs," he muttered. We were far from home. He'd never admit to Tutgual he was in need of a healer. I would need to fix him a poultice.

"Go slowly," I urged. Measuring my steps to keep pace with Father's, I battled the dread that rattled my resolve.

What did I know of making a man mad for me?

Maelgwn's face came before me and I blinked it away, counting the stone steps as the door to the third rampart came into view. Beyond the door, elms towered, their outstretched branches casting patterns of sunlight on the small, grassy plain nestled between the two mounts. Gooseweed and tufts of yarrow sprouted up the cliff side, good for eating and good for healing. A servant boy ceased filling his bucket from the depths of a well, watching as we passed.

"This way." Breg glanced over his shoulder, hurrying me along.

The thick scent of roasted meat wafted in smoky fingers from the squat timber building that housed the kitchens, and I caught a glimpse of slabs of beef and salt pork hanging beside neat strings of fish through the open door of the drying house. From a circular hut nearby came the persistent clang of metal: the smith was at work, whether on brooches or spear tips, who could tell?

My legs ached by the time we reached the last rampart. Here, gorse shot up in buttery sprays from weathered cracks in the rock, its nutty scent catching my nose. Dizzy with the height, I swayed a little as we ducked beneath the final door, emerging onto the peak of the hill.

"A moment, Breg." Father lifted his hand to signal a stop as he came to stand beside me.

We towered over a vast wilderness of watery sand and glittering river, where gulls spiraled against sweeping tufts of cloud blowing west toward the sea lochs. I tried to imagine pacing the fenced crescent of this hill in isolation as the world turned below me, a prisoner of Olympus.

Father gathered me close and pointed west, to the blue-green hills that rose in the distance.

"There you have the borders of Dalriada, land of the Scots," he said. "And those mountains mark the lands of the Picts." He gestured north, where the peaks rose in earnest, blurring the separation between rocky mount and sky.

"And there, to the southeast: you know those lands well."

I looked far in the distance, to the place where the lush fields of Cadzow rolled sweet and green. Never had I seen our lands from such heights.

"Look at our valleys, how fertile and green. They are bursting with crops, rich with grass for grazing—our own emerald sea. This is something our neighbors do not have, and they lust for it," he said. "Beyond our borders the world is rocky and inhospitable, where wind whips against granite, and crops, hard-won, are wont to shrivel and die. Our ancestors have given their blood to this land; elsewhere is harder living. Perhaps someday you shall see."

I scanned the horizon. Angles to the east. The cold mountains of Pictland looming beyond the great loch. The hills of Dalriada to the west, and beyond that, their kin, plundering from the great isle of Scotia, the Westland.

Lailoken swore I would be safe here, safer than the Borderlands, but as I took in the boundaries of our enemies from the teetering height of the great island, never had I felt so exposed.

"It is a lucky thing indeed that the kings of the Britons have been able to protect the boundaries of Strathclyde from this place for so long," I allowed.

Father looked at me sternly. "The men who rule Clyde Rock have no need for luck. The men of Clyde Rock have power."

CHAPTER 25

Tutgual's hall commanded the hilltop, its wooden pediments swirling with the ancient carvings of hound and serpent, eagle and swan. The heavy oaken doors of the hall were cast open and we entered into the flickering torchlight of a long, dark corridor.

Light and voices emanated from the corridor's end; my ears burned with the echo of my name in whispers. Lailoken placed himself before me, casting a steadying look over his shoulder.

"Remember, I am with you," he said.

Too soon we were at the corridor's end, and then the bannerman was clearing his throat and calling out, "Morken comes—son of Morydd, Chief of Stags, holder of the Great Fort in the Avon Forest, and king of all the lands of Goddeu."

I smoothed my robes as we emerged into a roar of golden light, clinging to the memory of Ariane's words.

We may not always have the choice we would like. But we always have a choice.

And suddenly I stood before the court of King Tutgual.

The room was vast, decorated with gilded shields painted in every hue known to the human eye. The soaring ceiling was edged by narrow slats hewn high in the stone to let out hearth smoke and give the room light. A throbbing sea of warriors, lords, and their richly robed wives, of monks and male Keepers all seemed to stare as Morken of Cadzow came forth to present his daughter to Rhydderch, son of Tutgual King.

I knew I should keep my head bowed demurely but, unable to stop myself, I risked a glance at the set of carved wooden chairs resting behind the high king's. I could be bound to one of these men until my bones turned to dust.

Two dark-haired forms were half-hidden in shadow behind the towering throne of their king. One was hulking, with the stout muscles of a bear, his bluntly cut hair terminating at eyebrows as thick as caterpillars. The other was of equal height and clearly strong, but not without grace. His brown hair fell in loose waves about his bearded face, and his eyes were steady and clear, the color of river rock.

Please, Gods, let that be Rhydderch, I prayed, returning my gaze to the smooth shale floor.

I waited, rooted, choking on my dread, as Tutgual spoke.

"Morken and his kin have arrived to Clyde Rock. Greetings, Morken. Do come forth."

"Tutgual, King." Father's voice echoed in the vast room as he strode forward. "We were gladdened by your invitation. You remember my son, perhaps? Lailoken."

My brother's body had been blocking mine like a human rampart, but as Lail moved forward to pay his respects to the king, he revealed me to the heat of a thousand stares.

Father could delay no further. "Of course we are gathered here so that I might present my daughter, the lady Languoreth."

I lifted my head as a river of jeweled garments and crimson-rouged faces swam before me. Everywhere the glint of precious stone and the shine of fine metal glittered. But nothing glittered as bright as the vulture-like eyes of the king.

"Come." Tutgual beckoned with a war-gnarled finger. Beside him stood his queen, Elufed, gray eyes watchful beneath graceful brows.

The room was so still, I could hear the rustle of my silk over the stone. I stood before the king and bowed my head, but Tutgual reached out to grip my chin roughly, as if he were inspecting a horse. I fought the instinct to jerk away.

"Pretty," the king allowed, studying me closely. "I remember her being a rather gawky little child. What richly colored hair she has. Red. Like her father's."

"Aye." Father moved to my side, protective, but his voice was agreeable.

"You have said they are twins," Tutgual continued. "Twins are auspicious. Yet they look nothing alike. One has red hair, the other brown."

"They are both tall, like the men of Morydd. And they share their mother's blue eyes."

"Aye, that I see." Tutgual's fingers on my chin were cold as a fish, and I struggled against the urge to resist him. The flash in my eyes did not go unnoticed.

"She's a spirited one, eh?" The high king's voice was hard. "Too much spirit, perhaps, to make a fine wife. We shall see."

He dropped his hand with a sniff of approval and gestured to the men sitting in ornate chairs behind him. "My eldest son, Morcant. And here is my second-born, Rhydderch."

I swayed in relief as the giant one merely grunted and the more refined brother rose, striding with purpose to stand before my father.

"Morken, King. It is an honor to meet you at last. I was reluctant to miss the war council, but my attentions were needed in Dalriada." Rhydderch's voice was measured. Fine lines creased the edges of his shale-colored eyes as he clasped Father's arm. He was more than thirty summers, older than Brant, older than Brodyn. But where his elder brother Morcant was overmuscled and clearly stout from overfeasting, Rhydderch had the lithe strength of a man of discipline, one who had burned through all his softness. Turning as if he could hear my thoughts, he locked his eyes on mine with a slight bow.

"Lady Languoreth. Since your arrival, Partick is enlivened by talk of your comeliness. I admit I did wonder if rumors do blossom on occasion from seedlings of truth."

Rhydderch's words caught me off guard until I realized he meant to test me. Ariane had warned me Tutgual's son was clever. Now, though his words paid compliment, his eyes posed a riddle. Clever Britons spent hours trading wits and words. They were puzzles, an art of sorts, and one in which Lailoken and I delighted as children.

Rhydderch was speaking not at all of my beauty; he alluded instead to the recent talk of my character. I bowed my head, trading riddle with riddle.

"You flatter me, Lord Rhydderch. I find rumors to be as enlivening as often as they are true. I'm afraid on this occasion, however, such talk cannot help but leave its subject wanting."

I watched to see if he caught my meaning—that rumors were neither enlivening nor true, and that the truth was always far less salacious than people liked to believe. But Rhydderch's eyes were shadowed snow in winter, just like his mother's.

Tutgual's chair scraped stone as he rose, impatient.

"Come. Let us offer some refreshment. This night you are guests of the Fortress on the Rock. Your chambers are arranged. Tonight we will feast!"

He gave an abrupt clap of his hands and called for music. A cluster of musicians beside the blaze of the hearth bowed their sweaty heads and began to play.

"Lady Languoreth." Rhydderch extended his hand. "Will you join me at the table?"

I inclined my head, feeling nothing as his fingers grazed my arm. He smelled of oil of juniper mixed with clove.

"Your brother will sit beside us," he said. A command, not a question.

"Indeed," Lailoken agreed protectively. "You will find I am like a lucky talisman. I turn up wherever my sister may go."

"I see." Rhydderch allowed a smile. "Well, you shall always be welcome in my court."

"And what of your father's?" Lailoken cocked his head. "For whilst I am grateful to be welcome at your court, the training of a Wisdom Keeper takes many years to complete. I wonder if by the time I have earned my robes the king will have seen fit to ban male Wisdom Keepers as well." Lail's sentiment was not all challenge; there was an ease to his wit that helped him get away with saying such things. If Lord Rhydderch was offended, he did not show it.

"Well"—Rhydderch smiled revealing strong white teeth—"then I suppose we must pray that will not be the case."

He welcomed my brother at his court in the same breath he resigned himself to his father's rule. He was spineless, I decided. Or was the prince being purposefully enigmatic? As Rhydderch led us to the table, I took his measure. His fingers upon my sleeve were callused, so he did his own fighting. The taut muscle beneath the blue fabric of his tunic told me he took meticulous care in training his body. Ordered. Even. Precise. And clever. Ariane was right: Rhydderch was not like most men. He was more difficult to figure. And that made him far more formidable.

Laughter rose over the cheer of pipe and drum. I watched as Tutgual's retinue found their seats, my father easing himself down in the place of honor to the right of the king. Poor father, besieged by the high king's brothers and nephews, his cousins and their wives, ladies with hair twisted and pinned with delicate bone fasteners, their filmy summer robes gathered and embroidered in the newest styles from across the sea. They looked cruel and peckish, like a flock of hungry chickens. As they sipped from exquisite goblets of glass, their eyes touched upon me before trailing languidly away, as if nothing of remark had captured their interest. Rhydderch followed my gaze.

"They see you as a country girl." He leaned in. "Naïve and overly accustomed to the coarser sorts of comforts."

Across the table Lail's mouth twitched with amusement at the flush in my cheeks.

"I suppose in that they are not wrong," I said. "I do not delight in finery and I have kept myself mostly far from the capital."

A servant came to fill our glasses, and Rhydderch turned to me. "Why is that?"

"I love my home," I said simply. Thinking of Cadzow, my chest swelled with longing. "*The wilds are in our blood*, my mother would always say. She taught us the name of every blossom, root, and tree. I know every crevice of Cadzow's shady cliffs. I know which pines glitter brightest with fallen snow in winter . . ." I stopped abruptly, certain Lord Rhydderch did not care to hear me rambling on.

"It sounds like a place I should like to visit," he said. "Though it must be easy to love a place when it is the only place you have ever known."

His condescension irked me, and I took a deep draft from my wine. "I cannot claim to be a world traveler. But Cadzow is not the only place I know. I have come to know Partick." I turned to him frankly. "And I do not love it."

"No?" Rhydderch's eyes lit with amusement. "You are unafraid to speak your mind," he said. "In court you may come to realize this is not always wise."

"Perhaps, at your elbow, I can learn the manners most needed to be accepted at court," I replied.

The king's son looked at me then, the weight of his scrutiny making my pulse race in my throat.

"You should not be insincere, Lady Languoreth. It does not suit you," Rhydderch said.

I was composing a response, when, blessedly, a figure over my shoulder caught his attention.

"Ah. Here comes my mother."

I turned to see Elufed sweeping across the room, the hem of her low-cut gown rippling over the shale like water.

"Lady Languoreth." She gave a perfunctory dip of her head, and I noticed the black sweep of kohl lining her eyes made them appear as translucent as glass.

It had been nearly five years since I'd last seen her, yet her flaxen hair was still as luxuriant as spun gold, not a single line having aged her face. I pushed back my chair to stand, but she pressed her pale hand to my shoulder.

"No. Sit, please." She smiled. "I do hope you are enjoying yourself."

"Indeed. I thank you."

"And this must be your brother, Lailoken." Her eyes raked him approvingly.

Lail rose to take her hand. "My queen."

"My *queen*," she repeated, her slim fingers still clasped in my brother's. "How charming."

"You must be pleased to have both your sons home from their travels," I said, in an effort to wrench her talons from my brother. "I heard Lord Rhydderch say he has most recently been abroad in Dalriada."

Elufed gave a shiver but her eyes were bright, as though the very thought excited her. "Yes, playing at niceties with the Scots. Our most unpredictable neighbors."

"For a Westman, Conall is not as unpredictable as he might be," Rhydderch said. "But his chiefs are strong and loyal, and the Scots yet have ironclad ties to the Scots of Ulster, not fifty leagues across the sea. Strathclyde must maintain a strong presence of ships on our coast if we mean to protect our trade routes."

"And what of Strathclyde's land borders?" I asked.

"The day Westmen cross the borders of Strathclyde in malice is a day they will live to regret." Rhydderch's eyes filled with a startling passion, but his mother only laughed.

"My son." She released Lail's hand at last. "You are truly our champion."

I watched Rhydderch stiffen almost imperceptibly. How curious.

"Well." Elufed settled her gaze on me. "I hope you will find everything to your comfort. Should you have need of anything, you must only ask."

"Thank you." I bowed. "I am glad we have met at last."

"Yes." She tilted her head. "I can imagine you are."

Elufed shot Lail a lingering look before turning to take her seat to the left of the king. I watched, my cheeks inflamed by the sting of her barb.

"It would seem your mother doesn't care for me," I said to Rhydderch.

He turned to me, his eyes for the first time appearing kind. "I wouldn't say that. After all, my mother was the one who sought to invite you."

I wanted to beat at my head in confusion. In this world at the top of the sky, nothing was as it seemed. I had thought surely Rhydderch had been the one to summon me. Or at least Tutgual, looking to secure Strathclyde's wealth and borders by joining with our rich lands to the south. But Elufed? What did this woman of snow and ice want of me?

I was sickened already by Clyde Rock's web and its weavers. Rhydderch read my face and took pity on me.

"Watch," he said, "and listen. It's those who are too eager to speak who make the most dangerous missteps in King Tutgual's court."

His hand was on mine, warm and reassuring. I took a breath and met his eyes. "Do you mean to say that your father's court is a perilous place to be?"

"It can be, yes. Quite perilous." His gray eyes were intent. "But not with me by your side."

• • •

The wine flowed like a ruby river. I watched as Lailoken and Rhydd-erch toasted and began to trade wits. Each time I imagined I'd emptied my cup, it was full once again, until the sky beyond the high windows had darkened to twilight and Tutgual's great room became a swirl-ing glow of music, hearth smoke, and wine. Straight-backed servants brought plate upon plate of delicacies on fine glazed stoneware. The flicker of oil lamps and hearth flame was mesmerizing, and I watched as brown-hooded monks and male white-robed Keepers moved about the room in a delicate dance of mutual avoidance. All the while I felt Elufed's watchful gaze upon me, tracking my every gesture.

I had been readied, told what to expect. But Tutgual was cruel.

He grew bored and set about arming his servants, commanding them to fight as his warriors bayed like wild dogs. My father and our retinue sat stonily, outranked and unable to object, until one poor steward lost an eye and Father took the chance to rise in fury, insist-ing the fighting cease lest any more blood spatter his fine clothing. My father was large and strong. No one assumed he was clever, too.

Rhydderch watched with immovable features. He was at one mo-ment approachable and the next a veritable wall. For a while I found it infuriating—before the liquor took hold.

I tried to temper my sipping, but the rich earthiness of the wine soothed my hot nerves. And so with each tip of my glass I became bolder, more cunning. Let Rhydderch think the wine had won me, setting my tongue loose to betray all my secrets. Though my head spun from keeping pace with him, my face was as calm as a forest pool. I smiled and laughed, willed my eyes to light with merriment. With intellect. And as the evening wore on, I willed them to smolder.

The chill of night crept in. Logs were tossed on the fire. Wasn't that his elbow skimming softly against mine?

When he leaned close to point out his sister, Gwenfron, hadn't I felt his lips nearly brush the lobe of my ear?

Lean closer, I urged him. *Smell the scent of sandalwood at the hollow*

of my neck. Breathe in the heady spell of the lavender water with which I
washed my hair.

Not because I wanted Rhydderch, but because this night I had seen
a world so much larger than any I'd known before. And I had found it
full of people with hard and frivolous hearts who should certainly not
be trusted with the well-being of a kingdom.

I had witnessed the power wielded by this merciless and violent
king perched at the top of Clyde Rock. Tutgual did not care for the
people of Strathclyde any more than he cared for my father or our
warriors, our farmers or our halls. He cared only for our wealth, our
land with its countless heads of prize cattle, our rich tributes of grain.
It was only because we gave it freely that he did not take it by force.

Now, at last, the path unfurled beneath my feet. I saw the place
for me beside the prince, and the way Rhydderch's eyes lingered on
the curves of my breasts. I saw my choice: depart tomorrow and risk
our family's fading into obscurity, or this evening strike and leave my
mark. Win the favor of Lord Rhydderch, and I would secure both my
family's and my people's protection for as long as we both would live.

And so I set my powers loose and bid them capture him.

In our world, kingship was earned, not given. It could be as easily
claimed by an uncle or a brother as by any of the king's sons. And there
was an aura about Tutgual's son that shone like a beacon. Rhydderch
was a man marked for kingship. When the time came for a new leader
to rule Clyde Rock, it could be none other than he. And I would be
the woman to stand by his side.

CHAPTER 26

I woke to a racket. Squinting in the weakly lit guest quarters of Clyde Rock, I struggled to sit and immediately identified the culprit: Lailoken lay sprawled on a fleece-lined cot beside the window, openmouthed and snoring. His wavy hair had turned squirrel's nest overnight, obscuring his face against the pillow.

He'd stayed with me, as was custom, to be certain my innocence was kept intact. But, truth be told, I was glad for his company. It had been so long since we two had shared a chamber. As a child, I would crawl in beside him to chase away my fear of foul spirits and beg him to tell me of the creatures in his dreams. Now he had grown into a man. Yet here, as he slumbered, I could yet remember the little boy who chased away my shadows, and my heart swelled with softness.

"Wake up," I said. Lail frowned in his sleep, his sandy brows drawing together disapprovingly.

"Lailoken." I reached a finger to prod his fine nose and he shot upright in bed, flailing for his sword.

"It's me! Only me," I said, then narrowed my eyes. "Do you truly believe an assailant would wake you by thumbing your nose?"

He frowned again before taking in the pallor of my skin, his face broadening into a truly obnoxious grin. "The drink's done you in."

"Hasn't," I said, my tongue stuck to the roof of my mouth. "I've only just woken is all." Disheveled as he was, his blue eyes were irritatingly bright.

"It concerns me how adept you've become at feasting," I said.

"I am the son of a king," he said. "Stomaching drink is what we must do."

Lail swiped at a wavy shock of hair plastered to his forehead. "So tell me, sister, what do you remember, then? For I shall wager it's not much."

Determined to prove him wrong, I scoured my memory, but the events of the previous night were consumed in fog. Scraps surfaced, and I collected them: the pounding of drums and racing of pipes. Lailoken and Rhydderch laughing and passing a cup. Spinning to the music with the women of court, my footwork fast, my dress twirling in a purpled cloud as face upon face gathered to leer at the daughter of the red-bearded king. There was Lailoken's arm in mine as we followed the bobbing lantern of Tutgual's servant across the wet summer grass toward the quiet looming guesthouse, the stars overhead swallowed by cloud.

"I do remember watching you talk idly with Rhydderch for quite some time, as if you were long-lost friends," I said. My voice was light but I had felt a sting of betrayal. It was not lost on my twin.

"I like him," Lail said. "In spite of myself. I want to dislike him, truly I do. But he's smart, Languoreth, not cruel like his father. I think someday he might make a fine king, if only his father would ever name him tanist. You could do worse than to wed a man like him."

I wrapped the coverlet more tightly around me and turned to the wall.

"You could scarcely stand as Desdemona helped you undress," Lail said.

"If that is your attempt at an apology, you might try again."

Lail came to sit with me, his eyes solemn. "I'm sorry," he said. "I know you want me to despise him, but I can't. And if I am right, do you not see what a world of difference a man like Rhydderch might make in place of his father at court? Do you remember the blood, the way it seeped over the stone, Languoreth? Or have you forgotten that, too?"

"Of course I remember," I said. Even the haze of alcohol could not make me forget.

"Then take heart, sister." Lailoken stretched to drink from a bedside cup. "You were captivating. You were clever. You were disarming. You've done it, or I'm a fool. You've won the favor of Rhydderch, son of Tutgual King."

I searched Lail's eyes to see if he could help me test the weight of it. But there was only a sinking in the pit of my stomach and the ghost of another man's kiss still burning upon my lips. My fingers traced them as if I could still find Maelgwn there. But I had spurned him. He was leagues away by now, and there would be another woman. I'd soon be forgotten.

Lailoken read my thoughts. "You think of him still."

"Of course," I said quietly. "Did you think me so fickle I might soon forget?"

The fire had gone to embers. I took the cup from my brother's grip and sipped, shivering in the morning damp.

Eager to distract me, Lail looked about the room and made a show of rubbing his muscular arms. "It's damn drafty on this hilltop. Where is Desdemona? Our fire's gone cold."

Her cot beside the door looked long abandoned.

"Off to sort breakfast, I'm sure, though I've certainly no stomach for it." I stood and moved to the window, unlatching the shutter.

"Close that thing, won't you?" Lail said. "Can't you see I'm half-frozen?"

"Oh, hush." I leaned on the sill. "The great warrior Lailoken."

Mist had settled in thick-bellied clouds on the summit of Clyde Rock, and the air was wet, heavy with the smell of seaweed and silt. I breathed in deeply and it cleared my head.

"I suppose it's not a horrible place to live," I allowed. "You can see all the world from up here."

"Yes, and much of that world would come right to your door," Lail said, still angling to cheer me. "Traders and merchants, chieftains and Picts. Life here would provide you an education greater than any Cathan might offer."

"No." I turned. "Not greater than Cathan might offer."

Lail avoided my gaze, leaping up as a brisk knock sounded at the door and Desdemona entered with a tray.

"That's breakfast, I'll wager, and thank the Gods. I could eat my weight in beef," he exclaimed.

"No beef," Desdemona said. "Salt pork wi' oats."

"And bannocks with butter!" Lail grinned, his mouth already full. "Desdemona, you're a goddess."

Desdemona's pale cheeks tinged scarlet as Lail leaned across to snatch a crusted roll.

"For goodness' sake, Lail. You act as though you've never eaten," I scolded.

"Chases the drink away." He inhaled the steam coming off the bowl.

"I pray you're feelin' better, m'lady," Desdemona said. "Will you eat?"

Nausea rose as the scent of yeast wafted from the tray. "No, Desdemona, thank you. I've no stomach for it."

"She will." Lail swiped a crusted bannock from the tray and pressed it into my hand. "Take one. You may not want it now, but trust me, you'll wish for it on the boat."

· · ·

We'd scarcely had time to dress when the low bellow of the horn sounded from beneath the banks of cloud. I smoothed my plait, my emotions churning, as Lail stood and brushed the crumbs from his tunic.

"The ship's at bay," he said. "They'll be waiting. Now we must only say our good-byes."

He gave me a reassuring nod and strode to the door to help me with my cloak.

Outside, I could hardly make out figures in the fog; then I saw Father standing in his rust-colored tunic and thick traveling cloak with our retinue beside the deep fortress well.

"Daughter." His face was etched with lines as if he'd not slept. He reached for my hand. "This arrangement will all soon be done, I can promise you that."

We waited in silence as Tutgual's men filed from the hall, backs straight and eyes too alert for men who had spent the night feasting. Rhydderch followed behind his father, his chestnut hair still damp from a bath. He was softer and less angular in the cling of morning mist. It was only his eyes that still felt stony and impenetrable.

"My lady." He reached to take my hand. "It was pleasing to meet you. Thank you for making the journey to Clyde Rock."

"The pleasure was mine." I bowed. A brittle silence descended before his brother Morcant stepped forward, his hulking shoulders hunched, wearing the same brightly woven tunic as the night before.

"I scarce had chance to meet the lady." His shifty eyes took in the length of me, bringing to mind a beady-eyed boar. "And still such a young thing."

His breath smelled of stale ale.

"Oh, come, now, brother," Rhydderch said lightly, releasing his grip on my hand. "There could be no loss of conversation here. The lady Languoreth is far too clever for you."

"Clever, eh?" Morcant shot a sharp look at his brother and expelled a humorless laugh. "A clever girl would do well to keep far from here. Clyde Rock is a place ruled by the wile of men and the brunt of our swords."

"Morcant." Elufed moved to stand between her sons, her fair hair beaded with mist. "Surely I have taught you a good woman is as valued a counsel as she is an ornament. You need only look to your own wife to be reminded of that."

Morcant looked to where his wife, Rhian, stood with her head bowed and snorted derisively. I'd noticed last evening she bore bruises on her wrists.

Elufed caught me staring and I looked away. As if the thought had only just struck her, she reached to tug the thick scarlet wrap from her shoulders.

"Lady Languoreth." She pressed the cloth into my hands. "A gift."

"I couldn't—"

"Nonsense," she insisted. "It isn't polite to refuse a gift. This fabric has come all the way from Iberia. Surely you possess nothing of its equal. Wear it in good health until we should meet again," she said.

I accepted the garment with a bow.

Rhydderch locked his gray eyes on mine. "My lady. I wish you safe travels home."

He spoke as if he were reciting lines from a tablet. Perhaps Lailoken was mistaken: I had failed, behaved a drunken fool.

"Gods keep you," I echoed. Shame began to creep into my chest, but I banished it. I met Rhydderch's eyes instead.

"The queen has done me an honor with this invitation to Clyde Rock. But I do pray in the future, if an invitation should come, it shall be sent from your hand alone."

Did something kindle behind his gaze? I couldn't be certain. Rhydderch only inclined his head and guided me toward my father. But I felt his eyes on my back as we began our descent down to the realm of mortal men.

I was so consumed in my thinking that the priest and I almost did not see each other. Had we departed that morning only a few moments earlier, our vessels would have slipped silently past each other as the river's current bore us back home to Buckthorn.

But there is nothing incidental about time. And so it was that I was descending the steps that led through the narrow chasm of rock when I heard the sound of voices from below.

I squinted in the fog to make out a trailing line of monks, heads bowed beneath the mist. *Telleyr must be among them*, I thought, scanning their brown hoods. *Surely he will greet us*. Here where the rock narrowed and the steps descended through the chute, there was not room enough for two parties to pass. And the monks had not yet halted their climb.

Up ahead, Father's bannerman stiffened.

"Step aside," he bellowed. "Make way for Morken King."

At this, the man at the front of the ascending party lifted his head slowly, raising a hand to signal the monks behind him to stop. He looked up and the blood slowed in my veins.

It was the man from Bright Hill.

The shock of recognition was nothing compared with that same instinct to run, to flee. It had been a fleeting moment, and I a girl of only ten. And yet his visage had been burned into my memory.

His brown robes yet hung from his skeletal frame, and his drooping blond mustache had grown into a fuller beard, but his sharp pale eyes were unchanged, and I watched them spark as he sized up my father.

This priest knew who our father was. And yet he did not bow.

I watched Lailoken's hackles rise as he pushed past Brodyn and Brant. "Monk. You do not bow your head in deference to this king."

"I mean this nobleman no offense," the man said, his voice smooth and even. "But I bow to only one king, and he is my god."

"This 'nobleman' is Morken, king of Goddeu." Lail's fist tightened at his side. "Perhaps in all your prayer you have forgotten your manners. Shall I remind you?"

The priest stiffened, and the look he cast my brother caused the hairs to stand at the back of my neck. At his full height he was tall, tall enough to level his hollow eyes on my brother's. "Strike me, chieftain's son, and you will regret it."

"Oh?" Lail gave a laugh. "The more you speak, the less I believe I will."

"Then strike and we shall see. I will look down from heaven upon your piteous moans as you blister in the fires of hell." The man's benevolent smile only served to incite my brother further.

"A zealot! Father, do you hear this man speaking? Allow me to—"

"Lailoken, leave him." Father strode forward. "I'll have no quarrel with these men."

My brother's eyes flashed. He stood, eyes locked on the priest, until I worried he may snap.

"Lailoken," Father warned.

"As you will it." Lail fell back in line.

"Lailoken," the man echoed, trying out my brother's name as if to preserve it. He shot my brother a satisfied smirk. "I'm certain we shall meet again."

"You should hope not, monk."

"Onward." Father gave Lail a stern look as he brushed past the hooded men. "Our ship awaits."

I had been watching, transfixed, unable to reconcile seeing the man who'd knocked my blade from my hand that day in the forest standing before me now, engaging with our party in such naked contempt. I'd been a child then. I was a woman now. But his presence within paces of me and my family made me feel like nothing more than a frightened little girl alone in the woods. As Lailoken reached a protective arm to escort me past, the man glanced up.

His pale eyes locked on mine with a flicker of surprise.

He knew me. What's more, I could see from the way his gaze turned keener that he saw the fear on my face and delighted in it. I moved past him, training my eyes on the steps beneath my feet. My anger swelled, but Tutgual's men escorted us, and I would not provide fodder for the king's spies. I said nothing, not until we were safely alone on board the ship. The moment we were river bound, I reached for Lailoken's arm.

"That man," I said. "The monk."

"Yes? What about him?" Lail's gaze sharpened. "I do not like the look upon your face, Languoreth."

"That is the man from Bright Hill."

Lailoken froze. "Are you certain?"

"Yes. The wood that day so long ago. It was he who had something to do with the felling of the trees. I know it. I knew him the moment I saw him."

A shadow crossed Lail's face as we watched the black island recede into the distance.

"And now it would seem he is in Tutgual's pocket."

"There can be no other reason for his presence on Clyde Rock," I said. "Ariane has told me Brother Telleyr has since fallen from Tutgual's favor. Perhaps this is what this monk planned all along."

Lail looked to where Father sat at the bow of the boat. "Father is so bent upon peace, he is blind to it. We must tell Father when Cathan is near. Cathan will make him see the truth of it. We must tell them everything you've spoken of, Languoreth."

"I agree. But who is this man? And how can a man with such darkness possibly be head of a church?" The man's hollow eyes returned to me and I shuddered.

"These are things we do not know," Lailoken said. "But I promise you, sister, we are going to find out."

• • •

Afternoon sweltered beyond Buckthorn's doors the following day, but the great room was cool and dark as we entered, answering Father's summons. We had spoken with him and Cathan long into the evening last night, and now Father sat at the long table, absently toying with his dinner knife.

"Good, you've come. I wanted you both to be present. Telleyr has just arrived and we've been speaking of this Mungo," Father said.

Cathan took a seat as Telleyr bowed in greeting. "The man your Father describes can be none other than Brother Garthwys," Telleyr said. "The man the people call 'Mungo.' But I would hear from Languoreth. My lady, you are certain this monk you encountered only yesterday at Clyde Rock was the same man you saw that fateful day upon Bright Hill?"

"It was he." I strode forward. "There can be no doubt of it."

Telleyr nodded, deep in thought. "When Lady Languoreth first described the man she saw upon Bright Hill, I had my suspicions. But Garthwys had only just concluded a vow of silence the fortnight before Fergus's death. I asked myself, *How could a man who has scarcely spoken plan a desecration on such a scale? No*, I thought. *It could not be he.* I was a fool."

"It would seem a fortnight of plotting with Fergus was more than sufficient," Cathan said.

"Aye," Telleyr said. "That can be the only way of it. Even in his silence he had drawn some number of followers to him, so beguiled were they by the fervency of his faith. As you know, Fergus was a zealot. It was likely his dying wish to be entombed on the hill and so claim it for the Christian way."

A vow of silence. This was why Mungo would not answer when I demanded his identity in the wood. Or perhaps he enjoyed frightening children of the Old Way.

"I cannot comprehend how a man such as he could come to inspire such a following," Father said.

"I blame myself," Telleyr said. "I saw no fault in it when Brother Anguen and Brother Garthwys made a petition to offer followers a . . . more ascetic sort of faith in their own weekly sermons. I was in need of aid in giving sermons, you might remember. With my flock growing and the building of the monastery, I thought it a heavenly gift of help. And Mungo has a way about him when he speaks to the people.

"Their weekly sermons soon became daily. I set my own sights on expanding the monastery: more buildings, clearing new fields for crops. Too late did I understand their radical view on the principles of the gospel. Mungo's faith is deep. It is a pity that his mind has warped it."

"The gospel?" Lailoken tested the foreign word.

"It is the Word of the Lord," Telleyr replied. "Brother Garthwys does not believe that men of Christ should marry or engage in . . ." He sought for the proper words, no doubt due to my presence. ". . . lustful acts. He deprives himself of such so as to be a beacon of right doing. He makes a show of piety, wearing a goat-hair shirt beneath his robes, and eats scarcely enough to live. They say he sleeps with a rock for his pillow. There are those who believe his ability to work miracles comes from his pure form of living." Telleyr looked up. "But Mungo's piety is not faith, it is madness. I know that now, and too late. I fear by now Mungo may even believe the tales told of him."

"I have gathered stories of these purported miracles," Cathan said. "The people believe he has restored a dead robin to life. That his breath alone has kindled fire. Stories all, put about to raise his standing. Not even I can perform such deeds—though I *am* quite good with a flint," he added, a twinkle of humor in his eye.

"You would jest?" Father frowned.

"The man is a blight. My humor sustains me. That and the drink," Cathan added, taking a deep draft of ale.

"Come now, Morken. I have put in my work. I have since traveled to the abbey to discover his past myself," Cathan said. "There I spoke to the abbot, an elderly man called Serf. When I told this man of our trouble, he displayed no surprise. He told me he raised Mungo as if the boy were his own. But whilst he was an avid student, he was detested by his peers; it seems he delighted in toying with his fellow students and making great mischief for them."

Father leaned in. "What sort of mischief?"

"Serf told me of an incident most disturbing," Cathan said. "The priest had a bird he was particularly fond of—a robin, I believe. Each day it would come to be fed from Serf's hand, and so it became quite friendly to people. But one day Serf went to feed his bird and found it dead in his courtyard, its head taken off. A student claimed he'd seen Mungo kill the creature, but Mungo replied it was done by the students to cast a stain upon him. It seemed to me Serf knew the truth of it. This was what caused Mungo to be cast from the monastery."

"Harming gentler creatures is sign of a sickness of mind not easily tamed," Father said. "I have encountered such men before."

I thought of Gwrgi and the chicken as Lailoken, who had been listening with intent, threw up his hands. "And now this twisted tale is being bandied about as a miracle? That this Mungo somehow brought the creature back from the dead?"

Cathan raised his brows. "For a young man so versed in stories, I would think you would understand their more fantastical elements, Lailoken."

"This man is a danger to Strathclyde," Lail said.

"That much is clear," Father answered. "But we must strive to keep peace! Already the Angles have established a kingdom at the edge of our eastern sea. I will not be the king to start a war within our borders."

Lailoken tossed his head back. "Father, if you do nothing, then he shall bring the war to you!"

Father shot him a look of warning. "This Mungo is under Tutgual's protection. Would you have me go to war with the high king?"

I heard a soft shuffle and Desdemona appeared with a jug of ale and an amphora of wine.

"No, Desdemona," Father said, dismissing her. "We have no want of that."

She bowed her head.

"And why are you bringing drink?" Father inquired, annoyed. "Can my servants not now carry out the simplest of tasks? This is Devi's duty when I am in meeting. You are a chamber girl."

"Devi's ill," Desdemona explained, eyes lowered. "He bade me serve you."

Father waved her off, and she went to stand beside the door, waiting to refill our cups. He turned to Cathan. "Have we any proof that this man is responsible for Bright Hill?" I could hear the edge that had crept into his voice, hungry for revenge.

"None save Languoreth's account."

"I *saw* him on Bright Hill that day," I said. "I will bear witness."

Father turned to me. "And you witnessed him felling a tree? Or perhaps instructing others to do so?"

"No, but—"

"It is not enough," Father said.

"He defied you openly," Lailoken said. "We could have made an example of him right then, Father, on Clyde Rock, and yet you forbade it."

"Lailoken!" Father's eyes flashed with anger. "My son, I fear you have long to go before you may offer counsel to a king."

Lail looked as if he'd been struck, but Father would see he learned a lesson.

"Even had I known it was he, you must never let a man within your borders know he is your enemy. Not until you are prepared to act. You've marked yourself now. I cannot make use of you."

"I can yet be of use," Lail said.

"Enough," Father said. "Tutgual plans to appoint a bishop for

Strathclyde, a leader for people of the Christian way. And this Mungo has already visited Clyde Rock." Father locked eyes with Telleyr. "If you ever held the ear of the king, you must travel to the rock and speak now, before it is too late. Tutgual must hear of your misgivings of this man. You must make it clear that you put yourself forward for this position of bishop."

"Yes. I shall speak to the king about my misgivings," Telleyr said. "But, Morken, you must believe that when it comes to a successor for Tutgual, Mungo will have his own designs for who best to raise to that throne. Rhydderch's brother, Morcant, is elder, and Morcant is of the Christian faith. Should Languoreth of the Old Way indeed be Rhydderch's choice, you'd be wise to remember it is not always the most noble-hearted son who is chosen to succeed his father."

I shuddered at the thought of Morcant's being named tanist, but Father only rose from his chair and walked to Telleyr's side.

"I cannot speak against Mungo. Not without witness. Not without proof. Even now we await Rhydderch's bid for marriage. If Tutgual does indeed favor Mungo, I cannot make an enemy of his chosen man. I must bide my time until I have something more actionable. But I promise you, brother, the moment that time does come, I shall act. And this Mungo shall know the meaning of my fury."

Telleyr took a breath and reached to clasp Father's arm. "I hear what you say, Morken King. This appointment may be made any moment now. I will bid you good day. I must hire a boatman. The tide is with me. If I leave now, I will arrive before dark."

"Very well." Father signaled to Brant, who was standing guard beside the doors. "Fetch Arwel and another—men Tutgual's soldiers may not recognize by sight," he said. Then he turned back to Telleyr. "You should not travel alone. I will send men to accompany you down to the quay. They can disguise themselves as hired hands. You needn't travel under my banner."

"I am grateful, Morken. But you cannot risk it." Telleyr adjusted his hood over his head. His brown eyes were kind. "I know the way well. I'll keep to the forest path until I arrive at the river."

"So be it." Father gripped his arm. "Travel safely, my friend."

A nagging sense made me stand. "Brother Telleyr, may I escort you out?"

"Of course," he said. "I should be glad for it."

Outside, beyond the courtyard, rain clouds billowed in the heat, and the sky had turned the color of molten silver.

"I must urge you to be careful," I said. "I cannot say why, but this whole circumstance has me very ill at ease."

"Thank you, my lady, but do not worry." Telleyr smiled. "You shall see: light always prevails. All will be right in the end."

I nodded but did not believe it. Hadn't Ariane warned of this? She had foretold of a darkness drawn by the Christians of Partick. Now that darkness had a face, one I was coming to know all too well. Would that Telleyr had never taken him in.

The monk looked up as rain began to splatter.

"I must be off." Mounting his horse, Telleyr gave a quick wave.

I lifted my hand in return and watched him ride, head bowed, into the coming storm.

CHAPTER 27

The rain swept in ceaseless billows from over the sea, gusting the thatch from roofs and drowning our high fields of oats and barley. It had been three days and still it had not ceased. All the while we had no news of Telleyr and his visit to Clyde Rock. Lailoken and Father joined the warriors in helping our tenant farmers dig drainage ditches in hopes of sparing the crops. Our wealth depended on our grain supply, and we needed a full summer's harvest. Rising water brought more power to our mills, but what good was more power if you didn't have grain enough to grind? The granaries were somewhat stocked, but without this year's harvest, come midwinter we would run dangerously low.

As waters turned puddles into lochs and grasses began to yellow and shrink, Ariane joined Cathan in seclusion on White Isle in hopes of discovering a remedy. There were sacrifices to be made, and in times like these our Keepers would spend long days in fasting and prayer. Of course, despite the wet and cling of the horrible weather, Lailoken did not miss the chance to point out that a few missed meals might actually do Cathan some good.

With the men out of doors, and the people of Partick hovered round their hearths to stay dry and keep sickness at bay, the world seemed awfully small. I sat in the great room with Crowan and Desdemona while the rain pounded down, every now and again lifting the shutter to watch sinuous streams of peat smoke rise from the huts like so many snakes.

"I hear rumors that in Pendragon's lands fighting has broken out with Hengist the Angle," I said aloud, my mind fixed on Maelgwn.

"Those men can keep their own," Crowan said, scarcely glancing up from her weaving. "Especially our Gwenddolau, eh?"

I felt a flash of shame that it was not Gwenddolau I worried over and closed my eyes, praying both he and Maelgwn would be kept safe. Sword, spear, or axe—in the blink of an eye a warrior could fall. One misjudgment of an enemy's hand . . . I'd witnessed the results. Maimed, blinded, suffering. To die was more fortunate.

Soon it would be Lughnasa, when our fortnight celebration of feasting and games would begin. Lailoken's favorite time of year. And yet, when my brother came home from the fields, he paced his chamber. He wanted to go to Gwenddolau. He wanted to join in the fight. I could feel the call to battle pulling him as if it were a need of my own. Why train to throw his spear in competition when it could be far more lethal in war? Why waste his muscle in digging drainage for fields when the Angle warriors raided and ravaged Britons in the south? As the days passed, I watched as Lailoken trained his mind for the tasks of a Keeper and his body for the tasks of war. He wore his hair longer now, tethered tightly from his face. He was corded with muscle, no doubt from goading Brant and Brodyn to swordplay long after they were spent, and from trudging out before sunrise to the targets to thrust his spear. His anxiety was smoldering, and I understood all too well as the rain continued to fall. After all, the weight of my own fate hung in the balance.

It was through these sheets of water that the messenger came from King Tutgual's court. My hand stilled at the loom as a shout rose up from the guard, followed by a thunderous knock at the door. I slipped from my chair and peered out into the corridor. The messenger was elegantly dressed but said little. I hurried back into the great room and wrung my fingers in my lap, waiting by the fire to receive him.

At last the messenger entered and bowed with great courtesy. Rising, he pulled a parchment from a thick leather case. It was sealed with the wax emblem of Clyde Rock and spotted from the rain.

I walked to the nearest table and set the missive upon it without another glance.

"Allow me to offer you a mug of ale by the fire," I said.

"I make haste to get home to the warmth of my own hearth, but I thank you, my lady." With that, he was gone.

"Who is it? Who's there?" Crowan called, rushing in from the kitchens. She stopped as she eyed the parchment, her thin fingers worrying at her face. "Sweet Gods, it's come."

"Yes."

"And you've not looked?"

"No."

"Lucky you haven't! Your father will want you to wait," she said. And so we sat by the fire, our gazes going in turns to the water-spotted parchment sealed with wax that awaited Father's return.

As darkness drew close, I looked at her imploringly.

"We dare not!" Crowan narrowed her eyes, but she was just as anxious. "Your father could be home at any moment, and more likely than not he'll be soaked to the bone. I'd be some sort of fool to test his love in this weather, and the same goes for you."

I went to pace by the fire. I was about to pluck the missive from the table and hold it up to the light, when the doors swung open and the men blew in, wet as a pile of half-drowned rats. Crowan gave a shout and our servants appeared, their arms full of dry linens. Father accepted one gratefully and bent to towel his hair.

"How did you fare today?" I asked, trying to keep the nerves from my voice.

Father shook his head. "Moving mud, that's all it is. The soil has collapsed, a stew of earth and water. But we got the last of the trenches in. Thank the Gods for that."

Father and Lail followed my eyes to the table. Brant and Brodyn stood utterly still, droplets of water beading into puddles on the floor.

"Tutgual's man was here?"

I nodded.

Father moved swiftly to the table, working his finger under the thick scarlet seal.

I watched as he let out a slow breath. Nodded. He handed me the parchment.

It rolled in upon itself like a snail in my hand. After waiting for hours to know my fate, I suddenly wished time to stop so that I would never have to know.

"Go on, Languoreth," Father urged. Reading the words would make them real. Taking a breath, I unrolled it, my eyes skimming the message written in Latin.

"Rhydderch will take me for his wife. A bride price of six hundred silver coins will be paid, and Father will be granted new tracts of land north of Cadzow. It is signed by Rhydderch's own hand." I set the paper down on the table and looked at him. "So the matter is settled."

"Yes, Languoreth. It must be so." Father's eyes touched on mine tenderly.

Lailoken looked to the ground. "And when will the wedding take place?"

"We will speak with the king, but I should think it must follow Lughnasa," Father said. My mouth went dry. Silence fell. I could be wed in less than one month's time.

Father sank heavily into his chair and called out in a voice that startled me. "Wine!"

It was meant to be in cheer, but his voice sounded hollow.

Servants appeared with cups and an amphora. When the wine was poured, he raised his glass.

"This is a great day for the house of . . ." His voice thickened with emotion and he shook his head. "Come, fellows. Let us drink. A cup for the bride. We shall celebrate my only daughter, our Languoreth. We shall honor the sacrifice she makes for this family."

"To Languoreth!" The cry echoed throughout Buckthorn.

I raised the cup to my lips and drank deeply, doubting there was wine enough in the world to drown all my sorrow.

As we sat at breakfast the next morning, Father's mouth was set grim. "It has been too long without news of Telleyr," he said. "Something has happened. Clearly I cannot send men."

Lail looked up from his porridge. "The rain has let up," he said, waiting for Father to tell him to go.

"Yes. It'll be a mucky ride down to the quay. But I thought you might manage it, Languoreth."

"Me?" I looked up from my plate.

"He cannot mean it," Lail said. "I'll ride out, Father. Let Languoreth stay here."

"Languoreth has occasion to visit the shops, and everyone knows she likes to ride," Father said. "It would not seem strange should she take the path through the forest."

"It would," Lail said.

"It would *not*," I argued.

I suddenly found I wanted more than anything to go on an errand for my father. Whether Telleyr had returned to the monastery or been delayed at Clyde Rock, he knew we awaited news. He should have sent word.

"It would not," Father agreed. "Men underestimate women. Stupid men, but men nonetheless. You must learn to use this to your advantage, Languoreth. Go and find our friend."

"Well, in the very least you cannot mean for her to ride alone." Lail stood.

"Lailoken, why must you bicker?" I said, my cheeks heating. "Don't you care at all for our friend?"

"No," Father said. "Lailoken is right. I pray you will not need it, but you should have your brother's protection. Lail, you may go. But on the condition that you will control yourself. No matter what you may find."

"I will. I swear it," he said quickly.

"Very well," Father said.

"I'll go and ready the horses," Lail said.

Father watched as Lail departed. As I stood to gather my things, he drew me aside.

"Bring your blade. Keep to the woods," he said. "And follow Telleyr's trail. I will trust you to keep a tight rein on your brother. He is too hotheaded for his own good."

"I will," I said.

The turf of the forest path had absorbed more water than had the river road, which, running south as it did, was a streaming rush of muddy water. It was overcast, and there was a coolness to the air that hinted of summer's end. As we ducked under the low-hanging branches of the canopy, I could not help but think of Telleyr riding alone toward the quay in the growing dark. The forest path was not much frequented, but since the flooding it had become a veritable thoroughfare. Twice we had to pull aside our horses to let lines of townspeople pass on foot, somber-faced men and women trudging ankle-deep through the muck. But on the third time I caught sight of a symbol resembling a stick figure strung round a woman's neck.

"Lailoken, her necklace," I said. I'd seen it before. Brother Telleyr wore just such an amulet over his robes. "It's the first two letters in the Greek word for Christ," I said. "Many Christians wear them."

Lailoken looked at the woman. "Pardon me," he stopped her. "Where do you travel?"

"To the monastery," she said, wiping her brow. The new monastery, she meant. At the foot of Bright Hill.

"May I ask why?" I said. "Is today some sacred day?"

"No, m'lady," she answered. "Not as such. We're going to visit the body of the monk. To pay our respects."

The monk. My heart thudded in my ears. "Which monk?"

"Why, Brother Telleyr, m'lady." She looked surprised. "There was none so beloved as he, save Mungo, of course. They found him yesterday just down the path, beside the river. Crushed by a tree that fell in the storm."

I felt a swift stab. A tree that fell in the storm? It could not be.

"Thank you," I said, dismissing her, and looked at Lail.

"A fallen tree," he scoffed. "So that is their tale?"

"I agree. It is all too convenient. We must go, quickly. We must see for ourselves." With a swift kick I swung Fallah round.

Her muscles strained as we trotted through mud, soaking my skirts with grime. At last we arrived at the little footbridge in the wood that led to the White Spring. I tethered Fallah and looked up at the sleeping mound of Bright Hill. There would be strange saplings now, planted in the holes where the oaks had once been. And new wooden crosses staked above bodies, grave markers for this decaying Hill of the Dead. Beyond the spring, where forest had stood for ages, a lofty wall of timber stakes stretched to encircle the monastery. The gate was unmanned, propped open to welcome visitors arriving to pay their respects. Still, we waited before crossing the bridge. We sought permission.

On the other side, forest had been cleared to make space for a cluster of buildings. Two long huts covered in whitewash were laid out in a fashion that called to mind the ruins I'd seen of an old Roman barracks: monks' quarters, most likely. A large rectangular building that looked like a kitchen and communal dining space sat not far from a church made of timber and stone, the symbol of Christ mounted above the door. People milled the grounds, some weeping, others in quiet contemplation, and from somewhere in the distance I could hear the sound of a single anvil striking stone.

A monk spotted us and began making his way across the field, the wet grass soaking dark patches in the bottom of his robe.

"Can I be of assistance?" As he looked at us carefully, his name came to me. Brother Anguen. It was he who led sermons with Mungo. He was quite handsome, with rich auburn hair and clear green eyes, but he had a spell-struck look about him, as if he drifted about in a thrall.

"We were on the road when we heard news of Brother Telleyr. He was a friend," I said.

"You are the children of Morken," Anguen observed.

"Aye. And what of it?" Lail stiffened.

"It's of no consequence, of course." A shadow flickered over the monk's face. "Brother Telleyr was a friend to many. A truly terrible accident. We are all beset by grief. As you can see, he was much beloved. We have been receiving his mourners since yesterday."

"It is strange indeed that we heard nothing of our friend's death until today," I said. "When last we saw Telleyr—"

Lail gave an almost imperceptible shake of his head and I switched course. He was right: we mustn't give too much away.

But it had been just enough. Something had sharpened behind Anguen's gaze. "Yes, he was found not far from the quay. It was a chestnut tree, fouled at the roots. It must have given way with all the wind and the rain."

"And what of his horse?" I pressed.

"Luckier than he," Anguen said. "Come. You've ridden all this way. You will want to pay your respects."

He turned to lead us through the sodden grass, hands clasped behind his back. "He led the building of this monastery with his own two hands. The granaries, the stables. The church. You should return for a proper tour. Today would not be a good day to show you our grounds. As you can see, we are all in mourning."

"Of course," I said. "I can assure you a tour is not necessary. We are well acquainted with the grounds of Bright Hill."

Anguen looked back, his gaze lingering on Lail. No doubt he knew of my brother's training as a Wisdom Keeper. But he said nothing, reaching instead to push open the heavy wooden door to the church.

I leaned in. "If Mungo is inside, we must not let him incite us to anger," I warned Lail.

Lail shot me a dark look and straightened his hulking shoulders. "I could say the same to you."

Inside the church, the stone seemed to remember the many days of rain. The temperature dropped and I felt a shiver travel my arms beneath my cloak. Beneath the room's only window, an altar glowed in the light of oil lamps and two dozen candles. Despite the flickering light, it felt cold and dark compared to the lush majesty of our groves or the cozy little open shelters where our people would sit to pray beside our wealth of sacred springs.

"This way." Anguen gestured. We followed him through a low doorway and I was startled to find myself suddenly standing in a small room amid a tight huddle of people. Some stood quietly, heads bent in prayer, while others wept openly, the press of their shoulders blocking the view of the wooden coffin that stood in the room's center.

A few mourners turned as we entered, but the man standing at the head of the table kept his eyes cast down. When he raised them, they were rimmed with red. If Mungo was surprised to see us, he did not show it. He had seemed so much older than me that day I first encountered him in the forest. But here in the candlelight, his hood resting at the nape of his neck, I saw he was only six or seven winters older than I was. He looked to Anguen calmly, as if awaiting an explanation. The brother approached him, bending to his ear to speak in low tones. Mungo nodded.

I felt the familiar mixture of fear and trepidation, but this time beneath it simmered a new and terrible fury. I strained to see past the horde of people but could only see the coffin's outline. Telleyr's body was hidden from view.

"I wish to see him," I said impatiently, breaking the silence. Faces turned in alarm, frowning.

"There are many who have come to see Brother Telleyr," Mungo said. "We will gladly make pardon for you, but we ask that you do not disturb our peace. We are grieving . . ." He said the words as if they were foreign.

You grieve nothing, I nearly spat, but bit my tongue. I felt Lailoken at my back, his rage billowing like a storm cloud.

Mungo turned to the mourners and spoke to them gently. "Brothers, sisters. These people have come to pay their respects. Let us grant them a moment alone. We shall meet for prayers at two."

Mungo watched them go, then bowed his head. "I will leave you, then."

Lail stepped forward, blocking his path. "You will stay."

"Your manners are no better than they were upon Clyde Rock," Mungo said. "Though I suppose that royalty and good breeding need not go hand in hand." His eyes flicked to me.

"I would be careful, were I you, with what you imply about my sister," Lailoken warned.

"You need not defend me, Lailoken." I turned to Mungo. "I should have gutted you that day in the forest," I hissed, before I could stop myself.

"I cannot figure what you mean." Mungo looked puzzled. "Are you implying we have met before?"

I pinned him with my eyes. "You would feign we have not?"

"On the contrary. I spend much time walking the wood," he said. "It is the place I feel perhaps closest to God. But I do not know you. You mistake me for somebody else."

I bit my cheek, struggling to control my emotion. Father depended upon me to be levelheaded. I could not let Mungo creep beneath my skin.

"Will you tell us who found him?" Turning to the coffin, I prepared myself to see the body of my friend. But the coffin lid was shut. "People have come to mourn. Why is Brother Telleyr's body not on view?" I asked.

Mungo sniffed. "It was the state of the body," he said. "Crushed, you see. I would spare the members of my flock the sight that I and my brothers were forced to see. As it was, it was three of our parishioners who discovered him," Mungo said. "By the time he was found, it was too late. It took two oxen to clear away the tree that had fallen upon him."

I watched as he spoke. Mungo was not telling the truth. He thought he was clever, but I read it plainly upon his face. As I stood listening to his lies, I felt the sting of tears imagining what Telleyr might really have suffered that day in the wood. I could feel the air beginning to thicken with our mounting fury. I worried for a moment what Lailoken might do—so much so that at the sound of my brother's voice I nearly jumped.

"Brother Telleyr must have been on an errand of some import," Lail said, fixing Mungo with a stare. "I cannot imagine why else he would venture out in the coming night."

Mungo raised a hand, flickering his fingers dismissively. "Who knows where the errands of God may lead us?"

I spoke quickly, reaching back to stay my brother. "I should like to say my farewells in private. Perhaps, Brother Garthwys, you might leave us after all."

"Very well," Mungo said, but he seemed suddenly suspicious. "See to it you let him rest undisturbed. Once was quite enough. I won't see you make it a habit to disturb good Christian men at rest."

He put before us the memory of Fergus as if to smear our faces in it, as if he meant to incite us to anger so he might force us to leave. There was something Mungo did not wish us to see.

"I am to tell you our father will see to the cost of Telleyr's burial," I said. "He was our friend. We would also make certain that arrangements have been made."

"I have personally taken care of the funeral expenses," Mungo said. "One of our brothers is a stone carver, and he's been at work this morning on a proper headstone. I shall see to it that Brother Telleyr has something far grander than this simple pine coffin. He shall be buried in a fine casket of oak."

Mungo's words were heavy with impunity, but his meaning was not lost on me. Oak being the sacred tree of our Keepers.

At last Mungo moved to the door. I felt the air nearly lighten with the departure of him but then he turned to loose one last arrow.

"Brother Telleyr will be buried beside Brother Fergus, you know. Up on the necropolis. I believe it was once called 'Bright Hill.' Perhaps you can visit him there."

There was a flicker of satisfaction in his eyes. I wanted to fly at him, to claw at his face with my fingers. I felt Lailoken's anger, the pent-up desire to lay this man flat right where he stood.

"Close the door," I said to Lailoken. Mungo's thin lips stretched into a smile, and with that, he was gone.

With the door safely shut, Lail moved hastily toward the coffin and lifted the lid.

At first I could see only that the figure of Telleyr was lifeless. His hood was drawn up around the warm face we'd come to know so well, his fingers knit over the crest of his ribs as if he were sleeping. I had never noticed how tall he was, how strong in the shoulders from years of farming and clearing land and building huts, all in the name of his God.

I'd seen too many dead bodies, but it was not the horror of death I found most startling. It was the absence of life. Pale skin once flushed by humor turned waxen. Never did the body feel more like a shell for the spirit than when emptied by death. Setting my jaw, I reached in to gently push back Telleyr's hood. It was then I saw the swollen eye. The purpled bruises. His face was covered in angry welts, and I drew in a sharp breath as I saw the place where the back of his head had fallen in, as though struck by some sort of blunt object.

I looked to my brother, my voice shaking in anger. "These are no injuries sustained from a tree."

Telleyr had never made it to the river. He had never gotten the chance to warn Tutgual of Mungo, to give voice to the terrible danger we all felt. Someone had intercepted him on the way. Someone must have been following him. Must have known where he was traveling. But who?

Lailoken's face went tight as he studied the extent of Telleyr's injuries with a warrior's eye.

"Yes," he said, bowing his head. "Brother Telleyr has been beaten to death. It is a terrible way to die."

CHAPTER 28

"Murder," I said, biting back tears. "This is murder."

We walked briskly as we could past the mourners and the kitchens toward the monastery gate.

"Yes, it is murder. And yet again we haven't any proof," Lailoken said angrily. I looked nervously over my shoulder.

"They mustn't hear you, Lailoken. They mustn't suspect."

"No." Lailoken ran a hand over his wavy hair in anger. "He is too smooth-tongued. Too treacherous. Even if we were to accuse him, Mungo would only say such wounds had come from a falling tree."

"We failed Brother Telleyr. We should have known it would come to this."

"And to stand here and do nothing!" Lail tightened his fists.

"But Father is right," I said, trying to convince myself as much as him. "Whilst Mungo does not yet know you, you will be at some advantage. You must play the part of impetuous young Wisdom Keeper. Reluctantly obedient son. He must not see our cunning. He must not know we are clever."

Lailoken flexed his fist and studied it. "He assaults my sister. He desecrates Bright Hill. He murders Brother Telleyr. And yet we cannot touch him. It is enough to make me think that his god does indeed protect him. I tell you, sister, this man, this Mungo, he is an enemy for the ages."

"I hate him," I said. The words were not enough.

"Yes," Lail said. "I hate him." Our words were like a vow. But as Lail looked at me, his anger drained and all that was left was worry. Worry for me.

"You do not have to say it," I said. "Of course I will see him at court. How could I not? He is Tutgual's pet."

"You must watch yourself," he said. "You must never forget what he is capable of."

I sighed with a nod. Strands of Lail's sandy-streaked hair had come loose, and he pressed his hands to his temples as if they ached.

"I cannot travel with such rage running through me. Let us sit a moment," he said. "Let us think."

"You are more levelheaded than Father gives you credit for," I said. And as we came to ourselves we realized we now stood within only paces of the White Spring. It trickled away softly as if untroubled by the events churning around it. Lail sat back on his heels beside the smooth stones at the edge of the pool where the water yet gurgled. A heavy stone cross had been placed upright at the springhead, but shiny bits of silver, glass, and precious rocks still glittered from the pool's bottom. Somewhere in those depths our pebbles of amber yet slept. In the blackthorn tree that kept watch over the springhead, colorful strips of cloth had been tied: hopes of healing that fluttered like wings when caught by the wind. I sat listening to the trickle of cold water issuing up from underground.

Lail knelt at my side in the mud, his eyes closed. I watched as his lips moved in prayer. Closing my own eyes, I felt the same sense of well-being wash over me that I had felt so long ago. Warm and pulsing. Like a mother. Like a friend. I soaked it in until I felt my lungs expand. Suddenly I found it easier to breathe again.

I opened my eyes to see Lail tracing tender whorls upon the stone beside the spring with his fingers. "Do you remember when we came here first?"

"I could not forget."

"That day was a perfect day," he said. "Before you saw Mungo in the wood, before the trees were felled. Now that I have come back here, I know that I will never return again. I prefer to remember it as it was, that first day we visited. Before all of this. The White Spring feels hollow now. Empty."

"And what of your Lady of the Spring?" I turned to him. "Would you abandon her, too?"

"The Lady of the Spring is sleeping."

"Come now, brother." I tried to cheer him. "People still visit the spring for healing; that much is evident."

Lail looked at the offerings scattered in the pool. "They call her by another name, a name that is not her own. And so she may become it, if she chooses, and her true name will be lost."

"What name do they call her, do you think?"

"They call her Mary, I have heard," Lail said. "After the mother of Christ."

"And what does that matter? The spring is still the spring."

"The White Spring is sleeping," Lail insisted. "Can you not feel the layers that now lie so thickly between you and the thrumming of her waters?"

"Perhaps she will stay asleep until one comes who truly remembers her. Then that one will call to her and she will awaken again."

Lailoken only shook his head, and I understood the difference between me and my brother then. I did not believe mankind could make magic flee from a place where it chose to manifest with such power. What we called that force did not so much matter. It was the honoring of the force itself, a longing man shared. Perhaps the Lady of the Spring did not belong to the old Gods or the new. Perhaps she belonged only to herself.

"Where you see sadness, I see hope," I said. "The people still visit her; they still pray on bended knee. We simple folk may call her by another name, but her power remains unchanged."

"We must each believe what we wish." Lailoken shrugged and picked up a nearby pebble. "Speaking of wishes"—he smiled a little—"what was it that you wished, all those years ago?"

I looked up, surprised. "My wish?"

"Or have you forgotten?"

"Nay. But Cathan advised we should not say."

"Well, I shall tell you mine, for I wished I would become a great warrior and a wise Wisdom Keeper, and that much has already come to pass."

I laughed despite my sadness.

"All right. Now you," he urged.

"Very well." My amusement dried on my lips. "I wished that someday I would be able to live as I please."

Lail's smile fell. We both knew I was to be Rhydderch's wife—that my life would be tied to his, no matter my wish. But did this mean the spring held no power?

I would not believe it.

"Perhaps the Lady of the Spring wields her magic still," Lailoken said. "Old magic takes time." I looked into my brother's eyes and saw the wisdom of other worlds reflected there.

A part of me wondered if some form of old magic had been set in motion that day we stood beside Cathan at the foot of Bright Hill on Beltane eve. But old magic was subtle and strange, I was coming to learn. It was the wind that moved the hair at the back of your neck; it was a stag drinking in the shallows. It was a vision of your departed mother, the haunting caw of a crow. Yes, my brother was right: old magic took time, but more and more, I was beginning to see it required surrender. For how else could the Gods and spirits help when we struggled so against their work?

"Come, sister," Lailoken said, helping me to stand. "Let us go home."

Home.

As we reached the footbridge, I looked back toward the water. Despite the overcast day, a glimmer of light caught the ripples of the stream in what looked like a wink.

Perhaps surrendering was all I could do.

"I sent him to his grave."

Father dropped his head into his hands and Brodyn tipped some whiskey from his flagon into Father's cup. We sat in the great room, our bones heavy from our slog back to Buckthorn in the mud.

"Uncle, you cannot hold the blame yourself. This Mungo has spies," Brodyn said.

"Surely you do not suggest it was someone within this house."

"Only one possibility." My cousin held up his hands in surrender.

Brant spoke up: "Or else he sent men to follow Telleyr to make certain of his silence. Either way, I agree. You cannot bear the blame upon your shoulders. You could not protect Telleyr any more than his own god could."

"I cannot bear the blame?" Father's hand tightened on his cup. "I could not send men to avenge Bright Hill. I could not send men to protect Brother Telleyr. Where does my power lie? At the foot of King Tutgual." His face flushed with anger. "I grow weary of feeling my hands are bound."

Father looked at me. "How much shall we deliver for burial costs?"

"Mungo says he has already made arrangements. Any monetary gift would only go toward lining his coffers."

Brant gave a sharp laugh. "Isn't he a sly bastard? He would have known how the people would love Morken, a king of the Old Way, for funding the burial of a Christian priest. Even in this he seeks to steal your power!"

"That is not the reason I sought to pay." Father stood abruptly. "Where is Cathan?" he demanded.

"I am here," Cathan called as he entered from the corridor, shaking water from his cloak. "We have arrived just now."

Ariane followed, her cerulean eyes finding mine across the room with a nod. Cathan sat heavily and signaled for ale as Ariane came to stand alongside me, laying a hand upon my shoulder in greeting.

"What said the Council?" Father asked.

"Tutgual has appointed Mungo as bishop. It is as we expected," Cathan said. "There is to be a naming ceremony to mark the occasion in one week's time and all are expected to attend."

Father banged his fist against the table. "Now that Mungo is backed by the king and his coffers, he will not need to grow his assassins from among his own flock; he may hire them with impunity! We must strike him where he stands, for he will soon be too armed to touch him."

Cathan shot him a look. "There is none who would like that better than I, but that is not wise, Morken. Think of all you might lose."

Father let out a growl and beat at his head with his hands. We waited until he blew out a breath and lifted his face to look at his old friend. "You are my counsellor. Surely there must be something we can do."

"Wed your daughter to the king's son. That much we have undertaken already." Cathan's eyes touched on mine in unspoken apology and I took a deep drink from my cup.

"And what of this naming ceremony?" Lailoken asked.

"We must go," Cathan said.

"Yes." Father took his seat once more, pushing away his cup. "Mungo has drawn the line of battle with the body of my friend. I will heed his call to war. No bishop shall hold sway over me," he said, his voice rising. "Oh, I will go to the naming ceremony. Let him look upon my face! I will see he understands a new kind of fear."

Next to me, Ariane lowered her head.

It had begun.

I could feel it creeping from the shadows, this strife among our people.

"Father, I loathe Mungo as much as you. But can you not see this is precisely what he wants?" I said. "Have we not known since the attack on Bright Hill that whoever was behind it meant to beget such a war? We are puppets playing his parts if we behave thusly."

"I agree with Languoreth," Lailoken said. "I loathe the man, too. But Mungo now wields the power of bishop with the backing of a sympathetic king."

Father looked between the two of us. "I do not recall naming either of you my counsellor."

"Lailoken and Languoreth are wise," Cathan said. "If Mungo finds no resistance, he must do something to provoke you, to draw you out. You and I are bastions of the Old Way. He will be unable to resist testing his new power."

"Yes. But at what cost?" Father held our gazes a long moment before nodding at Cathan with a sigh. "You are right, then, all of you. We will watch and wait, if only for now. I am coming to know his mind, I think. He will grow too bold with his power. He will make a mistake. That is when we must strike, and be rid of this Mungo once and for all."

I stared at the fire. As soon as I gained Rhydderch's trust, I would make certain he knew of Mungo's wicked part in this: Telleyr's murder, paying the burial costs, playing the part of sad brother-in-arms. Surely he would see that Mungo was only trying to increase both his power and his reach. For even now there were two factions of Christians in Partick: those who loved Telleyr, and those who flocked to Mungo.

By furnishing the cost of Telleyr's burial, Mungo not only sought to uproot any good deed by my father but also hoped to prove himself to Telleyr's community, thus absorbing it into his own.

Father rubbed the back of his neck. "Talk of Mungo sours my stomach. Let us discuss more pleasant news."

"Very well," Cathan said. "We are in a state of agricultural devastation."

"Ah! A lighter topic." Father shot him a look. "It is not so bad as all that. We have lost nearly half our crop, but we are better off than others. It will not be our strongest, but our tenants will yet manage a harvest, thank the Gods. We will be able to restock our granaries before winter, with some amount left to barter or sell."

"Your stores may be secure, but between here and the borders of Strathclyde there is little but dead and wilted fields, and there will be more rain to come," Cathan said.

Ariane spoke up. "Morken King, as you know I traveled with Lord Cathan to White Isle. Long we both sat, with varying methods, but the signs were all the same. There will be much rain this year and a very cold winter. With that comes worry of famine."

Cathan turned to Father. "Lughnasa will soon be upon us. We must guard your grain stores with care."

"I hear your warning," Father said, "and I thank you. I will double my guard. Brant will see to it."

A silence fell. Father squinted in the gloom. "Enough talk. I would have music. Summon Dane the Song Keeper. Perhaps he can soothe us all."

"A fine idea." Cathan nodded to our man Devi, who was posted by the doors.

Dane entered a few moments later, his kind eyes full of calm, white robes glowing in the dimming light of evening. As was custom, the king poured him a cup and offered it.

"A song, if you would so treat us?" Father asked.

"Indeed." Dane inclined his head and nestled his cruit upon his lap. We turned toward the hearth in silence as his nimble fingers tested the strings. "I will sing the tale of Lugh and his mother in honor of these high days of summer."

I sank back in my chair, closing my eyes as he began to play. It was a welcome invitation to lose my thoughts for a moment and dream of Lughnasa, my favorite festival of the year. It was two days' travel to the base of the mountain where we would settle into lavish tents for the fortnight of celebration. People would travel to the fields beneath the mountain from all across Strathclyde for spear throwing, swordplay, horse racing, and games. Song and dance. There would be sacrifices and offerings. A young bull. Incantations and tributes given in thanks for the harvest to come. On the final eve, we would keep awake the long night and, swathed in the blackness just before morning, begin our climb up the mountain.

It was a sacred pilgrimage, a punishing climb begun in darkness that finished with the rising of the sun. We offered Lugh's mountain our blood, and the mountain was greedy; it drank thirstily as we sliced our bare feet against the rocks, as the skin of our heels chafed against the hard-packed dirt of the trail. There were years when the wind would lash its way up the mountain pass as though it meant to sweep us from our feet, extinguishing our torches and leaving us fumbling our way through the stony morning dark. But always when we arrived on the summit, with all the world laid out before us and the first rays of daylight glowing like embers in the eastern sky, I knew I was as close as I would ever be to that unnameable power that lived in the Gods.

Dane's voice dropped. There was a moment of stillness as the room sat entranced, and then the final sweet reverberation of the cruit faded and my father stood and offered him a bow. The mood in the room had lightened, but my heart was yet a barnacled anchor sinking in my chest. Lughnasa was nearly upon us, and thereafter I would be wed. There was no ending more final than this. As conversation rose once more, I looked up to find Ariane watching me.

"Troubles with crops were not all the Gods showed me upon my visit to White Isle."

"I do not know if I can bear any more prophecy," I said.

"As you wish it. I shall not tell you, then, what I have seen."

I looked at Ariane, my face laid bare. "You know I cannot resist such a statement."

She gave a small smile. "Very well. You must take heart. For the warrior Maelgwn comes this way for Lughnasa. I have seen it."

I lowered my voice. "If what you say is true, then I am happy for it. But surely you would chastise me."

"I?" She gave a soft laugh. "No, not I."

Ariane leaned forward. "Languoreth, you have made such contracts as needed to be made. Your duty is fulfilled. You may be told where to live and with whom, but do not let fear get in the way of your heart's deepest yearnings. I have watched you since Midsummer. Any fool can see how this pulls at you. Let nature take her course. It will bring about more harm than good to fight it."

"Let nature take her course?" I echoed. "I am betrothed to a son of the high king. No. There is too much danger in this! Ariane, as my counsel, how could you of all people advise me so?"

Ariane fixed me with a stern glance. "Languoreth, in less than one month's time you will be given away, forced to live under the sleepless watch of a new court with hard rules of behavior and conduct the likes of which you cannot begin to imagine. You will be living a life of containment. Of servitude. Do not look at me so. You know it does not please me to say this, but you also know it to be true." She softened. "Time is what you make of it. Some things cannot be contained. Love is such a thing."

"I cannot maneuver my heart open and shut with the pulling of a lever. Even if I should follow my heart, I cannot see how—"

"There are ways," she said. "Ways to allow the things that belong to you to find you. Can you not see? The people and things that belong to you are not yours to decide in any case. Such things are decided long before we are born."

I stiffened. "I will not do any conjuring on him."

"Do not insult me," she scoffed. "And do not insult yourself. You have no need for witchery. This is something other. This is protection." Ariane observed my confusion with a sigh. "You and Maelgwn will be given the gift of time. If you desire it, I can arrange it so that no one will know you are missing. If he should desire you as you desire him, time will be yours to do what you will."

My heart beat in my throat. "You can do this?"

She gave a slight shrug. "I do only things I know are right. And this is right."

I blinked at the weight of it. "But what would the purpose be?" I asked. "It would all be for nothing."

Ariane blinked at the sorrow in my voice and reached to press my hand in hers. "Who are you to say what it will come to, what it will be? Do not deny yourself what little happiness you might find. For there are bound to be days in every lifetime dark enough to drown what little light we might gather." Ariane's clever eyes shone in the firelight. "You must trust me, Languoreth. You must trust in the Gods."

CHAPTER 29

I could hear the music beyond the skin of our tent. Whoops and hollers of delight echoed over the racing of the flute and the insistent pounding of the drum, filling me with a wild anticipation and the feeling I was missing all the fun. It was Lughnasa, and beyond the tents the celebration had begun. I wanted to be among them. And yet I had been plunked down on a wooden stool and told not to fidget as Crowan fussed over my hair.

"Stay still, won't you?" She poked at me playfully with a bony finger. "If this is the last time I'll be tending to your tangles, I shan't miss it, I can promise you that."

Crowan's tone was sharp, but I knew that behind me her small eyes were wistful.

She had readied me for Lughnasa each year since I was a babe, and this was to be the last. The task was to be Desdemona's now. Crowan's reminder brought a little swell of emotion and I bowed my head, acknowledging the familiar comfort of her bony fingers against my scalp.

"You see, Desdemona? This is how it's done." Crowan's hands trembled a little with age as she worked the delicate white bells of heather into the thick twists of my hair.

Desdemona looked up from mending the seam of my favorite green dress.

"Aye, m'lady looks fine indeed," she said politely. With Desdemona there was always a distance. It only made me dread Crowan's relinquishment of her old duties all the more.

Father's tent was vast—four furnished compartments separated by heavy bolts of stitched skin—and our servants had seen to it we had every amenity. Small tables were set about, piled with hazelnuts and cheese to nibble upon between feasting. At night dozens of oil lamps washed the tent walls with the soft glow of light, and garlands strung with sprays of wildflowers and colorful strips of fabric fluttered over our beds. I shifted on my stool as three haunting bellows sounded: the horn, announcing the beginning of the contests. Lail would be throwing his spear. He and Father had left some time ago. Ariane had gone off, too, to browse the traveling market that ran in the fields far from the tents. She meant to gather some supplies for a talisman, I knew. But I had little faith it might work.

"Are we nearly finished?" I asked. "I cannot miss Lailoken's toss."

"Yes, ready at last!" Crowan handed me the small mirror. As her gaze met mine in the bronzed reflection, she touched my hair lovingly. My cheeks were flushed with berry stain and my eyes were shining. Her eyes misted over as she reached to adjust my torque. "Not so terrible at all, my dove," she said.

"It's marvelous, Crowan." I pressed her hand to my cheek, then stood. "Thank you."

She swiped at her eyes impatiently. "Off we go," she said, "or we'll soon miss the contests altogether!"

Desdemona stood. "Are you wantin' my company, m'lady?"

"No, you needn't come." I turned. "Not if there's somewhere else you'd like to go."

"If you're certain?" she paused.

"Of course." I smiled. "It's Lughnasa. Enjoy yourself. I will see you back here before supper."

Desdemona ducked in thanks and retreated into the fray.

Outside it was a rare hot day, the sun pounding down upon the grateful upturned faces gathered for the festival. My pulse quickened as we moved through the crowd, following the sounds of shouts and the clash of metal to the contest site. Tables were scattered across the grounds laden with stout barrels of ale and mead, each chieftain having contributed dozens of barrels from their private stores. The smell of buttered crust and stewed gravy made my stomach tug in protest as we passed a banquet tray of meat pies, and I swiped one, delighting in the creamy decadence of flavor as I devoured it in three bites.

"You seem in fair enough spirits," Crowan observed.

"And why shouldn't I be?" I said. "I'm tired of moping about, worrying over things to come. Can't I just enjoy myself? It is Lughnasa, after all."

"It's always been our favorite festival, hasn't it?" The creases of her face folded into a smile, but even her watchful gaze could not prevent me from scanning the endless rows of tents for the banner of the dragon.

Surely Emrys and his men would be camped nearby. Outside the spacious tents the banners of boar, ox, bear, and lion flapped gallantly in the afternoon breeze. And at a distance from them all an impossibly white tent stood, grander than all the rest, marked by the figure of a swan.

Tutgual's camp.

The wind caught his banner in a way that made it look as though the great swan were striking out, hissing, and I turned my head, leading Crowan away.

It was only a matter of time before I spotted Rhydderch or a member of his family. Certainly Rhydderch would be looking for me here. But at least we had no worries about Mungo. The bishop and his most devout followers were spending Lughnasa in fasting and prayer in an effort to beat back the influence of our dark Gods, our blood sacrifices, and our barbaric rites, no doubt.

As festivalgoers in the crowd caught sight of me, they smiled and waved, called out my name, or reached to touch my shoulder.

"Lady Languoreth, come! Come and have a drink!" they shouted. I glanced at Crowan.

"Perhaps a drink is not a terrible idea," I said.

"Go on, then." She grinned. "Swipe me a cup."

I smiled and accepted two wooden cups from a toothless old man. The dark ale coursed down my throat, filling the hollow of my stomach.

"A fine spirit," I laughed. "No wonder our men drink so much ale before they ride off to raid." Around me a cheer rose up—a toast to Morken's daughter—and I smiled, wiping my lips with the back of my hand. The ale left me cool and spinning. My arms were bare in my light summer dress, and the sun had begun to feel hot on my skin.

"Let's hurry, now," I urged Crowan. "They'll be starting."

I gave a parting wave and we moved past the wicker fences that quartered off large tracts for the footrace and boulder toss, out along the edge of the racing path where muscled horses were being groomed, tossing their strong necks against their tethers. At last we came to the grassy meadow where the spear targets were laid out. Warriors milled in the expanse, testing the weight of their weapons or stretching the taut muscles of their throwing arms as they eyed the stretch of targets, each set farther than the next. I spotted Cathan moving amid a cluster of white-robed Wisdom Keepers set to officiate, and there Father sat upon the benches for the noble families, lined up within a spear's reach of the gaming fence. He'd kept an open seat for me, but I could not bring myself to sit among the crowd of painted women.

Crowan and I found a patch of shade instead, beneath a towering beech at the edge of the meadow. There was a mound at its trunk that offered an elevated view of the field. Crowan leaned back against the tree with a weary sigh as my eyes swept the crowd.

"Look! There he is—there's Lailoken. Can you see?"

Crowan raised her hand to shield her eyes from the surrounding glare. "He's just up," she exclaimed, and I helped her stand with some effort as Lailoken took his place at the center of the field.

My brother's wavy hair was tied back and he was shirtless like the other men, the only thing marking him as a noble being the flash of sunlight as it glinted off his heavy golden torque. Setting his spear on the ground, he gave an easy swing of his arm in practice, his handsome face intent on the targets.

At the sight of him, a tittering rose from a group of girls nearby, and they shot to their feet, craning their necks and nudging one another in a flutter of excitement.

"There he is," I heard one of them whisper. "Just look at his strong shoulders!"

"A warrior and a Wisdom Keeper," another said in a conspiring tone. "It's not often you find a man with so many . . . gifts." She widened her eyes with a seductive smile.

"That's my brother," I called to them. "I'll thank you to keep such talk to yourselves."

They whipped round and one had the courtesy to look embarrassed.

"Apologies, my lady." She bowed her head. "We did not see you."

I gave a slight smile. "It's all right. But you'd best watch now, or you're going to miss Lailoken's throw."

It was no secret my brother did not lack for female company. Willowy blondes, exotic brunettes, and curvy redheads came and went. I watched as the pattern unfurled before me: the coquettish looks that soon turned familiar and knowing would, inevitably, become cold and affronted, given time. My brother had not found his match. Truth be told, he wasn't at all looking.

I focused on the meadow as the crowd fell silent. Lail gave a light shrug of his shoulders as if to shake off the weight of the countless watchful eyes. *He's nervous*, I thought as he bent smoothly to retrieve his spear. I sent him my calm as he slowly drew back his arm, and then in a flash, his body plummeted forward as he sent the spear whipping toward the targets. It sank with a confident *thwack* at a very respectable distance indeed.

"Well done, Lailoken. Well done!" I shouted, though he was well out of earshot. Lail made a slow turn before his admirers, arms lifted, his face bright with triumph.

The farthest target remained untouched, its distance from the mark nearly too far to fathom. Few warriors had ever managed to strike it. But Lail had thrown exceedingly well, and Father's face was proud. The girls giggled and raced down the slope to the edge of the wicker fence, hoping to catch my brother's eye.

"Poor Lail," I said. "He'll never be rid of them now."

"Aye," Crowan said dryly. "And I'm sure he'll be troubled. Who approaches now?"

I stood on my toes to try to catch sight of the next warrior taking Lail's position at the mark. "I can't see."

Then the crowd shifted and I caught my breath.

Maelgwn strode forward, his dark brows drawn in concentration. A roar of applause rose so loud, it was nearly deafening. He was shirtless, and his breeches hung a little too loosely against his hips, as if he hadn't been eating quite as well as he should have been. His dark hair was shorter now, falling just clear of his powerful shoulders, and he'd pushed it back from his face with a rough leather strip he wore like a headband. My heart still hammered at the sight of him. But even in my state of distraction, I could not miss the way some of the chieftains and their lords in the crowd had stiffened at the roar of applause.

"It's as if they didn't know how beloved Pendragon and his men are to the people," I said.

Crowan eyed the nobles shrewdly. "That young man had best be careful. Those lords wear the look of envy."

"Perhaps, if they're envious, they should send their own men to guard the eastern border."

"As you say," Crowan said.

But Crowan was right: envy was a danger. Thankfully, Maelgwn was clever enough to know that popularity and pride made dangerous bedfellows. I watched as he nodded in respect to the noblemen on the benches, his eyes lingering for a moment on my father. Or was he searching the empty seat beside him?

I stared, willing Maelgwn to turn and see me standing beneath the beech tree. But he only flexed his shoulders as he moved toward the mark with his spear in hand, pausing to clap my brother on the shoulder.

How quickly the mood on the contest field had shifted. Crowan steadied herself on my arm, straining to see. The crowd had cast wagers. But this was no matter of gaming for Maelgwn; it was a matter of honor. Pendragon's title of "lord" was hard-won; it was not his birthright. In the eyes of too many nobles, Lord Emrys was a pretender. To lose at these contests and disgrace Pendragon's banner was a defeat no Dragon Warrior could suffer.

And here stood Pendragon's own young general, spear in hand.

My mouth tasted metal as Maelgwn took a breath and, on the exhale, drew his left arm back to throw. His muscles stretched as taut as a bow. He was just about to fling his arm forward and send the spear hurtling home, when a sudden jeer shattered the silence. The crowd gasped in collective shock, but if it fazed Maelgwn, he did not show it.

I searched the audience to pinpoint the sound and spotted none other than Gwrgi, son of Eliffer, leaning casually against the fence. Gwrgi bore the same eager look upon his face that he'd worn that awful day I'd encountered him in the market, the day he'd savaged that sweet bird and we had all left covered in blood.

"Gwrgi," I hissed. "No doubt it was he."

His brother Peredur stood beside him, his dark eyes slippery as eels.

Maelgwn lifted a hand to reassure the crowd and reset his stance.

I should have expected Gwrgi and Peredur would not miss the games, especially if they had heard that the Dragon Warriors would surely be in attendance. Their father had since died upon his stolen throne. What was ill-begotten ill begets. Ceidio, too, might have been gone, but now that Gwrgi and Peredur ruled the kingdom of Ebrauc, the war between brothers lived on through their sons.

I watched as Gwrgi gave a whistle, his eyes locked on Maelgwn's in a gleeful sort of challenge. Peredur leaned in to murmur in his brother's ear and Gwrgi laughed, picking at something in his teeth.

Maelgwn turned to face the brothers, his green eyes calm. "Have you something to say, lords of Ebrauc?"

I hoped for their sake they knew well enough to fear this tone in Maelgwn's voice. But Peredur only looked at him, running a hand through his long, thinning hair.

"I only wondered if perhaps your spear was too heavy," Peredur said, "for we have been standing here long beneath the sun and you have yet to throw it."

"Too heavy. I see." Maelgwn nodded. "I'd test its weight on you, but you stand far too close. Perhaps you would oblige me and go stand beside the farthest target."

Peredur raised his brows, smoothing his tunic. "The farthest target? You must be feeling the luck of the Gods. Perhaps you would make a wager."

"And what would you wager, Lord Peredur?"

"Your spear against my coin. Three hundred silver pieces."

I gasped. That was half my bride price! No warrior possessed that much coin. Maelgwn opened his mouth to answer just as a deep voice called out from the crowd.

"Are you certain you would not rather place a wager upon your lands?"

I looked up to see Gwenddolau swinging his long legs easily over the top of the fence, entering the field of contest.

"Gwenddolau." Peredur's voice was scolding. "I do not believe it's your turn."

Gwenddolau's comely face was framed by a pale beard, his light summer cloak pinned at the shoulder by a magnificent silver brooch. As he reached to touch the hilt of his sword, his linen shirt gaped open and the image of a dragon flashed beneath the fabric. Emrys bore the same mark; I'd seen it at Midsummer. It had been needled with skin dye upon his chest and could mean only one thing: Emrys had named Gwenddolau his successor.

Gone was the boy who had taught me how to tickle the bellies of trout. In his place stood a seasoned and warlike man, fit to defend a kingdom all his own. And his piercing blue eyes were fixed upon Peredur and Gwrgi with a fiery vengeance.

"Your lands," Gwenddolau repeated, moving to stand before Peredur. "Perhaps Maelgwn could win those back for you as well. Since I hear the Angles are pressing, and you and your squat brother seem so incapable of holding them yourselves."

There was a flash of metal and every man moved at once. Peredur mounted the fence, sword drawn, with the swiftness of a cat, Gwrgi at his heels, as Gwenddolau swung his sword to meet his cousin's. The clash of iron rang across the grounds, followed by a splintering crack. I rushed forward, but the struggle on the field of contest had been stalled. Something had kept them from fighting. It was Maelgwn's spear, the death-dealing tip of it within a hairsbreadth of Peredur's throat. The wooden shaft had fractured, but it held.

"Enough!" Cathan's roar sounded across the field as he shot to his feet. "Cease this at once!"

The men stood, eyes locked, each unwilling to be the first to cast down his weapon.

"You know well the consequence of breaking the peace at a festival," Cathan warned. "Lower your weapons. I'll not ask you again."

Gwenddolau took a step back and bowed respectfully to Cathan.

But Maelgwn did not move a muscle until Peredur had lowered his sword.

Cathan raised his hands to quiet the boiling crowd. "It's over, then. We may proceed. Maelgwn, Dragon Warrior," he called out. "You may select an uncompromised spear. Unless, that is, you wish to forfeit your throw."

Maelgwn frowned and shook his head, tossing his damaged spear aside. As he turned to signal for a new weapon, his eyes found mine across the vast distance of the crowd. At last. For a moment he seemed utterly struck. Then something behind his eyes kindled.

No, you mustn't do it, I thought. I swayed back against the tree trunk, shaking my head imploringly. Maelgwn gave a half smile, as if disappointed. When he spoke, it was to Peredur, not to Cathan.

"I will throw," Maelgwn said. "And furthermore, I accept Lord Peredur's challenge. Three hundred silver pieces on the last target. That is, unless Lord Peredur would indeed like to wager his ill-begotten land."

I buried my head in my hands.

"I accept the wager of coin," Peredur said darkly.

"The farthest target!" Crowan exclaimed. "In all my years I have never seen a man hit that mark."

I could scarcely stand to watch. But down in the meadow below, Maelgwn was easing his shoulders back, refocusing his gaze on the far end of the field. If he should miss, I knew he would accept no man's money in place of his debt—and it was one he could never afford to pay. Maelgwn gripped the spear, balancing its weight like a feather. Slowly he drew back his arm, until its deadly point was nearly level with his ear. And then, with a violent thrust, he sent the spear flying high into the summer air. The spear sailed across the great distance in a lethal arc. And then it buried its tip with a deep thunk, dead in the center of the farthest target's heart.

The crowd erupted in a frenzy.

The Dragon Warriors rushed the field with wild shouts, yanking Maelgwn from his feet and hoisting him up. He raised one arm in victory, but as they carried him past the fence where Gwrgi and Peredur were looking as mean as a pair of adders, Maelgwn's eyes were on me. I swallowed, my mouth suddenly dry.

"We should congratulate him," I said.

Crowan eyed me carefully. "Aye. If that's what you'd like."

"Yes, of course we must congratulate him," I said. "After all, he is three hundred silver pieces richer."

I led Crowan into the throng, where pretty maidens preened by the fence and drunken merrymakers were celebrating their champion with whoops and bellows.

"Go on, then," Crowan urged me, but her voice held a note of warning. "I'll be waiting just here."

Gwenddolau saw me first, sweeping me from my feet and swinging me round with ease. "Languoreth! Well met, sister. And what a throw, eh?"

"It was a throw such as I have never seen." At the sound of my voice, Maelgwn shook free of Pendragon's men.

"And to think there were those among the crowd who doubted me." Maelgwn's green eyes were fixed upon me, but Gwenddolau answered.

"Doubt you?" he laughed. "You have the strength of an ox and the sight of an eagle!" Gwenddolau smacked Maelgwn good-naturedly on the back, not noticing as the good humor of his friend faded.

"Come, now, brother," Maelgwn said. "The time for gloating is over. I would show more honor than the sons of Eliffer."

Gwenddolau fixed his eyes on Gwrgi across the field, watching him lift a drinking horn to take a deep draft as if nothing at all had taken place. "We will see that the debt owed to you is paid."

"Later," Maelgwn said. "We have traveled far for the festival, and it is Lughnasa. The Gods were watching. They know who broke the peace this day."

"As you say," Gwenddolau allowed. "You're the champion, after all. The Song Keepers shall sing tales of this throw for generations to come!"

"Yes," I agreed. "You shall have many admirers, no doubt."

Gwenddolau tossed Maelgwn a shirt. "Speaking of admirers, cover yourself up, brother. You can't greet those maidens so indecently. Look at them"—he smiled—"waiting by the fence for the favor of your presence."

Maelgwn glanced at me as he pulled the linen over his head. I turned toward the fence, where a dark-haired beauty was leaning forward to reveal the creamy rise of her cleavage.

I forced a smile. "Yes, it would be rude, after all, to keep them waiting."

I had no right to him, I scolded myself. And yet the way those women were swooning in their low-cut gowns, eyeing him as if he had already taken them to bed . . . I wanted to claw at their faces.

"Go, brother," Maelgwn said to Gwenddolau. "I'll join you in a moment."

"Very well. But do bring my little sister when you come. I would hear of your betrothal, Languoreth. You are soon to be princess of Clyde Rock."

"Of course" was all I could say.

Maelgwn's shoulders stiffened as Gwenddolau strode toward the fence without looking back.

"You look well," he said, his eyes sweeping the length of me. "Flowers in your hair and no target hay at all."

I touched the blossoms self-consciously. "Crowan's to retire from her duties, so she was determined to outdo herself."

"I would say she has succeeded," he said, but his compliment felt like time wasted. I could feel eyes upon us—Crowan's and my father's at the very least. We did not have long before people would begin their small-minded gossip. Maelgwn looked up as if reading my mind.

"You are not happy. When I heard of your match . . ." He faltered.

"Please." I locked eyes with him, imploring him to say no more. "It's a fine match. We all have our duties. It brings me joy to serve my family well."

Lies. More time ill-spent.

But Maelgwn kept his gaze on mine. "Tutgual can be a cruel master. It is only the ice of his queen that keeps him in line. I believe Rhydderch to be his own man, but hear me when I say this. If ever you feel frightened, or feel you are in danger, you must only send word. I and all the might of Pendragon will come to you, no matter the cost. I will not see you suffer," he said. "Do you understand?"

My vision blurred and I blinked the wetness away. "Yes. I understand."

The look upon his face was so certain and unflinching that my heart cramped. I wanted to tell him I would give anything if only it could be him I should marry.

But this was not love; this was torture. And I could not withstand it.

"I should greet my father," I said. I watched the wound deepen even as I caused it.

"Will I see you, then, at the feast?"

"Of course. I congratulate you again. It was a truly remarkable throw."

Maelgwn nodded as if he'd already forgotten. I turned to make my way through the sea of people cluttering the grounds, Crowan following close behind. Her clear eyes were troubled, yet she had the grace to say nothing. She took my hand and walked with me, her silvery plait bobbing with the quickness of our steps.

• • •

Soon sunset, so late this time of year, was upon us. Revelers had returned to their tents to doze before the feast; women sat under the patient and nimble ministrations of their servants; kings and lords drank or took their respite as the heat of the afternoon gave way to the chill that welcomed evening. Just before sunrise we would begin our climb up the mountain.

Having helped me change, Crowan was resting and Desdemona was yet away when Ariane ducked her dark head into the tent. She took in the sight of me in my low-cut blue gown and frowned.

"You look sad."

"Of course I am sad," I said. "Maelgwn has come, and my heart breaks in seeing him." I looked up at her, shaking my head. "Does nothing ever sadden you? Sometimes I wonder if you are even human."

Ariane gave a funny little smile. "Of course I am human. What a peculiar thing to say."

She opened the satchel she always wore at her hip and unfolded a piece of cloth.

"Look. I have brought something that may cheer you. A talisman. To work whatever ends are needed."

In her palm was the white-tipped feather from a falcon. It was strong and striped with varying shades of gray, deep twilight and stormy sea, knotted onto a simple leather cord. Her slender fingers traced its edges and then she lifted it to her lips. Blew softly upon it.

"Do not think the weight of the world is not felt by me, Languoreth. It is only that I have learnt there is little we can do but trust," she said. "We may fashion such things as might give us opportunities. For healing. For wheat to grow tall. For visions of what is yet to come. For love." She lifted her blue eyes to mine. "But there is always a measure beyond our control. The wind and the weather. The stray pierce of an arrow. Sickness. Death. A wise woman realizes this. She keeps her heart as full in times of pain as she does in times of good fortune. This is because her heart is full with trust."

She opened my fingers and laid the fragile talisman gently upon my palm. "We are meant to live our stories whether it pains us or no. Wear it and be done with this nonsense."

I looked down at the feather in my hand, its tip as white as a beacon.

"Very well." I said, slipping the necklace over my head. "I shall wear it." The feather fell lightly between my breasts.

"Good. Now come," she said. "We should go to the fields. Lughnasa has begun."

Torches blazed in the open, where more than a dozen fire pits dripped with the juices of roasting meat: beef, pork, and mutton. The heady smell of freshly fermented ale and fire-baked bread, the first from this year's harvest, traveled on the breeze. We wandered toward the feasting tables, searching for familiar faces in the masses that thronged, eating and drinking their fill. I spotted Father.

"There you are," he said, welcoming me to his table. "Come sit, daughter. Have some mutton. Enjoy the fine ale."

"Hello, Father." I sat and leaned to kiss his bearded cheek, exchanging pleasantries with the older chieftain who sat across from him. They'd fought together once, and soon they were lost in stories of times gone by.

I touched the feather at my neck, wondering if any such thing could truly conceal me from Rhydderch, from Elufed. From Tutgual and his many spies, if for no other reason than that this was Lughnasa, and I was yet free. I did not wish to carry my yoke of duty and obligation up the mountain tonight. I did not wish to be reminded of what was yet to come.

"Look."

I followed Ariane's gaze to the place where Gwenddolau and Lord Emrys sat across the grass, their features lit by torchlight. It seemed their celebration of Maelgwn's winning toss had continued, because their faces were ruddy from drink and the benches of their table nearly buckled with the presence of comely women. Maidens draped themselves over the warriors, filling their cups and laughing with heads tossed back, exposing the whites of their throats.

Beside Lord Emrys was Maelgwn, head bowed in conversation. But at his side the dark-haired beauty from the games sat like a cat, the curve of her hip pressed against his upon the bench. Her ruby-colored robe clung to her figure, and I watched with a rising sickness as she reached a playful finger to stroke Maelgwn's arm. I narrowed my eyes, consumed by jealousy.

"Must she sit so close? Surely he can hardly breathe. Who is that woman, anyway?"

"Who she is does not matter," Ariane said. "She is not you."

I watched Maelgwn run a hand through his thick black hair and wanted to believe her. But how could I expect Maelgwn to stay true when I was bound to another? When such real temptations were put right within his grasp? In cutting short our conversation, I had only done what I must. But perhaps I'd made him realize that our cause was truly lost. Our feelings could not be. Maelgwn was loyal, a man of integrity. One had only to watch him with Gwenddolau or Emrys to see as much. And there was no doubt there had been an exchange of feelings between us, no matter how brief. He'd said he meant to protect me, but perhaps he had meant it in a more brotherly way. He was being kind, I decided.

The feeling left me bitter.

But then Maelgwn suddenly looked up. He waved, as if motioning for me to come and join him. I was smoothing my skirts to stand when Father nudged me.

"Look, General Maelgwn waves to me," he said good-naturedly. "The champion. I told him he must find me. I wish to offer him a proper congratulations."

My face burned. Of course. Maelgwn had been signaling to Father, not me. I blinked, trying to quell my rising humiliation.

"Come on, then, Languoreth. Come join us," Father offered his hand to help me stand.

"No, thank you," I said. "I think I shall stay."

"Very well," he said. "I'll only be a moment."

Maelgwn looked up as Father stood, his green eyes flicking to mine as if in question. Had he indeed been beckoning me? But no, surely I had imagined that. For now his gaze *was* locked on mine, and there was no uncertainty to be found there. His stare was casual as he eased an arm back, slipping his hand around the dark-haired woman's waist. Watching my reaction.

"Bastard!" I cursed, pushing my drink away. Ariane looked between us.

"Oh, no," she said. "This is not so good."

"*Not so good?*" I turned to her, my face hard with rage. "Enough. I am done with this dalliance. Did you see how he looked at me? I've been a fool. Clearly Maelgwn is not the man I thought he was."

I stood, yanked the feather from my neck, and threw it to the ground. "Let the Dragon Warriors do as they wish. Come, it is Lughnasa. Let us celebrate. Let us dance."

Ariane frowned and bent to pick up the feather, tucking it safely into the folds of her blue cloak. "Very well. We shall dance. But I tell you, Languoreth: this man is your destiny."

I barked a laugh. Maelgwn was no different from all the other warriors: a womanizer, a trickster. A vain and lustful cad. Still, better I knew now that Maelgwn had played me for a fool. It could only make my path forward freer from the heartache such a union was certain to cause. I adjusted the neckline of my gown and thrust my shoulders back so that my hair cascaded down my back. Maelgwn leaned in close to the dark-haired beauty, unnoticing, as she whispered something in his ear.

I turned to Ariane, clutching my skirts with white-knuckled fists.

"Hear me now, Ariane. If that man is my destiny, I would rather drown in a sack."

CHAPTER 30

A chill mist snaked round my legs at the foot of the mountain, swallowing the tents pitched in the fields below. There had been feasting and spinning to the bodhran and contests of strength. Now the mood was reverent. This was a thin night, the Keepers warned. The moon was strong, and we would be climbing high into the Land of the Gods. When I closed my eyes, I thought I could almost hear the mountain breathing; it rustled the needles of the pines, sending a mourning dove tittering soft-throated into the night.

Ariane drew up the hood of her cloak. "I must leave you now. I will walk in the front, with the Keepers."

"Of course." I bent to unlace my slippers. "Don't worry for me. I know the climb well." Those who were wise walked without shoes for weeks before Lughnasa to harden their feet. Those who were foolish— or whose bodies were numbed by drink—could be seen hobbling, blood oozing by daybreak, down the mountain toward the women waiting to bandage their cuts. We gave the mountain our blood, and it drained into the soil below.

I'd made this climb at the end of each summer, yet on this night a bottomless anger drove my steps. I welcomed the sharp pebbles on the path below, my body hungry to feel pain outside instead of in, as if I could beat the very thought of Maelgwn from my body.

"There you are."

I turned just in time to catch the walking staff Lailoken tossed at me.

"Good catch," he said. "I could not help but notice you disappeared at the feast."

"I was with Ariane," I said. "Dancing and making merry."

Lail took my measure before bending to unwork the lacing from his boots. "You were jealous," he said. "It is only natural. But what do you expect? That Maelgwn should pine away with no prospects for himself whilst you—"

"Lailoken!" I said sharply. "You presume too much."

The shrillness in my voice silenced him. The mention of Maelgwn sent me plummeting again and I would not feel those things. Not on this night.

"As you say." Lail shook his head. Knotting his laces together, he slung his boots over his shoulder. Around us the crowd had begun to swell in anticipation, and the shouts of vendors hawking their wares echoed in the night.

"Torches and staffs! Staffs for the climb!"

A short distance uphill, the white robes of the Wisdom Keepers glowed eerily in the night. I spotted Cathan facing the great slope of the mountain, his silvery hair flickering orange in the torchlight. He stood so motionless that I wondered for a moment if he was still breathing.

"How does he know when it is time?" I wondered.

"I hope to learn," Lailoken said. "It is some strange alchemy of training, discipline, and gift."

"Someday you will walk with the Keepers."

"Yes," Lailoken said firmly, but his face was wistful. "Someday. But not today. Today I shall walk with my sister."

Nearly one thousand people had gathered at our backs by the time Cathan lifted his hand to signal the ascent. The climb began eas-

ily enough, but soon the trail became steep and craggy. The mountain was still shedding water after weeks upon weeks of rain. Rivulets
rushed down the path, pooling into moats at the trail's edge, where
pink-spotted foxglove and leafy fern sprouted against bleak, lichen-
covered boulders.

Father caught up to us, outstriding Brant and Brodyn with a boyish
grin.

"You would test us, Uncle," Brodyn laughed. "Well enough. We are
up to the mark!"

But soon we all slowed as the pitch of the trail thrust itself heaven-
ward before us. Father's face was pale. He blinked as if dizzy, steadying
himself firmly with his staff.

"You should have kept to your bed," I whispered.

"Do not insult me," he huffed. "I would never dishonor the Gods so."

We climbed higher and the mist closed in, wrapping us in a muffled stillness that amplified the smallest of sounds. All that could be
heard was the soft skittering of pebbles and our collective laboring for
breath. Even the shepherds and cowherds grew quiet from exertion.
Our limbs and lungs burned, and my hair began to coil into curls at
the back of my neck as the crystalline mist gathered on the sleeves of
our clothing and beaded in our hair.

Manannan's mist. They said Manannan, son of the sea, was as
gifted a god as the earth had ever known. He could summon the mist
to cloak himself in invisibility, or cast it about his people, leaving sea
raiders to splinter their boats against sharp knives of rock. I wondered
if he might have cast the mist upon us now, but to what end I could
not say.

I knew, if I chose, I could lose myself in it.

One slick step, and I could simply slip off the edge of the earth into
the land of the Gods, into the Summerlands, and join my mother. A
choice.

A gift?

It would be an unfettering from the timber and stone of this world, from all that would soon bind me to a stranger, to a future of sinuous control.

My head suddenly felt light, as if I'd been spinning. And all I could think was: *What if their princess fell from the mountain? Would that not be the greatest sacrifice of all?*

I swayed toward the edge of the path like a sapling in the wind. And then an iron grip clamped my arm, jerking me swiftly from the edge of the mountain and safely onto my knees in the wet grass.

"Watch yourself," Brant said, his quick brown eyes missing nothing. "For a moment I was quite afraid you'd fall."

I shook my head to cease the spinning, and had reached to accept his hand when I noticed the crest of a white-tipped feather half buried in the grass.

The talisman! But how had it ended up here on the path before me? I had watched Ariane retrieve it from the ground at the feast and tuck it into her cloak. She must have dropped it. Or else Ariane was determined I find it. I gritted my teeth in annoyance.

"What's that?" Brant leaned over, and I clutched at the feather instinctively.

"It's nothing," I said, folding it reluctantly into the pocket of my cloak.

"As you say." Brant fell into step with me. "You must be careful up here, on the mountain. Sometimes it's best not to open your ears. My mother used to say there were more spirits than Gods living on this hill. And not all of them wish us well."

"I never knew you to be superstitious," I said.

He smiled. "When you spend enough nights in wild places, you come to see there's little superstition in it. I've heard many a strange thing on a night's watch deep in the wood."

"What sorts of things?"

He searched the mist before answering. "Voices that belong to no earthly body. Ghostly music that drifts on the breeze. Once I saw strange lights in the trees." He looked away as if he'd revealed too much.

"My mother used to talk of spirit lights."

"Could be," he allowed. "I don't particularly like to question. Sometimes it's best not to open your ears," he repeated.

We caught up with Father, and I glanced over the trail's edge into the blackness, shivering to think I might have cast my body down the mountain. I touched the feather beneath the folds of my cloak. Perhaps it was good I keep it close. A talisman, Ariane had said, to work whatever ends were needed.

Had I indeed heard the murmurings of some wayward evil spirit? Or was it the keening in me itself that was a danger, a weakness?

Perhaps this was what Ariane knew but did not say. That a broken woman could never lead a kingdom.

Or perhaps she only knew I could not face the days to come as a fractured woman with a fractured heart. There must be something to ease this aching, or else it might cause my ruin. Taking a breath, I drew the feather from my cloak and slipped it once more around my neck. Up ahead a deep cleft in the mountain opened onto its vast and sloping spine.

The summit, at last.

We gathered at a distance from the Keepers. They stood beside a simple stone dais where Cathan waited, arms cast wide. Eyes fixed to the east.

The last stars of evening had buried their bright heads in the clouds racing overhead, and the crowd on the mountain was bathed in the purple promise of morning. Cathan took a breath, and the low-bellied chant rose up from the Wisdom Keepers in the ancient and rolling tongue of our people. The Call to the Sun.

We lifted our faces as the first brilliant rays reached us from the east. As the sun came up to light the earth, I felt its warmth flow through me as thick as honey. And then, as if by magic, the mist parted, revealing the rippling water of the loch below and the jeweled strand of islands rising from its midst.

A cheer rose from the mountain, the cheer of a thousand people lifting their voices in gratitude, in triumph. In hope and in peace. The wind whipped up over the mountain and the feather fluttered against my neck. And then I knew he was near.

I could feel the heat of Maelgwn's gaze on my back like the glow of a different sun. I turned slowly to see him standing in the crowd, barefoot in a soft gray tunic and trousers, his arms at his sides.

His eyes raked me over, and I wanted to pummel him.

I wanted to run to him.

I stood, torn between the two, as he closed the space between us.

"I did not see you after the feast," he said.

"I did not stay long."

"Languoreth, I—"

"You needn't explain anything to me," I said. "You owe me nothing."

"I did not take her to bed. I could have. But I didn't." His eyes flashed.

I felt embarrassed and selfish all at once. "Whom you take to your bed is no concern of mine."

"Oh, is that so? I think you are greatly concerned about whom I take to bed."

"Then you are wrong." I leveled my gaze on his.

"Sweet Gods, you're stubborn." Maelgwn cursed under his breath.

"Stubborn?" I leaned in so no one else might hear. "Because I refuse to be your plaything? What a prize I would have been, the daughter of a king! I saw the look upon your face—you were toying with me. You meant for me to see you with that . . . woman." My voice had risen in pitch and I glanced round, worried I'd been overheard. But no one seemed to take notice over the clamor of celebration.

"Yes," Maelgwn whispered fiercely. "I meant for you to see. I only meant to serve you what you've wanted, for we warriors are nothing more than wayfaring seducers, are we not?"

"If that is what you set out to prove, you've succeeded in making your point."

He threw up his hands, then stopped, letting out a slow breath.

"I've hurt you. It wasn't my intent. Perhaps there was a part of me that sought to provoke you, to know your true feelings. But I would never intentionally cause you pain. Not you," he shook his head. "Never you."

"What right have I to be hurt?" I asked. "And yet . . ." My cheeks flushed with the admission.

He took my hand, his fingers pressing my knuckles. "Languoreth, I am sorry." The touch ignited a heat in me. I did not want him to let go. "I assumed you had settled your heart," he said. "And yet I hoped you had not."

My eyes pricked with tears and I turned, not wanting him to see. But Maelgwn mistook my silence for something else and released my hand.

"Perhaps I'm the plaything, Languoreth," he said, as if trying to understand. "How long would you see me suffer over my love of you?"

His words hung heavy in the early morning air. I turned to face him. Maelgwn's eyes were fixed on mine, watching, naked, gentle.

"I do not wish to see you suffer," I said. "Not anymore. Not ever."

A look passed between us.

"Come down the mountain with me," he said. "Will you? Please? I know another way."

Moments ago it seemed that the world beyond us had entirely fallen away. I blinked now, suddenly remembering we were surrounded by a world of observers. Waiting for Father or Lailoken to admonish me. My every step had been under watch since I'd arrived at the games—

Look, there is Morken's daughter. There is the girl who'll wed Rhydderch— but now no one regarded us. It was as though we had slipped behind a veil and been rendered unseen. I had not believed it was possible.

"I shouldn't—" I began, then bit my lip. I wanted this time with Maelgwn with such ferocity, I had no choice but to trust it. "I suppose there can be no harm in climbing down a mountain."

"All right." Maelgwn gave a broad smile. "I mean, good. Follow me; it's this way."

I followed him across the summit. Beyond a hulking splinter of granite, a narrow sheep's trail led steeply downhill and Maelgwn extended his hand. I noticed for the first time a thick scar over the curve of his right knuckle, one wound of many in the lifetime of a warrior.

"From bracing my shield," he explained, following my eyes to our joined hands.

"That must have been quite a blow."

"Aye" was all he said, leading me gently down the trail. When we came to a muddy patch he slowed, his spear-hardened fingers warm and steady in mine.

"I'm certain you're a fair enough climber on your own, but if you're willing to accept my hand, I fear you'll find no shortage of offers for it," he said.

I arched my brows but did not release his hand. The last strains of laughter from the summit faded in the distance, and quite suddenly it felt as if we were moving through a dream. The slope sprouted with bell heather and delicate wild carrot, and I could hear the buzz of insects as I followed Maelgwn through the thick, wild grass into the quiet cover of woods.

"It's beautiful here." I drew my hand gently from his, looking up to where the trees knit their branches overhead, making me feel like a minnow darting through a channel of green gorge water.

"Yes." Maelgwn admired the branches overhead. "We had a wood like this behind our hut growing up. My brother and I would scarce have woken in the morning before we were out playing chase and exploring the wooded world, hiding when our mother called us to supper."

"You have a brother?" I asked.

Maelgwn squinted into the distance.

"I did, aye."

"He's gone," I said carefully. "I'm so sorry."

"Ah." He gave a small smile. "They say he dines in the Summerlands now."

"But you don't believe it."

"Not always." He cleared his throat and reached a hand to help me cross a mossy chain of rocks that led through a stream. "He was five years my elder. As far as I knew, he made the moon. My brother rode at Emrys's side."

"How did it happen?"

Maelgwn stopped. "For a long while I didn't know. Then, as soon as my fourteenth winter came, I rode to join the resistance. I wanted to be a Dragon Warrior like my brother." He paused. "It was Emrys who told me my brother hadn't died in battle."

I could see it pained him. I wanted to tell him he didn't have to go on, but Maelgwn bowed his head and continued.

"Gwenddolau had been captured, you see. He was only fifteen winters himself at the time, on his way to join his father in the Borderlands. They could see straightaway that wee Gwenddolau was a noble. He was no match for the brunt of an Angle sword. Don't know why they didn't kill him. They needed coin, perhaps, or cattle to get through winter. So they ransomed him. My brother was in the party that rode to collect him. The Angles took the coin and the cattle. But they would have their blood sport, too." Maelgwn's jaw tightened. "They demanded a man to take Gwenddolau's place. My brother offered himself up. What a right bastard he was." He fell silent, his green eyes on the rocky path before him.

"Gwenddolau was held prisoner?" I asked, astonished. "We never learnt of it. If he was fifteen, that would have been just as he left us."

"Aye. Being taken like that, it's hard on a man."

"But Gwenddolau was hardly grown from a boy! There can be no shame in that."

"For a warrior there is always shame," Maelgwn said. "Such things are always seen as weakness. We encounter Angles who taunt him for it still—until their breath is cut short."

I reached to touch his arm. "Your brother was brave. He saved Gwendolau's life." So this was the bond I had seen pass between Maelgwn and Gwenddolau on the night of the Midsummer feast. "Gwenddolau has pledged his sword in debt to you."

Maelgwn nodded. "He has sworn he would give his life to save mine. I told him there was no such need. But Gwenddolau carries my brother's death upon his shoulders. None save Pendragon and our men know of his pledge. And now you."

"And what of Pendragon? Did you not blame him a little for the loss of your brother? Could he not have traded another man?"

"It was my brother's choice, not Pendragon's. Men who rally to the standard know what danger it brings. My brother was clever. He knew that without the combined might of Ceidio and Lord Emrys, our resistance was doomed to fail. Gwenddolau was Ceidio's son. His heart. If Ceidio lost his heart, it might have all gone to dust. My brother is only one of many who have given their lives in defense of our land."

Our words fell away, replaced by the quiet rush of water. We rounded a bend in the trail to discover the stream had carved a narrow chasm into the side of the mountain where a little waterfall spilled down in a cold rush, clear as a crystal.

"A pretty spot," Maelgwn said. "Should we sit awhile?"

"I would like that."

I took off my cloak and Maelgwn spread it on the ground, gesturing for me to sit, but lowered himself onto a rock at a respectful distance, as if I were a doe that might bolt. I wrapped my arms about my knees and looked admiringly at the water.

"I've never felt so free. I cannot believe we were able to simply leave," I said. "Doesn't that seem funny to you?"

"No." He considered it. "Perhaps. In stories, we hear about heroes who climb a mountain or dive to the bottom of a loch only to find themselves in another land, where time is not counted in hours, and the weights of the ordinary world drift away like feathers."

Feathers. My fingers went to the talisman at my breast. Maelgwn leaned back a moment, regarding me. Dappled sunlight cast itself in slender beams from the canopy overhead, lighting his eyes like green amber. A gentle breeze came up off the water, blowing a strand of hair about my face, and Maelgwn reached to brush it behind my ear, his strong fingers surprisingly tender.

"I'm amazed I managed to hit the target yesterday. You were a right distraction."

"Maelgwn . . ." I paused a moment, searching his face. "That morning in the stables . . ."

"Yes?"

I swallowed. "Lailoken said you came to ask for my bride price. Why did you not tell me yourself? It was my hand you were asking for. Did you not think I had a right to know?"

"And what good would that have done? I was too late, wasn't I?" He glanced away. "It would have been too late whenever I asked. Your father was kind, but he said as much." Maelgwn gave a humorless laugh. "I do not blame your father. I am but a warrior. What is that when put beside a man who might someday be king?"

"Would that you had told me," I said quietly.

"And if I had? What would you have said?"

I looked into his eyes, my heart beating in my chest like a wild-winged creature. "I would have told you that Rhydderch may have bought my hand, but he cannot own my heart."

Maelgwn's eyes flickered with surprise. There was a moment when all we could hear were birdcalls. Then he lifted a hand to my face carefully, as if I might slip through his fingers.

"I do not know if I am under some illusion, if this is real or if I dream," he said.

"This is no dream." I swallowed my fear and reached to cover his hand in mine. "You said upon the mountaintop you wished to know my true feelings. It frightens me to say it, but when else might we have the chance? I am mad with love of you. I am mad with love of you and I cannot shake it. Truth be told, I haven't heart enough left to try."

Maelgwn pulled me to him, wrapping me in his powerful embrace. "Sweet Gods, how I've longed to hear you say it," he murmured against my hair. His linen shirt was soft beneath my hands as I pressed myself closer, running my hands down the curve of his spine and bringing them to rest on his lower back. He drew back to study my face, his solemn eyes questioning.

"And what are we to do, my love?" he asked.

I raised my face to his, my voice soft. "In a fortnight I will be wed."

Maelgwn winced as if stung, and drew back. "Yes. Of course." He dropped his hands from my waist, but I clutched at them, urgent.

"I am sorry to even utter it, but we cannot ignore it. I cannot fight it; I cannot change it. But I would be with you. Here. If this moment is all we might have, I cannot turn from it."

"This is a difficult decision," he said carefully. "Perhaps you are uncertain."

I shook my head, confused. "Don't you want me?"

Maelgwn sucked in a breath. "I want you," he said fiercely. "I want you more than anything."

I put my palm to his face, forcing him to look deep into my eyes. "There is nothing uncertain in the way I feel about you. I must have you. If only for today. It must be enough to last a lifetime."

My words were Maelgwn's undoing. He drew me to him again, this time almost roughly, his voice a raw whisper against my throat.

"If this is how it must be, so be it."

We came together with the fury of a storm. Our lips joined and I raked my fingers through his hair as we fell back onto the blanket of my cloak blindly, the mossy bank soft beneath us.

I arched against him, breathless, rising to meet the searching of his tongue again and again as his fingers traced my ribs and circled the curves of my breasts. Maelgwn broke away long enough to strip off his shirt and I let my fingers explore the hard muscles of his chest, pulling him back into me as he claimed my mouth again, sliding his hands smoothly up my legs and bunching the fabric of my dress around my naked hips. My body was hot with wanting and I pressed against him, gasping, impatient. He let out a low growl and I felt his body rise in response, his breath coming as quickly as my own under the dappled light of the forest.

His fingers brushed the feather as my dress fell from my shoulders.

"My love," he whispered against my mouth, pulling my hips possessively into his as he covered my body with the solid weight of his.

"Yes" was all I could murmur, his lips hungry against my mouth, my collarbone, the hollow of my throat.

I had known from the beginning it would come to this. That he would be mine. And I would be his.

CHAPTER 31

Far beyond the crowds, Maelgwn and I lazed beneath our canopy of trees, our fingers mapping the curves of each other's bodies. The final celebration would last long through the evening. We drifted between waking and sleep, knit together, sometimes dozing and then exploring again, until afternoon drew away and the evening air made us shiver.

"You're chilled," he said, gathering me closer to his chest. I pressed my cheek to it, listening to the muted thudding of his heart.

"I do not want our time to end," I whispered.

"Nor do I." He laced his fingers in mine. I closed my eyes against any thought of the world beyond the wood, nuzzling closer, breathing the scent of him more deeply, as if I could fix it forever in my memory. Maelgwn sensed the shift and reached to stroke my hair.

"Come away with me," he said.

I opened my eyes, my breath catching in my throat. "You know I cannot. And even if I could, where would we go?"

"We would ride south, into the lands of Rheged; King Urien is a friend. He would surely grant us shelter there until we could secure passage to Gaul. We'd set sail before your father or Tutgual's men could even reach us. You're a fast rider, aren't you, my love? And I could protect you. I could earn us a living there, hire out my sword."

I lifted my head to look into his eyes. They were shadowed with dreaming, as green as a winter sea. I slipped into Maelgwn's dreams like a seal, imagined waking with him on early winter mornings, warm beneath thick stacks of blankets as the wind tossed drifts of snow against our shutters. I saw us walking the shady paths of a forest in the sleepy days of summer and finding a cool patch of river where we could plunge to its pebbled bottom and rise like waterbirds, skin glistening, born anew.

I had only just felt the heat of his fingers on the small of my back, had only just tasted his kiss. I had only just discovered how perfectly our bodies molded together, as if we'd been fashioned, each for the other.

But it was only a dream. This we both understood. Maelgwn took a breath and let it out slowly.

"I am not the only one with obligations I cannot hide from," I said.

"No. I have pledged my sword, and it is an oath I cannot break. To abandon my brothers and our cause in such an hour of need . . . there is too much at stake."

Maelgwn wrapped his arms more tightly around me. Kissed the tender place behind my ear. "It seems I shall have to work to become even stronger, for now I have a reason to bring myself safely back home."

I went still in his arms. "I cannot be yours again. I will be . . ." I could not bring Rhydderch's name between us. ". . . a wife."

"Shhhh." Maelgwn's breath was warm against my neck. "Let us not speak now of such things, love. There will be time enough in days to come."

But there was not time enough. In a fortnight's time I would be bound to another man. And Maelgwn would be riding east, back to the Borderlands and a hard life on the Wall, where sword and spear were the only true kings and every man must bow before them.

A lump rose in my throat. "I would pray to the Gods every morning and night if I thought it could keep you safe," I said.

Maelgwn tilted a finger beneath my chin, forcing me to meet his gaze. "I have won your heart," he said. "No spear can pierce me now."

After a while, Maelgwn rose and bent at the edge of the stream. I watched as he cupped water in his hands and splashed his face. The muscles of his back rippled as he ran his wet hands through his hair, shaking off the water like a hound. I wrapped my arms about my knees, a smile playing at my lips.

He helped me stand on shaky legs to join him at the stream, and behind the cover of a rock I washed myself. As I did so, a thin rivulet of blood flowed down my legs. It struck me then, with a rush as cold as the water, what we had done. My stomach dropped, queasy. The dream was over. A soft flapping of wings startled me and I glanced up in time to see a crow take flight from the lofty branches of a pine.

Soon it would be night. I had been absent far too long. My father would be murderous. Worried sick. He would have sent men to find me. We should have been discovered.

And yet we were not found.

As if reading my thoughts, Maelgwn called to me. I slid back into my gown and went to him, folding myself into his arms again and breathing in the freshness of the stream. It mingled with the clean scent of leather I remembered from that day in the stables. He traced his thumb over my bottom lip and bent to kiss me again. When we pulled back, his rough fingers went delicately to the feather twisted about my neck.

"This is a curious talisman," he said. "Wherever did you get it?"

"It was a gift from Ariane." I met his eyes.

Surprise mingled with understanding. Maelgwn withdrew his fingers as if out of respect. "Then we are safe indeed," he said. "But we should return. Who knows how long this sweet enchantment was fashioned to last."

We walked hurriedly but with heavy steps, the leaves overhead rustling like papered silver. The sound of the stream faded and soon the tops of the tents came into view, their banners lit by torchlight and flapping in the coming dark. The scent of charred wood drifted from burning pyres. It had been a long day of celebration, and those who had taken full advantage would be resting. We moved in a nearly suffocating stillness as we drew closer to camp. But Maelgwn was right. Even the warriors we passed—those tasked with keeping watch—seemed to be slumped in upon themselves, their chests moving softly as if they were sleeping.

We reached my tent and Maelgwn bent his face to mine, the stubble on his jaw rough against my skin as he kissed me one last time. He leaned his forehead against my own.

"I will see you again," he said. "Until then I will be thinking of you. Always."

I leaned into him. "I will see you again," I echoed. "And you must know that nothing in my heart will change."

A tear slipped from the corner of my eye. Maelgwn wiped it with his thumb.

"Do not cry, Lady Languoreth. It will be my undoing."

I took a shaky breath. "I must go."

He nodded slowly. The tips of our fingers were the last parts of our bodies to touch as we pulled apart from each other, raw and wounded, empty and full. Maelgwn turned, and I watched as he moved through camp to the field where Emrys and the Brothers Pendragon were waiting, his shirt glowing like a spirit in the dark, until I could see him no more.

Crowan snored as I pushed through the thick flap of the tent and moved to my bed. Only Ariane was wakeful. She stretched her slender arms overhead on her cot and turned.

"Ah. There you are." Her teeth flashed white in the semidarkness. "Are you happy, then?"

"I am . . ." I looked at her. "Perhaps there are no words. Did no one miss me at the celebration?"

"Miss you?" she asked. "Whatever do you mean? Everyone remarked on what a fine dancer you were. And so full of wit. You shone as bright as a bird this Lughnasa. Certainly you made your father proud."

And yet I had been missing for several hours—a lifetime. I had not been there. I reached in the dark and took her hand.

"Ariane, I cannot quite figure how you worked this strange magic, but I thank you. I thank you from the depth of my heart."

Ariane pressed my fingers in return and was silent a moment. Then she cleared her throat, withdrew her hand.

"Languoreth. You know that I must leave you. I cannot journey with you to Clyde Rock."

Her words fell like boulders in the quiet of the tent. Crushing.

"Leave me? Of course you won't leave me. You may not be permitted in Tutgual's court, but that doesn't mean—"

"I do not leave because of Tutgual," she said. "I leave because of myself. Five winters I have been at your side. You promised me once the freedom to come and go without question. Now I must go. I have been away from my home long enough."

I shook my head in the darkness, panic rising. "But you can't go. Ariane, I need you. Now more than ever. Please. Please don't leave me." My voice broke even as I begged, tears rising into my throat. I had just said good-bye to Maelgwn and now Ariane would leave me, too? I could not bear it.

"Hush, now, hush," Ariane soothed, but the soft sound of her voice and the anticipation of its absence only made it worse. My breath came ragged as I tried to stifle the sound of my weeping.

"Please stay?" I asked, and I heard my own voice, as frightened as a little girl's.

Ariane shifted in the dark and rose from her cot. I nearly startled up to sitting, thinking she meant to leave that very moment, but her hand on my shoulder settled me back into my bed, nudging me over. "Make room," she said.

And Ariane lay down alongside me then, her slim body mirroring my own as she draped her arm over me, nestling her head to share my pillow.

In five winters I could have marked the number of times Ariane had embraced me; like a barn cat, she preferred to keep her own space. Now as she lay so close, it should have felt foreign, and yet I felt a deep calm settle over me.

What a thing it would be to sleep.

But so much had happened. Even as I lay there, I spun with it all.

"Hush, now," Ariane said. "You are so tired. You must go to sleep."

Ariane was right, I realized. I did feel tired, bone achingly so. I let my breathing slow, my eyelids drifting down.

"I will stay with you until the wedding," she was saying, her voice by my ear. "And then I must go." I wanted to argue, but my mouth was too heavy. And the coming night was so deep and soft, so inviting.

"You need me no longer, Languoreth. You are strong. Stronger than you know."

III.

There shall be a black darkness,
There shall be a shaking of the mountain . . .
–"Cad Goddeu" ("The Battle of the Trees"),
translated by Robert Graves, *The White Goddess*

III.

CHAPTER 32

Clyde Rock, the Rock of the Britons
Late Winter, AD 556

I rose slowly, inch by inch, in the dark, not wanting to stir Rhydderch from whatever dream may have found him. My body was not my own. I could feel the child moving again—a boy, Lailoken had wagered when he had visited too many moons ago.

I glanced at my husband as I wrapped myself in a fleece and settled into a chair beside the crackling heat of the fire. I'd woken to the soft unlatching of the door as a servant slipped in to feed the hearth and sleep had not yet found me again.

Across the room the bedding glowed like sifted pearl in the moonlight. The cleft that furrowed my husband's brow during the day was smooth in sleep, making him appear younger and unguarded—an illusion. Rhydderch was tender, but here on Clyde Rock they traded in many kinds of cruelty, and Lord Rhydderch's was distance. He had bedded me on our wedding night, as was his duty. He was gentle, polite. Perfunctory. Rhydderch had been pleased, in his own measured way, that his young wife so soon had been taken with child. But my new husband was absent for lengths at a time. When he returned, he sat beside me but did not touch me, spoke to me kindly but revealed nothing. He was a man of secrets who did not see me. I needed no talisman here to achieve invisibility.

Why have you chosen me? I wanted to scream. I was a stranger in this fortress, kept at arm's length even by my own husband. My ivory comb sat on the dressing table and my gowns inhabited wardrobes and trunks, but the three-room hut I spent my days in felt as lifeless as a tomb.

When Elufed's shrewd eyes caught sight of my thickening belly, I was no longer permitted to travel to Partick.

"You are a princess of Strathclyde now," Elufed had said. "The creature in your womb is our own family treasure."

But while she might forbid me from traveling to visit Lailoken and my father, she could not keep me indoors. I spent long hours wrapped in furs, standing upon the mount of Clyde Rock, overlooking the white-capped water of the rivers Clyde and Leven as they boiled out to sea. Ships came and went with the tide, and in moments I lived a waking dream about a fast horse and a ship to Gaul—a life I could have led. I would smooth my hands over the rounding of my belly and remind myself that I, too, had a secret. And it was my secret that sustained me.

I'd watched through the snowy months as my stomach swelled to accommodate the little form growing inside, until I felt the baby quicken, and it was in that moment I understood the gift I'd been given.

The child that stirred belonged to Maelgwn.

I knew this with a certainty that dwelled beyond reason—that I carried a piece of him with me now, a piece that would be mine to keep for always. My precious babe.

When news of my condition reached the world beyond Clyde Rock, I received a small package delivered by Brodyn, who agreed to travel with me as my newly appointed chief of guard. As my fingers unfolded the parchment, a heavy gold ring fell into the folds of my palm.

Embedded in its center was a simple but entrancing stone: round and deep forest green. An emerald meant to recall a day spent beneath a thick canopy of trees, beneath the shadow of a mountain.

The parchment was blank. Maelgwn would not risk my place here by putting anything to paper. But I kept the parchment because his fingers had creased it. The ring itself was an object of considerable worth and exceeding beauty, but I could not wear it. The craftsman Tutgual kept at Clyde Rock was one of the finest in the land, and my new husband had a keen eye for jewelry.

Since our wedding day I had been presented with jeweled cloak clasps and gold bracelets, bronze mirrors and glistening pearls claimed from mussels that dwelled in our cold northern waters. I wore them dutifully, and my husband knew the origin of each piece in my wooden jewelry chest. No stone of such beauty could go without notice. So I fastened the ring to a slender chain and kept it pinned inside my dress pocket, where I could slip my finger through it in secret, in times when I needed Maelgwn's comfort the most.

Now the late winter festival of Imbolc had come and gone, and still the heavy gray skies of winter were unrelenting. Icy winds whistled through invisible gaps in the thick timber palisades of Clyde Rock, breezing through the rooms of the hut to leave behind a hovering chill no number of hearths could abate. Gray in the sky and gray on the sea.

I ran my hands along the tight curve of my belly, pushing away a worry that had plagued me these past several months. *You have cursed this babe with your heartbreak. A shadow will follow him all of his days.*

I closed my eyes, hummed something soft and low to keep the shadows at bay. Beyond the halls of lords, there was talk that grain stores were running empty.

I rose from the chair by the fire and moved quietly across the planking to the carved wooden table that kept Rhydderch's correspondence. He'd left a missive unfurled upon the table after he'd read it. It was unlike him. Curious. As if he'd wanted me to pry. And so I took the parchment up now, studying it in the hearth light. The penmanship was beautiful, regal, and I recognized it instantly as Cathan's hand. A missive from my father.

Rhydderch Hael,

I have taken an audience at the behest of Mungo, and thought to advise you of my answer, for the bishop said he did come at the request of Strathclyde. The bishop came seeking grain. If it is grain Mungo seeks, he is advised to cast his burden upon the Lord. For does he not claim, in such bold tones as now echo throughout our once peaceful kingdom, that his Lord sustains him?

Has this bishop not chastised others, admonishing them to live in devotion to his God with the oath that all will be provided for?

Let his Lord, then, provide.

For I, as a king, provide for those good people who are within my chiefdom, of which Mungo is not a citizen . . .

It went on. It sickened me to imagine Mungo standing in the great room at Buckthorn. Had he sat in my vacant chair by the fire? Run his bony fingers over the spines of our books? I knew the rains had destroyed many harvests. And yet Mungo had not come to Tutgual, nor to any other lord of Strathclyde. He sought to take grain from my family's stores. This was a test of his power.

Rhydderch had left the letter in full view for a reason. Was it to detect whether I would spy upon his correspondence? A herring on a line, strung out to trap a stray cat? Perhaps he sought to discover whether I would interfere in affairs he deemed private, eschewing my role of dutiful wife when it came to matters of family.

I heard Rhydderch stir and moved silently to stand by the window. I could feel him narrowing his eyes, seeking out my form in the dark.

"Come to bed, wife, before you catch cold." His voice was tender and heavy with sleep.

"In a moment," I said. Beyond the small window the moon was nearly full. It shimmered in the high, rippling water of a high tide. Fat clouds raced over its face and westward toward the ocean, smothering the stars whose names I had learned as a child. I wanted to chant them so I would not forget.

I stood there until I began to shiver. The small bones of my feet cracked softly as I crossed the room to stand at the edge of the bed. Rhydderch's arm was raised overhead, his face so peaceful in sleep. I closed my eyes and reminded myself of my duty.

I did not look back at the silver promise of the moon. I did not allow my gaze to linger on the boats moored at the mouth of the river as I climbed gently back underneath the coverlet.

Far below, the boats bobbed steadily in the winter waters, content to have their sails tethered because they knew in the morning, they would set sail to the west. To the wild freedom brought only by the sea.

It was the sudden pain that woke me just before dawn, a searing so violent I woke with a cry, gripping my cheek as if I'd been wounded. Rhydderch startled instantly from sleep, knocking unlit candles to the floor as he groped for his sword. When he stood to find the chamber dark and deserted, he turned to me, urgent.

"What is the matter? Is it the child?"

My fingers searched blindly for the source of the pain as Rhydderch fumbled in the dimness to light an oil lamp with a reed from the fire. Nothing. The curved bone of my cheek was unblemished, and yet my face throbbed as though it had been sliced from temple to chin.

"It's nothing," I mumbled in confusion. "I'm sorry to have startled you. It was only a dream." My husband's gray eyes searched mine in the lamplight and I felt the stirrings of affection mingled with guilt.

"Are you certain you're well?" he asked gently.

"Yes, I'm well. I and the babe."

Rhydderch let out a breath, relieved. But my heart was pounding so loudly that I was certain he could hear it. "I'm sorry," I repeated. "Let us sleep."

I waited in the dark for an eternity. Foul weather had swept in and the wind was wailing as tiny particles of ice hissed against the shutter. When at last the rhythm returned to Rhydderch's breathing, I crept from bed. The fire had died down, and my fingers trembled as I dressed, pulling on thick woolen stockings and securing my warmest dress and fur-lined cloak with a sturdy leather belt.

Crowan, now my only constant companion, slept in the tiny room beside ours that she shared with Desdemona. But it was not Crowan I sought to wake. Crowan would only worry and raise such a fuss, she would never let me go. The floor felt like frost beneath my feet as I slipped into the dark, feeling my way to their door with a growing sense of disquiet. I stopped for a moment, suddenly unsure whether Desdemona was up to the task. But as I stood there in the dark, my face pulsing with a wound I could not see, I could doubt it no longer.

Lailoken was hurt.

I reached to stir Desdemona and she woke with a start. "Why are you no' sleeping, m'lady?"

I raised a finger to my lips, gesturing to Crowan. "You must ready yourself quickly. We are leaving now for Partick."

"But it's stormin' and bitter outside! It's no' yet mornin'!"

"It must be now, Desdemona. Something has happened to Lailoken," I whispered. "My brother has been wounded."

I saw the fear spring to her eyes; I knew she had long admired him.

"An' wha' o' the queen? She's forbid it." She glanced away. "They'll beat me."

"If they seek to lay a hand on you, they must first come through me. Please now. Fetch Brodyn. Have him ready a boat and enough men to row. Do it quickly. Go now!"

Outside, the stairs between the ramparts were slick with ice. I felt like a fly trapped in honey as we moved too slowly downhill by torch-light, frozen rain pelting at our hoods and hissing in its effort to extinguish our flames. We reached the lower rampart only to have two guards stalk from the warmth of the gatehouse, hostile and moody in the spitting cold.

"The lady is not to leave," the taller one said.

I stared ahead, refusing to meet his gaze. "How dare you question me! I am with child and in need of my healer."

His face blanched in alarm. "Then we must wake a priest."

"I will not see a priest." I turned to him, my eyes ablaze. "You would stand here and jeopardize Lord Rhydderch's heir?"

"If it is by your husband's sanction . . ."

"Where could I go without my husband's sanction?" I lied.

A look passed between the guards, but at last the taller one nodded, finally giving way.

Rhydderch's vessel waited at the dock's edge, six of our men hunched over their oars against the cold. They inclined their heads as Brodyn reached out to help me aboard, and Desdemona and I huddled beneath the small winter shelter secured on deck as the boat cut through the dark water.

"Did you do as I instructed?" I asked Brodyn.

"Aye. I left word for Rhydderch. But I warn you, cousin, your husband will be none too pleased."

"Then it is thankful that in this matter I do not seek to please him."

"Will you tell me now what this is about?" Brodyn's gaze went to

Desdemona, who sat shivering next to me under a pile of thick blankets. "You endanger not only yourself."

"Not even a tyrant would punish me for going to my brother's side," I hissed. "Lailoken is in danger. Something has happened."

"Lailoken in danger? Now you say! We would have gotten word of any strife, Languoreth."

"He is my twin, Brodyn. You must trust in me. I cannot say more."

Brodyn looked at me a long moment before bowing his head and tightening his cloak against the cold.

"How much farther?" I asked.

"It won't be long now. We should arrive by sunup."

I fixed my eyes on the glow of the eastern horizon. I could only pray, whatever had happened, sunup would not be too late.

CHAPTER 33

Up ahead the morning sky flickered with an orange glow. From a distance I almost mistook it for sunrise. But as the boat slapped through the wintry chop of the water I saw the ominous rise of black clouds.

Brodyn shot to his feet.

"Oars, men, oars!"

I rushed to the gunwale, straining to make out the source of the flames.

"Sweet Gods, it's the granaries," I shouted. "They're on fire!"

I could see the inferno licking the squat wooden buildings halfway upriver. Fire lit the dawn like a funeral pyre, smoke gusting downwind until I tasted the charred wood in the back of my throat.

"Faster. Faster, please!" I begged. Shouts and curses of men scrambling to put out the blaze carried over the water as we sped toward shore, nearly colliding with the dock. I blinked against the stifling billows, stumbling from the boat into a world of chaos.

Men raced from the river and back with buckets of brackish water, their faces blackened with soot. I braced my hands beneath the curve of my stomach and rushed uphill, Brodyn and Desdemona at my back.

"Lailoken?" I shouted into the crowd, my panic mounting. "Father!"

"Languoreth!" Brodyn called. "This way!" He cast his cloak over me to shelter me from a blast of heat as we hurried past the granary closest to shore.

"Brodyn!" Brant's voice carried over the crackle of flames, and I turned to see my elder cousin, ashes in his hair and a gash on his shoulder, calling to his brother.

"Whatever are you doing here?" Brant clasped Brodyn's arm, then looked at me.

"It doesn't matter now. Tell us what's happened," I demanded.

"It was a raid—a mob. Must have been near one hundred men. We'd doubled the guard, but what was twenty men to a hundred? I cannot think how word found you so quickly, but I am glad for it. Come, I'll take you to Morken. We are badly in need of hands." He looked over his shoulder as we hurried away. "And a healer."

"Who's been harmed?" I scrambled to keep pace. "And what of Thoma, Father's new healer?"

"Thoma lies wounded. Lailoken, too."

"Oh, no." I shook my head. "No!"

"Cathan is tending as best he can, but . . ." Brant trailed off as we ducked beneath a low door and into the smoldering shelter of one of the last remaining granaries.

My eyes swept the room, taking stock. Herbs and ointments were scattered across the floor. Many of my father's men lay wounded, and I glimpsed the bloodied white robes of Thoma, Father's new healer, who was splayed unconscious on the flagstone floor. Father paced like a wounded beast, his face black with soot and fury. I startled as he slammed his fist against the wall.

"I will have his head on a *pike*!" he shouted.

"Father!" I cried.

He turned and his rage collapsed into bewilderment as I rushed into his arms.

"Languoreth, this is dangerous," he said against my hair. "Whatever are you doing here?"

"Never mind it. I'm here now." I laid my head against his shoulder a moment before pulling back to search his face. "Where is Lailoken?"

His face darkened again. He nodded to the far corner of the barn.

My hands flew to my mouth as I spotted Cathan hunched over Lail's prone body, holding a blood-soaked rag against my brother's face. Discarded bloody dressings littered the floor. I nearly slipped on them as I rushed to my brother's side, his name a sob in my throat. "Lail."

"Languoreth, thank the Gods," Cathan looked up and I saw his face was bloody and bruised. The knuckles of his right hand had been smashed, but he was flexing them with a wince, preparing to do Lail's stitching.

"Your hand!"

Cathan frowned. "Don't fret over me; I will set it. I've survived many a kicking in my lifetime. I don't intend to stop surviving them now. Lailoken's bled too much. We need to stanch the wound."

I blinked in an effort to gain my bearings. Lail's lashes lay flush against his cheeks, his face waxy and pale. I could not yet see the wound that bled beneath the cloth.

I turned to Desdemona, who was staring at Lailoken as if she'd been struck.

"Desdemona, fetch clean linens," I ordered. "Quickly!"

"Yes, m'lady."

I swallowed. "And someone build a fire. I am not certain this is a wound that will stitch."

He'd lost too much blood; I could tell from the waxiness of his skin. If the wound was too deep, I could not risk it festering. I would have to clean it as best I could, then burn it shut. I rushed to Thoma's unconscious form, grateful to find his remedy sack still strapped round his waist.

"I'm sorry, but I must have this," I told him as my fingers fumbled against the buckles. "I'll help you soon as I'm able."

I upended its contents on the floor beside my brother, sifting through them, frantic. Oh, thank the Gods. Sphagnum and yarrow. Copper salts. Thoma had all the makings to clot the bleeding and ward off infection.

I looked to Cathan. "Let me see it."

Dried blood tugged at the cloth as Cathan pulled it away. I gasped as the blood spurted afresh and a wave of sickness rocked through me. It wasn't the blood—I'd seen plenty of it. It was the wound itself. The gash ran from temple to chin.

Lailoken's face had been carved with a wound the same shape as the scar my father bore. This was no accident. This was a mark made of hate. I blinked and pressed the cloth hastily back to the wound, preparing to clean it.

"Cathan, the wound is too big; we cannot stitch it. It will have to be sealed with fire. It's the only way." I looked up. "Who has done this? Tell me they have been punished."

"Oh, the men who did this have been punished." Brant knelt by Lailoken, voice low and his dark eyes fixed on my brother's motionless face. "Do you hear me, Lailoken? The men who did this have been punished. The first man slain was the one who sought to hold me back. Next among the dead were the three I discovered holding you down. But the man brandishing the knife . . . Well. I showed him what his weapon could do."

Cathan rubbed his temples with the heels of his hands. "Dead men cannot speak, Brant."

"Oh? And did we need them to speak?" Brant challenged. "It is no great mystery who sent them. And where do you think they have taken our grain? To Mungo's lands upriver, that's where. Easy as you like on the tide, and on one of our vessels, too."

I could not think of it. Not now. I fumbled through the spilled contents of Thoma's sack for a flask that I hoped held vinegar. I sniffed to make sure before pouring it onto a linen and pressing it to the weeping gash. It would have burned like fire, yet Lailoken did not stir.

"I should have liked to have questioned them," Cathan said angrily. My fingers shook as I struggled to focus on the wound.

Desdemona reappeared, her face tight with worry, a stack of clean linens in her arms. "Please, m'lady. Let me help."

"Find me a place where the fire burns hottest," I said. Taking my blade from my belt, I handed it to her. "Hold this over the flames until it is glowing red. Glowing with red, do you hear? Then bring it back to me right away."

Desdemona nodded and I could have sworn that her distress seemed driven by something deeper. But whatever Desdemona felt, I did not have time to consider it. Lailoken began to stir and shift on his pallet on the floor.

"Your son is strong." Cathan looked to Father. "Come. We must hold him."

Later, when it was done, we sat beside my brother's still body and spoke at last of what had taken place. Lailoken had gone unconscious from pain. A blessing, for I hoped he would never remember what I could not forget: the smell of his burning flesh, the pitch of his screams. This was not a pain that could easily be borne by any man. Not even a warrior.

Anger boiled in a sickening vat in my stomach. This could not go unanswered.

"Tutgual's men were posted on the ramparts," Father growled.

"The storm was pelting," Cathan said. "They will say they were closed in the guard huts. They will say they saw nothing."

The silver-tongued bishop had inspired a mob to raid my father's stores. They had disfigured his only son and escaped in one of our vessels.

I could almost laugh at the absurdity of it. "So this is how Mungo would find his grain when his people are starved. An armed mob of one hundred." This carried out by a man who followed Christ.

It had been a span of only months since his naming, and already Mungo had sought out our sacred shrines and springs, claiming them as property of his church. He had hacked up our tribal land into arbitrary tracts now called "parishes," placing each under the jurisdiction of a priest. He had even gone from hut to hut disavowing marriages among Strathclyde's tenants and warriors that were not conducted by a monk. All of this had been done under the sanction of Tutgual.

Brant rubbed a blood-streaked hand over his face. "They were armed with sharpened sticks. Hay forks," he remembered. "Spears, stones, knives. Not one in twenty had a sword. But they came in scores. Men willing to kill for food."

"Lailoken was full of fury. He rode out faster than any of us could mount," Cathan said. "We were too far behind."

"This cannot go unpunished," I said. "Surely Rhydderch cannot stand idly by whilst such vile men attack my own brother in such a brutal and unforgivable act! I am a princess of Strathclyde. I will not rest until I see that wicked man pay. Surely Tutgual—"

"Tutgual?" Cathan scoffed. "Tutgual will sit upon his ornately carved throne and do nothing. And you will not so much as move your lips in protest."

I looked at him, my eyes ablaze. "Why else have I been given to Rhydderch if not to use my influence to protect my family?"

"You? You have no influence. Not yet. When you do, we shall use it. But you will make no allies in your new household by acting as such. We have our ways of dealing with such matters. You will see."

"I should have been with you," Brodyn said. His voice was tight. It had not been an easy choice for Brodyn to leave Father and Brant to captain my guard. I waited now for Father to allay my cousin's blame, but he only looked at him. At last Father bowed his head.

"Your place is with Languoreth, Brodyn. And Lailoken's justice has been served. The men who marked him are dead. My son is strong. He will yet live to see this man Mungo cast from our kingdom."

"Is that so, Father? And what will you do?" I challenged.

"I have rage enough to wage ten wars," Father said. "But the bishop's mouth is a yawning maw. Did we not predict that no matter how much of our world he swallowed, he would hunger for more? Yes, the cost has been great. But Mungo has overstepped himself now. I do not agree with my counsellor. I have a different mind." Father nodded at Cathan in respect. "I believe Tutgual will be forced to act."

The Wisdom Keeper only raised a brow and flexed his fingers, examining the damage done to his hand.

I looked to Father. "Kill him and be done with it. Mungo will never cease."

"You think I do not wish him dead?" Father turned to me. "Think it through, Languoreth. You are cleverer than this."

"Morken cannot kill Tutgual's appointed bishop," Cathan said. "To do so would force Tutgual to retaliate. He would raze Cadzow. Any who swear fealty to your father would be put to the sword. And then there's Morken's own daughter," he said. "Kept so close in Tutgual's own fort."

The harsh light of a winter's dawn showed the age on Father's face. My eyes fixed on the mottled scar only partly concealed by his thick, reddish beard.

"But look what he has done to your son." My voice broke. Father blinked and glanced away.

"Look! He's stirrin'!" Desdemona suddenly straightened. "Lailoken's waking!"

"Please, give him air," I said. But I'd nearly lost my brother, and now

I wanted no one closer to him than me. I had packed a poultice gently to Lail's face, securing it with two long bandages, one knotted round his forehead and the other wrapping the oval of his face. It would need changing soon. My breath hitched as Lailoken's eyes eased open.

"Lie still. Don't speak," I said.

His blue eyes roamed the world from his pallet on the floor and he winced with a moan, reaching for the wound on his face.

"Don't! You've been . . . injured," I said. "I've sealed the wound and dressed it, but you mustn't touch it, please."

At this he rolled his eyes. With some effort he worked to loose his tongue from the dry roof of his mouth. "You dressed it? Then I am truly in trouble," he said.

I shook my head as Father knelt beside us.

"You bore it well, my son."

Lail glanced up at the half-burned ceiling and looked at my father incredulously. "We'll leave that. And what is she doing here?" He nodded to me, jaw clenched against the pain.

"You are truly unbelievable," I said. "You're lucky I came."

Our eyes met, and I read Lail's question.

You felt it?

I gave an almost imperceptible nod.

"And in your condition . . ." His eyes traveled to my belly.

"Don't be foolish. It wasn't your fault."

Lail sank back and closed his eyes. A tear escaped, slipping down the pale skin of his cheek.

"They are dead, Lailoken, the men who did this to you," I said. "Brant saw to that."

"No. Not all of them," Lail said. "Not yet."

I bit my lip. Of course. It was not only my brother's face that had been wounded. There was also his pride. He strained and pressed himself up.

"Lailoken! You cannot yet move. You've lost so much blood. You could have—" The words lodged in my throat. "Please, I beg you. Lie still. There's a cart outside. You'll go home to Buckthorn. All will be well."

"Lailoken," Father said. "You must regain your strength." My brother said nothing but eased back down, staring at the scorched thatching overhead. I reached to knit my fingers in his. He did not draw away, but his hand was limp, lifeless as a corpse.

"You must go, Languoreth," Lail said. "You should never have come. You have endangered yourself. And your babe."

"And I would do so again," I said. "Do not worry for me. Just rest, please, so that you might heal. I've seen to Thoma and he's even now readying a cart. He'll know what to do."

At the thought of my departure, the consequences I'd set aside since feeling the searing pain of Lailoken's wound upon my own face resurfaced. I would have to answer to Tutgual. I was a disobedient hound who had slipped her leash. My husband would have woken by now and found me absent. Rhydderch would be fuming. Furious. And anxious for my return.

News would have reached them by now of Mungo's raid. I thought of the missive left open upon Rhydderch's table, and a fresh surge of anger rocked through me. Had Rhydderch anticipated this, he should have warned me. He should have warned my family.

"Languoreth, your brother is right. We must see you back to Clyde Rock, and quickly." Father helped me stand. "Brodyn," he called. "Ready her boat."

Three granaries smoldered in the dawn. Smoke stung my eyes as Father walked me to the river's edge. Men from town had come in droves to help extinguish the flames, and many of them sat now atop empty buckets, shoulders sagging and faces solemn as they took in the devastation. What the thieves could not abscond with they had burned. We were in the midst of winter now. If Father could not recover his grain, it was our people now who would face starvation.

"There is still the granary and mill at Cadzow," Father reassured me as if reading my thoughts. "Look for me soon. Tutgual will call a meeting. Then I will deal with Mungo. I will recover my vessel and my grain. Until then, you must take care." His dark eyes were tender. "I nearly lost my son today. I do not need to tell you that carrying a child is a dangerous endeavor."

"I will take care, Father. I promise."

"Keep to yourself. Be clever. You are your mother's daughter."

"Perhaps," I allowed. "But it seems I also carry my father's stout spirit."

He touched a callused hand to my face. "Then I pray it serves you as it has served me. May the Gods keep you, my daughter."

"And you."

I took Brodyn's hand and stepped aboard the boat as Father lifted his arm in farewell. "I will see you at court."

I took my seat, my swollen feet pulsing in my boots. Yes, news of the raid would have spread by now, and with it word of my brother's disfigurement. My father was much beloved as a king, and the men of our tenant garrison had watched Lailoken playing at swords as a boy; their loyalty to our family ran deep. Now the grain they'd given their sweat and blood for had been plundered. The son of their king disgraced. Father had doubled the guard as a precaution—but how could he have conceived of such an attack so close to the capital's own walls?

My heart sank as I thought of returning to Clyde Rock. I belonged with my father. With my brother. As we took the first bend in the river, I turned to look back one last time.

Father stood at the water's edge wrapped in furs against the cold, the wealth of his kingdom smoldering behind him.

The muscles that carried the growing weight of my belly throbbed with a dull pain, and I closed my eyes to it, letting the sound of the waves against the hull lull me. Desdemona woke me what felt like a moment later, the fear in her voice making me sit up too quickly, leaving my head spinning.

"You'll want t' wake now, m'lady." Her eyes were fixed on the shore beyond.

I blinked and rubbed a hand against my head. "What is it?"

I looked downriver. Clyde Rock loomed, its dragon-backed summits covered in snow. And standing upon the docks at the great island's feet were Tutgual's soldiers, clad in scarlet, their faces hard as they waited for the woman who had dared disobey their king.

"Don't be frightened, Desdemona. It isn't you they want."

I scanned their cloaked forms and nearly swayed in relief as I spotted Rhydderch standing among them, his own sealskin cloak thrown hastily over his shoulders and dark shadows beneath his eyes. Breg stood only one step behind, his sharp jaw set with purpose.

Brodyn placed his hand protectively on my shoulder. "Give me the word and I will strike."

"No, Brodyn. We mustn't let it come to that. Lord Rhydderch will not harm me."

"It is not Lord Rhydderch I worry about."

Tutgual, of course.

My cousin's mouth formed a thin line as Tutgual's men came forth and yanked our boat into the dock.

I had been ordered to confine myself to Clyde Rock. Wives had been thrown into pits for lesser displays of disobedience. But to disobey the high king? I could only thank the Gods I was with child; surely there was protection in that.

Rhydderch's eyes burned into mine as Brodyn stepped onto the docking, offering me his hand. I'd been Rhydderch's wife for six moons, and still his stony gaze was unreadable. He gave a curt bow of his head and took my hand from Brodyn a little too firmly.

"I can only assume you absconded to Partick," he said.

"I did."

"And your brother?"

I met his eyes. "He would have died if not for me."

Rhydderch exhaled. For the first time, I saw the strange look of fear flicker behind my husband's eyes as he ushered me toward the ramparts, the dock planks trembling beneath our feet.

"In leaving the fortress, you have disobeyed the king," he said. "I cannot protect you now."

CHAPTER 34

Four soldiers suddenly closed in, and Rhydderch stepped before me. These men were not the soldiers I sometimes chatted with, the ones who manned the lookout near the sloping boulder where I often perched to gaze out to sea. These men were bred with no room for niceties.

"She carries my babe, Breg," Rhydderch reminded him.

The captain of Tutgual's guard gave Rhydderch a hard stare. "Aye," he said. "A fact she might have considered before taking her leave of the fort. We will escort her now."

Rhydderch planted his feet, his eyes stony with warning, but I knew he must step aside.

"Come, my lady."

I set my jaw and followed Breg uphill. They pushed me up the slick stone steps until my breath came in gasps and my legs nearly gave way.

"Let her rest." Brodyn's angry voice came from below. "The woman's with child!"

I held up one hand to silence him. I did not want to test them.

By the time we reached the peak of the hill, I had stripped off my fur cloak and my dress clung to my back with sweat. I struggled to catch my breath as we moved into the entryway of Tutgual's hall, the hot blast of hearth air stifling my lungs. I heard the buzz of voices as Tutgual's men hurried me onward toward the great room. It was to be public, then, my shaming. The king would chastise me in front of his court.

So be it.

I steadied my chin and moved as gracefully as I was able toward the imposing doors. As the hinges swung open, the room fell silent. Morcant and his warriors. Elufed, standing beside the king. I could feel their eagerness as they perched like ravens on a battlefield, their eyes greedy for a corpse.

"How dare you," a woman whispered as I passed.

And then, to my horror, I spotted Crowan pressed between the iron-armed grips of two of Tutgual's men. Her gray hair was disheveled; she had been pulled from bed in her nightdress and brought before court, her thin legs visible beneath the worn fabric. My face must have crumpled, because she shook her head, her hazel eyes grim with determination. I could not let them harm her. I would not let it come to that.

I trained my eyes upon the floor as my feet plodded toward the heavy wooden throne where Tutgual sat. I dared not look up, but I could almost feel him cock his birdlike head. I knew his eyes upon me were as sharp as any dagger.

"My king." I dipped my head low.

"*My king*," he echoed thoughtfully. "Am I? Am I your king?"

"Father—" Rhydderch spoke up, but Tutgual silenced him.

"I am speaking to your wife," his voice boomed. "Now. Look at me."

I lifted my head. Tutgual's face was hard but his blue eyes flickered with something that neared excitement. Beside him, Elufed's pretty face was a mask of pity.

"Who knew of your plan, this plan to defy me?"

Tutgual's eyes scanned my retinue, shifting from Desdemona to Brodyn. Settling on Crowan. "Bring forth her maid."

"No!" I shouted as the soldiers lifted Crowan by her fragile arms, dragging her feet. Tears of panic clouded my vision. "No, please! She knew nothing. It was my doing. Mine alone!"

Tutgual considered me a moment. Then snorted derisively and gestured to Crowan. "Beat her," he commanded.

Crowan stiffened her little body like a rod, her mouth firm as the warrior lifted his arm to strike.

"No, please!" I sobbed, falling to my knees. "Please don't hurt her!"

Tutgual lifted a finger, and the soldier looked to the king, pausing. The high king shifted his vulturish eyes to me.

"Don't hurt her? We shall see. Come," he said.

I scrambled to my feet. Fixed my eyes on the embroidery of his winter robe as I moved to stand before him. Tutgual took a slow sip of ale from a nearby cup and handed it to a servant, wiping his mouth on the edge of his sleeve.

"Lady Languoreth. You have arrived back to Clyde Rock. And how was your journey?"

I summoned my strength. "My journey was not a happy one, my king."

"Was it not?"

"No."

"Go on."

"I arrived in Partick at dawn to find my brother nearly bled to death inside my father's granary." I swallowed my fury, forcing my voice even. "Surely you received word of the raid on my father's stores of grain."

Tutgual steepled his fingers, peering at me with curiosity. "We were informed of the raid only hours ago. And you have been gone since before first light. Tell me: How could this be? Who could be your messengers, that they could bring news to you, unbeknownst to us, with such inconceivable speed, for I would have such lightning men carry news for myself."

Laughter rippled from court, and Tutgual raised his hand amusedly to silence them.

"I had no messengers, my king."

"You had no messengers," he echoed. "What am I to think of a young princess, so newly wed to my son, who flees from my court under the cover of darkness without my permission? What am I to suppose, other than that you disobeyed our orders? That you had run away?"

I faltered, my eyes fixed on the ground.

"Speak!" he boomed.

"I did leave word with my husband. I would never flee, my lord."

"I will ask you again: How did you know that this raid had taken place?"

I lifted my eyes to meet his, defiant. "I knew nothing of the raid, my king. I only knew my brother was in danger, and from no source of messenger save a sister's love of her twin. I woke in the dark from a pain not my own. I did not seek to discover the reason. I knew only that I must go at once, before it was too late!"

There was a long moment of silence as the king weighed my answer.

And then.

I had not realized how close I stood to the high king until my body slammed into stone. The blow knocked me from my feet, sending me prostrate on the floor. My face against the shale, I blinked as my vision blurred, pain exploding across my cheek.

Tutgual's voice was calm. "Stand," he commanded.

Swallowing my tears, I reached instinctively to touch my face. Never before had I been struck. My cheek stung as though I'd been slapped with a fist full of needles, and my wrist ached as if it might have been fractured from bracing my fall.

"Stand," Tutgual demanded once more.

I blinked and pushed myself up on trembling arms, my hair falling around my face. The crowd in the hall stood silent at my back. No one came to my aid, not even my own husband. I took a breath, bracing to be struck again, my arms shielding the life in my stomach. But no further blow came.

At last Tutgual sniffed.

"Handle your wife," he said to Rhydderch. "You would do well to teach her who her true family is now."

Rhydderch came forward. I wavered, reaching out for him to steady me, but he pulled his arm away, nodding toward the door.

"Go," he said.

My face burned with fury. Go? I wanted to run. I wanted to race from this horrid hall and out onto the hill where I could sob beside the wintry shadow of the boulder and fix my eyes on the sea. If I could feel my brother's pain, could not my own lover then feel the roiling emotions that pulsed within me?

Come to me, Maelgwn. Save me, I pleaded.

But only Brodyn came to walk with me. I held my head erect, kept my footsteps measured as I made my way through the crowd. As I reached the door, rather than open it and release me from the endless shame and humiliation, two of Tutgual's men stood, unyielding. Brodyn cast them a look that could splinter stone and they stepped aside at last, the door closing behind us. My fingers found Brodyn's sleeve and I fell against him, my tears silent and shuddering.

"It's over now, it's done." My cousin's voice was thick as he wrapped his arm around me.

I moved my feet blindly as Brodyn guided me out into the cold, then into the warmth of my hut, where I fell upon the bed and wept. The door opened and shut. Brodyn reappeared with a linen knotted around a thick mound of snow.

"Here, little cousin. Put this against your face. It will help ease the swelling."

"I hate him," I seethed. "I hate him. That tyrant! That—"

"No, Languoreth, you mustn't," Brodyn clutched me. "There are men all around."

I pressed the snowpack to my cheek. It was some time before I could breathe evenly again.

Even as exhaustion took over, even as I slept, my cheek swollen and my bed linens damp with tears, I kept the embers of my hatred for Tutgual close, where my breath could fuel them, fan them, keep them from extinguishing. He may beat me but he could not rid himself of me. Rhydderch must only be named tanist. I would stay at Clyde Rock and Tutgual would die. Someday I would rule.

I was still cradling my anger when a knock came at my door.

So Rhydderch had finally come. I pulled myself to a sitting position, but it was Elufed, not my husband, who stood framed by the door.

She raised a delicate eyebrow in concern. "How is the babe? I trust you have rested?"

The queen took my silence as agreement and nodded at Brodyn to close the door. Her pale hair was twisted into sweeping coils, her long, straight nose and proud cheekbones conveying her high breeding even where fine jewelry and lavish dresses could not. It was her clear gray eyes Rhydderch had been born with, so difficult to measure, ancient and impenetrable as slate. Elufed gave a practiced smile as she came to stand beside the bed and reached to touch my face, gently tilting it to the light.

"He has a skilled hand," she said, dropping her fingers. "It won't leave a mark."

"Even Tutgual King, then, abides by the law," I said.

"Indeed." Elufed smoothed her robes to avoid creasing before sitting at the edge of the bed. "The laws of the Britons declare a man might strike a woman so long as it does not leave a mark. But where I hail from, if a man strikes a woman, they cut off his hand."

I looked at her in surprise. Elufed rolled her eyes. "Do you know nothing of the Picts?"

"I know a little," I said.

I did not care for a lesson on Picts. I only wanted her to leave so I might be alone. Elufed seemed too at ease in my room, as if she belonged there, just as she—with her regal bearing and heavy-lidded eyes—seemed to belong so naturally at court. Hosting feasts, standing in deference at the elbow of such a despicable king. She made me feel feeble-legged and gawky, like a newborn foal. I still had my anger, though, and fixed my eyes on the coverlet, my fingers picking at a loose thread.

"That blanket was embroidered by my mother's hands," Elufed said.

My fingers ceased.

"You cannot take much with you when you leave home. But you know that." She smiled and waved a hand, as if her husband had not just slammed me to the ground before all of his court. As if my father's granaries had not just been raided by force, my brother's face not just butchered like a side of beef.

"She was a Pictish queen, my mother," Elufed continued. "This is why I was married to Tutgual, of course. The Pictish people honor the mother's line, not the father's. Rhydderch and Morcant, my daughter Gwenfron—they may be Britons, but they will always be Picts because they are mine." She sought to catch my eyes. "My mother and father sought peace with Strathclyde and so I became their holy token. Just as you are ours."

I looked up angrily. "I am no token."

"Oh?" Elufed laughed. "And what else might you be?"

I searched but could find no answer. I reached instead for the copper pitcher beside the bed and poured water into a cup.

"It is said the people have to hear you utter nary a word before declaring their love for you," Elufed said, studying me. "Mungo is much beloved, too, by the people of Strathclyde. Since his arrival the Christian cause has found a new champion. He feeds the hungry. He has more than tripled the church's numbers. His priests move about the countryside doing great works. He is a pious man who converses with great charm and lives humbly by example. Merchants, traders, and men of stout means shower him with goods and coin."

"Mungo feeds the hungry with stolen grain," I said. "He spreads his faith by blood and intimidation. He is a twisted zealot and a power-monger whose web is made of lies. His priests are paid highwaymen who barge into people's homes and disavow their marriages. And I am certain that any goods in his coffers will only further his own gain."

Elufed's gray eyes lit and she smiled. "Yes, all this is correct, too." She gestured at my cup. "May I? I do have a terrible thirst."

I passed her my cup. She reached for it gracefully, and as she did, the silky fabric of her robe slid up her arm. A wide silver cuff caught the light, enameled with strange creatures the likes of which I'd never seen. She lowered the cup, her eyes on mine.

"Tell me, Languoreth. Do you think me a Christian?"

I looked at her carefully. I knew the Picts were an ancient and mysterious people. Cathan spoke of wind-tossed islands in the far reaches of the north, with holy temples more ancient than any in our land, with circles of stone that stood three men high, and tombs nestled into the cliffs and the earth, where they worshipped and consulted the bones of their dead. But the new religion had found them, too, or so I thought. Even if this bracelet marked Elufed as a woman of the Old Way, she had spent far too many years at the side of a power-hungry king.

"I would not assume otherwise," I said, looking away.

"No, of course not." Elufed smiled and leaned back on her hands. "You know, my husband was not always so sympathetic to the Christian cause. But these merchants and traders and men of wealth—they are the ones who take our goods overseas. And for every good that goes in or out of our ports, this family takes a sharing in tax. In tribute. Our kingdom and our wealth is built upon the merchants' backs. Wine, silver, salt, spices, tin. Our beautiful fabrics. Trade must continue, at all costs."

"No," I said. "Tutgual does not kneel at the altar for trade."

"Oh?" Her clever eyes sparked with interest.

"In the Christian view, it is the king who is said to be closest to their god. Not the Wisdom Keepers, as my people believe, who have the ear of the Gods and answer to no one, not even a king. Priests may give counsel, but the king has dominion. How much easier it would be to rule with Wisdom Keepers stripped of their power."

I heard the bitterness in my voice too late and stopped, frightened I'd said too much. But Elufed's face was as calm as a pool.

"Perhaps it would be easier," she allowed. "But there are thousands throughout this land who yet honor the Keepers of the Old Way. Our prosperity depends, too, upon our allegiances and our army—our petty kings and chieftains who call up their war bands to take weapons in hand when our kingdom is in danger. Our supply of cattle and grain. So you see, a balance must be struck. Mungo has tipped that balance. My husband will not be pleased."

"What will Tutgual do?"

Elufed looked at me sharply. "I have not come to give away the high king's secrets. I only meant to see how you fared."

She stood and smoothed her skirts. "I go on too long. Rhydderch will soon be here." She glanced at the door and then turned to me, smiling almost tenderly.

"Here upon Clyde Rock, wives and mothers are replaceable," she said. "I should hate to see you replaced. You must remember that Tutgual is your family now, and you would do well to please him. No more of this . . . nonsense."

Her gray eyes met mine and she reached to touch my cheek, murmuring something in the Pictish tongue. "All things heal in time. That's what my mother once said." Though her face was smooth, her voice was hollow.

Lailoken had told me Elufed was given to Tutgual quite young. And for a moment I saw a flicker of the little Pictish girl she might once have been; she yet haunted the shadows behind Elufed's eyes.

Do you think me a Christian?

I looked at the queen as if seeing her for the first time.

What horrors had awaited her as Tutgual's child bride? She had meant for me to see her silver cuff, I knew. But to what end? It was Elufed who'd been behind my first summons to Clyde Rock. It had been Elufed's keen eyes that had lighted on me that day of the Gathering, when I was but a girl. Had her wisewomen foreseen the tipping of the balance and sought to place her, just as Cathan and Ariane had sought to place me?

"My queen . . . ," I began, but a knock sounded at the door and her gray eyes silenced me.

"There is my son."

"Mother." Rhydderch seemed surprised to see her. Then I felt his eyes settle on me, heavy with betrayal and disappointment. Perhaps this was his power: a look that could feel worse than any blow. Brodyn stood beyond the door, watching, wary.

"I will leave you," Elufed said. "I am certain you have much to discuss. You should rest, Lady Languoreth. And take some nourishment. For the babe."

"Yes. I will."

My throat went dry as Rhydderch ducked beneath the lintel, then turned. "Brodyn," he said, "I would speak with my wife."

Brodyn looked at me, waiting until I nodded. "It's all right, Brodyn. You may close the door."

"So be it." He bowed, but his frown let me know he'd be waiting just outside should I need him.

Rhydderch came to squat beside the bed, his gray eyes studying me. "Are you yet in pain?"

"Nay," I reached to test the spot, the skin swollen beneath my fingers. "It doesn't hurt."

A lie.

He rose and moved to the window, shaking his head. "I have heard of twins who can feel each other's wounds, but it is the stuff of fireside tales. Tell me, wife, and let it be the truth. Did all happen just as you said?"

"You were with me when I woke in the night. You heard my cry. I had to go to him. Lailoken would have done the same had it been me."

Rhydderch weighed my words. "And yet you did so without waking me. Creeping from our dwelling like a thief in the night. Lying to the guard." His voice went quiet. "You could have killed our child."

I reached instinctively to cradle my stomach. "It was a journey by boat; there can be no danger in that! Far more dangerous was being marched like a prisoner up the high stairs of Clyde Rock. Being struck to the ground by your father. And you let it." My voice shook with anger. "You, who swore an oath to protect me."

"Aye," he said angrily, "but it seems I cannot protect you from yourself."

I gave a bitter laugh. "You left that parchment for me to discover. You knew something might happen. Did you imagine it would be this?"

Tears rose and I bit my lip to keep them from taking hold. "My brother nearly dead. My family raided, disgraced. And all this by a man your father has declared bishop. When will this madness come to an end? What more must come to pass?"

"I did not imagine Mungo could wreak such violence." Rhydderch rubbed his jaw in frustration. "I did leave that parchment in sight, but only because I thought to extend you the courtesy of reading your father's missive yourself. It was not intended as permission to do as you please."

"How was I to know? You with your guarded mind and your weighted looks. You expect everything, yet you tell me nothing! Well. You must be happy now that my punishment has been measured out."

Rhydderch turned to me. "Do you think it pleases me to witness my wife struck down before court when she is with child? To see her treated like a common prisoner?"

"I cannot say. I cannot say what pleases you or does not please you at all. I sleep at your side each night and wake to you each day, and yet it does not seem to me you care overmuch whether I stay or go."

Rhydderch's eyes were stormy. "You are gravely mistaken if you assume I do not care."

"Care," I said. "And what of love? Does a man like Rhydderch, prince of Strathclyde, feel love for anything but his kingdom? For his own wife? For I have given my life over to you as is expected. And you give me nothing but silence."

Rhydderch's shoulders dropped. "Is this what you think? That I am incapable of love?" He lifted his head, and for the first time I saw his hurt.

"Someday, wife, you may be glad of my caution. For I possess it where you haven't any. I will concede I have been guarded. And now I wonder if I was not right in being so. You flee from our fortress in the middle of the night, carrying my heir, against the wishes of this family. Worse is the danger in which you put yourself. You could have met with raiders. The boat could have capsized in wintry waters. Had you arrived a moment sooner, you could have been beaten or raped by the mob, or given a mark to match your brother's."

"And what else should I have done?" I asked defiantly.

Rhydderch looked at me sidelong. "Languoreth, I have trusted you. Is this how you show me where your loyalties lie?"

I thrust the coverlet aside and flew from the bed, my face hot with anger.

"My brother is filleted from temple to chin! I spent the early hours of morning slipping about a chamber slick with his blood. Mungo's men did this. Tell me. What will be *your* answer? What will be the answer of your father? Tell me!" I shouted. "Is this how you show me where *your* loyalties lie?"

"Stop this. Stop this at once!" Rhydderch's jaw clenched as he caught my wrists. I glared at him, struggling against his grip as he yanked me toward him, pinning my arms against his chest.

"Listen to me. *Listen.*" He shook me and I stilled. "Do you wish to protect your brother, Languoreth? Do you wish to protect Cathan? Your kin? Yes?" He bent, forcing me to meet his gaze. I pursed my lips but let my body go limp, too exhausted to fight any longer. Rhydderch dropped his hands to his side.

"You would be a fool to think Mungo the most fervent among Christians. For if you think Mungo is fervent in his faith, perhaps you have not yet spoken with my brother, Morcant. Eh?" he said. "Morcant is my elder and more experienced in war. He is stronger. He has no qualms about doing what must be done to protect this kingdom. It appears you believe my position as tanist to be secure. But you and I now stand on a blade's edge. One slip this way, or one slip that, and we will fail. Then who will protect your people of the Old Way from conversion under the might of Mungo's mobs? Who will protect the rights of Keepers and freemen alike, their wives and children, when Morcant's men come calling, seeking to beat the devil out of Strathclyde? Answer me, wife. Do you dislike these ideas? Does such talk frighten you? Answer!"

"Yes," I said, my voice shaking. "Yes. It frightens me."

"Good." His face fell in relief. There was a long moment of silence before he reached carefully to take my hand. Rhydderch's voice was demanding, but his eyes pleaded.

"You must know that before the battle for my father's throne is over, I may have to do many things—say many things—that you will not like. But I will do it. For I would not see my people, my wife, or my children live in a kingdom ruled at the tip of Morcant's sword. You ask if I love you. I love you as much as I know how, in my own way.

You ask where my loyalty lies. My loyalty lies with you and with this kingdom. The power I believe in does not favor one way of believing over another. To my mind, all paths lead to God. But these are times unlike any we have seen. If I am to succeed in protecting our people—not just the people of Cadzow or of Partick but all the Britons in this hard-won land—you must never go against me again."

I blinked. Looked at the floor. "You let him strike me," I whispered.

"Yes," Rhydderch said. "And I would do so again, if it would keep you here."

I went to pull away, but Rhydderch cupped my face in his hands.

"You are my wife. One day, if the fates allow, you will be my queen. But you must act accordingly. I cannot protect you if you run away. You must have faith in me, Languoreth. And I will have faith in you. Next time you will wake me. I have men I trust. Next time you will take them. And from this day forth, you must do all you can to avoid angering my father. At all cost. For without Tutgual's support, all will fall to ruin. I would not wish the children of an enemy to live in the country where my elder brother might rule. And neither should you."

His beard brushed my chin as he leaned in to kiss me gently. When he withdrew, his face was shadowed.

"Sit now, and rest. I have spoken with the king. You will stand at my side on the morrow when Mungo and your father gather here to come to terms. But you must swear to me that whatever is done, and whatever is said, you will say nothing."

"Mungo will come here?" I looked up. "What does Tutgual mean to do?"

"I cannot pretend to know my father's mind." He stared at the flames licking against the hearth. "He has become increasingly unpredictable of late. He is no Christian at heart—that much is certain. But I think he was moved to test the limits of its power."

"So he set Mungo loose on Strathclyde."

"What are his lords and chieftains to him other than gaming

pieces?" Rhydderch bowed his head. "It is much like when he pits one slave against another: he is curious to see who is strong enough to slay whom. In the eyes of my father, Mungo has won. Your father must strike back. We must both of us wait and see what the morrow brings."

I looked out the window. "Father would slit Mungo's throat if he could."

Rhydderch closed his eyes a moment, and I noticed the dark circles of sleeplessness beneath them. "It will be deadly if he does. It could be deadly if he doesn't. Your father is a strong man with a clever advisor. He will find some way to settle the matter. But enough of this talk." He straightened and offered a faint smile. "I, too, have been worried for Lailoken. I sent for news; he is arrived at Buckthorn and is resting. We will hear more on his condition tomorrow, I am sure."

"Thank the Gods." I let out a breath and sank back on the pillows.

"Now you must rest." Rhydderch opened the chamber door. "Our lady will have a bath," he called out, then turned to me. "Dine here tonight. Sleep. In the morning you will be by my side when we return to court. It's done now. By tomorrow all will be forgotten."

Forgotten? I nearly said. *By whom?*

My shame and my fury still burned; my face yet pulsed from Tutgual's blow. But my body was racked with hunger, so much so that I felt sick. Desdemona entered with a plate of food, and suddenly I could do nothing but try to satiate the sudden and ravenous demand of my body, soaking up the meat's juices with hunks of warm, crusty bread.

Exhaustion claimed me. I finished eating. I bathed.

I slept until morning, my hand resting protectively upon the curve of my stomach.

CHAPTER 35

Father and Cathan were late.

All morning, far below Tutgual's great hall, boat after boat had glided toward the fortress carrying councilmen and merchants, chieftains and lords. They shuffled in with solemn faces, surrendering their weapons to the soldiers standing guard over the armory drop. It brought me some satisfaction that the assembly could not be held in Partick; the risk for riot was far too great. But as the appointed time came and went, Tutgual's thin lips grew tight and his fingers traced the carvings on his throne in growing agitation. At least my father and Cathan were not alone in their tardiness; there was still no sign of Mungo.

The thought of laying eyes upon the bishop made me sick with rage. Truthfully, I did not know if I could control my emotions. But a score of Tutgual's roughest men stood waiting, eyes watchful and spears sharp. Conformity, I decided, could make a most useful costume. I had taken great care with my hair. I had applied kohl to my eyes and berry stain to my lips. I would allow neither Mungo nor the king to see how they had affected me with their violence. Perhaps I was learning at the elbow of my husband after all.

Around me the women chattered about a shipment of perfumes that had arrived from Galatia. The blow I had suffered by Tutgual's hand was nothing compared to the wound dealt my brother. I closed my eyes and tried to follow my connection to Lailoken, searching some inner landscape that traveled across the distance.

There. Was that a pulsing I could feel upon my cheek?

I am with you, brother, I tried to tell him. *You are my twin. Always I am with you.*

Across the room Elufed was seated behind Tutgual's throne, her pale fingers resting on her lap as she listened in apparent earnest to Morcant. He had the vulturelike eyes of his father, close-set in a way that pinched his features in perpetual meanness. His face was smug, and though I could not hear him, I knew he was ranting. About the righteousness of Mungo's cause. The injustice of this accusation. As he glanced up and caught sight of me, his eyes glinted in the light and I looked back unflinching, disgust pooling in my mouth.

"You look lovely." A timid voice stirred me, and I turned to find that Rhian, Morcant's young wife, had come to stand at my side.

"As do you." I smiled in spite of my nerves. Rhian deserved every kindness. She was pretty—fair-haired, with large blue eyes and a bow-shaped mouth. Her frock was tailored perfectly to highlight what curves she possessed on her girlish frame, but she was frail and bruised easily. Perhaps Morcant enjoyed that—that others could see the marks he left on her body. The purple splotch below her elbow, the twin thumbprints now fading yellow above the hollow of her throat. By law Rhian could leave him. I knew she never would.

"I was very sorry to hear of your brother," she said, her eyes full of sympathy.

"Thank you. He will heal in time. I suppose it could have been worse."

Her eyes flicked to Morcant. "That's what we say, isn't it? That it could have been worse. But truly it is always bad enough, just as it is."

"You're right." I followed her gaze. "It is bad enough, just as it is."

Rhian glanced away, frightened we'd come too close to the truth of it. "What do you think will happen today?" she wondered.

"I cannot say. I only pray that justice will be served."

"Then I will pray with you," she said resolutely. My heart swelled at her kindness even as, across the room, Morcant settled his hard gaze on his wife.

"You should be careful in speaking with me," I said. "Your husband does not like it."

She swallowed but straightened her shoulders. "We are sisters, are we not? Surely we must speak with each other."

"Of course." I reached to touch her hand. "Otherwise I should be very sad indeed."

Rhian smiled at this, but her happiness turned to alarm as she glanced over my shoulder at the door. "He's here," she whispered. "The bishop is here."

I turned as a score of brown-hooded monks entered, Mungo at their center. He walked contemplatively, head bowed and eyes downcast. His finely embossed bishop's robes hung limply from his slender frame, but I noticed his once simple wooden shepherd's crook was now cast in fine silver. Mungo bowed low as he greeted the high king. His eyes touched calmly on Morcant's.

He harbors no fear, I thought. *He imagines his position in this kingdom to be that secure.* My anger threatened to boil as I took in the merchants who stood at the far end of the great room. In their thick satins and flowing tunics, in their cloaks trimmed in exotic embroidery, they watched the bishop reverently, as if he walked upon water, while their wives studied the handsome Brother Anguen by his side beneath lowered lashes. It seemed Mungo had more than one weapon in his arsenal, and I doubted he was unaware of it. I glanced impatiently at the doorway.

Where in the name of the Gods were they?

Please, Father, be clever, I begged. *Don't keep the king waiting overlong.*

Just as I thought Tutgual was going to stand and call the Gathering at a loss for my father, the slow troop of footsteps sounded from the corridor and the crowd fell silent.

I turned to see Cathan, his thick gray hair woven neatly into a plait and his sloping shoulders drawn tall, moving with purpose through the entryway. Brant came next, followed by the rest of our retinue. At last my father appeared, face grave and mouth set firm.

His wavy auburn hair was loose and his torque shone heavy about his neck as he strode casually to the armory drop to deposit his sword and two knives, bending to adjust the lacing on one of his boots.

When he straightened, his dark eyes found mine and he gave me a reassuring nod.

Tutgual warned my father even as he greeted him. "Morken. You have kept us waiting overlong."

"My apologies, my king." Father moved to the center of the room. "But as you well know, I am short one vessel, and today I travel in large company."

If Father's tardiness was intentional, his words were inspired. He reminded the king of the injustice we'd been dealt, and that a king of the north was no longer safe within the walls of Strathclyde's own capital; he must travel with greater guard.

"As you can see, I have come without my son," Father continued, clearing his throat. "Lailoken is not yet strong enough to travel."

Perhaps a prod too much. I glanced nervously at the high king, but Tutgual only bowed his head in a display of pity. "May he recover soon."

Tutgual gestured to the center of the room. "I have called you together in hopes of finding a peaceful resolution to the strife between you and the bishop. This time is yours. State your grievance."

Father had yet to acknowledge Mungo. Now he turned his broad back to him as he addressed the king.

"Some weeks ago, this Mungo—"

"You shall address him as Bishop Kentigern," Morcant interrupted, lurching forward like a bear.

"Kentigern" was the name Brother Garthwys had been given at his naming ceremony. But Father only snorted, then continued.

"Some weeks ago, this *Mungo* arrived at my hall. His crops had failed and he demanded that I should come to his aid out of my abundance."

"And you refused this request," Tutgual said.

"Yes."

"It would please me to know why."

"Why?" Father looked up sharply. "First, because neither Mungo nor his monastery are within the confines of my lands. Of course this means by law I am not beholden to come to his aid. Second, because my own grain stores are low, and I must ensure that proper provisions are available to those who have pledged their fealty to me. Third, because this Mungo has been collecting taxes these past months on behalf of his church from the broader regions of Strathclyde. Why could he not buy or trade for the grain he wished for rather than demanding I provide it?"

Father cupped his hand to his mouth, whispering aloud. "He did not offer me any coin when he made such a request, though I have it on good account that his coffers are overflowing."

Some in the audience snickered, and Tutgual swept the audience with an ill-tempered look.

"And fourth"—Father turned, pinning Mungo with his stare— "because I do not like him."

Laughter rippled through the crowd, and my father gave a wry smile, but his eyes were rimmed with exhaustion. He'd had little sleep for two days. His son was wounded, and now he'd been summoned to the high king to arbitrate a violence that under any other circumstance would have been answered by instant death. And still no one had asked why Tutgual, in all his wealth, had not come to the bishop's aid himself.

Father straightened his shoulders and continued. "Two nights ago there was a raid on my grain stores. My sacks of oats and barley were plundered, my barns were burned, and one of my vessels was stolen; my men watched it departing upriver, toward the monastery at Bright Hill. As you know, my son is skilled with spear and sword. He rode out at the head of our men to defend my property only to find himself outnumbered." He paused, his jaw working silently. "For his troubles he was given a scar to match his father's."

Father touched the old wound, and the atmosphere in the room turned stormy.

Tutgual leaned forward in his seat. "And can you prove that Bishop Kentigern was responsible for this raid? Have you any witnesses? Any who saw him at your granaries that night?"

"This is not a man who fights his own battles," Father grunted. "Why should he sully his hands when he can incite others with empty stomachs to carry out his violence for him?"

He turned to face Mungo, jabbing a thick finger toward the bishop.

"*You shall not pollute the land in which you live, for blood defiles the land, and the land cannot be cleansed of the blood that is shed except by the blood of he who shed it.* This is a teaching of your faith, is it not? And yet men died for oats. For barley. Your own god calls for your blood." Father's mouth twisted. "Shall I let him have it?"

Mungo raised his arms in a gesture of capitulation, his pale eyes wide. "I do not wish a violent outcome to this matter any more than I wished violence upon your son."

"You *lie!*"

The mention of Lailoken snapped any measure of restraint my father had left. He crossed the room in five big strides. The first blow doubled Mungo over. The second, dealt with the force of a seasoned warrior, slammed Mungo to the ground. I gasped as the great room erupted into turmoil. Father's men bolted to his side as Tutgual's soldiers rushed in, swords drawn, from the edges of the room. Father's men formed a wall before them as the soldiers fought and shoved their way toward the bishop.

"Stop!" Tutgual shouted. "Cease this at once!"

I heard Mungo grunt as Father's boot collided with his ribs. Rhydderch sprang from his seat and pushed himself between the factions, arms thrust wide to keep both sides at bay.

"Steady, now," he said, voice low. "Steady all, steady."

Father raised his hands in mock surrender and backed away. Mungo lay curled like a wounded fox, but Father's eyes remained locked on him with a predatory gleam.

"This man peddles a belief built upon compassion. Yet, since his arrival in Strathclyde, our kingdom has seen nothing but violence!" Father bellowed over the shouts of the crowd as he pointed at the bishop. "Our sacred groves are felled. Good Christian men are found dead. His priests come into our homes and tell us our wives are not our wives! That our heirs are illegitimate! He says one thing, yet his deeds say another. This man is not a priest. He is a coward and a power-hungry fool. I am Morken, son of Morydd, and a king of the north. My grain stores were robbed within the walls of our own capital. My own son was mutilated. And in this matter I will have justice!"

I balled my hands into fists, my eyes brimming with tears. The room had fallen silent now, enraptured by my father.

"Enough!" Tutgual barked. "Morken. You have broken the laws of treaty. I will not warn you again."

Father smoothed a hand through his thick, wavy hair. Brother Anguen rushed forward, but Mungo stood on his own, addressing the high king.

"I am not injured." Mungo lifted his chin and winced, turning to the men and women who watched anxiously. "This wicked king has seen fit to cause me shame. But I would joyfully suffer such humiliation in defense of my Lord. In defense of my belief!"

Father's dark eyes narrowed in disgust. "Those blows were not for your God," he spat. "They were for your thievery and your malice."

"You call me a thief," Mungo said. "I shall let the king deliberate on the falsehood of your claim. But I would ask: Who is the thief, when children starve whilst this man is feasting through the long winter nights?"

Father stood tall. "I do not bow to your God, nor do I seek his justice. And yet I am increased with prosperity and abundance in all things. My Gods smile upon me. You call yourself a Christian. You are no Christian. You may have slithered your way into a bishop's seat, but you are full of lies and false miracles. Your faith is empty and your preaching false."

"Enough!" Tutgual thundered again.

Father turned and fixed him with a stare before finally bowing his head, giving way to the king.

Tutgual sat back angrily and beckoned to Mungo. "Bishop, come forward. You may address these claims."

Mungo touched a slim hand to his ribs as if to remind us of the blows he'd just been dealt, sweeping the audience with soulful eyes.

"It was Matthew, a disciple of Jesus who said, 'Do not be anxious about your life, what you will eat or what you will drink, nor about your body, what you will put on . . . Look at the birds of the air: they neither sow nor reap nor gather into barns, and yet your heavenly Father feeds them. Are you not of more value than they?' "

He paused, steepling his fingers. "It is true I visited this chieftain Morken, beseeching grain. And though I have children in my care whose stomachs roil with hunger, I was told to cast my burden upon my Lord. This man, Morken, scoffed at me, asking did I not travel these lands preaching that my God would sustain me." He smiled to himself. "Sometimes the voice of God can come from the most mysterious of places. And so I turned my thoughts to this man's message, though it was delivered in spite.

"Did I not believe my Lord would sustain me, and his people, in our time of need?" He tilted his head. "I prayed in isolation, taking no sleep or sustenance for days on end. And on the seventh day of my fasting, I heard a voice. It said unto me, *Worry not. For the waters of the Clyde will rise up, and the grain you seek shall be miraculously delivered to your people.*"

"Miraculously delivered." Tutgual blinked. "And you say this was so?"

"I have many witnesses who will attest to this fact, for we all rose together, and were equally humbled by the miracle that had appeared before us." Mungo spoke softly, his voice full of wonder. "Where my grain stores had been empty, now they were full." He stretched his thin arms wide.

Father scoffed. "He would deny his role in the raid that has taken place!"

Mungo looked up. "I leave it to my king to deliberate on such slanderous and outrageous claims."

"No more," Tutgual warned the bishop. "I have heard enough." Mungo's light eyes flickered between my father and the king, and for the first time I saw fear in them.

"I have reached a decision," Tutgual said solemnly. He cast his eyes upon the bishop, and I noticed with disgust that they were full more of disappointment than with anger.

"I find King Morken's grievance is not without reason. The bishop Kentigern shall henceforth return the grain by sundown on the morrow, along with the vessel his disciples have plundered to transport any goods."

Shouts of dissent and wild applause broke out all at once.

"But this was a miracle of God!" Mungo lifted his head angrily. "My king, you know not what you do. We have committed no thievery. This is a mistake! You would shun the hand of God for supplying grain to the needy!"

"Silence," Tutgual demanded. "Silence!" The clamor dropped, and the king turned to my father. "Morken. Does this resolution satisfy you?"

"I am glad you have ruled thusly," Father answered. "For this very morning I struck out and recovered my grain. I recovered, too, my vessel. There were a few . . ." He paused, studying his fingers. ". . . injuries. But none, I believe, are dead."

Mungo turned his head, rage contorting his face. "You have already acted thusly?"

The king pinned my father with a dangerous look. "Morken, you test the limits of our friendship."

"It did not gladden me to do so," Father said. "But no man shall steal from me without answering for it."

Tutgual considered him. "Now, then, you have been answered. You will leave this matter. It has been settled."

"Settled, perhaps," Father said. "But you ask if I am satisfied, and my answer is no. My son's wound is a debt yet to be paid."

Mungo looked anxiously at the king.

"This man is yet the bishop of Strathclyde," Tutgual asserted, "and as such, he will not be harmed. If any violence should come to him, I can assure you my actions will be swift and unforgiving."

The bishop stiffened beneath the weight of Father's stare.

"So be it," Father said at last. He strode toward Mungo, but three of Tutgual's men stepped in front, shielding the monk. Father raised a brow at them, then leaned forward, getting as close to the bishop as he was able.

"But I warn you, Mungo. You should keep yourself from my sight. Keep your monks from my tenants; keep your ghoulish face from my door. For if I should catch sight of you on my lands or near any of my people, I can assure you *my* actions will be swift and unforgiving."

Across the room Elufed's eyes touched on mine. I could not quite see, for her face was cast in shadow, but I could have sworn her mouth parted in the barest hint of a smile.

CHAPTER 36

"It is not enough," I said. The guests who had stayed had dined and gone to bed. Father and Cathan had chosen to sail home with the favorable tide. I stood before my dressing table as Desdemona helped pull my nightdress over my head.

Rhydderch looked up from his parchment, his eyes lingering on my figure. "It is all it can be for now. Morken did test my father. I worried for him. It is not a game he should play."

"Father could not afford to appear weak. Not in front of his men, nor in front of the bishop." I sat at my little pine table and studied my fingers.

"It matters little now." Rhydderch looked back to his parchment. "You heard my father. It is done. Neither party can act lest he face severe and sudden punishment. Surely there is a measure of safety in that."

"I wish I were so certain," I said. "Word will spread of Mungo's beating at the hands of my father. His followers will be vengeful. And as Cathan is his counsellor, everyone will know it was truly Cathan's words behind my father's speech this day. Isn't that the way it goes with kings and their Keepers?" I picked up my comb and set it down again. "Perhaps Tutgual will find he cannot so easily extinguish the fire he has kindled."

"My father can extinguish any fire." Rhydderch looked up darkly. "And we would all do well to remember it."

I swallowed and rose with some effort to stand behind him.

"There is something I would ask of you."

"What is it?" His voice was already weighted with dread.

"I wish to go to Partick."

Rhydderch looked up. "Why?"

"Can you truly ask me that? Why am I here on this rock? Each day my belly grows fuller with child. I should be in town, where I am closer to a healer."

Where I am closer to my family, I did not say.

"We have healers here," he said gently. "There will be priests to assist you."

"Priests," I said firmly. "What do they know of a woman's body? Ariane has left me. That cannot be helped. But let me at least retire to your father's hall in Partick. Surely it would be safer to labor there."

"You are here on this rock"—he used my words and they sounded petulant—"because the capital harbors sickness and disease. And now there is civil unrest. Armed mobs attack your father. Who is to say they would not strike out in search of you?"

"*You* are to say. Do you mean to tell me you believe any wife of Rhydderch, any daughter of Tutgual, could ever be in danger? With all your military might?"

Rhydderch's gray eyes pierced mine. "Languoreth. Tell me what is truly at the heart of this request."

"I want to be close to my brother," I said. "Lailoken needs me. You have not seen it. This wound and the way he bears it. His face may be scarred, but the wound runs much deeper."

Rhydderch studied me. "Do you believe this will make Lailoken an enemy of the Christian cause?"

"An enemy of the Christian cause?" I gave a humorless laugh. "Lailoken is that much already. Mungo has made certain of that." I looked at him, imploring. "You talk of causes and allegiances. Have you forgotten? Over these past months my brother has also become your friend."

"Yes. In his visits these past months, Lailoken has become more to me than my own brother, I cannot deny it. But I have seen such scars of war, and I know their price. I do not know that any man has the power to ease the bent of Lailoken's mind. And at what cost to you? No, you must allow Lailoken to come to it himself."

I refused to look away. "But I shall be quite safe at your father's hall."

Rhydderch sighed. "Very well. I can see you will not be swayed. So be it."

"And nearer to a healer of my choosing," I added.

"Languoreth, do not test me." Rhydderch eyed me warily and pushed back his chair to stand. "I will secure my father's permission. But when it comes to the birth of our babe, the child's birth must be attended to by a priest. Morcant's babes have been so, and our child must be, too, if he will stand a chance to rule." He leveled his gray eyes at mine. "If I consent to Partick, you must promise me that."

I paused, weighing it. I knew enough of healing that I could at least prepare some medicines for pain and numbing in advance. I could raise my child on the stories of our gods and our people. But Lailoken. I had heard from Brant he wasn't eating, that he spent hours upon hours staring at the fire.

I reached for Rhydderch's hand and traced my thumb over the curve of his knuckles.

"Very well, then. A priest. I can agree."

"And Tutgual will not be eager to let you have your way," he warned. "You have angered him. Now you give him an opportunity to deny you."

I looked into his eyes. "Then we will speak first to your mother."

"My mother?" he laughed. "And what makes you think she would come to our aid when it was she who first demanded you stay on Clyde Rock?"

I looked at him, curious. Could a man as clever as Rhydderch truly be blind to the true nature of his own mother? I nearly said as much, but Elufed had granted me her confidence and I dared not press my fortune. Betray her, and I did not doubt she could destroy me in ways I could not yet imagine.

"She has been mother to a babe three times over," I said instead. "Surely she will understand the strength of the desires that accompany a woman with child." I waited, my heart pulsing in my throat.

"Very well," he conceded. "But I warn you: Do not set your mind to it. We will speak to her in the morning."

Tutgual's hall was near the center of Partick, as if the village had seen its majesty and risen up to surround it. I had only ever glimpsed it from the road; the leering soldiers posted at its corners had always caused me to quicken my horse. Now that I was married to one of Tutgual's sons and nearly seven moons with child, my days of being leered at were behind me. Here, out of the way of sea gales, the high king had spared no expense. Pearl white and braced with dark timber uprights, its windows were cast in thick green glass that gave the impression, when standing inside any of the six private chambers, that one was drifting beneath summer water. They were the work of a Roman glazier, no doubt, most likely from overseas. The great room was decorated with oil lamps and a glittering array of silver-tipped shields. Sumptuous fleece-lined couches and elegant tables lined the room, which could feast close to one hundred, and the two rectangular stone pits set side by side in its center provided warmth. Beyond the great room stood a buttery and larder, where food from the kitchens was dressed and brought in to be served. Another small hearth burned with peat there; it was where the servants laid out their cots to sleep at night.

"It has been too long since I've had occasion to visit town," Elufed said as we stepped onto the shelter of the porch. Icicles hung from the thatch and glinted in the afternoon sun, their spindly horns dripping onto the planking where the soldiers stood alert.

"Do hurry up, Breg. I'm entirely frozen." She blinked impatiently as Breg moved forward to open the heavy doors. He gave a curt nod and Elufed stepped inside, dropping her cloak into the waiting hands of a servant.

"And stoke the fires," she called to no one in particular. "They may have been set, but they are not nearly hot enough. We have guests coming this night. I want to feel these fires blazing."

"It is most generous that you have invited my family to dine with us tonight," I said to her as Desdemona helped me and Crowan with our cloaks.

Elufed was already drifting toward the great room to inspect its cleanliness.

"It's true," she called over her shoulder. "I don't like the trouble of moving residence in winter, but I always prefer the busyness of town to the snow and sleet on that despicable rock."

Out of the corner of my vision I could see Crowan taking in every detail of the high king's hall. The finely woven tapestries, the decorative railing on the stairs that led to the private chambers, the Roman statue that stood garish and out of place just beyond the king's oaken throne at the head of the room.

Behind me, two servants entered carrying my trunks, and Elufed turned suddenly, eyeing my stomach. "And with Rhydderch's travels, you cannot be expected to spend your days here alone. You're with child, after all."

"That's very gracious of you."

"Yes," Rhydderch said. "I hope you'll find some pleasant diversions, Mother."

"Oh, I expect I shall," she said, sinking onto a couch beside the fire. Her eyes trailed to the door, and I wondered if Elufed dared take a lover while she was out from under the watchful eyes of the king. As if reading my thoughts, she turned to me.

"Everything will be in order for the arrival of your father and his retinue this evening. They'll spend the night, I expect." Her stormy eyes lit; she was thinking of my brother, no doubt. I stiffened.

"Yes, if it is no trouble. It is so kind of you to entertain us. Lailoken, especially, has kept to his chamber since his injury. It is difficult to believe it was little more than a fortnight ago." I locked eyes with her in the hope my meaning would not be lost.

"Such a handsome young man. It was all such a pity." Elufed frowned, her elegant nose wrinkling at the thought of it. "Still, we shall be glad for some company."

I cast Crowan an incredulous look before turning to Rhydderch. "I'll retire to our chamber now, if it pleases you. I must see to our things."

"Very well." He looked at me solicitously. "But do not exert yourself overmuch. You must rest before supper."

I watched as he glanced about the room and settled into a chair at a safe distance from his mother.

"Why do you sit there? I haven't got the plague," I heard Elufed complain as I slowly climbed the stairs.

"Of course you don't, Mother."

My heart swelled with pity for my husband; she had already worn him weary. Outside, the sky darkened and snow began to fall.

It was going to be a long confinement indeed.

Snow had piled thick on the branches outside by the time I heard the horses. I lay down my sewing and rushed to the window. The green glass distorted the snowy world beyond, but the white flanks of Cathan's horse glowed in the darkness, and I could see the bulky wooden cart that my brother had come by.

Crowan lifted her head. "Are they here, then?"

I nodded and she stood on stiff legs, worry lines creasing her face.

"Come, now, Crowan, he's all right," I assured her. "You know it drives him mad when you fret. Surely Thoma would have forbade him from traveling to town were he still unwell."

"Ha" was all she said, and I knew she was right: few could tell Lailoken what to do.

The plucking of the cruit sounded from the great room, and I glanced down from the stair to see Elufed draped over a couch with an embossed silver cup in hand, her golden hair loose in waves about her shoulders. In the trance of evening firelight she looked somehow softer, more inviting. Then a rush of wintry air gusted in as Father ducked through the door, brushing snow dust from his hair.

"Father!" Ignoring the order of things I rushed past Rhydderch, breathing in the familiar scent of him as Father gripped me close.

"Morken. Welcome." Rhydderch strode to clasp Father's arm, his eyes intent. "I hope all has been peaceful in your corner of the world."

"Peaceful enough," Father said.

Elufed rose from the couch, her pretty lips in a frown. "It was an ugly business. Let us speak of something else. It is bitter cold outside and you have traveled in the dark. Come and let our servants tend to you."

Father bowed to Elufed as Lailoken stepped in from the porch. He scuffed the snow from his boots, the hood of his cloak still obscuring his features. I took a tentative step forward.

"Brother." I smiled. "I'm so glad to see you. Here, let me help you with your cloak."

His blue eyes were somber as I reached to tenderly push back his hood. Behind me Crowan let out a gasp and I cringed, wishing I could have silenced her. It wasn't the wound, though it was an angry, boiled welt. It was the burn itself that was the worst of it. Small bubbles of fluid had risen in a mottling of pearls down the side of his face, hanging from his jawline like sacks of dew. These blisters, I knew, carried the worst risk of infection, but they did not look unwell. I kept my face emotionless even as my heart convulsed at the sight.

"You're healing well," I said too brightly. "I've missed you."

I reached out to help him unfasten his brooch, but he jerked away. I dropped my hand to my side as Brodyn came to grip Lailoken's arms, his voice painfully cheery.

"Cousin! At last, you are among the living. Come and sit by me. I'll show you the way of it."

"Oh, he knows his way well enough around a cup these days," Brant said dryly, shrugging off his cloak.

"Pay him no mind." Brodyn threw an arm around Lail's shoulders, guiding him toward the fleece-lined couches. "You're entitled to your drink, cousin, that's what I say. Tell me, Brant misses me, does he not? He is never forthright with his feelings . . ."

Lailoken mumbled something I could not hear as Cathan appeared and embraced me, his hair smelling of snow.

"Lailoken does not seem to know the trouble I've gone through to arrange this," I said.

The Wisdom Keeper's eyes trailed my brother. "Give him time, child. I know it does him good to see you. Just now he cares for no other troubles than his own. We must try to have patience." He gave me a gentle smile. "I, for one, am glad to have you in town once more."

"And I you." I clasped his hands. "But your hands are cold. Come, warm yourself by the fire."

Cathan cast a weary glance round the room, his eyes lingering on the Roman mosaics and the gilded shields. "I will need some drink."

Elufed overheard him and gestured languidly. "Drink. Of course. Bring our Wisdom Keeper and the great chieftain Morken some ale! Come, we will sit."

Across the room, Lailoken stared vacantly into the fire as Brant and Brodyn chattered on. His wavy hair had grown longer and was yet brown streaked with blond, and he wore it loose about his shoulders. I could see where it had nested in snarls at the base of his neck.

I moved to stand beside them, throwing a pointed look at my cousins. Brant looked up. "Come, Brodyn. Show me these fine shields you've been speaking of."

Brodyn straightened. "Right. The shields."

"You needn't treat me like an invalid. Or a dullard, for that matter." Lail gave them a dark look.

"He's been like this." Brant stood and spoke low as he nudged Brodyn toward the shields mounted on the wall. "Supposed to leave home soon to begin his training on White Isle, and now he's even talking of setting it aside. You'll set him right."

Suddenly I wasn't so certain I could have any influence at all. Perhaps Rhydderch was right. The scar had been dealt. My brother must face his darkness alone. And yet I could not bear the thought of it.

"May I sit beside you?" I asked. Lailoken watched me with a stranger's eyes. I cleared my throat. "I hope you know the lengths I went to keep Crowan from flying at you with her comb."

Lailoken did not smile.

Fine. If he would have no humor or niceties, I would get straight to it. I let out a puff of air. "Brant tells me you have set aside your Keeper's training. I told him I could not believe that to be true."

Lail gave me a black look before settling his gaze once more on the fire, and I felt my anger mount.

"Would you truly sit here in my own hall and refuse to speak to me, brother? Do you have any idea how difficult it was for me to escape a confinement on Clyde Rock? What I had to—" I bit my tongue.

Better Lailoken not know the bargain I'd struck.

Lail turned. "Tell me how difficult it has been for you, sister. Was it difficult for you, too, when you branded my face?"

The blaze from the fire suddenly nauseated me as I remembered the clammy grip of my fingers on my knife, the sickening smell of burned flesh as it met open wound.

"That is a cruel thing to say. What would you have had me do? Would you rather I'd let you die?"

"Aye." He tossed his head. "It would have been kinder. Now no man will look me in the eye. None who know my name will ever shrink in fear of me. What king will want me for his counsel when I was pressed down in the hay and slit like a sow for the slaughter? Song Keepers in faraway courts tell my tale even now."

"So you pity yourself, then? And you would make all of us suffer whilst you commit yourself to a wasted life staring by the fire? Sweet Gods, Lailoken. Are you so vain you cannot see beyond your appearance to the wound that festers within?"

"You know nothing." He turned away, his deep voice bitter.

I fought to keep my voice even. "I know you are yet handsome, Lailoken. Your scar and your burns will heal. Some may mock you. For this you would give away all ambition for the life of a warrior, a counsellor, and a Keeper that you have always wanted? If that is so, then you are not the man I once knew."

Lail scoffed in disgust.

"Yes. You will be forever scarred. But so will the tales the Song Keepers tell of you if you shrink now from your destiny," I said. "Mark me, Lailoken. If you do not cease in this self-pity, then Mungo's infection will only spread. Is this what you desire? To let him bend and twist you until you are unrecognizable even to yourself? Even to your own sister?" My voice broke. Lailoken risked a glance at me from the corner of his vision.

"You needn't shriek like a harpy. I will come to it," he said gruffly, crossing his strong arms against his chest. "I need more time."

"That may well be," I said. "But whilst you sit and stare into the flames, there is a deadly world of rough men and raiders whose shadows daily creep closer to our doors." I stood to face him so he could not avoid the warning in my eyes.

"I only pray you will not wait too long. For you are Lailoken, son of Morken, son of Morydd, son of Mor. I know in my heart you are bound for something greater. The Britons need you. *I* need you," I said. "How do you want the Song Keepers to tell your tale? You must decide that this will be the beginning of your legacy, my brother. You cannot allow it to be your end."

Lailoken looked up, and I thought I saw his eyes flicker before he fixed his gaze over my shoulder. I felt the cool fingers of Elufed on my arm.

"Elufed." Lail stood. "My queen."

"Come and join us," Elufed said. "The table is set with wine and ale. Lailoken must be ravenous. It is time to eat."

"Of course." I dipped my head, and Elufed slipped her arm into my brother's. "I have been goading Lord Rhydderch to tell me of his recent dealings with Aedan mac Gabhran, king of the people of Manau," she said. "He's a Westman, you know. Just last week we nearly caught fifteen of his men attempting to raid our cattle."

My brother bent his head politely and escorted Elufed to her seat. The meat was served and soon talk of politics consumed them.

The meat was tender and my body seemed to crave it, but after a while my head began to spin from the wine and the heat. I drew a hand across my brow to wipe the perspiration away.

"It is blazing in here," I whispered to Brodyn.

Across the table, Cathan looked up. "Languoreth, you look uncomfortably warm. Have you eaten your fill?"

I nodded.

"Good. Then come and take some air with me."

I gladly reached to accept his hand as he helped me from the table. It was gnarled now, lumps forming on the fractured bone as it healed like galls on a tree. It would be difficult for him to track his observations of the stars now, with his quill hand misshapen and bent. He should have allowed me to set it.

I looped my arm through his as we made our way past the musicians and out onto the covering of the porch. Outside, I took in a deep breath of winter, closing my eyes as the welcome chill cooled the flush of my face.

"You look well," Cathan said, appraising the length of me. "With any luck the babe will arrive after Beltane."

"With any hope." I reached to touch the swelling of my stomach. "But Ariane always said first babes are ever late or early."

"Ariane was a loyal friend," Cathan observed. "It's only natural you shall miss her. But Wisdom Keepers will wander. You can't have expected that she would stay with you forever."

"You have."

"Well." Cathan stroked his beard with a laugh. "Your family has made me fat and overly comfortable." He glanced at me. "The truth of it is, I grew too fond of my old friend Morken and his rascal children."

A silence fell between us and we leaned against the Hall to watch the snowflakes fall. After a moment Cathan turned to me.

"Have you considered where the child will be born?" It was the way he asked, hushed in the snow; there was something beneath it.

"Rhydderch has asked he be born with the aid of a priest, and I have agreed," I said.

"A priest." Cathan said. "But he is his father's son. As such, should he not be born under the Old Way?"

"As his father's son . . ."

"Come now, Languoreth. Do you take me for a fool?" His voice was gentle but his gaze piercing. I looked at him.

"Of course." He bowed his head. "We shall not speak of it here. But I do not ask out of mere dalliance. It's the child."

I eyed him warily. "What about the child?"

"You must know I look after you, even when we may be apart," Cathan began. "I did not wish to speak of this. I had hoped we could make arrangements without such discussion . . ."

My mouth suddenly went dry. "Cathan, speak, I beg you."

He closed his eyes a moment, the lines etching his face making him appear suddenly quite tired. "I have had a dark Knowing, Languoreth. If we are to try to prevent what may come, your child must be born on White Isle."

"White Isle?" I straightened. I had never even set foot upon the sacred isle. Now I was to travel there to bear my child? I shook my head. "This is impossible. I have sworn Rhydderch an oath. The child is to be born under the care of priests. I cannot risk his displeasure in this."

"An oath. I had hoped some such thing would not be the case." Cathan fixed his eyes on the snow, thinking. "You will have to break it."

He spoke as if it were the simplest thing, like drawing breath. "Languoreth, you know I would not ask it of you if I believed there was another way."

I blinked a moment, my world spinning. "Even if I acted against Rhydderch's wishes, they would come searching for me. They would send soldiers . . ."

"To White Isle?" Cathan stepped back. "I'd like to see them try. I don't know a man in Tutgual's guard fool enough to trespass on my land. No," he assured me, "once you are arrived safely, there would be no more trouble to be had. You'll bear the child, and what is done is done."

"So you may think, but you are wrong. Tutgual would not forgive such an act. Nor could my husband. Rhydderch is a man of his word, and I have given mine. I have already abused his trust once."

Cathan studied me. "I hear fear in your voice. I know Tutgual is frightful. I know you are loyal to your husband. But I must ask you, Languoreth. Do you love this child?"

My hands again cradled my stomach. Did I love my babe? This child that now tossed and kicked inside of me was all that bound my heart together. More than a living memory, this babe was made of me and of Maelgwn, and the ferocity with which I felt its presence nearly took away my breath.

"I love this child more than any living thing. But what you ask is too much. If I must risk this—if I must agree to risk everything—you must tell me, Cathan. What did you see?"

He turned to me, his eyes shadowed in evening snow light.

"It was my hope that you could take me at my word. Once told, such visions can be haunting. They can be . . . impossible to forget."

I looked at him expectantly, and the Wisdom Keeper looked down, rubbing the dry skin of his knuckles. "Very well. As you wish it.

"I sought the fortune of the child you now carry. But where I had hoped to find blessings, the Gods showed me a vision of a fortress in flames. Men were shouting. Bodies were piled. Rivers of blood soaked the soil. In the midst of it all, I saw your son drowning in fire."

I clutched for the porch post.

"Ho, now." Cathan reached to steady me. "Not everything I see takes root in this world. If you bear him on White Isle, the Gods may protect him. That is my hope. It is a place between worlds, sacred ground, steeped in the rituals of the ages. If he is born there, I can beseech the Gods' blessing." Cathan covered my hand with his. "If he is born there, it is possible the event I have foreseen may never come to pass."

"Possible?" I shook my head. "All this for *possible*? No. There must have been some error. You say you saw my son. But we do not even know if this child I bear will be a son or a daughter." I spoke out of desperation, as if I could wave it away. But Cathan turned my face to his, his blue eyes intent.

"The child you carry in your womb is a boy," he said. "The son of a Dragon Warrior. And if he is not born on White Isle, I fear he will not live long enough to become a man."

CHAPTER 37

I did not speak of what Cathan had told me to anyone. I moved through the evening and the following day with my head full of fire and the haunting memory of the crow's call. The thought that the bird had come that day to warn me of my child's death made me suddenly sick, and I leaned over the washbowl in my chamber, retching until there was nothing left to purge.

As I wiped my mouth with the edge of a linen, I knew I had no choice. I must go to White Isle. For if I did not, and my child suffered the death Cathan had foreseen, how could I carry on breathing?

I glanced at the bed where I lay each night beside Rhydderch. I had sworn him an oath, and promised to come to him first should I ever be in need.

Perhaps I had not seen proof enough of miracles to risk the betrayal this would be to my husband. But had I not walked the slopes of a mountain on Lughnasa, seemingly unseen, a talisman at my breast? Who was the specter those at the festival saw that day, laughing and drinking, while I lay beneath a canopy of trees with Maelgwn?

The babe in my belly was proof of the Gods' magic.

Yet Rhydderch would never give way when it came to the Christian birthing of our child; he'd made that much clear. What if I told him of Cathan's vision and he forbade me to go? I could not risk it.

This warning was a gift. If the Gods had seen fit to send Cathan a Knowing, how could I fail to protect my child?

No. It did not matter what punishment Tutgual would exact, or what Rhydderch might do. Beat me, imprison me. Take away my life. In an instant everything had changed. So long as my child should live, it no longer mattered. That my child would not suffer—I would sacrifice anything for that.

But my journey would need to be timed down to the moment. Leave too soon and I would þe discovered before the child was born. Too late and I would not make the journey through the forest and onto the boat in time to bear the child on sacred land. Cathan would need to escort me, and Crowan . . . Tutgual knew I cared for her. I could not bring her with me, but I could send her on some errand. Ensure she knew nothing and was occupied or safe. I would not tell her of Cathan's Knowing; she'd fight me tooth and nail for fear of my health. Brodyn, likewise, would fear too much for my safety.

I would need someone to send word to Cathan when the time came, and there was only one person I could rely upon to do my bidding. I found her in my chamber and she looked up from her mending with a flicker of annoyance.

"Desdemona, I would speak with you."

"M'lady?" She finished her stitches and set down her work. "Are you needin' me to stitch another frock?"

"No." I lowered my voice. "I fear I must ask you something much more dire. I must ask you to do something for me. There is none other I can trust."

Her eyes shifted, but then she said, "Aye, m'lady. Tell me wha' I might do."

"I need you to get a message to someone when the time comes, no matter how dangerous. Can you do that?"

"If it be dangerous . . ." She swallowed in hesitation. Or perhaps it was in fear. "Might'n I know wha' it's to do with?"

"I'm sorry, Desdemona, but I cannot yet say. Please, I beg you. You are the only person I might trust."

She looked at the ground but dipped her head nonetheless. "Aye, then, m'lady. I'll do it."

"And you must swear you will not speak a word of this to anyone. Not to Crowan, not to anyone."

"Aye." She fixed her dark eyes on me. "I swear it."

"Thank you." I touched her shoulder and bowed my head. "Desdemona. I am grateful to you indeed."

The snows melted and tender shoots of fern began to spike up through the soggy springtime ground. Nearly nine moons had passed since I'd lain with Maelgwn. From my chair under the shelter of the eaves I watched the rain fall in thin sheets of mist and prayed he was keeping warm. Word came that Emrys had brokered a peace with the new Angle king, and since then there had been an eerie sort of peace in the Border-lands. But not knowing if and when I should ever see Maelgwn again left a feeling in my bones like a fracture that ached before a storm.

I had taken to sitting outside regardless of weather. Inside the hall the air was cloying and Elufed's eyes scarcely left me. Inside, I had to be careful not to sink my hand into my pocket where I could close my fingers around the soothing metal of Maelgwn's ring.

"Why have you always got your hand in your pocket?" Elufed had asked one dreary afternoon as we sat weaving in the front room.

"Habit, I suppose." I didn't look up. "I like dresses with pockets. It gives them a purpose."

She had shaken her head, but her eyes had rested on me a mo-ment too long. Since then I had been more careful to keep my secret close. It was not beneath Elufed to send a servant rummaging through my things. I had thought that, being shut indoors together for the last months of winter, we would come to know each other; but in all the hours we'd spent in Partick, she hadn't breathed a word of much significance. Nothing of her past, nothing of her people. Nothing of Mungo or the Old Way. She spoke of fabrics and fashion, and delighted in hosting elaborate feasts featuring spices from the Orient and dates from the sun-drenched shores of the Mediterranean that were so sweet, they made my cheeks pucker.

I let out a sigh as a shuffle sounded from over my shoulder. The door swung open and I turned to see Desdemona peering at me like a mouse.

"Hello, Desdemona." My voice sounded tired. "What is it?"

"The queen, m'lady." She squared her shoulders. "She says your husband and the king'll be here. She's wantin' you to come in an' dress."

I glanced out into the yard where Tutgual's men stood stiffly at their posts, blinking in the rain.

"Dress. Of course," I sighed, and pushed myself up with some effort.

"You must be bright an' glad to see Lord Rhydderch again," she said as I shuffled reluctantly inside. "If you like, I'll fix a fetchin' plait in your hair."

"To what end?" I was well aware I had let my appearance go to seed, but I did not need reminding of this from her.

She shifted uncomfortably. "What wi' you bein' with child and all, m'lady, an' your husband travelin' so oft—"

"My husband has no taste for strange women," I said sharply.

What business was it of hers? Rhydderch cared for me. He was loyal to me. The pounding of my husband's pulse was reserved for politics. He kept me safe, and when he was home he sought to teach me about the maneuverings of the world beyond Strathclyde's borders. He thought well of my intelligence and treated me as his equal. For that reason alone, I owed him my fealty and—I supposed—the respect of appearing presentable when his father and his retinue arrived to take up summer residence in the hall.

I turned to Desdemona. "My apologies. I did not mean to be so harsh."

"It's no bother, m'lady. You've much weighin' on your mind of late."

"It's no excuse for ill behavior."

Desdemona smiled gratefully as I gestured for her to lead the way down the corridor. I had scarcely reached the stair when the call came up from the guard.

Desdemona's eyes widened. "Sweet Gods, is tha' they, come so early?" She rushed back to the door, peering through the crack. "Stay back, m'lady," she said when I tried to look. "We mustn'a let 'em see you in such a state!"

"Very well," I sighed. "Who is it, then?"

I watched as she squinted, then frowned. "Not the king. It's only a single rider." She drew in a breath. "It's . . . a Wisdom Keeper! I— I canna see his face; he's got a hood up 'gainst the weather . . ."

"Oh, this is foolishness. Let me see," I insisted, opening the door. I stepped out onto the porch to see a white-robed figure lift a hand in greeting to the soldiers. I would recognize his outline anywhere, but the sight of him in crisp white cloth, his brown and golden-streaked hair shaved into a tonsure at the forehead and plaited neatly away from his face, made me wonder if he wasn't some sort of apparition.

"Lailoken."

My brother's handsome face creased into a smile at the sound of my voice. He ducked under the eaves and out of the rain, knocking a clump of mud from his boots. His wound was a deep red gash that traced the curve of his cheek, mottled and angry, but it was healing. I was so relieved to see that the glint of good humor had returned to his eyes that I nearly forgot to congratulate him.

"You've been given your robes!" I exclaimed, rushing to embrace him. "You look so well!"

I held him at arm's length. "So this is it, then? You're to begin your training in earnest?"

"Aye." He grinned.

"And when will you depart for White Isle?" My pulse raced with hope: that Lailoken would be there to greet me; that I could bear my child among family there.

But his face shifted. "I depart even now, sister."

"Now? You leave for White Isle now?"

"No, not for White Isle. There is a master in the north, deep in the mountains, whom Cathan greatly admires. He has sent word to arrange it. He expects me even now."

I stared at him. "Up north? But Cathan has said nothing of this. Why would he send you away?"

"Each Keeper must find his own master. Cathan has been a teacher to me these many years, but he cannot take me any further. The man I travel to see—he is the one I must train with now."

I swallowed. "But . . . you will miss the birth of your nephew."

"Yes."

I closed my eyes. "I do not want you to go."

"Eh?" Lail said. "But wasn't it my own sister who said I must complete my training?"

I looked at him standing there, so proud and strong in his robes, and gave a sad smile. "I know you must. And I am proud of you, brother. It is only that I shall miss you so."

Lailoken met my eyes. "Then we will not say good-bye. We shall only say farewell for now. When my training is complete, I will return home and find my calling in the land of the Britons. We will be close to each other again. And I shall meet my nephew." He smiled at the curve of my belly.

"Then this is how it shall be," I said.

"This is how it must be." Lail looked up, offering me his hand, and I took it.

"But there may yet be a spot of sun in my departure," he said.

"Nay, there is not."

"Indeed. For I will first travel south, to set sail from Rheged. There is a student there called Taliesin. We are to travel together. I will rest a few days at Emrys's camp before traveling on to Rheged. Surely there will be those among Emrys's retinue who will be glad to have some news of you." Lailoken's eyes locked on mine so I could not miss his meaning. He would carry a message to Maelgwn.

I glanced over Lail's shoulder. One of Tutgual's men stood with his back to us, his eyes set on the road but his ears pricked like a hound's on the hunt.

"Then you must tell our brother Gwenddolau that not a day passes that I do not think of him. Tell him I think of him every time I look out to sea," I said carefully. "Tell him I keep our memory of the forest tucked away in the safety of my pocket."

Lail's eyes questioned but he nodded all the same. "Very well. This I will tell him."

"Thank you." I looked at his face as if I could press it into my memory.

"Don't look at me so," he scolded.

"How?"

"Like I am either an earthbound god or some condemned mortal. Men have sought their souls in the mountains since time out of memory."

I forced a laugh. "Well, you are certainly no god."

"So you might say, but I know many a fair woman who might disagree."

"Incorrigible." I managed a laugh, but my brother's eyes were fixed on Tutgual's hall. Our smiles faded.

"It's dreadful in there," he said. "It is the only reason I hesitate to leave."

"Yes. And the high king will return now for the season."

Lailoken's face was grim. "Sister, you must promise me something."

"I would promise you anything."

"Whilst I am gone, you must not forget who you are."

"Oh? And who am I?" I asked, in an effort to make light.

"You are Languoreth." He gripped my hands, squeezing them almost 'til they hurt. "You are daughter of the great chief Morken and the Wisdom Keeper Idell. The Old Way flows through your body; it lives in your very veins. There is power in that. You must never doubt it. When it comes to these people, you must never give way."

I drew back. "You think that of me? That I could set aside my family, my blood, all my learning?"

"I do not think that. I fear it. I have visited this court of merchants and priests. I know Tutgual rules by the strength of his sword. You are no longer with us, and now I am leaving. If the tide should turn—"

"I am no fair-weather seaman, Lailoken."

I wanted to tell him of the baby and White Isle, but Tutgual's man was listening. And perhaps I didn't wish to know which my brother valued more: my life, or that my child be born of the Gods of the Old Way. My eyes went to the welt on his cheek, and Lailoken bent his head in acknowledgment.

"You were right, sister. They meant to take away my power, yet they have only made me stronger," Lail whispered. "When I return to Strathclyde, I will be a Wisdom Keeper the likes of which Mungo has never known. Let him try to rise to me then. I will crush him where he stands."

The guard did not hear. My brother spoke of power gained, but we shared the same sickness: our hatred of Mungo. I could feel in my body where his deeds had darkened me, too.

"Then I will wait for you," I said.

We pressed our hands together, sealing our vow. Lail looked up, scanning the dull sky for the promise of sun.

"I must go," he said, drawing up his hood. "The morning's half-gone and I have a long day's ride ahead. But I could not leave without saying farewell."

"You are right on that count, for I never would have forgiven you."

"Nay. The truth is you will forgive me anything." He winked and ducked off the porch and into the rain. Giving his horse a swift pat, he pulled himself astride.

"We are brother and sister, after all," Lail said. "We must always forgive each other. It is what we must do."

The way Lail said it—as though it was not entirely in jest—made me shiver a little to think what his words might foreshadow, and I wrapped my blanket more closely around me.

At the gate, my brother turned and lifted his hand in farewell. I thought he might have said something, but I couldn't hear against the sound of the rain, and his face was blurred by the ocean of my tears.

Inside, I blotted my face with my sleeve, leaning for a moment against the solid wood of the door.

"And who was that?" Crowan called, sticking her head over the railing. She blinked so expectantly, I couldn't bear for her to know Lail had come and gone and hadn't bothered to tell her good-bye. *Tomorrow*, I thought. *I will tell her tomorrow.*

"Nobody. Just a Wisdom Keeper who'd lost his way."

"Doesn't sound very clever for a Wisdom Keeper." She frowned. "Did he figure out where he belongs?"

"Yes." I looked up. "I believe that he did."

"Well, then. Are you coming up, or would you see Desdemona old and gray first?" Crowan thumped her little foot impatiently. "Poor thing's been waiting to ready you!"

I sighed, too wrung out to say anything more. Upstairs, I traced the teeth of my ivory comb as Desdemona bustled, laying out a woolen dress the color of sorrel and pulling green amber from my jewel chest to match.

By the time I was ready, I could hear the crowd gathering outside along the road. The rain had let up and a cheer sounded as I followed

Elufed onto the porch. Much of Partick had turned out to welcome the high king. I lifted my hand, offering a smile. Somewhere from the midst of the throng, music began. I shifted my weight between my feet, puffed like rising dough above my tight leather shoes. Desdemona looked down.

"Your feet—they're so swelled, m'lady. Here, lean on me."

"Thank you." I took her arm gratefully as the low rumble of carts sounded in the distance. At last Tutgual's retinue came into sight. I spotted Rhian, her golden hair spilling in waves from beneath her cloak. The king rode haughtily on his black mount with Morcant beside him, his eyes glinting with pleasure at the shouts from the crowd. Just beyond them followed Rhydderch, his dark head bowed graciously as the people of Partick caught sight of him and cheered. I could not help but notice how Morcant's face darkened with envy to see how the people loved his younger brother.

You should *be envious, you horrible monster*, I thought. Morcant locked eyes with me then, as if he could somehow read my thoughts. A wet gust swept through the courtyard and I shivered, forcing myself to bow in deference to the king as he swung from his horse and adjusted his sword.

Gathering my skirts, I greeted Rhydderch with a kiss.

"You look well." The fine lines around Rhydderch's eyes creased with his smile as he embraced me. His beard was damp and smelled of horses.

"And how is our babe?" he asked.

"Kicking," I smiled.

"Good."

He turned and gave a respectful nod to the crowd before offering me his hand and leading me inside, into the warmth.

• • •

"Will you not go and sit with the other warriors?" I asked Brodyn. He sat beside me in the great room later that night, tearing rather moodily into his portion of beef.

"I am in your guard, Languoreth, not the king's." He took a deep draft from his cup.

"But would you like to sit with them?"

"Ha." He glanced up, taking in their scarlet cloaks and thick armor. "Would I like to sit with them? My sweet cousin, there isn't silver enough in all the land."

"I thought as much. Then stop your staring. You're going to cause a fight."

A crash sounded, and I looked up to see that a cluster of Tutgual's soldiers had gotten into a skirmish without Brodyn's help. They laughed as blood spurted onto the stone from an unlucky warrior's nose and Brodyn's dark eyes flashed with disgust.

"My little cousin's gone off to the mountains and I'm here, watching these cockwarts wrestle."

Of course, I should have known. Brodyn was a true warrior, and here he was, taken from Father's service and placed with me while Lailoken sought his fortune and his brother, Brant, got to raid and to fight.

"Your sword was of great use to Father," I turned to him. "But it is of even more use to me."

"My hope is that you will never have need for my sword, and yet I admit I am suffering to use it. I long to fight," he said.

I threw him a look of pity. "Cousin, I—"

A thunderous pounding sounded on the hall table and silenced the room, interrupting us. The king would speak. I looked up as Tutgual smoothed his graying hair and looked out over the crowd of drunken warriors.

"It has been a long winter," he said. "Now spring has come, and the blood of the Britons heats with the warming of the land. Soon it will be time for raiding our enemies and claiming our spoils!" A roar went up from his men and Tutgual's thin lips spread in a smile of satisfaction. He lifted a hand for silence.

"I have watched you grow fat this winter on my mead and my meat. Beltane nears. Now I would see which of my warriors are yet fit enough to fight. We will have our fire festival here, but in the name of Christ. And one week from this day I will host the races to please him. The champion's prize will be no less than ten heads of cattle, ten silver pieces, and one-tenth of this season's spoils." He raised his silver goblet aloft. "May my best warrior prove himself worthy of honor!"

The hall thundered with a resounding cheer.

The horse races. It was like an omen from the Gods themselves. The races lasted the length of the day and the feast would be held in the fields beyond the race path. Our servants would be occupied in cooking and preparing the comforts of camp for Tutgual and his retinue. It would have to be then. If only the babe would wait. There could be no better chance to slip away. I could scarcely believe my luck.

Across the room Tutgual's men hawed about this one who loved his stallion too much, or that one who'd gotten himself impaled before the race had even gotten under way. Brodyn watched with a scowl.

"You say you yearn for a fight, cousin," I said. "I just might be able to give you one."

I leaned in, and told him of Cathan's warning, of my plan. I could see his eyes spark, but then he shook his head, reaching for his cup.

"I do not like it, Languoreth. Something in this makes me uneasy. If you must ride out, I must go with you."

"But you will be with me, cousin. I'll be only a moment's ride ahead. Tutgual's men who must stay behind will be drunk; we both know this. Please. I only need a few moments' distraction. You will find me in no time."

He ran a hand over his face, considering. "And you say I may beat them as much as I please. So long as they are not dead."

I nodded. Brodyn's white teeth flashed in a smile, but it faded just as quickly.

"But what of Rhydderch? Surely he will not sanction such a plan. You've told me yourself he wishes the child to be born with the monks. Wives have been thrown over for less. You must speak with him."

"How can I speak with him? Rhydderch may care for his babe, but he thinks only of maneuvering. Now more than ever his mind is set on securing a kingdom for this child. No, he will not understand what is at stake."

Brodyn leveled his gaze on me. "Do not underestimate what a man may do when his wife goes missing whilst heavy with child."

"I tell you, Brodyn, I have gone over it time and again. There is no other way. I will not risk the life of my son."

"Very well. I will do it. But I have one condition."

"Name it."

"You must agree to wait for me beyond the tree line. Do not depart for the boat without me. I will sort Tutgual's guards, and then I will come for you. If I know Cathan, he will not wish to draw attention; he will travel alone. I must ensure that you both arrive safely to White Isle."

"Very well," I said. "You have my word."

I touched my cup to his.

"Oh, did you hear? The races!" Rhian beamed, her fingers nearly fluttering with excitement as she came to sit beside us. "My father would never let me attend. How I longed to see the horses gallop . . ."

Her eyes were shining and her fair cheeks flushed with excitement. Brodyn's dark eyes swept her appreciatively and I stiffened. Goodness, no. Nothing good could come of that.

"Whatever will you wear?" she wondered.

"Well, I suppose it doesn't much matter; I cannot go," I gestured to my stomach and she blushed.

"Of course. How foolish of me."

"It's no matter, truly," I said, hating to dampen her spirit.

"If you cannot go, then I shall stay with you," she said. "You'll be in want of company. The races are a bloody business anyway. Galloping or not, I should be glad for some peace and quiet."

"No, Rhian, you mustn't." I smiled through my mounting panic. "I'll be well cared for here. And I'm sure your husband will want you in attendance. I couldn't bear for you to miss any fun on my account."

"Nonsense. I'll speak to Morcant. He'll see the sense of it, I'm sure."

Yes, he likely will, I thought gloomily, *if only so he might whore with other women.*

"So it's settled, then?" Rhian looked at me expectantly. "We shall spend some time together?"

"Of course." I squeezed her hand. "I shall be glad to have your company."

She stood with a smile. "Good. Then you will excuse me. Mention of the races has my husband in a fair humor. I'll speak to him now."

Our eyes met. "Very well, but please, Rhian, don't press him."

"Don't think of it," she said softly. "I've come to know him well enough."

I watched as she gathered her skirts and walked away.

Brodyn drained his cup. "Well, that's not good. I suppose you will want me to distract her, too. I'll do it if I must."

"Do not jest," I said firmly. "Any man would be a fool to touch Morcant's wife. Besides. Rhian needn't suffer any more heartbreak. She deserves a man who would love her."

Brodyn said nothing, but I couldn't help but notice the way his eyes followed her as she crossed the room.

• • •

Later that evening Desdemona stood at my back, helping me undress. I'd tried to rush Crowan off to bed but she'd lingered, chatting about the richness of the stew, and did I see the cloth of Elufed's gown? How fine it was! At last she yawned and shuffled away. The moment the chamber door was shut, I glanced up, catching Desdemona's eyes in the mirror.

"Desdemona. Do you remember our agreement some days ago? What I asked of you?"

Her face paled ever so slightly but she nodded. "Aye, m'lady."

"Good. I need you to get a message to Cathan first thing in the morning. He'll be at Buckthorn with my father."

"As you say. I'll do it."

"What is it?" I turned to her. "Are you frightened? Surely we've traveled that way through town hundreds of times before."

" 'Tisn't that, m'lady. It's only . . ." She glanced away. "Well, am I right in thinkin' m'lady doesn'a want me followed?"

"Followed?" I frowned.

"There's a man, ye see. Sent after me! Crowan, too, when we're off to market. Anyplace, truly, if m'lady's set us upon it."

"What do you mean, a man? A soldier? One of Tutgual's men?"

"Aye."

"Why haven't you told me of this?"

"Beggin' your pardon, m'lady. I s'pose I didn'a think anything o' it. I thought they were protectin' us is all! But now I ken it's somethin' secret, I thought you should know."

"Elufed," I muttered. It had to be. First the rifling through my things, and now she was having my servants followed. I rubbed my temples. "Of course. You have told me now and I am grateful. But what am I to do?"

Desdemona stared at me blankly.

"Tomorrow is Sunday," I said, "is it not?"

"Aye, m'lady."

"There will be Christian services beyond the Gathering Place then, won't there be? They gather to hear Mungo spout his vitriol one day each week."

"Aye." She looked away, suddenly uncomfortable. "I mean, I'm nae certain . . ."

"Some of the servants go; I've seen it. You could accompany them. Elufed's man will follow, but once the sermon commences you could slip out. You could be back before it ends and none will be the wiser. I realize I am asking much of you," I said. "But I would not ask it if I did not believe you could do it. Will you do it, Desdemona?"

Her fingers worked a loose thread on her dull gray frock. "Aye," she said after a moment. "An' wha' will I tell Master Cathan?"

"Tell him I will meet him beyond the tree line in the forest after the sound of the first horn of the races. He will know what to do. And, Desdemona?" I took her hand in mine. "No one must hear of this. Do you understand? No one."

"Aye, m'lady. I swear it." Desdemona went to my bed and lifted back my coverlet. I watched as she touched the back of her hand to the heated rock at the foot of our bed. "Aye. It's hot the now," she said.

"Desdemona, you've been very good to me." I looked at her as I eased my way beneath the covers. "You must tell me if I've upset you," I pressed. "Is it the Christian service? You must know, it isn't betraying your gods, Desdemona. You needn't stay, after all. You needn't be baptized, for goodness' sake!"

I smiled but she didn't return it, moving instead to blow out the wick of the oil lamp.

"Nay, m'lady. Do na worry yerself o'r me. Get your rest, then. I'll see you in the mornin'."

CHAPTER 38

The day of the races came cool and clear, a crisp spring breeze rippling the dark glass of the river. The hall had been in a frenzy for weeks, and somehow the babe had not yet dropped. Father was in Partick for the races and had come to see me.

"Let the lords think I've come for the races." He'd winked. "I'd not want to miss the birth of my daughter's first child." My belly was still round and high, and when I gently prodded my opening with my fingers, I was relieved to find it had not yet softened. But it would have to be today. I would not have another chance.

Rhian leaned against the porch post beside me in a scarlet gown, watching the men mount their horses.

"They are already in their cups," she said, casting a nervous glance at her husband. Most of the servants had traveled ahead to be certain the ale was flowing when the king and his retinue arrived. The grooms would soon be departing, too.

"Then 'tis a pity Morcant isn't racing," I murmured. "I should hate for some accident to befall him."

Rhian's eyes widened and she reached for the Christ symbol she wore about her neck. "Pssht! You mustn't say such things! Someone might hear."

I lowered my voice to a whisper. "They say your god is one of compassion, and yet he lives."

She bowed her head quickly to conceal her smile. "Do not jest," she scolded. "You had best be careful or *she* will hear. She is always listening."

She looked at Elufed, perched gracefully on her dappled horse as her servant arranged the drape of her cloak over the beast's smooth haunches.

"So I am not the only one she has set her spies upon."

"Spies?" Rhian looked alarmed. "I don't know about spies, but she did follow me one night when I left my chamber to visit the privy!"

"You see? That's precisely what I mean," I gave a small laugh, wishing I hadn't said a thing. I pointed. "Look. I think they're ready to depart at last."

The gate clattered open and Rhydderch turned his chestnut mount back toward the hall.

"Wife! If we should have any happy news, send a rider straightaway," he called out. His gray eyes, once so shuttered, were so warm and open that it made my stomach swim with sickness. Would he ever look upon me like that again? I forced a smile and lifted my hand, waving them off brightly.

Soon the courtyard was empty save four men posted at the gate. The race would begin in the wood that bordered the eastern edge of town. I would be riding in the opposite direction. Brodyn was to saddle Fallah, then clear the courtyard of the men posted at the gate, all without being seen. Desdemona stood nearby. She'd been quiet all morning but had assured me she'd reached Cathan with word as I'd planned. There was Crowan to manage and now Rhian. Already Crowan had been watching me as if she could smell something foul on the wind. She jostled Desdemona aside to stand at my hip even now. And all of this was to take place in the instant I heard the first far-off blow of the horn.

Cathan would be waiting.

In my chamber I'd packed a satchel with birthing herbs, a clean dress, and soft woven swaddles, bundling the whole packet tightly in one of my traveling cloaks. The hilt of my knife had dug painfully into my stomach as I bent to stash my bundle beneath one of the fleece-lined couches in the great room, the one closest to the door that led to the kitchens. I'd prayed when it came to the knife, I'd have no need of it.

"Well, that's it, then," Rhian sighed. "Let's go inside. You should rest. Look, your feet are so puffed."

Crowan led the way and I took the arm Rhian offered, feeling wretched for deceiving her. "You're such a kind sister," I said. "Better than I deserve."

"Nonsense," she said. "You're the one who's been kind to me. Now let me look after you!"

"Very well." I smiled. "What shall we do then to pass the time? Shall I show you my weaving? I've been working at it these long, slow months."

"Yes!" She brightened. "I've yet to see your loom."

"It's in the chamber off the great room," I said. The truth was, it was a dim room used for storing wet-weather gear and not fit at all for weaving, but Tutgual wouldn't have a loom in his great room, even in his absence. We passed two servants still cleaning up breakfast, the younger one nearly tripping as she rushed past us with the heavy wooden serving board.

"Put the meat up," the older girl called out. "Hurry, then, or we'll miss the start o' it!"

"Watch where you're going, now," Crowan scolded. The girls looked up in horror as they caught sight of us, dropping their heads in a curtsy.

"Unless you'll be needin' anything at all, m'ladies," the older one flushed.

"Nay. We are quite all right, thank you," I assured them. "Off you go."

They raced off toward the kitchens and I heard the telltale slam of the door that led out to the stables and the midden heap, the route I hoped to take. My eyes went to the couch where my things lay waiting in the shadows. I hadn't much time now.

"The purple!" I threw up my hands. "Rhian. You must see the purple wool. It's dyed with whelk and Rhydderch acquired it at some expense. Crowan, will you show her where to fetch it? It's in my chamber, in the trunk with my skeins."

"The purple?" Crowan wrinkled her face. I hadn't a purple wool, but poor old Crowan wouldn't remember.

"I'll go wi' 'em, m'lady," Desdemona said quickly. She was too full of nerves. I wanted to reassure her that all would be well, but what could I say?

"Right you are." Crowan nodded as they led Rhian away.

I waited 'til they had turned the stairs before hurrying across the great room and ducking clumsily beneath the couch to gather my belongings. Fastening my cloak with trembling fingers, I had just concealed my satchel beneath its folds when a voice came low at my ear.

"And where might you be going, Lady Languoreth?"

I spun to find Morcant standing within a hairsbreadth of me, his eyes lit like those of a wolf who'd just cornered a hare.

"I knew you were fixed to do something you should not," he said. "It's as though I can sense you. The way your mind works." He closed his heavy-lidded eyes and leaned in to breathe the scent of me, his nose sickeningly close to my neck. "You are disobedient. A savage." His hand shot up and gripped my chin even as I tried to pull away. "Stay still, now, little rabbit," he scolded. "I'm going to decide what must be done with you."

I knocked his hand from my face, trying to sound braver than I felt. "Release me at once or you'll rue the day you did not."

"Oh, I'll rue it, will I?" Morcant gripped me again, his face darkening with rage, and I swallowed, bracing myself to be struck.

"Crowan sent me down to inquire which trunk—" Rhian blanched at the sight of us, her eyes flickering over my traveling cloak. Morcant's hands fell to his sides but he did not back away.

"Husband," Rhian said. "You are due at the races."

"I left my sword behind," Morcant lied. It was yet housed in the baldric at his shoulder. He had come to catch me out; he and I both knew it.

"The lady Languoreth seems to be stealing away. And what might you know of this?" He lifted the edge of my cloak as if some game were afoot and turned his eyes upon his wife.

Rhian brushed boldly between us, drawing me away.

"She is cold, that is all. I told her I'd fetch her a blanket, but this cloak brings her great comfort. It belonged to her mother."

"Is that so? Have you caught a chill, Languoreth?" His eyes roamed my body. One flick of my cloak and my satchel would be revealed; a trained warrior, he would not miss the outline of my knife.

"I have caught a chill." I raised my chin, pulling my cloak more tightly about me. "I would have told you as much myself had you given me the chance."

Morcant looked as if he would say more, but Rhian laughed, a sound so odd, it startled me.

"Hot in winter and chilled in spring! But what do I know of pregnant women?" Her smile was innocent—it did not falter—yet I glimpsed a hard resignation behind her eyes. Rhian was offering herself up as whipping horse. It drew Morcant as she intended.

"What do you know indeed." Morcant took three menacing steps toward her, turning his back on me. "Did you tell your sister Languoreth that you are barren? Did you tell her of all the times I have taken you, you lying beneath me, a wanton whore, only to have you leak your blood month after month like a worthless sow?"

Rhian's smiled faded but she did not shrink away. Her eyes met mine and looked mortified, frightened. For me. I wanted to intercede, but I could only make matters worse.

"Come, now, husband. Such talk."

She lowered her gaze, peering at him sweetly from beneath her lashes. "And you are cutting such a powerful figure today. Sure the races are bound to begin any minute, but couldn't you miss out on a moment's revelry? You can be certain you'll not regret it."

"Lord Morcant."

Rhydderch's brother stiffened as one of his men strode into the room.

"Here," Morcant said, his eyes never leaving us.

"Are we to stay as you commanded? The race is about to begin."

Morcant looked between the two of us for a long moment, then snorted dismissively.

"No. We are leaving."

I exhaled as he turned to walk away, but he stopped beside Rhian, his face pinched with disgust. "I've wasted enough of my seed on you."

The door slammed behind him and Rhian wilted against the wall, boneless.

"Thank you, Rhian, I am so sorry—"

"Never mind it. You are leaving. Do not tell me where. That way he cannot beat it from me." Her voice was clipped. "Only tell me: Is it with good reason?"

My eyes fell upon the symbol at her neck. "I do it for my child."

She nodded. "Then it is reason enough for me. And you will come back?"

"I will come back." I took her hand. "I pray he will not strike you . . ."

"It doesn't matter." She pressed my hand before glancing up at the railing. "You had better go. Crowan does not know?"

"It is safer for her that way."

As if Crowan could sense us, she stuck her graying head into the upper hallway to holler from my chamber door, "Whatever are you gabbing about? Shall I come down or stay up? There's no purple up here, not that I can see!"

"Tell her I'll be back," I said quickly. "Tell her that I'm sorry."

"I will tell her nothing, for I did not see you leave. Now go!"

Wasting no more time, I rushed past her and through the kitchens and out the midden door. Brodyn had saddled Fallah as promised, and my horse shifted now, edgy, as I heaved myself upon her. From beyond the fields at the western border of town the solemn blast of the horn sounded.

"Go, Fallah, Go!" I urged her.

My stomach seized in pain as I kicked her into a gallop, one hand bracing my unborn babe as I streaked toward the gate.

"M'lady! Stop! Halt!" one of the guards shouted, lifting his spear before he was silenced by a stout knock from the hilt of Brodyn's sword and the gate was shoved open so I could pass. I glanced back over my shoulder to see Brodyn had drawn the other three to him already, his taunts fading beneath the beating of Fallah's hooves. As I cut due west through town, past shuttered shop fronts and temporarily abandoned halls, there was no one to see me except Partick's wandering ghosts. I did not slow until I reached the fields, and only then because otherwise I was certain to injure myself or my child. My breath was coming shallow and fast as I entered the dappled shelter of the wood.

At last.

Here I was at the tree line, but I could see no sign of Cathan. Suddenly a flash of white caught my eye. There was the old Wisdom Keeper, emerging from behind an oak on his trusty mottled gray horse.

"Languoreth! Thank the Gods, you've made it. Are you unhurt?" His face was creased in worry. I nodded and gave a dismissive wave as I pulled Fallah to a halt beside him, still catching my breath.

"Very good." Cathan reached a tender hand to pat my hair. "Then we must hurry now. My boatman will be waiting. You cannot trot, and we must make haste." He swung his mount round and I turned quickly, scanning the field beyond the trees.

"We must wait for Brodyn," I said. "I swore to him we would not leave."

"No." Cathan tightened his grip on the reins. "It's no good. We cannot wait."

"But I promised—"

"It does not matter what you promised, Languoreth. If we are to save the child, we must go now."

I swallowed my sense of unease and swung Fallah about onto the soggy forest trail. There was no turning back now, and Brodyn would catch up to us soon. With his protection I would feel more safe.

"The timing of this . . . How did you know Tutgual was going to host the races?" I asked as I ducked beneath a low-hanging branch, wanting to distract myself.

"I did not know, but I hoped," Cathan said. "Winter with its sea storms has been too long, and like that of all kings, the blood of the high king thirsts for violence. There have been no Westmen to cut down, no raids to be had. He must have some blood sport before the season begins. He cannot help but whet his appetite."

A shiver traced my arms. "Father's blood does not thirst for violence."

"Your father is just. He does his duty for the land and the Gods, and in turn the Gods protect him. He is an honorable man and better than most. If I did not believe that, I would not have counselled him for so long. But all leadership is blood, Languoreth." Cathan looked at me. "Whether king or queen or chieftain, you cannot come to your seat without being willing to spill it. Your own and that of others."

We fell into a solemn silence as we rode side by side, listening to the soft trill of birdcalls in the trees overhead . . . then, from somewhere far off, the rasp of a crow. After a moment Cathan turned to me, his blue eyes as watery as the sea.

"Truth be told, I am blood sick and weary," he said. "Sick to my spirit with war. All of this nonsense over whose god is true. Gods rise and fall away. Such is the way with gods. Our gods replaced that of the ancients, and now there is a new god who comes from over the sea. So was it ever."

"How can you say such things?" I asked. "You above all, who have always spoken of our gods' magic?"

"When you have lived a life as long as mine, you come to understand that all gods, and all stories, are different names for the same thing. Beneath it all, there is one god with many faces, but always one god. There is one story with many variations, but always the same ending."

"And what is the ending?" I asked.

"Death," he answered simply. "Oh, do not look at me so, Languoreth. For we all know as surely as we are born, our time will come." Looking at him now, I could see his clear eyes were rimmed pink by exhaustion. He shook his head as if to clear it.

"I look at you now and I see a young woman. Why must everything age, and so quickly? It was only yesterday you were a little girl, sitting in your lessons with me high above the river. Now we travel to White Isle so you might bear your own child." His voice grew thick and he turned back to the trail lest he be overcome.

"Yes," I said. "Time passes too quickly."

The Wisdom Keeper only gave a satisfied "Hmph" and unbuckled his saddlebag with some fiddling, retrieving a crusty loaf of bread and a hunk of cheese wrapped in cloth.

"Here, eat," Cathan said, handing it to me. "Agnes baked it off this morning and just for you. Soon you may labor. You shall need your strength."

I accepted the loaf, reveling in its yeasty smell, but ate uneasily, half listening for the sound of Brodyn's horse.

"He should have joined us by now," I said. "He was to follow on my heels."

I glanced up as a dark silhouette caught my eye and I spotted a crow gliding onto a high branch overhead, bobbing its head with a startling caw. It made me cringe in my saddle, plucking at my already disquiet nerves. Cathan looked up, curious.

"If Brodyn is not yet with us, it is for good reason," he said, watching the bird. "In any case, a little ways yet and we'll be at the water's edge."

"As you say," I flinched involuntarily as the beat of feathered wings sounded within inches of my head and looked up to see another inky form settle in the treetops.

"That one nearly hit me," I said.

The Wisdom Keeper glanced up. "They're gathering." There was a note of warning in his voice. An omen. A bad omen.

My skin pricked into gooseflesh and yet they kept coming. Bird after bird flocked to the canopy overhead, their fathomless eyes fixed upon us. Soon the trees were thick with them, nodding and squawking. I looked at Cathan only to find his bearded face had gone grim, his eyes searching the brambles ahead.

"So, then," he said, as if to himself. "It is to be now."

"What is happening, Cathan? You frighten me."

Cathan turned to me as we tightened our grips on the reins, nearing a sharp bend in the trail.

"Guard yourself, Languoreth," he warned over the racket, but there was no time for anything more. There was a streaking figure, and then Cathan's mount reared up with a terrified whinny as a man with a spear sprung out from behind a tree. His shout had startled Cathan's horse, and, caught unawares, the Wisdom Keeper sailed from its back, cursing as he came down on his shoulder with a sickening crunch.

"Go, Languoreth, ride!" he shouted as he scrambled to his feet, staff in hand.

But I could not leave him. Spinning round I saw more men rushing from the forest wearing heavy, coarse wool tunics and brown trousers. Thieves. Fallah twisted, bucking beneath me, and I clung to her with my thighs, my teeth gritted as she came down hard. I gripped Fallah's reins and rounded on them with a cry, but a flash of metal and a sharp sting made me gasp.

"Stop!" a male voice demanded.

I yanked the reins, pulling Fallah to an abrupt halt. A ruddy-haired man with a pockmarked face had appeared seemingly out of nowhere.

"Drop your reins," he said. He motioned with the spear that had pierced me. A warm trickle of blood seeped between my fingers as I reached to touch my throat and blinked against the pain of it, raising my hands. The spear tip had grazed my windpipe: half an inch deeper and it would have impaled me completely. The man stepped forward and tore Fallah's reins from my grip.

"You're in want of riches. Take my jewelry," I said. "I will hand it over freely. But leave the Wisdom Keeper. He has nothing."

"Languoreth!" Cathan's voice was sharp. I swallowed as a hulking man stepped forward, clearly their captain. He had an underbite that made him look brutish and wore his yellow hair in a bowl cut like Morcant's. His eyes lit with amusement at my offer.

"Your jewelry." He looked as if he might laugh.

"Did you hear me?" I demanded. "I have rings. An amber hair comb—"

Cathan turned to me, his voice low and fierce. "These men have no interest in riches, Languoreth. Listen to me now! You must do nothing foolish. Think of the child and do exactly as they say."

Cathan maneuvered himself between me and the ruddy-haired spearman, addressing their captain.

"Nine men," he said. "You must tell your lord Mungo he flatters me."

My stomach pitched. These were no common thieves. These were Mungo's men. Cathan and my father had beaten Mungo at his own game. They had struck and humiliated the bishop. Now he would have his revenge.

"Shut your mouth, old man." The captain motioned for his men to surround us, their blades flashing in the filtered light. "Drop your staff."

Cathan's eyes were full of a deadly fire as he tossed his staff away. "I will give you no fight. And you, in turn, will not harm this girl. You know who she is, do you not?"

The captain raked his eyes over me. They settled on my torque.

"Yes, this is the wife of Rhydderch," Cathan continued. "Daughter now to King Tutgual. Harm her, and they will not only come for you. They will come for your wives. For your children."

The captain gave a hard laugh, looking at Cathan a moment as if deciding what to do.

"I said shut your mouth," he sneered suddenly, and in one swift motion he had ducked down to grasp Cathan's staff, swinging it up with a thwack that sent Cathan sprawling back into the mud, blood spurting from his nose.

"Cathan!" I shrieked. The Wisdom Keeper touched a hand gingerly to his face, then waved me away.

He stood with some effort, wiping his nose with the back of his sleeve. "You call that a blow? Pass me my staff, fool, and I'll show you how to use it."

"Cathan, no!" I called out. The captain lifted a brow and cracked the staff round again, doubling Cathan over with a grunt.

"Stop it, please stop!" I sobbed. Cathan staggered to stand before another blow sent him plummeting onto his knees.

At the sound of my voice the captain turned as if he'd only just remembered my presence, jerking his head. "Get her down from that horse."

"You heard him." The pockmarked man jabbed me with his spear. "Get down or I'll spike you."

I came down too hard on wobbly legs and stood helpless as he whipped the shaft of his spear against Fallah's flank.

"Get on!" he shouted. Fallah had never been struck. The blow sent her careening into the undergrowth. I wrapped my arms around myself as I watched her gallop away.

Brodyn, Brodyn, Brodyn, I chanted, as if he could hear me. But what good was Brodyn against nine armed men?

The captain strode toward Cathan once more, testing the weight of his staff in his hands. "This is a fine staff," he said, leaning in close, his face within inches of my beloved tutor, my dearest friend. Cathan's head lolled at an unnatural angle. His snowy hair had come loose from its braid and was streaked with blood.

"Yes, I like this staff. I think I'll keep it." The captain straightened, looking at the men. "String him up," he commanded.

"No," I shouted. "No!" I watched in horror as one of the men took a heavy coil of rope from behind the towering old oak we stood beneath and I realized what they meant to do.

My hand flew to my knife. Drawing it from its sheath, I slashed out with a cry and felt the satisfying yield of skin as the pockmarked man cursed, dropping his spear.

"Cunt!"

The spear tumbled to the forest floor and I snatched it up, moving with an agility that belied my condition. The yellow-haired captain looked up in surprise as I held the tip of the spear against his throat.

"Step away," I demanded, my eyes darting wildly around the circle of men, my knuckles white on the shaft of the spear. "Step away or I'll kill him."

The captain looked at me, but his face was impassive. "Grab her," he said.

They came at me in a collision of bone against flesh, knocking the breath from my lungs as I landed in the mud. My stomach spasmed in pain and I gasped, openmouthed like a fish, clutching my belly.

Hands yanked me up by my hair, pulling me to my knees.

"That'll show you, making me bleed," the pockmarked one spat at me, twisting my arms behind my back. I cried out as the captain surveyed the forest, his hard eyes impatient.

"Hurry up," he ordered. "Do it now! You," he commanded the ruddy-haired man. "Hold her down."

"Don't touch him! Don't you touch him!" I screamed, bucking against my captor. He wrenched my arms back, impossibly tighter.

"Oh, we plan to handle him; that we do. And you'll watch it all," he hissed in my ear. "You will watch your friend swing like a cow."

With a great heave, one of the men tossed the noose over the sturdiest branch of the oak, slackening the rope until it dangled within reach. Two men with eager grins hiked Cathan up by his elbows, knotting his hands with a length of cord behind his back.

"No, no, no . . ." I could not stop saying it, my mouth open, tears and saliva dripping down my face.

"Shut her up," the captain yelled. "I said hold her down!"

Brodyn must be coming. Someone must hear me. I opened my mouth and let out a scream as two more men came forward and grasped the dangling end of the rope. They meant to haul him from his feet in a slow and agonizing tug-of-war rather than grant the Wisdom Keeper a swiftly broken neck.

"My family will find you, I swear!" I shouted. "I will watch as they kill you!"

"Languoreth!" Cathan's voice stilled me.

I looked up and our eyes met. His beard was rusty with blood but his face was pleading. He shook his head.

He did not want me to fight for him.

My chest collapsed and I went limp, silent tears coursing down my cheeks as they forced the noose over his head.

But the men were growing nervous now. The crows were cawing in the trees overhead. I had forgotten their presence in the chaos, but they were cocking their heads at Mungo's men, watching with beady eyes, their cries nearly drowning out the human voices below.

Cathan lifted his blue eyes to the treetops. His swollen face stretched into a smile of delight. "You see that, fools? My gods are watching . . ."

"Stop his mouth! He would curse us!" a man shouted. Cathan's smile faded, his eyes finding mine.

"Look away, Languoreth," he commanded. "I would not have you remember this."

I shook my head, my tears a burning river. I could not look away. I would not leave him.

A curse rang out from one of Mungo's men who stood beside the Keeper.

"It's the blasted birds!" the man shouted. Splatters of bird droppings were raining down, caking their eyes with white and streaking their hair and faces as they retched, clutching the rope at the base of the tree.

Now there was panic in the captain's voice. Fear.

"Do it now!" he shouted.

Cathan's stormy eyes widened in surprise as he was pulled from his feet, gagging as his own body weight tightened the rope around his throat.

I closed my eyes against the horrible sight of his agony, but I could not drown out the sounds: the gurgling that went on and on as they held him suspended from our sacred tree like butchered meat, the heaving of my breath as I bent to retch into the forest muck.

I could not drown out the sounds, so instead I let them fill me, and they filled me with such torrents of hate that I began to think my body could not possibly bear it. I did not open my eyes because I did not need to. The faces of these men were etched in my brain.

And I swore that if they did not kill me, they would regret the day they let me live.

CHAPTER 39

When it was over, I found myself staring at the captain's battered leather boots planted in the mud before me.

"Leave her," he said. "She won't get far."

My captor let go of my arms and I collapsed onto the ground, my body gone slack. My skin felt waxy from shock and my throat was still bleeding. The crows had scattered in a great torrent of feathered wind. I fixed my eyes on the forest floor, still splattered white with bird excrement, until the hurried footsteps of our attackers faded into the wood.

There would be no White Isle. Cathan was twisting in the breeze overhead. I pushed myself up onto one elbow and forced myself to look, sobbing again at the sight of him. The slack end of the rope had been knotted round a neighboring tree so that the Wisdom Keeper would dangle in perpetuity.

No. I would not have it.

They had taken my knife, and the loss of it meant I had no means to sever the rope.

I lifted up my skirts and ripped a strip of cloth from my ivory shift beneath to bind the graze on my neck. The ground beneath me pitched as I stood, and I leaned with my hand against the tree to stop the forest from spinning so I could focus on the task at hand. It was a shipping rope, coarse and thick, so the knot was large, but the strain of Cathan's body had drawn it impossibly tight. Gritting my teeth, I wrapped my hands round the taut line of rope and pulled with all my might. Nothing. Roaring in frustration, I searched the forest floor, at last unearthing a sharp-edged rock. Splintery fibers of rope embedded themselves in my palms as I gripped the rope in one hand and sawed furiously with the other. I worked through a blur of tears for an eternity, his body jerking on the other end of the rope. At last the rope severed, the momentum sending me crashing back as Cathan's body collapsed on the forest floor in an unnatural heap.

"Cathan." I dropped to my knees beside him, buried my face in his robes. The smoky smell of incense still clung to them, but it mingled now with the soiled rust of blood. Our gods had abandoned us.

Cathan the Wisdom Keeper was dead.

I opened my mouth to cry out for help, but just then a sharp pain in my womb caused me to double over.

"No, no, not here," I cried.

It was too soon, too soon. A sudden wetness trickled between my thighs. The babe.

My labor had begun.

When at last the sound of trooping hooves came, it had grown cold, so cold. My body shuddered. The wringing of my womb had been coming for hours in the twilight forest. I came to myself to find my face burning hot but my body shaking in chills. Somewhere in the thicket I heard the rustle of an animal. Then one of Rhydderch's men called out and I rolled onto my side with a groan.

A voice sounded from the wood. "I've found her! I see her!"

Arms came underneath me. I struggled to discern their shapes until they fell into familiar forms: Rhydderch wrapping a cloak around me as he lifted me up, cradling me like a child. My father's shadow etched like a giant against the failing light, the feel of his weathered fingers on my face. Behind me, I knew white robes glowed eerily in the dim.

Father's eyes widened in bewilderment, and another wave of labor gripped me.

"Cathan," I said through gritted teeth, trying to master the pain.

"Already your father sees to him," Rhydderch said. "You've lain too long exposed to the elements; you're burning up. We must get you back, my love. We've brought a cart. Lord Cathan will not be far behind."

Arms came beneath me once more, cradling my shoulders as they eased me onto a pallet in the bed of the cart. Brodyn climbed in beside me, his long dark hair tangled and loose from its leather binding.

"I failed you, cousin. I failed you." His face was split, battered, his eyes nearly swollen shut. He swallowed with some effort, his voice low with strain. "There were men in the forest," he said, "waiting beyond the tree line. They knew I was coming. I fought them, but I could not get to you. I'm sorry, cousin. I couldn't get to you . . ." His face contorted and I reached to touch his hair as he laid his head on my chest like a bewildered young child. It was a strangled sound, his weeping. Never before had I heard Brodyn cry.

It was easy, then, for my body to split open. I reached out blindly for something to grasp as my world became a blur of agony, sound, and motion. The seeming endless journey over tree roots and rutted road, the heavy wooden clamor of gates, the sudden blare of torchlight, and the rush of Crowan's voice as I was carried into a chamber and lowered onto a bed. My chamber. My bed.

Eyes squeezed shut, I burrowed deeper as the torrents of pain came to claim me, crying into the depths as they rose in swift waves to swallow me. I cried out until my throat was raw.

From the bottom of the blackness I called out for Ariane.

And suddenly she was there, hovering over me like a white gull in the darkness, a wet cloth in her hands as she cooled the fever overtaking me, her pale skin beaded with sweat in the lamplight. She had come. She was with me. I had not been forsaken.

Many hours passed before the relief came. At last my body collapsed at the sound of a cry. I lay on the sweat-drenched pallet, lids heavy and eyes wrung dry, as a hot little weight was placed on my chest. I could feel the delicate breath of the babe on my neck. Its newborn skin was like petals and smelled of pine needles and rosemary soap. A tear slipped between my lashes as I clutched the tiny body to me. A cool hand pressed against my cheek and I struggled to focus my vision.

"Ariane?" I blinked, her name a rasp from my throat.

"No." The voice was firm. "It is Elufed."

Confused, I squinted at the form seated beside me. Slats of light came through the wooden shutters. It was daylight. Elufed reached for a damp cloth and pressed it to my forehead.

"You are delirious with fever. But you've given birth to a boy."

"A boy," I mumbled, even as I sank away from her, back into the murkiness, my body wrung out. In my dreamless sleep I heard the sharp caw of the crows and the feathered flapping of their wings. I woke to find Brodyn standing guard beside my door. He nodded with a sad smile at the bundle in my arms. I was still clutching my babe; he breathed softly in sleep on my breast. My fingers went instinctively to tuck the blanket beneath his chin, observing him clearly for the first time. His head was covered in thick dark hair, his skin soft and smooth as fruit. His lashless eyes were folded tight, swollen from his journey. His tiny chest rose and fell in his dreaming.

A rush of feeling washed over me such as I'd never known before. I had thought I'd felt love, but looking at my son I realized with wonder that I had never known the true meaning of it until this very moment. Hesitatingly, with awe, I brought my lips down to rest on his downy head. My nostrils flared, catching his scent, imprinting it, and I drew him closer, protecting him within the circle of my arms. This babe was made of me, of me and of Maelgwn, and yet he was more, so much more than I could comprehend. Tears filled my eyes, this time not of sorrow or rage. In this sacred moment of bonding, I shed the tears of a mother's devotion, of a new purpose in life, of a love that could not falter.

I drew him even closer, longing for my own mother.

But when the door to my chamber opened, it was Elufed who stood before me. Strands of her flaxen hair had slipped loose from her plait, and though she wore a clean frock, I could smell the soft musk of her sweat. It was she who'd sent the priest away, I remembered now.

"Woman's work," she'd said, and in aiding my labor she'd been nothing like I'd known of her. Solemn and quick, she'd tended me with patience and skill that startled me.

Now she came to stand beside the bed and placed a cool hand on my forehead.

"Your fever has abated. Good. I shan't stay long. Rhydderch is waiting."

She gazed at the child in my arms. "I have borne three children, and each time I see an infant I am reminded anew what tiny little seedlings they are," she said. "A whole life exists already complete within them: their fates have already been written. They grow and stretch until they have burst open their pods. And each time we must let them walk the paths set before them."

I held my babe to me as if I could tuck him back into my body for safekeeping. "Not always," I said. "Perhaps not all fates are decided."

"Yes. All," she insisted. But as she stared at my baby her face softened.

"We found your boatman, Languoreth. He was quite willing to speak plainly when he heard of his master's death. I know what it was you intended to do."

My heart skittered through the lingering fog of labor and exhaustion, but I met her eyes. "Christian or no, would you stand before me and tell me you would not have done the same, if you thought it might spare the life of your child?"

Elufed studied me. I thought for a moment I saw a shimmering wetness fill her eyes that nearly resembled tears.

"I learnt long ago there is little sense in twisting the hand of fate," she said. "But it is not for me to pass judgment on what a mother feels she must do. I have not told my husband. But you must tell Rhydderch. My son deserves to know the reason you would endanger the life of his child."

"I will tell him," I allowed. "I know I must."

"Good." Elufed's smile was perfunctory. "Then we must only discuss the issue of Desdemona."

"Desdemona?"

Elufed's cool gray eyes observed me with the patience of a tutor as I came to realize the truth.

Sweet Gods. Brodyn and Desdemona were the only living souls who'd known of our meeting place. I swallowed the sudden urge to be sick, and Elufed smiled without humor.

"Ah, now you've come to it."

"Oh, no. No . . ." The events began to shift and come together in my mind, and I shook my head. "But . . . why? How could she do such a thing?"

"You can never trust a servant," Elufed said. "Not truly. Especially not one raised up beside you as a child. She must scrub pots and serve wine whilst you eat and drink and wear fine things. How can she not envy the life that you have? Now, Crowan, she's another matter. You could have sent her. But she wouldn't have let you go, of course. And you're too soft to disobey her. *Better she not know*, you thought. Well"—her fingers fluttered dismissively—"I suppose you did not know Desdemona was a Christian?"

"A Christian?" I echoed dumbly, even as my chest began to seethe with rage. No, she'd gotten it wrong. It was I who'd sent Desdemona to hear Mungo speak, but she hadn't lingered . . .

"Yes." Elufed narrowed her eyes. "Why, I believe she was baptized last summer. My man spotted her. I always send a man to watch the baptisms. *Isn't it odd that Languoreth's maid should want to be Christian?* I thought. A servant from your family. Your own chamber girl. And now your friend Cathan lies dead."

She spoke as if I were a child late to bed and I needed no reminder of what I had lost. Blood pulsed hot against the bandage bound at my neck.

"Do not speak of him. You know *nothing* of what Cathan meant to me. You cannot know—" I bit down on my lip to silence my cry. I would not weep with my babe in my arms. Already he had known too much horror, far too much grief.

Elufed folded her hands. "I am sorry to see you suffer," she said.

"You're sorry to see me suffer?" The idea was so preposterous that I nearly laughed. "Do not play with me, Elufed. You knew all of this, and yet you set us up to march like game pieces! You could have spared his life! I and your grandchild, we could have been slain." I leveled my eyes on hers, my face burning hot with fury. "Let us speak plainly and agree that you are sorry for nothing."

Elufed raised her brows, incensed. "Do not put Lord Cathan's blood on me. I may have spies, but I am no god. I could not know those men intended to assassinate your Keeper. All I have done has been necessary," she said tightly. "You know nothing of being wife to a high king. You will never learn to rule if you are coddled, warned of treachery at every turn."

"You speak of lessons?" My ears pounded so furiously, I could scarcely hear. "A great man is *dead*. They lofted him from our own sacred tree, where he swung, kicking, and I watched his face go purple as he choked—"

"I tell you again I did not know," Elufed hissed. "Nay, not me. Languoreth, it was you who did this. And all because you would battle the fates. A mother loves her child and she believes this is beyond any power. This is not so. This babe is my child, too! Do you think such visions bring me pleasure?"

"Visions?" I sank back against the pillows. "What visions? Speak plainly, Elufed, for I have nothing left. I cannot play your games any longer."

The babe kicked and let out a wail and Elufed looked at him, the flush of red fading from her cheeks. She turned her gray eyes to the window, her voice so faint I could scarcely hear.

"In my dreams I see visions of fire," she said. "A fire so hot it melts even rock."

I covered the baby's head to shoo her words away, as my mother used to spit and chase off a curse. I could not think of it. I could not bear to.

"Is this your secret? You are a seer, then?" I did not mask the bitterness in my voice.

She lifted a hand to silence me. Striding across the room, she shut the door before returning to sit uninvited beside me. Her eyes did not leave mine as she bent her head, sweeping aside her hair to expose a symbol I had never seen before, a symbol she had kept so fastidiously covered. Etched into her skin with blue ink, a horse raced for eternity against the fragile bones of her neck.

"You will not know this mark," she said. "It is the mark of a priestess. I am a daughter of Cailleach Bheur, just like my mother, and her mother before her. Our line stretches back to the very first circle, the rocks that stand on the Twilight Isle, deep in the north. What I know, I learnt from watching her." Her voice hardened. "I had only just performed my rites when Tutgual caught sight of me. A girl of eleven. He took what he wanted."

"I did not know."

"Of course not." She frowned. "No one knows, save that I am Pict-ish and a royal by birth. That much is true. Many of us carry markings. But there are yet secrets among my people. We Picts are not like the Britons, who give away their power. We keep our secrets close. And we keep our enemies closer."

The king, she meant, but would not say.

"And what of me?" I asked. "Am I your enemy?"

"No," she said. "Not unless you grow careless with my secret. For my husband does not know its meaning and I will not have my husband fear me. Tutgual kills what he fears. Anyway"—she waved her hand—"the truth of the matter is that you are my ally, and together we will bring about what must come to pass in ways only women can. I knew when I saw you. You were nothing more than a girl, but I knew. You were to marry my son. Your people and mine—we were both put here to protect the Old Ways."

I met her eyes. "Then I will keep your secret safe. I swear it."

"I believe you." She stood. "And I will advise you most plainly now, so it cannot escape you: you must deal with Desdemona. No more softness. Or it will be the death of you."

Just then a knock sounded at the door, rankling my nerves like a chain.

"Come," I called. It was none other than my chamber woman her-self, dipping her dark head as she entered, clay pitcher in hand.

"Water, m'lady?"

Instinct flared and I pulled my baby closer to my breast.

"I'm sorry, m'lady. I didn'a mean to startle you." Desdemona's puz-zlement was so earnest I blinked, struggling to believe she could have caused all this bloodshed. But then her smile flickered, and behind her eyes I saw fear.

I needed nothing more.

"I will take my leave now." Elufed slipped through the open door.

Outside, Brodyn stood guard in the corridor. Though his strong back was to me, he shifted his weight in a way that let me know he was listening. Could he suspect her role in this?

"Here, you must take some drink," Desdemona said, reaching to fill my wooden cup.

Three silver coins for the death of a slave girl. That was the penalty, the price by law. I would gladly empty our coffers into the Clyde if only to watch a blade come down upon her neck. I looked up. "Summon my husband, please."

"Lord Rhydderch was only waitin' for the departure o' the queen." Desdemona set the pitcher down. I could feel her unease mounting.

"Just bring him," I snapped. "Bring him to me now."

Brodyn turned at the sound of the edge in my voice, dark eyes questioning.

"Aye, m'lady, I'll fetch 'im, o' course." Desdemona turned and I locked eyes with my cousin, shifting my gaze meaningfully to the back of Desdemona's head.

Traitor, my look said.

I saw the blood beast that lived within Brodyn quicken as Desdemona brushed by, hurrying down the hall.

"Let me," he said.

Revenge. He was hungry for it.

"No," I said. "Do nothing yet. Follow her; make certain she does not flee. I must first speak with Rhydderch. There is much we must discuss."

"As you will it." Brodyn turned on his heel. I heard him offer his congratulations to my husband as they met in the corridor. A shuffle in the doorway a moment later announced Rhydderch. I looked up to find his dark hair tousled and his eyes rimmed pink with exhaustion. It struck me then what I had put him through. Still Rhydderch smiled at the sight of me, transfixed by the babe wriggling in my arms.

"A son."

He closed the distance between us, shutting the chamber door behind him.

"Already he is nursing," I said.

He reached to stroke the child's cheek. "Aye? That's good luck."

Rhydderch's voice was tender but full of weariness. He looked away from me as if he, too, had only just remembered all the events that had come between us.

"And what would you call him?" he asked.

I studied the babe's face, but I already knew. "Rhys, if it please you. In echo of Rhydderch. And Emrys, to honor the Britons' great hero."

Something flickered behind his eyes but he bowed his head. "A fine name."

Then without looking up, he asked me, "What were you doing in the wood?"

We had come to it, then. I opened my mouth to speak, but Rhydderch silenced me.

"It does not matter. Already Morcant is calling for me to set you aside. He saw you preparing to leave. You have betrayed my trust. Your head of guard attacked my men. Women have been beaten and returned to their fathers for far less. Tutgual will soon know of it. You have made me a fool."

"And for this I cannot even ask for forgiveness," I said.

Silence fell between us. I closed my eyes against the weight of it. Regret. Grief. Exhaustion. Guilt. Even then, from a fluttering fold of my heart, came the image of a sail snapping in the wind as a ship set its course across an open sea.

I could be cast away, only let me take my son. In the midst of everything, I held the sweet, sleeping bundle made of Maelgwn and me and felt a shameful stirring of hope that his father and I might be together at last.

"You are within your rights to do what you must," I said. "You will hear no complaint from me."

"No complaint." Rhydderch nodded as if to himself. "Right. Are you so unhappy, then, that you would rather return to Cadzow in shame and utter disgrace than to state your argument to the contrary and have a hope to stay with me?"

His gray eyes flashed with anger, with hurt.

"I meant only that I will bear whatever punishment you find just," I said, but there was no eagerness to please, nor quickness to quell the question I now saw stirring round his brain.

"You do not love me," he said. A statement, not a question.

"And do you love me?" I replied, unable to turn back. "For if you said so, I would be startled to hear it. You show me tenderness and respect. You treat me as your ally and your equal. But do you burn from the nearness of me when I am lying beside you? Does your heart drum faster at the thought of my touch? Kindness alone is not love, husband. There are times I have wondered if you are even capable of it—"

"Stop." I was silenced by the sudden ferocity of his kiss before he pulled away just as quickly. "Do not say any more, for I will never be able to put it from my mind."

I drew back, startled by the pain in his voice.

"You ask if I love you," Rhydderch said. "I love you as any man has loved a woman, Languoreth. I love your wit and your beauty, your fire. And, damn you, even your stubborn will. But I cannot change the elements of my being. I am not like you, composed of passions. I am built of steadfastness. Logic and solidity. I . . . suppose I struggle in expressing such things. But have I not provided for you in every way a man can? I have given you jewels and fine clothing. I treat you with consideration and with kindness. I have gotten you with child."

Unable to hide my guilt, I looked away. For once his keen eyes did not see.

"You have wronged me, hidden secrets from me," he said. "You have broken your word. But I love you still." Rhydderch blinked a moment, stiffening as he continued.

"I know that I love you because I cannot bear to set you aside. If you consent to it, I will offer Morcant a payment. The king will hear nothing of your role in this matter. My brother may be coarse, but in this I believe he will keep his word. If nothing less, it will give him some power over me. I hope he shall not have occasion to use it."

Rhydderch looked up and my heart twisted in my chest as he said the last of it.

"But I will not do this until you tell me this is what you wish. And I will have the truth as to why you have brought this tragedy raging to our door."

Never had my husband's eyes been left so unguarded, so naked to me. A tear slipped down my cheek. I did love him. Perhaps it was not the smoldering, desperate sort of love I felt for Maelgwn, but wasn't this love, this feeling of warmth overcoming me?

Perhaps love was made up of more than just passion. Rhydderch offered me kindness and constancy. Loyalty. His heart. And passion was a cruel master—I had learned as much so far. I reached for his hand.

"I did not wish to betray you. Please. I want to stay."

Rhydderch's tall shoulders slumped in relief. "Very well," he said. "Then tell me. I am listening."

CHAPTER 40

Rhydderch sat beside me as I told him of Cathan's vision and my deceit of Morcant, my escape into the woods. I told him of the men, the oak, the crows. Of cutting the rope and the way Cathan's body had plummeted to the forest floor like a child's broken puppet.

He sat quiet a long moment after I'd finished, then gestured for our son. Rhys was so very light. A bundle of feathers as I eased him into Rhydderch's arms. As he studied the babe, a shadow crossed his face. At last he spoke.

"We cannot raise this child in a cage. He is a boy, and the first of my name. If the kingship falls to him, he must be able to claim it. If war threatens our borders, he must be able to fight. I will do everything I can to ensure that when that day should come, he will be ready. I will protect this child with my dying breath. This I swear to you. But we can do nothing more."

"Surely he would make a fine king," I began, unable to keep the desperation from my voice. "But should he choose to enter the Keeperdom, or even the priesthood—"

"Languoreth. If death is to be his fate as Cathan foresaw it, who is to say it will not find him wherever he travels? King or Keeper, bishop or priest, we cannot say what the outcome will be. You cannot send a boy out into this world without knowledge of a sword. I can offer him fighting men, a warrior's training. He will have the might of Strathclyde at his back."

I looked at the infant nestled in the crook of Rhydderch's arm and realized the futility. My heart would now be coursing rivers of blood in a body outside my own forever. No matter how much I wanted to wrap my child in swaddling from the world, Rhydderch was right. He would be better armed against his fate as a fighter than not armed at all.

"Here . . ." Rhydderch settled the babe gently against my chest. "He belongs with his mother."

My body relaxed as I took him, and the baby slept on.

"We have said so much," I began. "And I am so very tired. But now I must speak to you of something even more urgent." I paused. "The men in the woods. This murder was carried out by Mungo's hired men. Cathan said as much, and they did not refute it."

Rhydderch rubbed his jaw. "Aye. And now it is my turn to tell you what has come to pass."

He reached into the pocket of his tunic and drew out my knife, dropping it on the bed beside me. "There are so few golden knives such as yours."

He had cleaned it of blood, but I could not bring myself to pick it up.

"The moment I saw you safe, I rode out with my men. We scoured the woods and villages, piercing hay piles and knocking down each door between here and the Molendinar Burn."

"Are they dead, then?"

"Some are dead. A few are yet hiding, but we will root them out." His eyes found mine. "The bishop waits at my father's hall. He will be exiled on the morrow, of this I assure you."

I sat up. "Exiled?" My mouth went metal with disgust. "He is a murderer, an assassin! He must pay for what he has done! He hunted down the head Keeper of Strathclyde and had him strung up like butchered meat. The people will never forgive this. My family will never forgive this!"

Crowan stuck her head into our chamber, her thin lips in a scowl. "What is all this shouting? If you've got rotten things to discuss, give me the babe. He deserves a little peace after his journey. And you"— she pointed a finger at me—"with the fever that nearly done you in! You're to be resting now, not shouting!"

"You're right, then, Crowan. Take him. I promise I will rest, and soon."

Rhydderch stood as she departed, shaking his head. "Languoreth, I will only tell you what is true: Tutgual will not kill him. Not whilst he may yet be of use. Mungo has powerful connections to the merchants, to the townsfolk, and now also to Rome. Tutgual will send him away. His exile must be the end of it."

"My father will not stand for it. Mungo has murdered his counsellor. Morken's retribution will be swift and without mercy, I am sure of it."

"If Morken values his lands and his own life, he will not lift his sword against the order of the king. Tutgual will deal in this matter. Morken must abide by his decision, as must any other king or Keeper, and so must you. You are no longer only the daughter of Morken, a man of the Old Way. You are also a princess of Strathclyde. Whether they follow the old gods or the new, these are all your people now. Christians are mothers and babies, too. Mothers and babies on both sides, homes burning, their bodies impaled on ends of pikes. This is what war looks like, Languoreth. I have seen it, and I tell you, there are horrors you cannot imagine. Think of that and tell me once more you'd see Mungo hang."

"I would see Mungo hang."

I had only just handed away my own child, bird-boned and defenseless. But my grief was a wild and stricken thing; it cried out for blood. "But if I cannot yet reach him, there is another who must pay."

I told him of Desdemona's suspected betrayal.

"And, sweet Gods"—I remembered—"it was Desdemona serving wine the afternoon Brother Telleyr visited Buckthorn. She knew Telleyr rode out to warn the king."

Rhydderch's gray eyes went hard. "If it was she, Desdemona has brought about the murder of two good men and nearly caused the death of my wife. She endangered the life of my son. If all this is so, we have suffered too much bloodshed by the hands of your servant . . ." He stopped. "You are pale. You must drink something, Languoreth. This has all been too much."

He handed me the cup and I drank greedily, the wound on my neck burning like fire when I swallowed. My body still throbbed with pain from the birthing. Rhydderch's worried eyes took in all of me as I lay there, spent.

"I will handle this," he said.

"No," I insisted. "I must hear for myself why Desdemona has done what she's done."

"Very well. Then I will fetch her."

Rhydderch leaned out the chamber door and a moment later a shriek sounded from the hall. Brodyn appeared, gripping Desdemona's wrist as if he might crush the bone.

"Your lady would see you," he said.

He released her too roughly and she stumbled into the chamber, her dark hair hanging limp about her face. Seeing her handled in such a way, I was struck with such pity, I nearly told Brodyn to stop. But how many more would betray me if they knew the true nature of my heart? There could be no more softness.

"Desdemona," I began. "We know what you have done. Unburden yourself now, for this is the only chance you shall have."

Her mouth twitched uncertainly a moment before her face fell and she erupted into tears. "It weren't as they said, m'lady, please! They weren't to touch you. They promised me you wouldn'a be harmed . . ."

"I would not be harmed? And what of Cathan? He was meant to be harmed, wasn't he?"

I drew myself up with some effort and swung my feet onto the floor. "How could you? Cathan was kind to you. And you repaid that kindness by setting his murderers upon him! You have betrayed me and my father, the very family that took you in."

I went to her and bent with some effort so that she must look me in the eye.

"You have taken the lives of two good men with your treachery. You will pay the price."

"Nay, m'lady, I beg you!"

"Beg? You do not get to beg. You will tell me what you have done and I will decide what's to become of you. For you are my servant. It is I who decides your fate. Speak, now. Or shall I have Brodyn aid you?"

Her eyes darted between Brodyn and me like a lamb cornered for slaughter.

"She's not speaking," Brodyn said. In a flash he'd gripped a fistful of Desdemona's dark hair, yanking back her head to expose the pulsing artery of her neck. I winced as she cried out, looking at me. But where there had been fear, there was now a flicker of expectation.

"M'lady, you must hear me. I'd ne'er forget what you've done! I told 'em you were not to be harmed!"

She did not think I would do it.

She did not think me capable of taking her life.

Rhydderch shifted his weight to remind me of his presence should I need it.

"I commanded you to speak." I nodded to Brodyn.

With a jerk of his arm, Desdemona's neck was strained as if it might snap, her arms pinned against the small of her back.

"He loves me!" she shouted. "You canna understand. He loves me! An' Lord Cathan meant to send 'im away, 'im an our Mungo!"

"*Who* loves you? Whom do you speak of?" I demanded.

"Brother Anguen," she cried. Brodyn released her abruptly and Desdemona fell to her knees, rubbing her neck.

"Brother Anguen?" I took a step back. "Explain yourself."

"It's th' truth: we've lain together." She said it with an air of satisfaction, but pain also lurked in the depths of her eyes. It brought to mind the way I'd seen her look at Lailoken all this time.

"You've always admired Lailoken," I said, half-astonished. "And what? He spurned you? Yes, he would have. So you went straight to our enemies. They took you in readily, no doubt, once you'd told them where you'd come from. Which family you served."

"Nay, it wasn'a like that! I mean, I did go to 'em once Lailoken sent me away. But then I listened t' Mungo, and what he spoke—like a caring da he was. The stories Brother Anguen would tell, 'bout women like me, servants, slaves. We've a place wi' Lord Christ in the afterlife. I am just as equal as you. We're all beloved in the eyes of God!"

"Are you not equal and beloved in the eyes of our gods? The gods who saw you delivered out from under Angle spears and the wolves of the Caledonian Forest into the safekeeping of our family? Where you were fed and nourished, clothed and sheltered, always considered a part of our community? Has your life among us been such a trial, Desdemona?" I reached to steady myself on my dressing cabinet. "No. Do not speak to me of love. You could have joined Telleyr and his followers had you truly chosen the way of Christ. Instead you acted in spite. You offered up Telleyr to Mungo. You betrayed my trust and caused the murder of my most beloved friend."

I looked at her. "You think you control these men but they have used you—used you to their ends. I have heard of Brother Anguen and his charms. You are not the first woman in Strathclyde to claim them. You have been a fool, Desdemona, and I am doubly sorry for it. For now you must pay a fool's price."

"No, m'lady! Please . . ."

"Enough." I looked at my husband. "I have heard enough."

Rhydderch nodded. "If the matter is decided, you should not make her wait."

Now? It was to happen now? My heart pounded between my ears as Desdemona's dark eyes went wild.

"Morken should be here," I said. "If only to see justice served."

"He comes this way already," Brodyn said. "He'll be here shortly."

"Then take her outside."

Brodyn nodded, gripping her arms as she kicked and sank again to her knees.

"No. No! M'lady! Languoreth!" She used my familiar name, as she had when we were girls, and my stomach pitched. I closed my eyes a moment, unable to look. Then I grabbed my cloak and made for the door.

Crowan met me on the stair, her hazel eyes frantic and the babe tucked in her arms.

"Keep him here," I instructed. "Keep him away."

"Desdemona?" she asked. "Was it truly her, dove? You've known her since she was a child . . ."

I held up my hand. "Know her? No, I do not know her. She's betrayed us all, and she will die for it."

We crowded onto the porch as Desdemona's screams brought the servants gawking and stumbling from the kitchens. Rhydderch's men fell into line between us, watchful, but they trailed our procession at a distance, as if Desdemona were plagued. Rhydderch had slipped his sword in its baldric over his shoulder and strode now through the grassy plot behind the hall, toward the old stump where our servants split wood.

So be it.

Desdemona was weeping. I prayed for her sake my father would not make us wait. Then, as if in answer, we heard the sound of horses.

My father had come to see my child, but would witness an execution.

In a moment I recognized Father, Brant, and Father's man Oren slowing their mounts by the gate. Father bent to speak with Rhydderch's guard. Then across the expanse of the yard I saw him straighten and kick his horse into a run. His dark eyes were fixed upon Desdemona.

I raised my hand in greeting as he drew close, and the crowd of soldiers and servants parted. Father dismounted heavily and placed his hand warmly on my shoulder, but his brown eyes would not look into mine.

"My daughter. Are you well?"

I had not seen him since he appeared to claim Cathan's body in the wood. He was angry with me. I could not blame him.

"I am sorry, Father. I am so sorry. Neither Cathan nor I was willing to sully your hands." He nodded, studying the ground a moment before lifting his face.

"I do not thank you for your protection, but all is forgiven," he said. "Now tell me."

I leaned my forehead against his cheek and told him what had transpired. He looked to Rhydderch.

"Will you do it, then?"

Rhydderch nodded. "Unless you command otherwise."

My husband's voice was even, but I knew he was not eager to bring his sword down upon a woman's neck. He would do it for me. For Cathan. For my Father.

"Nay." Father shook his head. "Let it be you."

Rhydderch spoke quickly. "Desdemona, you have admitted freely to acting a spy, betraying the confidences of your household and your lady. Your actions have brought about the murders of Brother Telleyr, priest of Partick, and of Lord Cathan, head Wisdom Keeper of Strathclyde and counsellor to Morken King. Have you anything to say before justice is done?"

She looked up at me, panicked.

"I'm sorry, m'lady," she said. But her voice held a fragile hope. A question. The horror of the moment displaced me. I shook my head. Desdemona's weeping became feral and strange, like a wounded deer's. I stood outside my own body as her hands were bound behind her back, as she was guided to her knees in the grass. The wind picked up and the air smelled suddenly of rain, and for a moment I stood once more in the slickened mud of Cadzow's courtyard, clutching the hand of a dying boy. I stood beside Desdemona in the barn, eyeing her dirt-streaked face and her soiled doll.

I could lift a finger and put a stop to all this madness.

The blood for blood for blood that this action would beget. But all leadership was blood. Cathan had said as much. Now I knew it to be true.

"Languoreth."

Rhydderch's voice brought me back to my body. I looked up. Behind me, servants were crying. Rhydderch stood, blade drawn, waiting.

"Do it," I said.

I did not flinch as he brought down his sword.

IV.

Swiftly came Maelgwn's men
Warriors ready for battle, for slaughter armed.
For this battle, Arderydd, they have made
A lifetime of preparation.
— *The Black Book of Carmarthen*

CHAPTER 41

Seasons rose and fell to the earth. I learned that horses, loved ones—even heroes—cannot live forever. I lay in the hay beside Fallah, my head on her snowy flank as her beautiful dark eyes went sightless. I held Crowan's frail hand in mine as she wasted away to nothing in her bed, until her chest had ceased its rattle in a sigh that felt like summer. I cradled my father's head in my lap as his disease finally took him; I felt the moment his body became a shell. We buried him among the oaks at Cadzow, close to Mother's healing hut. Cadzow was under my care now, and we spent summers there. Time passed and Mungo remained in exile. I became wise at court. I watched and I listened upon the arm of Rhydderch, at the elbow of Elufed.

But I did not forget.

With Father passed, my cousin Brant rode to join Pendragon's cause in the Borderlands. Not long after I received word that Lord Emrys, too, was dead. Lailoken had returned home from his training in the mountains of the north only days before he answered Emrys and Gwenddolau's summons to be their counsellor at the Wall. Lailoken was thickly bearded and thought long before he spoke. His time in the mountains had changed him. But perhaps Elufed had been right about twisting hands: even my brother's newfound wisdom could not stay Emrys's fate. Gwenddolau and Emrys were battling advances in separate parts of their kingdom when the mighty Pendragon fell sick. In a distant town he found refuge at an inn. A healer was called for. He wore the robes of a Keeper and spoke like a Briton, but a slow-acting poison was his remedy. By the time Pendragon's convulsions began, the assassin had long disappeared into the forest. Maelgwn went on the hunt, and though he could not turn up the man himself, he discovered he was an Angle named Octa, skilled in the knowledge of deadly plants.

And so Gwenddolau succeeded Lord Emrys as head of the Dragon Warriors. As word traveled throughout the kingdom of his bravery and strength, the people loved him and they called him by a new name.

Uther Pendragon.

The Other Pendragon. Now more than ever, Gwenddolau wore a target on his back.

To the east, the Angles had dug their iron roots deep and a new kingdom had risen. The lands once known as Bryneich were now called Bernicia.

Lailoken visited as often as he could. But now his presence was urgently needed at Gwenddolau's side, and for me his absence tingled like a missing limb.

But my world was not made only of longing and loss; there was such joy in it, too.

With Mungo in exile, peace had come at last to Partick. My body swelled thrice more with child: a scholarly boy named Cyan, a sensitive girl called Gladys, and last came Angharad, a girl all fire and grit, with reddish hair like mine and a smile that could melt the sun. My eldest, Rhys, grew tall and muscular, with nimble hands and eyes the color of leaves in summer. He was a good boy, kind to his brother and gentle with his sisters, even when they hung in peals of laughter from his elbows or clung to his legs like caterpillars on a tree. But within Rhys the heart of a warrior pounded its deafening beat. When he practiced, I watched the shadow overtake him. Already his skill with sword and spear was nearly beyond Brodyn's teaching. Sometimes I would catch a glimpse of him training in the yard and my breath would catch as if Maelgwn himself stood before me once more.

It had been seventeen years since I had seen Rhys's true father. And yet each summer when we packed our trunks to stay at Cadzow for the season, I remembered him everywhere.

I looked now to where my boys stood, sparring in the long grass of Cadzow's pasture. Cyan, still a lanky tangle of limbs at twelve; Rhys, a strong young man of sixteen. It was the time to gather yarrow before autumn came, and my arms were full of their golden sprays. The breeze off the Avon was thick with the green smell of summer. Gladys and Angharad chased each other in circles, breathing it in with exaggerated sighs like two forest nymphs drunk on honey.

"Ow!" I startled at the sound of Cyan's cry and turned to see him cradling his side.

"Mother, he struck too hard." Cyan glared at his elder brother.

"Cyan, my love, you cannot cry to me every time you get a good whacking. Keep your shield arm up as your brother has shown you."

Cyan would rather have his head buried in some ancient text, but Tutgual King was growing old. Soon my children, too, would ride with targets on their backs, and because of this, Cyan must learn how to fight.

Rhys lowered his practice blade. "Cyan, you cannot think a Westman or a Pict would be any kinder. Come, now. You must try again."

I shook my head. Hadn't I been standing just there, a girl of ten, when Brant told me the same? I looked to the empty patch of grass where my girls had been playing. Gladys had given up the chase and now sat close by with her feet tucked beneath her, weaving a crown out of yarrow. Across the field, Angharad was circling the same tree she always seemed drawn to, her tawny head bent as if she were listening.

"Angharad, come away," I called out. "It's bad luck there. Come away, now. Quickly."

She looked up, her gray eyes questioning, and for a moment I felt as if she were peering straight through me.

Gladys wrinkled her delicate nose and balanced the yarrow wreath atop her dark head.

"I don't know why she likes it there. It's just a thorn tree, after all."

"Gladys, you're meant to be minding your little sister," I said. "You know I don't like her playing just there."

"But why do you say it's bad luck, Mother?"

I glanced at the place where so long ago the little boy named Drustan had clutched at my arm and I had looked down to see him bleeding in the mud. A thorn grew there now, just at that spot. And sometimes, on a summer night, when it bent in the wind, I could swear I heard the soft sound of weeping.

"Sometimes events happen that people can forget, but the landscape does not" was all I said. "Now, go and fetch your sister."

Gladys sighed, stood, then squinted. "Mother. I think Aela is waving at you."

I shielded my eyes and spotted my fair-haired servant lifting her skirts to make her way through the tall grass, her freckled face anxious.

"Aela, what is it?"

"A messenger's come, my lady. It's Uther Pendragon! He rides this way even now, toward Cadzow!"

I dropped the yarrow in a heap at my feet. "Here? To Cadzow?"

"Even now!" she exclaimed. "The messenger says Pendragon comes to treat with your husband."

I brushed back the wisps of my hair that had come loose from my plait and glanced back at the hall, my chest a cage full of birds. "Do my brother and— Do all Gwenddolau's men ride with his retinue?"

"I imagine so, my lady, but our man did not say."

"Sweet Gods." I threw up my hands. "Of this Lailoken could not have sent notice? And they will plan to spend at least two nights. We must ready the guest rooms. Fetch the spare sheepskins from the loft and sweep out the warriors' chambers. My husband's men will sleep in the great room whilst they are here. We'll need to slaughter more meat and set it up to roast right away. Go tell Cook. Bid her see to it."

Suddenly the singsong of my girls chasing in circles rose to a nerve-clattering pitch and I rounded on them, shouting.

"Angharad! Gladys! Enough of that noise. Get inside and get cleaned up. Guests are coming. Important guests." My hand flew to my throat, fingers drumming against my collarbone.

"Who is it?" Rhys sheathed his sword. "Who's coming?"

"Your uncles ride this way," I said carefully, so that I would not say the one name circling round and round my brain.

Maelgwn. Maelgwn.

"Lailoken comes? Truly?" Rhys had been so serious of late. His smile now was bright with sun, and it soothed me a little.

"Yes, even so. He rides with Uther Pendragon to speak with your father."

"The Dragon Warriors." Rhys's tone was one reserved for miracles and acts of witchery. Perhaps I was to blame, raising my children on stories of Gwenddolau and his bird, indulging Rhys when he bade me recount endless times the moment I'd first seen the Dragon Warriors riding full tilt across the fields of Cadzow.

The first moment I'd seen his real father.

But Rhys belonged to Rhydderch now, in spirit if not in body. It was Rhydderch who'd bounced him on his knee and told him stories. It was Rhydderch who'd first watched him stand on fat, wobbly legs, who first showed him how to spar, to strike, and to parry.

I tried to smile. "Do not be so awestruck. The Dragon Warriors are men, just like you."

"If Pendragon is our uncle, too, why has he not come before now to meet us?" Cyan asked. He swung his shield idly now, his wavy brown hair all tousled.

"It is no fault of his. War has kept him away too long."

"Not war. Not exactly, Mother." Rhys looked at me. "Cyan should know the truth of it."

"Very well." I bowed my head.

"Gwrgi and Peredur are raiding Uther Pendragon's lands as of late," Rhys said. "Pendragon dared not leave his fiefdom. Perhaps Gwrgi and Peredur intended this. Their raiding keeps Pendragon from Partick. It is difficult to make allies when you cannot even visit their courts."

"Yes," I agreed. "Perhaps it is so."

"Even so, I think they are fools provoking Pendragon and his men," Rhys said.

"Gwrgi and Peredur are not at all foolish," I said. "They are black-hearted men, and clever in the ways they seek revenge, and you would do well not to forget it."

Rhys frowned at my tone, but Angharad had come racing over, breathless, and smiled.

"Lailoken is coming? Mother, do you think he will take me for walks in the forest again?"

I bent to pluck a leaf from her hair. "Do you not enjoy our walks in the wood?"

"Of course," she said. "But Lailoken knows such stories. He tells me the story of every tree and plant and wonder we see . . ." Her voice trailed off. She did not want to say how forgetful her mother had become. Tutgual had long declared now that priests were the only sanctioned healers at court. It was a bitter decree and I had been forced to swallow it. At first I had strived ever harder to retain my skills, but with four children, the running of Father's lands, and no tutor to question me, my knowledge was slipping.

"You must be patient, my dove. We know not what brings him here. His time with us may not be his own."

"But why does Uther Pendragon ride here to speak with Father?" Cyan asked. "Why would he not treat with King Tutgual instead?"

"I cannot say. That will be between Pendragon and your father. Enough questions, now. Go and ready yourselves." I shooed them toward the hall. "And whilst they are here, you must not speak out of turn or place yourself in matters above your standing."

"But I will treat with the warriors," Rhys said quickly. "I've discussed it with Father."

"You will not. You are yet children, all of you, and you are to watch. Is that understood? To watch and to listen."

Anger flashed in Rhys's eyes before he turned away, shaking his head. "Come now, *children*," he said, ushering his brother and sisters across the field.

Aela, who had been standing at my side, let out a breath.

"Rhys is no longer a child, my lady. You know as well as I that he is grown to be a man. Two years now he's been fighting at his father's side. I know you don't wish to think of it, but after this winter's sea storms have abated . . ." She meant to say that Rhys would likely be given his own retinue of Rhydderch's forces to command soon.

"Please. Don't speak of it." I held up my hand. "Not now. Not yet."

"As you say." Aela bowed her head. "Shall we get you dressed, then, my lady?"

I slipped my hand into my pocket, where it closed tightly around my green ring. "Yes, I had better ready myself."

As we hurried toward the hall, the cool, familiar comfort of the metal pulsed against the cushion of my palm. Inside the hall I was greeted by chaos as servants swept the slate floors and brought in armfuls of summer greenery to deck the tables. Aela closed my chamber door and I fought the sudden urge to lean against it to keep the world at bay. Instead I sat on the edge of my little pine chair watching Aela heave open one of my trunks and rifle through it with practiced hands.

"And will you wear the green robe?" she asked, drawing it out.

"The green?" My voice was too sharp, and Aela turned, studying my profile.

"It's only that it's so lovely with your hair . . ."

Of course. She couldn't have known it was the color Maelgwn had favored on me so long ago.

The ring suddenly burned like an ember and I drew my hand from my pocket. "No, not the green," I said. "I am the wife of Lord Rhydderch. Any day now he shall be named tanist. Tonight I will wear the color befitting a royal. Tonight I'll wear the purple."

After the ring had come nothing. It was the last of anything I'd had from Maelgwn. Lailoken visited us at Partick and at Cadzow, his pockets stuffed with secrets and sweets, but he never brought one word from the man I loved.

At first I begged for news, for any small detail of Maelgwn. How were his new men training up? Was he keeping his feet dry in all the autumn rains, the winter snows? I sent messages by Lail full of love and reassurance. Again and again I was met only by silence.

At first it was merely puzzling. There was a time I would never have doubted his love. Surely there was good reason Maelgwn had not sent any word. But time passed and resentment sprouted, binding my insides like a disease. Look what a desperate woman he'd made of me. No, this was my doing. Hadn't I been playing the part of the warrior's wench all along?

In the end, perhaps I took pity on my brother. The pain my own suffering caused him was plain upon his face, and he had such pressures now in the Borderlands. There were only so many times I could ask my twin to feel my own heartbreak.

"I have delivered each message. I swear it," Lail assured me.

At last he'd said gently, "Perhaps it is better this way."

And so nearly seventeen years had passed. I was thirty-two winters now. I had borne four strong and beautiful children. I had given my faith to my husband. All was as it should be.

But as I lifted the bronze mirror from my dressing table, the expression that met me was furrowed. I turned my head to the left, then the right, my fingers exploring the smooth skin of my cheek. I supposed I did not look so very different from when we'd first met. Tired about the eyes, but my softness had been replaced by lean muscle from chasing my children and lack of good appetite; I was hungry for a food I could never consume. A caring wife if not a happy one. I loved Rhydderch in my way, but he could not fill me.

I was dutiful but hollow-hearted.

Try as I might, I could not part with the little green ring. And so Aela knew that in each robe or new frock that I bought, whether it be of silk or wool or finest linen, a pocket must be sewn, though she never asked why. Attached to a slender chain and fastened by a pin, I kept the ring safe in that pocket, close to my hip, where Maelgwn's head had once lain.

Seventeen years. I had been such a fool.

I set down the mirror and, reaching into my dress, gave the golden band a sharp tug. There was a satisfying snap as the pin ripped loose from its anchor in my pocket, and I set the ring down on the table before me, the little chain dangling like an umbilical cord.

"Yes," I repeated, straightening. "I'll wear the purple. The new robe with the gold embroidery. Let them see me for the woman I have become, not the foolish little girl I once was."

Darkness fell, and still Gwenddolau and his men had not arrived. I waited with the children for the call of the watchman's horn in my weaving room, my fingers clumsy at the loom. Rhys was in the great room beyond with our warriors, where the tables were decked with late summer blooms and drinking horns, where the firelight flickered and our musicians sent sweet strains echoing beyond the Hall into the dusk. In the corner, beside the lamplight, Angharad hummed the kennings I'd taught her. Not the words—those she knew must be kept secret—but the melodies. I'd kept them in my memory from Ariane all these years. Now I knew they were meant for Angharad all along.

The children grew hungry, and I sent for some bread.

"What are you weaving, Mama?" Gladys came to sit beside me, her pale fingers reaching gingerly to trace the threads.

"Who can tell?" I murmured. "Busywork, that's all weaving is. It keeps a woman from going mad."

I looked at my hands on the loom, crisscrossed with tiny lines, each one a story of time gone by. Just then the call came up from the watch. I looked up.

"Our guests have arrived. Come, then. We must greet them."

I took my place beside Rhydderch, to the right of his great oaken chair. His gray eyes swept my face and he reached back to touch my hand, reassuring. We had not had time to speak of what this might mean, this sudden and unannounced visit. And now outside the Hall came the heavy sound of boots as the men dismounted from their horses.

My long auburn hair was shiny and plaited, pinned with combs. My purple robe skimmed my figure, the intricate embroidery drawing the eye to the curves of bust and hip. My eyes were lined with kohl, my freckles powdered pale with lily root. There was a dull ache at the thought that three men I'd once been inseparable from had become so distant from me now as I stood waiting, a polite smile upon my face.

Rhydderch's wife, the lady of the Hall.

I felt like a rose clinging to a woody stem in winter, faded and used up.

What had I done to fulfill my great destiny? What revenge had I exacted to right the wrongs done to my family?

I had aged and borne children. I had entertained rich lords and helplessly witnessed their maneuverings. In the world of the high king, a woman was an ornament to be tossed on the midden pile once her enamel wore off. But just as I thought that, I loathed myself for it. If I succumbed to that belief, then Tutgual's reign had done its work.

Elufed and I knew a woman's worth.

My husband's mother had become a trusted friend, and more than anyone she had guided me well. Did I not have my husband's heart but also his ear? Had I not grown wise in all I had seen? Did I not work each day to be a model of intelligence, grace, and kindness to all of our people?

I imagined my backbone built of iron. I had taken on my roles to the best of my abilities. Seventeen years of silence had taught me I owed Maelgwn nothing. Then the footsteps were sounding. The voices were dropping. The servants were craning their necks. The Dragon Warriors were coming.

The doors opened and I saw their figures etched against the darkening sky, the first stars winking beyond their silhouettes in pinpoints of light against the azure of the coming night. Gwenddolau entered, flanked by twenty solemn-faced men, scale-bellied in their ebony lamellar armor, shields slung over their shoulders, eyes hard and wary of strangers. They smelled of mud and sweat and leather.

I scoured the ranks until I found him, Maelgwn, my living ghost. He wore his thick black hair long now, held back by a golden ring, but it hadn't a trace of ash in it. His olive skin had weathered from the pelt of rain and snow, but his face . . .

His eyes . . .

The quiet assuredness that breathed from him . . . I had summoned him a thousand times alone in the dim: green eyes, strong brows, straight nose, even mouth. The vines that had bound me twisted. Then gave way.

My *love*.

It was as if I'd spoken the words aloud: Maelgwn's gaze tracked me like a falcon's. Our eyes met, and time fell away. I read him like a parchment and his body told me the story of the Dragon Warriors: seventeen years of warring, raiding, and tribute. The power and wealth the Pendragons had amassed was evident in General Mael-gwn's golden armband and masterful cloak clasps, in the rare indigo dye of his tunic; the cost of that power in the hardness that now clung to him, black as hearth smoke, in the set of his jaw, in a new scar that arced above his right eye, a sliver of white cutting through his dark eyebrow like a crescent moon.

All this had changed. But the look in his eyes was unmistakable.

You, it said. *It has always been you.*

My heart flipped like a wounded rabbit and I tore my eyes from his. If this was so, then why had he tortured me with his silence?

You mustn't stare, I warned myself. *No one must see what's passed between you.*

Gwenddolau strode forward to clasp Rhydderch's arm, and I watched, unhearing, as words passed between them.

Uther Pendragon.

Somewhere beneath this man's leather scaled armor and impen-etrable countenance was the boy who'd carried me up from the river on his shoulders. Gwenddolau was just as golden now as he'd been then, his pale hair long and loose about his shoulders, tangled from the wind. There were small braids plaited throughout, secured with golden rings that caught the gleam of the oil lamps as he bowed his head in greeting. His forehead was tan, dust from the road lining its creases, but it held more furrows than a man of forty winters should wear. And the wrinkles at the corners of his eyes—there were stories here, too.

Not crow's-feet from laughter. These were of a different sort of bird: hunchbacked, vulture-like, they were watchful lines that came from searching the hills for any flicker of movement, squinting at every shifting shadow in the underbrush.

Uther Pendragon's face was that of a man with too many enemies.

The Dragons who stood before me now guarded significant treasure. But gold always came at a cost.

Behind Gwenddolau the men hefted trunks: gifts for Lord Rhydderch, who might someday be king. I could see now how Gwenddolau bent a little as if cradling his ribs. His blue eyes were rocks, but behind them I sensed something cavernous. The human body yet spoke to me in a tongue I could not forget, and Gwenddolau's body was worn through.

"Languoreth." Gwenddolau's eyes were trained on me now, awaiting my greeting.

"Gwenddolau, my brother." I rushed forward to embrace him, and beside the summer hearth the musicians struck up their instruments.

He drew back to look at me. "Sister. It has been too long. It does me such good to see you."

"And you." I squeezed his callused hands. "Are you well, truly?"

He raised a brow but allowed me to inspect him. "Have the years truly treated me so poorly?"

"No, no," I said. "You seem tired is all. Yours was a long journey."

"There is no need for politeness, little sister. Not among family. I know how time has worn me."

"Time has worn us all," I said. "We all wear our histories, whether it be inside or out."

"Not you," he said. "You have not aged one single winter, I could swear it."

"Come, now. You needn't flatter your host. But you!" I turned to Lailoken, who stood waiting impatiently. "You look worst of all."

"You should watch how you speak to a Keeper." He smiled and leaned in to kiss my cheek just as Gladys and Angharad broke the line and ran to wrap their arms around their uncle.

"My littlest ladies," he groaned beneath their weight as he hefted them. My brother, at least, was blissfully unchanged. Though he, too, wore his hair long, the front of his head was shaved in the style of a Keeper and plaited as Cathan had done, in a braid down his back. He wore a full beard that now partially obscured his massive scar. And while Gwenddolau's eyes had dimmed, Lailoken's glowed with a warmth and charm that was captivating, contagious. He lumbered forward to greet Rhydderch with a crooked smile, Angharad's legs wrapped around one hip and Gladys clinging awkwardly to the other.

"Daughters," I called after them, "you are nearly eight and ten. You mustn't hang on your uncle so. You're going to break the old man's back!"

Lailoken threw me a look but straightened in relief as his nieces dismounted. I kissed my cousin Brant, graying at the temples but much unchanged. I could feel Maelgwn's eyes on me as he stood with his shoulders square, waiting. I should greet him. As lady of the house it was my duty, was it not? But just as I moved to welcome him, Rhydderch placed his hand on the small of my back. It was strange and unsettling to have the two of them standing face-to-face, equal in height but different in every other aspect. Maelgwn was broad where Rhydderch was narrow. Maelgwn's hair was dark as peat, while Rhydderch's was oak, threaded now with thick strands of silver. But both pairs of eyes belonged to men who missed very little.

"Lord Rhydderch." Maelgwn bowed. His green eyes touched on mine. "My lady."

Rhydderch's hand went protectively round my waist. "General Maelgwn, you are most welcome. But I cannot help but notice. You look at my wife as if you are acquainted."

"Indeed, for we have met," I said quickly. "Maelgwn visited my father on a few occasions at our hall."

Maelgwn blinked at my half truth but dipped his head gracefully. "It is so. You look well, Lady Languoreth."

"And you," I said, then turned to my foster brother. "Come,

Gwenddolau. You must meet my children." I gestured for them to join us before Rhydderch could observe anything more.

"Children, come and meet your uncle, Lord Gwenddolau," I called. "And this is Maelgwn, his general and second-in-command."

The children clustered round like seabirds, and I spoke their names as they bowed, the blood pumping in my ears. I could not help but wonder if with one look Maelgwn might know. Rhys's eyes, green as pine. But his skin was mine, fairer than his father's, and he had the shape of my face about him. I watched like an eagle as Rhys clasped Maelgwn's thick arm with a nod of admiration. Then Maelgwn stepped back, his eyes sweeping our son's face as if he were figuring a riddle.

Beyond the pulsing in my head, Rhydderch was welcoming the men with lifted cup, the warriors were settling onto sturdy benches, the servants bringing out the platters of beef and salmon trapped in our waters.

Maelgwn cocked his head as if to say something, but I reached out to smooth Rhys's checked tunic with a smile.

"Come, Rhys, you have a place beside your father. Our servants will show General Maelgwn the way. It is late now, and time to eat."

Rhys bowed his head and went to the table, but Maelgwn caught my sleeve, his eyes flickering in the lamplight.

"I have not set eyes on you in nearly two decades and you treat me like a stranger."

"Are we not strangers now," I asked, "after so much time?"

"Nay, Languoreth. I could never be a stranger to you."

"Is that so?" I suddenly wanted to strike him and clutched at my skirts to stay my hands, turning to him instead. "How dare you speak to me now as if we are familiar. In fact, it would please me most if you would not speak to me at all. You're practiced at that, are you not?"

He drew back with a look of consternation. "What I did, I did for your protection. Surely you must know—"

"Please take your seat," I said, turning away. My cheeks were flushed with heat and I could feel Rhydderch's eyes upon me across the room. This was dangerous—too dangerous. I took a breath to calm myself and crossed the room. Gathering my robe, I sat gracefully beside my husband.

"You are upset," Rhydderch said. "What were you speaking of?"

I knew my husband would not be fooled by smiles and platitudes. "An old disagreement," I said. "One better left buried."

"And is it, then?" he watched me. "Buried?"

"Yes." I met his gaze. "In truth, it was buried long ago."

"Very well, then," Rhydderch said. He lifted his spoon, urging me to do the same. "You must eat something, my love. Autumn is coming and it will be cold. You are growing too thin."

Later, Lailoken and I sat side by side looking out over the great room as empty platters were taken back to the kitchens and glasses and drinking horns refilled.

"It worries me that Tutgual has not yet named Rhydderch his tanist." Lail said. "Did not this past birthday mark Tutgual one thousand years old? I am beginning to think he sips each night on some magical elixir."

"It is no laughing matter," I said. "It seems the king's health will not falter. There are things I wish . . . but we mustn't speak of that here. Tell me," I said, observing Rhydderch and Gwenddolau at the head of the table, "why does Gwenddolau sit so stiffly beside my husband?"

"Gwenddolau does not trust the lords of Strathclyde."

"Then why has he come? Rhydderch is my husband. Can Uther Pendragon not even show his host some good favor in conversing?"

"Good favor." Lailoken's echo was hollow as he set down his cup.

"Brother"—I searched his face—"tell me the reason you've come. You have heavy matters on your mind. How might I ease your burden?"

"Yes, he is silent." Lailoken stared at Gwenddolau and Rhydderch, unhearing. "To have come all this way, and our brother sits silent!"

"Gods, speak plainly, Lailoken. I am your sister and your ally, or have you forgotten?"

"By the time I have spoken my piece, you will see I have not forgotten." Lailoken took a deep draft from his cup. "You have heard, I am sure, of the raiding by Gwrgi and Peredur?"

"Yes, of course."

He set down his cup, eyes fixed on the hearth. "When Emrys rose up, he was lord of nothing: a burnt-out fortress and smoldering fields. Now look at the golden clasps in Gwenddolau's hair, the jewels in his brooch. We have fields bursting with crops. Endless heads of fine cattle. We have chests of silver and gold, booty and coin such as even you cannot imagine. The lure has become too great."

I frowned, impatient for my brother to reach his point. "Surely, to be robbed of booty and livestock is a blow—"

"Booty and livestock?" Lail's laugh was bitter. "Nay, sister. Perhaps that is how they began . . ." His eyes touched on Angharad and Gladys. Their faces were bright across the room, heads raised to the high thatching as they twirled to the beat of the bodhran.

"Only days ago we came upon our village of Sweetmeadow. They had rounded up the women and the girls." Lailoken's jaw twitched, and he looked away. "Perhaps it is better that at last Gwrgi killed them, for I will never forget what I have seen."

"Children? You cannot mean . . ." Lailoken locked his eyes on mine and I pushed away my plate, sickened.

"We mean to show the sons of Eliffer that harming little children is not a sport," he said.

"But what will you do?" I asked. "How will you answer?"

"It will come to war. Already we fight with the new Angle king. I fear a war with the sons of Eliffer might break us."

There was a shadow of fear in my brother's eyes unlike anything I'd seen before. Lailoken feared nothing. And yet he feared this.

"Then you cannot fight them," I said. "There must be another way. Double your men. Triple your patrols."

Lailoken looked up angrily. "You speak as if this has not already been done! They mean to incite us. For twenty-three years the Dragon Warriors have bled to protect the people of Pendragon. Emrys rose up to fight when their own king would not. Under the Pendragon banner the people have prospered. Under the Pendragon banner the people have been safe. We cannot fail them now."

"You must appeal to Tutgual," I said. "He may be a tyrant, but surely even he would see the evil in their ways. You need the might of Strathclyde behind you."

"Our lands are beyond Strathclyde's borders," Lail said. "Yes, Tutgual would be all too happy to exact tribute upon us—to expand his influence over our trade routes, too, if only Gwenddolau would bend his knee in fealty. But that is something Uther will never accede to."

"Then you must tell Rhydderch what Gwrgi and his brother's men have done. He will speak with the king. Perhaps something can be arranged. You must treat with Rhydderch right away."

Lailoken blinked. "You think I tell you of things your husband does not already know?"

"No." I shook my head. "Rhydderch could not know of such horrors. He would have spoken of it. Surely he would have ridden out!"

"Sister, I sent word of Sweetmeadow to your husband myself. Perhaps you do not know him as well as you think."

I looked at Rhydderch, his gray eyes intent as he watched the bards play. No. Rhydderch could never stand by after learning such atrocities were taking place. And yet . . . I knew such an arrangement would be at great cost to my husband. He was not free to align himself with whomever he chose. The throne could go to any male heir. First Tutgual would have to name Rhydderch tanist, his chosen successor. Then Rhydderch must be elected by the Council. Supporting the cause of a man who would not pledge fealty to his father would be unacceptable. Unless, of course, Gwenddolau would pledge fealty to Rhydderch.

"You know as well as I that Rhydderch can do nothing without first securing Gwenddolau's fealty himself," I said. "An allegiance is a costly thing: vessels, food, and weapons. Horses. The lives of men. Rhydderch cannot risk himself if Gwenddolau is not under his command."

"It is as you say, but I fear he will not do it," Lailoken said. "No Pendragon has ever sworn allegiance to a king. And, truth be told, I am with Gwenddolau. What do the Pendragons owe to a king? One king fled as his people were cut down to nothing. Another pits his servants against one another for sport. No, I cannot blame him. Yet I fear it is our only hope."

As I watched, Gwenddolau nodded curtly at Rhydderch and stood, striding to join his men on the fleece-lined couches by the wall.

"But Rhydderch is a good man, and true to his word," I said.

"You ask why we have come. Gwenddolau thinks he comes to treat with Rhydderch. In truth, I have brought Gwenddolau here so that he might speak with you. You must persuade Gwenddolau to swear his fealty to Rhydderch."

"And what will Gwenddolau care for my thoughts when he will not even heed the word of his own counsellor?"

"Counsellors and kings do not always agree. You know as much. You are Gwenddolau's own sister, and you have lived beside Rhydderch for many winters now. I can only hope Gwenddolau will hear from you what he cannot from me. Too many wait to catch sight of the chink in Pendragon's armor. Look at our brother and the price he has paid. He cannot go on like this. His body has been mended so many times, it is ripping at the seams. He must make an allegiance, and soon."

Across the room Gwenddolau sat hunched with his elbows on his knees, his eyes lost in the fire. I could see how tired he was, how used up. If I had seen it so plainly when he arrived, I could not have been the first to notice.

"I will speak with him, and with Rhydderch," I said. "But it will take time. How long can you stay?"

"Three days, perhaps, maybe four. Long enough to rest the horses and our men's tired feet and not a moment more. We must strike within a matter of weeks. The atrocities of Sweetmeadow cannot go unanswered. If we attack, even in defense of our people, it will be nothing less than a call to war." Lailoken fixed his gaze on his fingers, anxiously rubbing his knuckles.

"But what if he will not listen? He seems a different man from the one I once knew."

When Lailoken looked up, it was the face of a Wisdom Keeper, not my own twin, gazing back at me.

"I can only hope that he will heed you," he said. "The wolves are circling and evening has come. It is time for the Dragons to find a safe haven."

CHAPTER 42

I thought on my brother's words late into the night. If only Gwenddolau could become better acquainted with Rhydderch. I would organize a hunt for the pair of them and then speak with my foster brother at day's end. Surely by then Gwenddolau would see that Rhydderch was deserving of his fealty. That he was a man who could be trusted. And yet, why hadn't Rhydderch told me about what had taken place at the village of Sweetmeadow? What Gwrgi had done to those innocent girls . . . children. I could not imagine.

The summer skies were gray and foreboding, rain misting in fine swaths beyond the shuttered windows. I sent a man to Gwenddolau's guest quarters, as was custom, to determine how he would like to spend the day.

Did Lord Gwenddolau wish to hunt?

He declined.

Surely then, he would like to watch a race? It could be organized quickly and with little effort; we maintained a good trail that ran clear through the pastures behind the hall. Again his response came back that he thanked Lady Languoreth and Lord Rhydderch, but what he would most prefer was to spend the day in his quarters.

"He comes to our hall only to refuse our invitations." Rhydderch gave me a look before striding toward the door. "I'm riding out to visit with the tenants. Rhys, come with me."

I twisted my fingers in my lap as Rhys followed his father out the door. Poor Rhys. He'd made such heroes of the Dragon Warriors. Now they'd hidden themselves away in our guest quarters like a bunch of petulant old men. The visit was going badly, but I could not let Rhydderch discover just how badly things truly stood.

Gwenddolau had never had much patience for playing politics. He must have already decided he would not pledge himself to Rhydderch. Now he would avoid his host and stay only long enough to get what rest he needed for his men.

"Is Father upset?" Gladys asked, watching her father and brother go.

"No, my love. It takes a great deal more than this to make your father upset, but Lord Gwenddolau has certainly insulted him with his refusals."

"It *is* insulting," Cyan said darkly. "He could at least suggest an activity that would better suit him."

"But why does he keep himself away?" Angharad complained. "Uther Pendragon is our uncle, yet he won't even come to us."

I bent to brush her hair behind her ear. "Your uncle is tired. He has had a long journey."

"He isn't our real uncle, anyway." Cyan narrowed his eyes. "He's only your foster brother."

"Foster siblings are no less legitimate than our own kin. It is an oath, a binding of family!" I spoke more sharply than I intended. I had not realized the depths of my own sadness. Gwenddolau was my brother, and I could not stand to see him coiled up in our guest quarters like a wounded old dragon.

Angharad fixed her eyes on the ground. "I want to see Lailoken," she said.

"You are right." I stood suddenly. "They have come all this way, and who knows when we shall see them again? Let us go to them, then. We shall go and see both your uncles right now."

Aela stood hurriedly. "My lady, if you mean to visit the guest quarters, perhaps you should send Brodyn first. The men may be . . . otherwise occupied."

Women, she meant. Most likely nude.

"If that is the case, I have no doubt Brodyn is already there," I said frankly. Tapping my cheeks to bring some color to them, I gestured for the children to follow me out of our hall and into the rain.

Droplets splattered down my bodice from the thatching overhead as I lifted the iron latch of the guest hall and thrust open the door.

Inside, the quarters smelled of stale mead and unwashed bodies. There was a flash of naked flesh as my eyes adjusted to the weak light and I heard a curse. Squinting into the gloom, I saw a yellow-haired warrior yank up his trousers as he swiveled to frown at me.

"Wait here a moment, children." I pressed them gently back.

The Dragon Warriors were scattered about the main room in varying states of undress, the prettiest whores of Goddeu come to sit astride them or bend provocatively to serve them drink. Gaming pieces were scattered on the tables, and smoke trailed from the wick of an oil lamp that had just exhausted itself. As if entirely too accustomed to his surroundings, Maelgwn sat at the long table in the center of the room, studying a map by candlelight.

"Greetings, General Maelgwn."

At the sound of my voice he rose too quickly, bumping the table and tipping the candle in its holder. Hot wax splattered across his knuckles and he cursed, frowning at his company.

"Cover yourselves, all of you. There is a lady present."

Cyan pushed in beside me, his gray eyes widening as a blond woman with berry-stained nipples reached languidly for her dress.

"Lady Languoreth. What brings you here?" Maelgwn asked. For a moment I imagined his eyes flickered with hope.

"I am looking for my brothers."

He gave a curt nod. "Gwenddolau is in the back chamber. Lailoken left earlier, I presume for a walk."

"I would speak with Gwenddolau. It is a matter of much import."

"Gwenddolau does not wish to be disturbed," he said carefully. "Perhaps I might be of service."

"No. You cannot be of service. I must speak to my foster brother." I planted my feet. Maelgwn studied me a moment before raising his brows with a nod.

"Very well, then. You can answer to him. Come, I will show you the way."

"I thank you, but there is no need." I held up my hand. "This is my guesthouse, after all. Come children, follow me. We're going to speak with your uncle."

Maelgwn did not give way as I brushed past him. I willed my cheeks not to flush at the nearness of his body to mine in the confined quarters of the room. The Dragon Warriors looked on—some in disbelief and some in disdain to have their revelry disrupted, and by the lady of the hall, no less—as I led the children past the smoldering hearth pit and rapped at Gwenddolau's door.

"What is it, then, are you ill?"

I thrust the door open but stopped at the sight of him.

Gwenddolau sat propped up in bed, his golden skin pale and his clear blue eyes rimmed red. He tried to stand at the sight of us but winced, doubling over, his hand cradling his ribs.

Angharad looked at him as she came to stand beside me.

"He has a wound," she said, tugging at my fingers. "On the outside it is healed, but it festers from within."

"How do you know this?" Gwenddolau demanded. Angharad shrank behind me, disappearing behind my skirts. I reached back to squeeze her little hand.

"It only matters if it is true," I said. "Come, brother. If you are injured, you must let me see."

"Mother," Gladys said meekly. "Perhaps we should wait outside?"

"Not me," said Cyan. "I want to see."

"Of course you may stay." Gwenddolau's laugh came easily but turned to a cough as he gestured to the stools perched beside his bed. "It gladdens me to see my nieces and my nephew."

"If you are certain," I said. I looked to the empty stool at his bedside. Lailoken had been there. His presence lingered upon the seat, and I wondered what they had been discussing.

"It's no trouble," Gwenddolau said. "Besides, such wounds of war will come. You would all do well to watch your mother at work."

"I'm afraid my healing skills have fallen out of use," I said. "Will you still let me?"

His eyes locked on mine. "You and no other."

"Very well."

"Cyan"—Gwenddolau bestowed a charming smile upon him— "you must tell me what you've learnt of Pythagoras of Samos whilst your mother pokes and prods at me. Lailoken says you are already a great student of philosophy."

Cyan beamed, then became suddenly quite serious. "Certainly, Uncle. You see, it was Pythagoras who first discovered that everything given to us by God was made up of numbers."

Gwenddolau's smile faltered as readily as it had come. "You mean to say the Gods."

I turned quickly, giving Cyan a reassuring look.

"Cyan is currently tutored by priests," I said. My eyes beseeched Gwenddolau not to berate his nephew for a fault not his own.

"Of course he is." Gwenddolau bowed his head. "Please. Continue, then, Cyan. And forgive my interruption."

I drew up Gwenddolau's shirt as the children began arguing over the role Pythagoras's disciples played in his work and Aristotle's thoughts behind his *Metaphysics*.

Gwenddolau watched them with amusement, but his blue eyes kept returning to Angharad. "It would seem your youngest possesses her mother's gift," he said.

"Nay. She is far more gifted than ever I was."

He sucked in a breath as my fingers tested the flesh between his ribs.

"Sorry, brother. Only a moment more." I leaned in to study the pink scar I found there, alarmed to feel the heat emanating from beneath. "This wound—what was it?"

"A spear," he said. "But it was some years ago."

The scar was the size of a game piece, but where the tissue should have been firm, there was a softness beneath it like rotten fruit. Angharad was right, not that I'd doubted her. Gwenddolau's old wound was festering from within. And the tightness in his cough—I worried for his lungs.

I lowered my voice. "When you cough, is there blood?"

"Some." He gestured at a rag beside the bed and I saw it was soiled with bright streaks of rust and phlegm. Our eyes met.

"Gwenddolau. You must tell my husband you are not well."

"No."

"Rhydderch thinks you insult him."

Gwenddolau rubbed a hand over his pale beard. The children had gone quiet, listening now.

I turned. "Children, perhaps you should go find your uncle Lailoken. General Maelgwn mentioned he'd gone off for a walk. Bid Aela go with you. And mind you fasten your cloaks and draw up your hoods so you don't get too soggy."

"Yes, Mother," Cyan and Gladys said, obedient. Only Angharad peered reluctantly over her shoulder as she followed them out the door.

With my children gone, I turned back to Gwenddolau.

"Lailoken has told me of your predicament," I said. "I know you place no faith in kings, but you must trust Rhydderch. Please, brother, I beg you. Tell him of your condition. Pledge your fealty in exchange for his aid."

Gwenddolau would not look at me. "You make it sound so simple." He reached for a bedside cup, his eyes lost in memory.

"Tell me, sister, do you remember the day we first heard that Vortigern had fled? The day we first heard of the great hero named Emrys?"

"Of course I remember. It was just after Mother died."

"Aye." He nodded. "Morken summoned us all to the courtyard. I had been training with my sword. That day I could not hack hard enough. I had lost so much, I wanted revenge. I could not know I was preparing for the day when I would fight at the side of that very same hero: the Great Pendragon, the man who summoned an army from the wilds. He taught me that only small men fight for revenge. Honorable men fight for something far greater. They fight for freedom.

"Shortly after I joined Emrys at the wall, his men made him their king," Gwenddolau went on. "A Wisdom Keeper had come. She hailed from the north. She consulted her oracle and conducted the sacrifice. She led Lord Emrys into his tent, and when they emerged some time later, he bore a mark just like this."

Gwenddolau slid back the loose collar of his shirt. There upon his chest was the massive likeness of a dragon. It was this I had glimpsed so long ago on the contest field at Lughnasa, but to see it up close was astonishing. Its talons gripped the smooth flesh of Gwenddolau's torso, its serpentine body twisting between the peaks of a mountain scene, claiming its land. The artistry was fearsome and of such tremendous skill that the dragon seemed to breathe with each rise and fall of Gwenddolau's chest.

His blue eyes pinned mine. "Your son is tutored by priests. Have you, Languoreth, so soon forgotten the Old Ways? Emrys is dead. I am the Dragon of the Isle. I have long sworn my oaths. My fealty is to the goddess of my land. I have bedded her. I have bled for her. And in return she has given me and my men her protection. I will not forsake her. We have carved out our own kingdom; we have made our own fortunes. I owe fealty and tribute to no one. Do you not see, little sister? If Uther Pendragon kneels before Strathclyde, I will not be the disappointment of a generation. I will be the coward of an era. The last Pendragon, the one who turned belly-up at the royal table."

"And what choice have you?" I asked.

Gwenddolau let his eyes drift closed as if he did not hear me. "I am not afraid of death. I feel that it comes. When the time comes, Maelgwn will succeed me. He will take the oath and become the third Pendragon. He is more than ready."

I reached for his hand. "Brother, please. You must listen to me now. Your men may be the fiercest of warriors, but your enemies are too many! Would you send your men to their deaths in payment for their loyalty? What of our own brother? What of Maelgwn, your most loyal friend?"

Gwenddolau yanked his fist from me and pounded it on the coverlet. "I will not trust a man who keeps the company of priests!" he shouted.

"If this is what it comes to, then you are a fool." My voice broke. For a moment I thought he would command me to leave. But he only closed his eyes and sank back against the pillows.

"I do not wish to fight," he said.

"Nor do I. But you must know that Rhydderch is a fair man; he is no zealot like his father. He married me, a princess of Cadzow and a daughter of the Old Way, did he not?"

"Who is to say that Rhydderch would aid me even if I should disgrace my legacy and swear him my fealty?" Gwenddolau said. "Rhydderch will not be named tanist if he displeases the king. And Tutgual is no friend of mine. He shelters my enemies, Languoreth. How many times have you seen my 'cousins' come to court? No. Gwrgi and Peredur are in the pocket of Strathclyde. Even if I did see fit to pledge Rhydderch my fealty, he would never make war against his own father."

I wanted to protest, but Gwenddolau was right. Tutgual was still far too powerful, and Rhydderch could not risk losing the Council's appointment of tanist. In Tutgual's eyes, and likely in the eyes of the other lords of Strathclyde, the Pendragons were an unruly threat that needed to be tamed, while lords like Gwrgi and Peredur bowed and simpered. Tutgual had long given preference to the lords of the east. I looked at Gwenddolau, his body gone slack against the pillows, and I could see how our conversation had taxed him.

"I am sorry," I said. "You must rest."

Gwenddolau's shoulders eased and I took his hand once more. "I will make you an elixir. It will help fight the festering and keep your cough at bay. But it cannot do its work if you exert yourself. You must stay another few days at least. I will speak to my husband. Tell him you've merely fallen ill. Rhydderch will make no demands on you."

Gwenddolau nodded, wary. "He is your kin, and I do not wish to insult him. He has been a most generous host. But we must leave on the morrow. My people are in jeopardy even now. I left strong men but took with me my general."

My heart sank but I nodded. "Of course. I understand."

A knock sounded at the door and Gwenddolau looked up. "Come," he said.

Maelgwn entered, looking between the two of us. "How are you, brother?"

"Hale as ever." Gwenddolau did not smile. "Languoreth is going to heal me up."

"Then you are in good hands," Maelgwn said, then looked away. "The servants have come with food. Shall I have them attend you here?"

"No. We cannot risk it. Have them leave my fixings by the main hearth."

"Very well." Maelgwn leaned out the door and said something beyond hearing. One of his men grunted and I heard the warrior address my servants. Gwenddolau was taken by a sudden fit of coughing and Maelgwn moved swiftly to conceal the sound by shutting the door.

I stood and smoothed my skirts. "I should see if the rain has let up. I must fix you that remedy and will need to gather some plants."

Gwenddolau nodded, but Maelgwn shifted his feet. "I will come with you," he said.

"I can assure you there's no need."

"I am sorry, but I must insist," Maelgwn said. "Sister or no, if you intend to make a remedy for Uther Pendragon, it will be under my watch."

"So be it," I said. I was too spent to be insulted, and besides, it had been just such a "remedy" that had caused the death of Lord Emrys. I could not blame the Dragon Warriors for being careful.

Gwenddolau smiled. For a moment the candlelight chased the shadows from beneath his eyes and I saw for the first time in too long the face of the brother I once knew.

"I am sorry I raised my voice," he said. "You must know how much I care for you."

I swallowed the lump that rose in my throat. "Yes. I know. I'm sorry, too."

"Well, then," he said. "I am eager to take your elixir when it is ready."

Gwenddolau bowed his head in thanks as Maelgwn held the door for me. In the main room he pulled his cloak from a hook on the wall as I turned to our servants who were laying out the midday meal.

"I'm going to gather some supplies. I'll be quite safe, but General Maelgwn has insisted on accompanying me. Tell Aela when you see her."

They bowed and I ducked outside into the wet.

"What will you need, then?" Maelgwn asked. We walked side by side past the stables and the apple trees growing heavy with green fruit, beyond the patch of grass where the elm had sprouted and into the wood.

"I need some oxeye. It's a certain type of daisy that may aid with his cough. I'll need to mix it with elderberry and some other remedies for the tincture, but I've plenty of all that."

The sky was still misting. Rain whispered against the leaves of the forest in a thousand tiny fingers, but the afternoon didn't yet carry the chill of autumn. Rather than look at Maelgwn, I tried to listen to what the rain might say. But the rain spoke of forgiveness, and the heart that thudded in my chest was far too wounded from years of silence to heed its urging.

I could feel my bitterness even now, leaking into the pit of my stomach. I stepped over a rain-drenched root that resembled an adder.

"You know Gwenddolau cannot fight this festering, don't you?" I asked.

Maelgwn bowed his head. "If you mean to say Gwenddolau is dying, then, aye, I'm aware that's the case."

"This tonic, it may help him for a few weeks. Into autumn, even. But it can only help a body that wishes to heal."

"You think he is used up, then?"

I did not have to look to know Maelgwn was studying the contours of my face.

"Yes."

"If that is so, I reckon any strength you can offer him will be a boon," he said. "He'll have to travel again soon to collect our rents. The people will want to see him."

I thought of my foster brother suffering in his bed. "It pains me to see how his destiny has used him."

Maelgwn looked at me. "Do not pity your brother. Gwenddolau

knew the demands; we all did. He would do the same again if given the chance."

"And what of you?" I trained my eyes on the wet ground before me. "Are you prepared to take his place?"

Maelgwn's answer was swift. "Aye. I'll do what must be done."

We spoke of such matters, but all I could feel was his nearness. I cursed my own stupidity, my insides pitching like a ship tossed at sea. I knew well enough where the bank of oxeye had sprouted; I did not have to fetch it myself. Maelgwn could have just as easily accompanied one of my servants to collect it. I should turn and hurry back to the hall before the fissures running through me cracked and all I knew I could not say rushed out.

But I could not turn back.

How could he have hurt me so? The air between us was piled thick with the weight of years gone by and too much left unsaid. No matter the danger, no matter the price, I could not leave. I deserved an answer, did I not? But I could not begin it. I could only walk, eyes fixed on the forest thickets. Just as I thought I would surely explode, Maelgwn stopped suddenly under the shelter of a silver birch.

"I know that I should be worrying for Gwenddolau, and I am," he said. "But my thinking's gone sideways being here with you. It has been impossible to find a moment to speak with you alone. And you have been too full of fury to even look upon me."

I turned to look upon him as he bade but said nothing. Maelgwn ran a hand over the shadow of stubble on his face. "So that is all? You will stand here with me and say nothing?"

"What would you have me say?" I asked, determined he should not see my hurt.

"Languoreth, if you only knew how long I've waited to see you once more, you wouldn't have the heart to behave like this. Please." He held out his hands and I stepped back as if he'd doused me in cold water.

"Do not touch me. Don't you dare. Seventeen years without a

word. Seventeen years in which you broke my heart over and over with each passing day, and now you say such things?"

Maelgwn dropped his hands to his sides as if stunned.

"Have you truly thought all this time I didn't love you? Sweet Gods, Languoreth. Everything I've done, I've done for the love of you."

"Love?" I exclaimed. "What you have done to me is not love. You left me to live a life I did not choose without even the slightest message of hope from the one man I believed my heart was made for. If you only knew how many nights I lay awake and wept, and still I heard nothing. To think I once thought you the bravest man I'd ever known. Well. I am glad I know now. You have shown me you are nothing more than a coward."

Maelgwn blinked, as if he had suddenly stepped from shadow into blazing sun.

"You think me . . . a coward."

I swallowed the tears that rose in my throat and stood there trembling, my breath shallow with anger. "And what else would I think? You knew your words were safe with my brother, and yet you chose to remain silent. Cowardice or lack of love—what does it matter? You should have had heart enough to spare me from such misery. Instead you did nothing. Said nothing. You abandoned me to seventeen years of silence and I was left with nothing but the ache of you. To love me in spite of the distance, to love me as I loved you. That, to me, would have been truly brave."

Maelgwn wiped the rain from his dark lashes, his eyes fixed on the ground.

"Perhaps you are right. Perhaps I have been a coward."

He shook his head as if thinking aloud. "That morning we parted at the foot of the mountain, I thought nothing could tarnish my love for you. I used to throw myself into battle with little care for my safety. Suddenly each battle took on a new urgency, because I knew that I must find my way back to you. What did it matter if you were wed to another when I knew, in truth, your heart was wed to me? The messages you sent were a balm, and I sent you the ring as a symbol of our promise. With each night that fell, it was as if I could sense you lying in the coming dark, thinking of me across the distance. But what good were messages of love when they could never be realized? To feel you but never again be with you? To think of you, but never again touch you? I thought I could handle such witchery, but I was wrong."

Maelgwn looked up, his eyes kindling with hurt and with anger. "You say I left you to live a life you did not choose. But you made your choice, that day in the wood. You chose a life apart from me. And as the days became weeks, and the weeks became the turning of a year, the words that once sustained me began to burn like a poison. Each missive I received was a reminder of all that could not be. I told myself I was doing what I must in remaining silent. I knew at first it would wound you. But I was certain that as time passed, it would save you from the suffering I felt. That you might at least find some happiness, if not with me, then with a man who might be king. But I see now that I was wrong."

He stopped, his face wet with a sheen of mist, looking at me as if I were some sort of earthbound goddess.

"Yes," I said. "You were wrong. So very wrong."

He reached to take my face between his hands as I stood, motionless, unable to break the spell.

"Look what I have done." He traced his thumb over my cheek. "Look how we have wounded ourselves. I told myself that this was the best way for you, but now I realize I did not do it for you. I did it for me. I failed you, my love. But I swear to you now, I will never fail you again."

My chest heaved with the sob I had been holding in the pit of my heart for too many years. I thought surely, if released, it would break me.

But then Maelgwn drew my face to his and kissed me.

I had forgotten what it was like, to say so much without speaking. Our lips spoke in volumes as my fingers roamed his rain-slicked hair, his sturdy jaw, the velvety lobe of his ear, his stubbled cheek. His breath was hot against my cheek and he tasted of spice and the sweet ferment of ale. It could not even occur to me that I was blind to the danger of discovery, my head so consumed in this fog of urgent desire. The only thing that mattered was that I taste Maelgwn and be tasted, that our bodies, which had been withering each day from being split apart, could meld together once more.

Maelgwn gripped my bottom roughly and I gasped as he pulled me into him, his hands roaming as if they could not fill themselves with enough of my flesh, his mouth hungry for the feel of my skin. I shivered a little from the rain as he pushed aside the fabric of my cloak and pulled at the lacing of my bodice. My dress was down around my shoulders and he broke away, his lips almost touching mine.

"Stop me now or I swear I will take you right here."

"I cannot stop you. I will not."

I reached for his face hungrily and drew his lips back to my own. It was all the assent he needed. He lifted me up, carrying me over the wet ground until my back was bolstered against the solid trunk of an oak. There were brambles that scratched at my flesh, but we were sheltered as he slid my skirts up around my waist and pushed inside me.

"I love you," I whispered, my forehead pressed to his. "I love you."

"I am sick with love of you." His voice was hoarse as he thrust against me. I cried out, my body erupting in pleasure, and my mind went empty. My body squeezed his in a hot and frenzied fury, my hair catching on tree bark as he pounded into me until I came to pieces again and again, his deep voice in my ear.

"Come for me, my love. Come for me again."

It was over too quickly. And as our chests heaved to recover in silent time with each other, Maelgwn lifted his head and scanned the forest protectively, as if it had just dawned upon him how risky our lovemaking had been.

"I do not want to move," he said, our bodies still locked together.

He shifted inside me and I gasped again. Maelgwn closed his eyes as if tucking the moment away in his memory and then moved to withdraw from me. I felt the loss of him instantly and pulled him back.

"No, no. Not yet."

"I don't care who should see us," he said, smoothing back my hair. "But you. You stand to lose everything."

"Shh." I covered his mouth with mine. I could not speak of it. Only one moment ago I had felt so whole, and now each word, each small span of distance, felt like a chisel chipping at my spirit.

At last he sensed I was ready and drew reluctantly away. His spear-hardened fingers were tender as they brought my dress up around my shoulders. The hem of my skirts fell back to the forest floor, the only memory of our coupling the quieting throb of my heart and the lingering wetness between my legs.

I looked at him and he nodded slowly, reaching for my hands. "Come. We must find that flower. We need not think of parting just yet."

His strong hand pulsed in mine, giving me strength. "It's this way."

Maelgwn followed me through the brambles and back onto the path, but a sharp rustle in the undergrowth made me stop and hold up my arm, stopping him in his tracks.

"Look," I whispered. "It's a stag."

Its chestnut fur was giving way in small patches to the darker hair of the coming winter, the velvet on his newly formed antlers all but gone. Maelgwn froze with the practice of a hunter and we stood in silence, watching as the young buck bounded gracefully over a great rotted log and disappeared into the greenery beyond.

"Beautiful." Maelgwn's deep voice was full of reverence. "Surely that's a good omen, aye?"

"Surely," I echoed. But as my eyes followed the buck's movement I could not ignore the deepening pit in my stomach. He was bounding south, toward the lands of Uther Pendragon and the Borderlands. Yes, he was fleeing south and east, toward the Wall.

CHAPTER 43

Moon daisy, Ariane had called it. The thin, velvety petals glittered with rain as I drew out my knife and harvested what I needed. The rain had given way to murky skies by the time we reached the green sloping bank dotted white with oxeye. It was late in the season, but there were plants enough, and I turned to Maelgwn as I shook the water from the stems, tucking them gently into a piece of cloth. "This is what we seek, though you wouldn't know a toxin if you saw one."

"Did you think I was truly worried?" he laughed. "How else was I to get you alone?"

"You're a terribly good bluffer."

"I wouldn't be much use as a general if I wasn't." He smiled and folded his arms across his broad chest. It was the same self-satisfied expression our son Rhys wore when he'd told a good joke or bested Rhydderch in gaming.

"What is it?" Maelgwn shifted. "Why are you looking at me so?" His smile faded as he studied my face. "There's something you wish to tell me."

I wanted more than anything to tell him of Rhys. I knew he suspected as much already. But I didn't want to hurt him anymore, ever again. And I just didn't know how to begin. I took a breath. Better to just come straight out with it.

"You're right. I wanted to tell you—"

"Mummy!" I startled and looked up to see Angharad racing toward me along the forest path, her arms flung out in delight. Lailoken lifted a hand in greeting, Cyan and Gladys at his side.

"We'll come back to it," Maelgwn assured me.

I gave a slight nod as Lailoken called out, "Your wood nymphs have found me and I am returning them unharmed!"

Angharad grinned up at her uncle, her pale face dusted with summer freckles.

"We were catching moths in our hands, like this!" She cupped her hands and made a show of peeking inside the cage of her fingers.

"I see. You're a pack of rascals," I said, smiling, and bent to snare her in my arms. "Did you know that if you knock the dust from the wings of a moth, it can no longer fly?"

Angharad stopped.

"It's true," Gladys said. "I told her not to do it. She never listens."

"You would do very well to listen to your elder sister," I said, drawing back to look at her. "And what have you got in your pockets?"

I waited as Angharad dug for her treasures.

"Ah, green acorns," I observed. "And a very pretty jay feather. And this . . ." I took the red-bulbed mushroom between two fingers. Some of the white warts had worn off in Angharad's pocket, but Lailoken should know better.

I looked into her slate-colored eyes. "This toadstool is poison, Angharad. It can kill you."

"That's not what our uncle said," she protested. "Lailoken told me the Wisdom Keepers eat this mushroom and it teaches them how to fly."

Maelgwn chuckled. I looked at Lailoken with a frown. "Your uncle said that, did he?"

"To other *realms*," Lail said, waving it away. "She knows it cannot teach you to flap like a bird."

"And did he also tell you that only a Wisdom Keeper knows how to prepare it thusly?"

"Of course I did. But Angharad's no fool. She knows not to eat it, don't you?" Lailoken tousled her auburn hair. "She admires the colors is all."

"Doesn't matter." I took the toadstool firmly in hand and looked at her. "This has no place in a little girl's chamber. Toss it away, please."

Angharad's little face reddened with shame and I tamped down a swift surge of guilt. I felt the weight of Lailoken's gaze upon me as she took the mushroom gingerly from my palm and tossed it back into the forest.

"Come now, children. Let's walk back to the hall."

Lailoken came to walk beside me as we moved along the forest path. "That was cruel," he said softly so the children would not hear.

"You cannot allow children to collect poisonous mushrooms." I looked away and beckoned for Cyan and Gladys to join me. "So," I said brightly, "tell me of your adventures. Where have you been this morning?"

We walked back together through the wood, Angharad trotting closely behind with Maelgwn. He smiled as she rattled on about the wild creatures they had seen and the tales Lailoken had told them.

"Did you know that it takes thirty petals to make a daisy?" she asked. "And twenty-four grains of pollen can be carried on the belly of a bee."

Later that evening, long after dinner had been served, I sat with a cup of wine on the slope of grass in front of our hall where I could look out over the river. I could feel the press of ruthless men on Gwenddolau's borders as if they shadowed my own. Tonight I would speak with Rhydderch. There had to be a way. Several paces away, Rhys practiced with his sword, and watching him brought me comfort. Soft strains of music sifted through the twilight. Though Gwenddolau had again been absent from dinner, the Dragon Warriors had found an ease with Rhydderch's men, and I could hear deep rumbles of laughter as they passed round the ale horn, trying to best one another with stories. Amid it all I waited for Maelgwn to come; I'd felt his gaze upon my back as I'd turned to leave. But our men were everywhere. Rhys was here, swinging his sword. And anywhere else we might possibly escape to would be too private to be seemly. I could hardly admit Uther Pendragon's general into my private chamber.

In the end, it was Lailoken who found me instead.

"You're missing great tales about goats." He crouched down beside me, cup in hand.

"Ah, then I've left just in time."

My brother plopped down heavily beside me in the grass. "I owe you thanks. Gwenddolau told me of your discussion. He seems much relieved by your medicine. He was even able to prop himself up for dinner."

"Though not in our hall," I added.

"But you spoke with Rhydderch, did you?"

"I told him only that Gwenddolau had fallen ill on his travels. You know more than anyone that Rhydderch is shrewd. I cannot say he believed me. I rather think not." I glanced at him. "I have not yet spoken to Rhydderch about Gwenddolau's allegiance. I will do it this night."

I thought again of the little girls. Perhaps Lailoken was right. Perhaps I did not know my own husband after all. The thought gave me a sudden chill.

"Are you cold?" Lail asked, wrapping a sturdy arm around me.

"No. I was only thinking how much I miss you."

"And I you."

"Things haven't been the same since you left."

"I suppose we've both grown up, haven't we?"

I looked down. "Sometimes, when it's quiet here, I think about our childhood days at Cadzow with such longing, I could weep. It doesn't feel right that we should live so far apart, you and I. You're half of me, you know."

Lailoken looked out over the edge of the gorge in the fading light, his thumb absently tracing the finger where we'd pricked our oaths so long ago.

"Nothing can touch those days," he said. "The earth here remembers. We remember." He looked up at the first stars of twilight. "Someday we shall live together again. When we are old and wrinkled. You can build me a grand house up on a hill, somewhere I can observe the stars, and we shall drink wine and hobble about and bicker, just as we do now."

"Sweet Gods," I groaned. "Pray someone strike me dead before all that."

Lail laughed, a sweet, rich sound that eased the pulsing of my heart. From behind the hall, the low call of our groom sounded as he summoned the horses to the stable for the night. Rhys was a shadow against the fading sky as he sheathed his sword and swiped at his brow.

"Are you finished, Rhys?" I called out.

He looked over. "In a while, Mother. There's light enough yet to toss the spear."

"He is a strong warrior already," Lailoken observed, setting down his cup. "Much like his father."

"Of course. Rhydderch is a prince, after all."

Lailoken's eyes softened. "It will only become more apparent the older he gets. Surely you must have considered this."

I glanced over my shoulder. "He is nearly seventeen winters and no one is yet the wiser. This secret shall not leave us. Is that clear?"

"Do not doubt it," Lail said. "I worry for the boy is all. He is a fish out of water at Rhydderch's court."

"Not so long as he swims in his mother's sea."

"And will he keep to his mother's sea when the men of his family drink from the baptismal font? His father is of the Old Way. Our way."

"Rhys is strong and wise and blessed with a kind heart. Religion will not change him."

"And what about Angharad? Would you see her raised a Christian, too?" Lail looked at me keenly. "Come, now, sister. You must have realized by now that she is Chosen."

My ears pricked like a mother lion's. "So now we get to the heart of it. Yes. I suppose it is plain enough to see."

"The Gods have marked her, Languoreth. This is a call greater than any mortal man or woman can deny. I thought as much before, but now I am certain. She has our mother's gift. The one you could never realize. She needs proper training. And yet you chastise her."

Lailoken's words stung, and I drew away.

"How might I encourage her, Lailoken? Tutgual King cares not what mortal men can or cannot deny. He would never consent to have Rhydderch's daughter trained as a Keeper. Zealotry aside, she's too valuable a pawn. He'll want her wed. And Rhydderch would never consent to send his favorite daughter away. He is most attached. No. I will not see her heart broken over this."

"As yours was?"

"I think you remember how I felt." I fell quiet.

"The call was not yours to receive. But it is your daughter's," he said firmly. "I prayed you had made peace with this some time ago."

"I've made peace with a great many things," I said.

"Indeed? You talk of Rhydderch and Tutgual, but I think there is a deeper reason you have not heeded Angharad's calling."

The truth poked my soft places like a stick but I shook my head.

"She is nearly eight winters, but it is not yet too late," Lailoken said. "Let me take her. I will love her and foster her, and above all I will ensure she receives proper training."

"Take her?"

The thought of Angharad being taken from me brought on a wave of panic so swift, it was as if someone had thrust a hand into my body and ripped the womb from my belly. "She is a child, Lailoken. She cannot be taken from her mother."

"Children younger than Angharad have heeded the call. Already she and I are bonded. Surely you can see that, too."

I looked up, bewildered. "And what do you know of raising a child?"

"I am a man of thirty-two winters and head counsellor to Uther Pendragon," Lailoken said. "Since joining our brother in the Borderlands, I have initiated scores of young men and women into the Keepers' fold, and yet you look at me and all you see is a boy, your twin. I am grown to a man, Languoreth, and I am not incapable of raising and loving a child. What I do not know of being a father, Angharad would teach me, and I would be her most ardent student."

"Let it lie, brother," I said, my voice full of warning. "I will not discuss this any further."

"I only ask that you hear me." Lailoken shifted to crouch before me, his face earnest. "I swear to you, Languoreth, I will love Angharad like my own. I will lay down my life to protect her. I promise you, no harm will come to your daughter in my care."

"I am sick of Wisdom Keepers telling me what I must sacrifice, of taking every last thing I love away!" I turned away, tears spilling onto the fabric of my robe.

The air between us was charged as if by a storm. Lailoken pressed his lips together, and I saw the mottled pink patches where his beard would never grow. The seal I'd made with the branding of my knife.

"You asked if I remembered how you felt," Lail said. "I remember you felt robbed of your greatest desire. I remember you felt as if you were nothing more than a game piece." He looked up. "Is this what you wish for your daughter? This is Angharad's destiny. She will wither without it. Angharad is meant to be a Keeper. Please. Do not be the one to stand in her way."

I dropped my head into my hands. "I cannot say good-bye to her. Not my little girl."

Lailoken waited.

When at last I spoke, it was in a whisper. "If she goes, when might I next see her?"

"It will be some time. If I am to foster her, I could not bring her when I came to your court. It would only confuse the child. She will need to be immersed in her training. She could visit when she reaches fifteen, but not before."

"Seven years." I nearly choked.

"Seven years and she will be free, living the destiny the Gods have carved for her," Lailoken said. "What is seven years in exchange for that?"

"Seven years is a lifetime in a mother's heart." My voice was bitter, my stomach cramped as if she had already been wrenched from my arms.

Lailoken bowed his head. "I understand."

"I do not believe you do."

A straw moth flicked past my ear, drawn to the gold embroidery of my robe. I watched as it settled on my bent knee and folded its papery white wings over its back.

"I will speak with her," I said at last. "It must be her choice. Angharad must understand what it means. She must know what she will lose."

"Of course," Lail said.

"And what of Rhydderch and the king?"

"Leave it with me. I will speak with your husband." Lail stood with ease and extended a hand to help me to my feet.

"You must never lose faith in the Gods, Languoreth. Angharad is marked to become a Keeper. What is meant to be will come to pass, I can promise you that."

The bodice of my robe felt suddenly tight as I entered the hall, as if it were pressing the breath from me. Maelgwn sat beside the hearth surrounded by a group of twenty men, all of whom seemed to be vying for his attention. He looked up and his face stirred at the sight of me, but his green eyes were sad.

He could not break free without being noticed, and I could not risk a message, written or not. Women had been executed for less deceit than I was guilty of. And what might become of Rhys if it was discovered that he was not Rhydderch's natural son? Banishment, if not death.

No, the truth of the matter would have to go unsaid. Tomorrow, if all went as the Gods seemed to will it, I would be forced to say good-bye not only to my lover but also to my child. I turned as Lailoken strode past the hearth and bent to speak low in Rhydderch's ear. I could not bear witness to this—any of it. Rhydderch stiffened, his gray eyes settling on me, and I wondered if he could see the guilt that clung to me like leeches.

I signaled my retirement for the evening to my husband and climbed the stairs, knowing eventually he would follow.

What answer would he give Lailoken? Perhaps he would not answer him at all. My chamber was a sanctuary of stillness. I draped myself over the bed, half-extinguished. I must have closed my eyes, for when I opened them, Rhydderch was sitting beside me, his bearded face watchful.

"You fell asleep," he said, his voice even, his eyes unreadable.

"Has it been long?" I pushed myself up with some effort.

"It has been a long night for me," he said, his voice not so much weary as oddly numb. "I have only just come from speaking with your brother. You know what he asks?"

"I do."

"There were days when one could not refuse the call of a Keeper, or so Lailoken reminds me."

"Yes."

"And you, as Angharad's mother, you would part with her?"

I closed my eyes. "I would. Though it would shatter me."

Silence hung heavy between us until at last he looked up. "Then Angharad will leave with your brother and the Warriors Pendragon in the morning."

My heart swung between uncertainty, loss, and relief. "And you?" I asked. "Is this what you wish?"

Rhydderch bowed his head. "The old laws are not yet gone from here. But now new laws rise, too, laws I do not always have a taste for. I love Angharad. I love my child," he said. "But I have seen her speak to things that I cannot see. I have watched her fascination as she walks in the wood. I know there is no place for our daughter in a land of priests. The old laws are no more mine to break than are the new. My only hope is for our daughter's happiness."

"But your father . . . What if he does not consent?"

"I have considered it, believe me, wife. There were days when Tutgual still visited the temples of the forest, just as I yet do. But my father is not sentimental. His zeal will not prevent him from seeing a purpose when that purpose presents itself. Your brother may be a Wisdom Keeper, but he is also head counsellor to Gwenddolau. Uther Pendragon may never swear fealty to my father, but Angharad's fostering would create a bond between Strathclyde and the Pendragons. It may someday be of use to him, though he may not know yet to what end."

"Then it is done," I said.

He traced his thumb over the back of my hand. "Yes. It is done."

Until this moment, my skin had borne only Maelgwn's touch. Rhydderch's fingers brushed the enchantment away like dust from a moth's wings.

I drew my hand away gently. "I should go to her. She will be sleeping soon. Will you come?"

"Nay. Let her hear it from her mother. I will be better fit to see her off in the morning. Besides"—he cast a gloomy look toward the door—"we have guests yet in the great room. I must return for a while before I can retire to bed."

I nodded and Rhydderch turned to leave, but I knew I must ask him the question that had been haunting me since Lailoken's return.

"Husband. I would rest better for my part if I knew you had no knowledge of the most recent dealings of Gwrgi and Peredur."

He looked at me, his gray eyes tired. "I will not aid Gwenddolau. I cannot. Do not press me, wife. For tonight, I have given you enough."

Rhydderch had answered. I had no choice but to leave it for now, but I vowed to bide my time. Perhaps there would yet be a way to make my influence felt. And, truth be told, I had no argument left in me. I was to say good-bye to my daughter on the morrow. Tonight I would tell her that in the morning she'd be leaving.

Cyan was already asleep against his pillows, but he shifted a little, restless, as I kissed him and blew out his candle. In the room beyond I heard Gladys and Aela softly laughing and the slap of water as it spilled over the edge of the wooden tub and onto the floor. I found Angharad in the chamber she shared with her sister, her nightdress bunched up around her knees as she crouched on the bed like a magpie, sorting her woodland treasures.

She glanced up. "Hello, Mama."

"Hello, little dove." The hay in the mattress made a shushing sound as I sat down beside her and smoothed back her hair, still wet from her bath. Her skin smelled of pine needles and rosemary soap. Was this how my own mother felt when she had to break my heart? She had been firm, too firm, and at the time it had seemed needlessly cruel. Now I sat before my own daughter with happier news, yet it was not happy at all.

"Something has happened today and I must speak with you," I began. "There is no easy way to discuss it. You and I, we both must be brave. Can you do that?"

Angharad went still, her hand hovering uncertainly over a pine-cone. "Mama, what is it?"

She sat back on the coverlet and looked up at me, suddenly seeming so much older than her years.

Say the words, I urged myself. *Then it will be out. It will be done.*

"I have always known you were special, and your uncle knows this, too. Lailoken would like to take you with him when they leave in the morning. He would train you as a Wisdom Keeper. You would be trained like my mother, the lady Idell, was before you. You could learn all you wished about healing and plants and the gods of our people."

"Me?" Angharad blinked. "A Wisdom Keeper?"

"Yes." I fought to keep my voice measured. "But do you understand what this would mean, my love?"

Her gray eyes fell to the coverlet, her voice a whisper in the firelit chamber. "My uncle would take me away from you."

"That's right." I nodded and pursed my lips, busying myself in tucking her coverlet snugly about her. "He would foster you and love you as his own."

"But I don't want to leave you, Mama!" It was the panic in her voice that made me suck in a breath, fighting to keep my voice steady.

"I know, my darling." I pulled her to me so that she could not see my tears, but was almost undone again breathing in the scent of her.

"I cannot bear the thought of your leaving. I cannot tell you how much I wish for you to stay. But, Angharad, we must both be strong. We must think of your future. You must listen to me." I drew back, taking her little face between my hands. Her cheeks were hot beneath my thumbs as I wiped away her tears.

"Your elder sister, Gladys, will be raised in court. When the time comes, she will be married and sent away, the bride of some unknown lord or chieftain. This is her duty, as it was mine. But Gladys's path is not made for you. As a Wisdom Keeper you would come and go as you pleased. You could make your home in whatever court you so chose.

To see the wide world, protected under the mantle of a Keeper, is an honor and a privilege many Britons only wish to have."

She looked up, fearful. "Do you . . . wish me to do it?"

I swallowed. "I will not lie to you, my dove. I am at war with myself. Truth be told, if you should leave me, I do not think I could survive it. And yet, survive it I will, because I *do* wish this for you. I wish this for you more than anything."

Angharad picked up her jay feather and studied it, considering. "But . . . cannot Gladys come with me?"

"Gladys's path is hers. This path belongs only to you. Besides. Marrying a far-off lord or chieftain isn't so dreadful. Look how it brought me all of you."

I forced a smile and took her hand, smoothing it as if rubbing away a blemish.

"We may be apart, but nothing will alter the fact that I am your mother. And I will love you to the ends of the earth and back, wherever you should go. My blood flows in yours. You carry half my spirit in yours. In this we will always be together, do you understand?"

My voice broke and I squeezed my eyes shut. "You must always remember that."

"Don't cry, Mama, please don't cry." Angharad's voice was small, her slender body now shaking with tears.

"What's happened?" Gladys stood in the doorway, stricken, Aela close behind.

I opened my mouth to speak, but Angharad drew the wings of her shoulder blades up.

"I'm to be a Wisdom Keeper," she said, even as her sister's face fell. "I am to leave with Uncle Lailoken in the morning."

CHAPTER 44

I lay awake the long night. Perhaps I thought if I did not sleep, morning might never come. Rhydderch came to bed smelling of peat smoke and ale. In the hut across the courtyard, I could feel Maelgwn lying awake, too, his thoughts trained on me, but there was no place for him where guilt did not devour me. My daughter was leaving when next I opened my eyes. What was the loss of a lover compared to that?

At last, out of the eerie morning stillness, came the screech of a barn owl; a call from the dead. My mother would watch over her. I closed my eyes and dreamed of feathers drifting from the trees overhead, landing at my daughter's feet.

When I woke, I stood numbly as Aela helped me dress, my naked body pricked with gooseflesh. *Odd that the sun is shining*, I thought, *when my heart has been split and butchered in such a way.*

Angharad woke and I hovered over her, helping her dress, fastening her brooch with trembling fingers. "Will your gray cloak be warm enough? There will be wind, and the chill comes at night. Perhaps you should wear the fur."

Rhydderch touched my hand. "It is yet summer, my love. Our daughter will be warm. And she rides with Lailoken. She'll have use of his cloak."

"Yes, of course."

I watched as he bent and drew Angharad to him. She buried her face against the crook of his neck.

"There, there, my littlest love," he murmured. "You have made us so proud."

Angharad's face was calm but her fists were white-knuckled. I looked away and led her down the stairs and to the door. Outside, the men were waiting. It would be a long ride before they rested at sundown.

Aela and I had packed what things Angharad might need in one of my sturdiest trunks.

"This is the trunk I brought with me when my father first took me to Partick," I had told her. "Now it will carry you on a journey all your own."

But I would give her one last parting gift. The sun glinted off the dragon hilt as I unfastened my knife from my waist and pressed the gift into her hands. The belt buckle was most worn on the smallest setting, the hole that fit the waist of a little girl once no more than ten.

"Wear it, my love, and may it bring you luck. There is nothing in my life I have kept closer, save you," I whispered, securing the belt at her waist. "Ask your uncles. They will teach you to wield it."

Then the courtyard, the horses. Parting gifts of bread and cheese and salted pork. Wine in flasks. The bustling of servants and the ominous scraping of trunks on a cart. Cathan had told me once that farewells took practice, but I knew now it was only a ploy designed to appeal to my logic—a distraction for his most ardent student.

That sunny, late summer morning, I knelt and told my daughter the truth.

"Angharad, the heart is a bird pricked full of feathers. And each time we say good-bye to someone we love, a feather will fall. One for a friend, two for a lover, three for a child."

I took Angharad's face in my hands. "This means that whenever you should find a feather, you will know it is from me. It has fallen from my heart. Pick it up and keep it close, for it carries with it all my love for you. If you believe this, if you remember this, these feathers will protect you and keep you safe."

Angharad blinked. "But, Mama"—her gray eyes clouded—"what happens to the bird when it loses all its feathers?"

I considered this a moment, caught by surprise. "A bird can never lose all its feathers," I said. "New ones always sprout in return."

Gwenddolau emerged from the guest quarters, his hair freshly plaited and his shoulders squared with purpose. The golden hue had returned to his face, and I watched as Maelgwn clapped him on the back.

"Ready, then, brother?" There was a tightness in Maelgwn's voice, and as our eyes met, I knew I was the cause of it.

I lifted my hand to my collarbone and let it rest there just long enough that he might spy the green ring that glinted on a finger of my right hand. Maelgwn's eyes kindled and he gave a faint smile. I closed my eyes, pressing the sight of him into my memory. His black hair, tied partway back, his scaled leather armor. His broad shoulders and callused hands. The crescent scar that now marked his brow, and the way his eyes pierced me to the core.

I crossed the courtyard and embraced Gwenddolau, passing him a fresh bottle of the tincture I'd made.

"Thank you, little sister. I am grateful for your care."

"I was glad for your visit, whatever the circumstances. But now you leave and you take with you my child," I said. "Watch out for Angharad. Mind that my brother takes good care of her."

Maelgwn spoke instead, his eyes locked on mine: "We will guard her with our lives. I promise you no harm will come to Angharad whilst I live and breathe."

"I thank you."

As Gwenddolau looked between us, I saw realization flicker at last.

He angled his head, a look of warning to Maelgwn, but swung astride his dappled horse and called out to his men.

"Mount up. It is time to ride."

The passing of hours had been like wading through honey, and now the moment had come.

My fingers clutched at my dress. "I am not ready—"

"We are ready," Maelgwn whispered, his fierce voice reassuring. "You know how I feel. Time cannot alter it."

There would be messages this time. Perhaps there would be a way yet to tell him what he deserved to know.

I tested the buckle of Lailoken's girth as he helped Angharad astride, nestling her in front of him. "If she grows tired, let her ride in the cart."

"I will." He took my hand. "We will send word when we reach the fort."

"May the Gods keep you close," I said. "I love you, my little dove."

Angharad looked down at me uncertainly now, as if she might have changed her mind, but in the same moment Lailoken gave his gelding a swift kick. I climbed the wooden platform of the rampart and watched until they disappeared from view. The last thing I saw was Angharad looking over her shoulder, her tawny hair streaming across her face, clinging to her tears.

"Mother." Rhys's deep voice brought me back to myself.

Had I other children? I blinked and pressed my hand to my stomach as if to keep my innards in.

I did have others, and now they had come to stand beside me. Gladys was leaning against me, her face swollen with tears. Cyan was looking out over the field, a fierce look upon his face and a tremble in his lower lip. My sob came before I could stifle it, a keening that caused me to clutch at my skirts, doubling over. Gladys swayed with me and I wrapped my arms about her, burying my face in her smooth fair hair. We stayed like that for some time, the four of us. The court-yard emptied behind us. Rhydderch stood below for a while; when I next looked, he had gone.

Days passed, and it was soon time to return to Partick. The leaves of the trees above the river burned gold and the pines had begun drop-ping their cones. I busied myself overseeing the packing of our trunks to keep from the hole that Angharad's departure had left. Macon was an old man now, but I trusted no other to keep Cadzow slumbering on tightly through the winter. It soothed me to use my body, and the ser-vants indulged me as I helped move the horses to pasture so we could clean out the stables and checked and rechecked the hay stock and food stores. The men always cursed their luck, because even though our forest was thick with deer, no spear or arrow seemed to catch them when I was in residence. Now that I was leaving, the deer, too, would be left to fend for themselves.

Rhys rode with me down to our little quay on the Clyde to chat with our tenants as they hoisted heavy sacks of flour and grain onto my father's old boats.

I turned to him. "Do you like it here?"

The wood smelled of freshly fallen leaves, and Rhys was riding with his face tilted up to the sun. "Like it?" He opened one eye in a child-like squint that made me smile.

"Good. Someday it shall all be yours."

He straightened then, as if suddenly remembering the burden of adulthood, and I cursed myself for speaking.

At sunset on the eve of our departure, I went to sit beside the mound among the oaks that held my father's body.

"I'll come with you, my lady." Aela set aside her sewing to help me with my cloak.

"No, Aela, thank you, but I wish to go alone."

Alone. It wasn't the truth. At Cadzow I was never alone. I was surrounded by ghosts: the spirits of the dead and the memories of those yet living. Their shadows were soaked into stone and earth and wood. Here was the field where Maelgwn had caught me in his arms, barefoot with soot upon his face. Here was the hut where Cathan had sat, his open hands resting on his knees as he taught us of laws and nature and man. Here was the mortar and pestle gripped by Ariane and, before her, by my mother. There in the Hall were the shields painted by Brodyn and Brant, and the coverlets sewn by Crowan that yet warmed the beds.

I rounded the bend on the forest path and spotted the oaks up ahead. They stretched their timeworn limbs, welcoming me like an old friend. The sentinels of a great king. The grassy mound where his body slumbered was lit like a torch by shafts of sinking sun.

I circled the mound sunwise until I reached the spot farthest from the path where I could sink into the grass and be hidden, my knees tucked to my chest and my back bolstered against the depths of earth piled between us.

At first, as always, there was only me. I set the little spray of golden leaves and rowanberries I'd gathered on my walk upon the grass next to me and let my eyes fall closed. My lips moved in a prayer for my parents, for Cathan and Crowan in the Summerlands, for the ancestors who had come before them. I pulled the flask from my cloak and poured the wine. And then a soft autumn wind rose and rustled in the trees. It played at the wisps of hair at my ears and suddenly I felt them gathered close, if only for a moment. As if my mother's love and my father's body sleeping below could stir the winds of the earth to touch my cheek one last time. Cathan had once promised me that the dead never leave us. In this moment I felt that it was true.

"Please protect my loves," I whispered. "Please keep them safe."

The only answer was a drop in the breeze and the plaintive call of a ewe who'd strayed too far from her flock. Then there came a rustle in the hedges. I bristled at the sudden wave of discomfort. As if the very air in the wood around me had grown thin, and I was suddenly no longer alone.

But what did I know? I was no Wisdom Keeper. And though Ariane had promised, she had never taught me the language of the wind. I gathered my things and stood too quickly, breaking the evening spell.

Winter came early, with snows piling past our horses' knees and, with it, the season of stories, of Clota and the Seven Geese, of Brân the Blessed, son of Lir. There were new tales, too, as Song Keepers traveled between courts spreading news and stories about the kings, Keepers, and warriors of our land. I wondered what the Keepers in Tutgual's court were saying of Gwenddolau and Lailoken, for even the Song Keepers knew better than to sing their praises before Tutgual King.

Angharad sent word that Lailoken warmed her bed with a hot stone on cold nights, and Maelgwn sent word that the Dragon Warriors were charmed beyond belief; the brave men of Gwenddolau's fort were wrapped round my daughter's little finger. It somewhat eased my mind to think she was so well loved by my brother and his men, safe under not only Maelgwn's hawk-eyed care but also that of some of the most famed warriors of our island.

And as Rhys's seventeenth winter came and went, his father took him to the mountain for three nights. He returned, his fingers and toes burned by frost, but he'd been made into a man. He would not speak of what had transpired, but he stood straighter and spoke with more care. Village and noble girls of Partick alike began to appear wherever Rhys went, their eyes lit with romance at the sight of him, and I could not blame them. With his dark hair falling to his shoulders and his sea-green eyes, he was the very image of his father.

As the snows receded, fiddlehead ferns began to poke up from the

earth. Summer came, and then the first days of autumn. I pushed
Cathan's prophecy from my mind until one fall morning, more than a
fortnight before Samhain, when my weaving was disturbed by the in-
cessant cawing of a crow beyond the shutter. Elufed sat beside me, her
smooth brow bent over her work until she looked up in annoyance.

"Well, go see to it, will you? It isn't here for me."

"Do you mean the bird?" Gladys stood and Elufed cast her an impatient look.

"Never mind it, my child. This is for your mother."

Gladys glanced between us uncertainly before taking her seat.

"Don't worry, Gladys. I'll only be a moment."

Elufed need not say what I already knew. There were few times I
spotted a crow without thinking of Cathan, but even as I wrapped a
woolen shawl hastily about my shoulders and stepped outside into the
autumn gloom, I shivered a little with a sense of foreboding.

The crow sat on the slender ledge that trimmed the window, its
black feet planted stubbornly.

"Very well. What is it?" I whispered, too aware of the gate guards
with their crosses pretending to be good Christian men. The bird
whipped round and regarded me with a tilt of its head, the lids blinking over its inky eyes. Then, as suddenly as it had appeared, it lurched
toward me with a great "*Caw!*"

"Sweet Gods!" I cursed and shrank back, heart racing as the bird
took flight over my head. The gateman spun on his heel, spear in
hand.

"No, it's all right," I assured him, placing a hand to my racing heart.
"It was a bird is all."

He gave a curt nod. I watched the crow's dark silhouette glide high
over the gate as if in warning. Someone was coming. Someone with ill
intent. I would not have to wait long, for the next moment a rumble
sounded like distant thunder. I looked to the tarnished sky in search of

rain before I realized it was the thrumming of horse hooves sounding from the road.

The sentries squinted and gathered together, testing the heft of their weapons in their hands as the riders approached. I heard a great thudding of hooves come to a stop.

"Announce yourselves," the sentries warned. Then I heard a man's harsh voice call out, "It is Lord Peredur, son of Eliffer, in the company of his brother."

I tugged my shawl more tightly about me and hurried inside, back to the weaving room.

"Gwrgi and Peredur have come," I warned. "They travel in great company."

Elufed lifted her hands from her work. "And this was warned by the crow?"

I nodded.

Gladys looked nervously to the shuttered window. "What does it mean, Mother?"

"It means we must ready the feast hall and the guest quarters right away." Elufed stood abruptly, summoning her serving woman.

"Mother." Gladys fixed her eyes on me. "What does it mean?"

"It was a warning no good will come of this visit," I said, my stomach churning beneath my robe. "Your father is in the great room. Go and tell him who has arrived."

"And shall I tell him of the crow?"

"Goodness, no," I said quickly. "Tell him nothing of the bird. And, Gladys," I added, causing her to pause, "do not come outside. Find your father and then go to your chamber."

"But, Mother, won't it be rude?"

"Don't argue, now," I snapped. "Obey me. Is that clear?"

Her cheeks reddened, but she dipped her head in quick assent as she turned to go, and I felt a stab of regret. Too often of late Gladys had borne the brunt of my sharpness. But I had seen the way Gwrgi's dark eyes pricked with delight at the sight of my eleven-year-old daughter, and I would not provide him another glance.

Elufed finished directing the servants and sent them away, cursing under her breath. "Why were we not forewarned? I do not like surprises. My man shall know my displeasure when next I see him." Her eyes were icy with her threat, but beneath them I saw a flicker of fear. Elufed had watchers everywhere. Never before had they failed her. She caught me looking at her and straightened.

"Don't fret, Languoreth. Corpse birds should warn of Gwrgi and Peredur wherever they go. Perhaps this is nothing so special," she said, trying to soothe me in her way, then touched her coiled hair. "We must greet them, I suppose." My mouth must have curved in disgust, for she frowned.

"Give them a warm welcome. You show your displeasure too readily upon your face."

"Gwrgi and Peredur know that I despise them. In fact, I rather think they enjoy it," I said.

"All the more reason." Elufed fixed her pretty mouth in a smile as a servant helped her with her shawl. "Why would you endeavor to provide them with even a moment's pleasure?"

I drew myself to my full height and took my place beside the queen as the sentries admitted the men on horseback into the courtyard. I counted more than forty in number, wearing their fur-lined autumn cloaks, their leather boots stained dark from muck and weather, faces dirty and hair unwashed. Among them I spotted square-faced Gwrgi as he gave a violent yank on his horse's reins, and Peredur, his long hair hanging limply beneath the hood of his cloak. His dark eyes were slippery as he scanned the courtyard, dismounting and removing his riding gloves. A fat man wearing a torque followed, sniffing loudly with his bulbous nose. He had golden rings jammed upon each of his pudgy fingers and a licentious look about him. I knew him only by the final chieftain who rode in their company, a man with keen eyes and angry splotches of red marring his stubbled face, who could be none other than Cynfelyn the Leprous. This meant the fat lord was his cousin. I had never before met them, but I knew they were petty chieftains of the south, their narrow swaths of land pressed between the new Angle land of Bernicia to the east and the lands of Uther Pendragon to the west.

"My lords." Elufed bowed as they neared. "Your visit is not forewarned, but nonetheless you are most welcome. I see you have with you Cynfelyn and Dunawd. You must travel on a matter of much import."

Peredur mounted the step and I inhaled the rancid stink of the goose grease he used to slick back his hair.

"We are grateful for your hospitality, my lady." Peredur ignored her bid for information. "I take it the king is in residence?" He peered behind Elufed into the yawning corridor of the hall.

"Indeed. You will find him in the feast room. Come in, dry yourselves. I trust you will stay the night?"

"Provided it suits the king."

"I'm certain it will."

Behind Peredur, Gwrgi fixed his eyes on me and tipped his head back, giving a soft howl like a wolf.

"You must excuse my brother," Peredur said. "He is in want of wine and a willing woman, if it can be arranged. It will settle him, I'm sure of it."

Elufed blinked. "Of course."

Gwrgi meant to remind me of all those years ago, at the market. Good. Let him search my eyes now. He would find only disgust lingered; I had no tolerance for fear. As Peredur brushed past, Gwrgi did not miss his chance.

"The lady Languoreth," he said. "How fine you look. I am sorry to hear that your brother Pendragon is in such poor health."

"Uther Pendragon?" I gave a laugh. "Nay. Why, Lailoken joined him on a hunt only days ago. Wild pheasant, it was. Pendragon won the day; it was quite a slaughter of birds. They are far tastier than chickens, I think. Pendragon likes to leave the heads for his dogs."

I watched his face shift as he caught my meaning.

"Such talk of hunting must stir your stomachs," Elufed put in. "Come, come, now. Our grooms will see to the horses. Your men can clean themselves in the guest quarters before they join us in the hall."

Dunawd and Cynfelyn, Gwrgi and Peredur.

Half the lords to the south had arrived at our door unannounced. The only notable lord in absence was Uther himself.

When the last of the men had disappeared into the hall, Elufed turned to me. "That was foolish. You think you deliver a blow, but you only excite him. Unless you wish to be the woman I must deliver up, I suggest you be more careful what you say."

"Let him dare to touch me," I said. But Elufed only scoffed, ushering me into the warmth.

"You'll want to warn them, of course you will," she said in a whisper. "But don't be too hasty. A messenger with no information is just as deadly as no messenger at all."

CHAPTER 45

I needn't have worried about Gwrgi laying eyes on my Gladys, for no women at all were permitted in the great room that night. As we traveled down the corridor, we found ourselves suddenly moving against a great human tide of unwashed men as the warriors of Tutgual, Rhydderch, and the four southern lords were sent from the room. They parted—so as not to dare touch us—as we moved toward the door, and I caught the discernible hardening of Elufed's face as her man-at-arms brushed past her, their eyes meeting with a solemn look.

"Damn him," she muttered. Tutgual had sent him away with all the others. There would be no chance of information coming to the queen.

I saw a face I recognized and caught the sleeve of my husband's man.

"What is happening?" I whispered. He was Rhydderch's kin and third in his guard. He'd always been kind.

"The king has called a war council," he said, nervous someone might hear.

"A war council?" I said. "And what of my son? Is he in there still?"

"Aye." He gave a short nod. "His father will want him to witness, no doubt. You'll pardon me now. We're to wait in our quarters 'til they're through."

He dipped his head and carried on, leaving me stunned in his wake. Elufed's eyes were narrowed, fixed on the door as if she could see beyond it.

"This can be nothing good. No such secrecy would be needed if there were trouble with the Angles," I said, trying to stifle my panic. "Can you not discover something?"

She turned to me with a stare. The king's men yet moved all around us. *Be quiet*, her look said.

I tugged at my plait as the corridor emptied of the last warrior and we were left in eerie silence. Brodyn came to lean against the wall, his brown eyes watchful as we shifted anxiously between the weaving room and our chambers. An hour passed. There were no shouts of dissent. I waited on a thicket of stinging nettles as the low hum of voices carried on behind the heavy oaken doors. At last I shook my head and went to the guard barring the door.

"My son is in there."

"Yes, my lady."

"Well? When will he be coming out?"

"Can't say," the man replied.

"You cannot say, or you do not know?"

"Can't say," he only repeated.

"Of course you can't," I said angrily.

War with the Scots wouldn't bring lords from the south. If it were war with the Picts, our neighbors in Manau—the lords in the north—would be darkening our doorstep. Even as I reasoned, the sudden drop in my stomach cried louder than any logic.

The crow had come, hadn't it? Cathan's bird, a sign from the Summerlands.

I could deny it no longer. It could only mean war against Gwenddolau.

War against my brothers.

A sickness began to spread like poison as the reality of it settled.

Rhydderch's men thrusting spears against a shield wall held by Lailoken.

Rhys bracing against blows from Dragon Warriors he'd sparred with at Cadzow only seasons ago.

Maelgwn cutting through man after man to protect Angharad, his weapon perhaps even slashing his own boy.

Brother against brother.

Uncle against nephew.

Father against son . . .

And in the middle of it all, Angharad, terrified and alone in the mad hell of war.

Sweet Gods. I looked at Brodyn and turned for the stair, and he pressed off the wall to follow.

The queen looked up then, turning to Aela and her own maid. "Wait outside Lady Languoreth's chamber door. I will see to her."

The sudden silence was deafening as Elufed pressed my door shut behind the three of us. I placed my hand to my stomach, certain I would be sick.

"They are planning an attack," Brodyn said. "We must send word now. We cannot delay."

"I know we cannot delay. But what would you have me do?" I snapped. "If I warn my brothers, it will be Rhys who pays the price. If I fail to send warning, it will be Angharad whose life is in danger!"

I tore my hands through my hair.

"Sit. Calm yourself." Elufed came and pressed me onto the bed. "This is no time to lose your head."

"I can go now," Brodyn said. "You've only to say the word. We cannot worry for Rhys. I have trained him myself. He's a strong warrior; he can fight. But what chance does Angharad, a girl of only eight, stand in a fortress besieged?"

Tears were coming heavy now, and I lifted my head. "Brodyn, you ask me to choose between my children."

"Enough." Elufed placed herself firmly between us. "Languoreth, you are right. Either choice brings a consequence. And you"—she thrust her palm against Brodyn's chest—"do not be so eager to ride to your death."

A look passed between them, one of lovers. I had suspected as much for some time, but now I was certain.

"Any man wishing to kill me would have to catch me first," Brodyn replied, but his humor was gone.

"Of course they will catch you," Elufed snapped. "But even should you evade the notice of the sixscore warriors milling about our gate, you would only reach Pendragon hours, at best, before battle."

Elufed shivered. "It's cold in here. Add more peat to the fire."

Brodyn frowned but crossed the room to do her bidding, his brow furrowed in thought.

"Even if Brodyn can escape the front gate, there will be questions," Elufed reasoned. "You, Languoreth, will be brought to blame. You'll be locked up, and when Tutgual returns he will not hesitate to kill you. So the only real choice you must make is whether to send a messenger or no warning at all."

I stared at her. "How can you speak of this so evenly when the lives of my children are at stake?"

"Because I have seen the Gods' magic, even in times such as these. What is meant to be will come to pass," she said.

"I am sick to my core of the Gods and things meant to be and coming to pass," I said angrily. "How many times has Cathan or my brother said the same? One envisioned my son burning in flames and the other has taken away my daughter. Why must they always *take* from me?" My voice broke. Elufed came to sit beside me.

"I do not pity you," she said. "I cannot know which circumstance will bring about catastrophe for either of the children. But you must make a decision, and quickly. Death comes for all of us; none can escape it. You must decide for yourself what you can live with."

She reached to smooth my hair, a perfunctory motion, but in it I felt love.

"I know that you, too, have seen the benevolence of the Gods. You, too, have felt their magic. Spirit never dies, Languoreth. Just this morning it was Cathan himself who showed you as much, did he not?"

I closed my eyes a long moment and tried to steady my breath. When I opened them, I had my answer.

"I cannot live knowing I did not try to spare them," I said, "no matter the consequence."

Brodyn cursed and tossed two hunks of peat on the fire. "Yes, but Elufed is right. I cannot go. It would only implicate you."

"Wait a moment." I twisted my fingers, thinking. "There is yet one of my grooms in the stables. We took him in when I was little and he has always been loyal in return. His wife is with child. They live at the edge of town in a little hut by the wood. I can tell the guard he must go to her."

"A dangerous task for a stable hand," Elufed said. "He would have to be convincing. And even so, it is two full days' ride to the Borderlands."

"He is quite clever, and the stables will soon be in chaos readying the horses."

"And this groom," Elufed said. "What makes you think you can trust him?"

I set my jaw. "Loyalty, that's what. You were not there that day. You did not see what I saw, what the Angles had done. He is not like Desdemona. If I entrust this man with a task, he will find a way."

"Then I shall pray to Epona that his horse may be swift. And you"—she looked at Brodyn—"you will be content to stay here?"

"No, I am not content." He paced. "I want to ride to the Borderlands and warn my brother. I want to fight. But if my absence would put Languoreth in harm's way, I am left with no choice. We must have faith the Dragons can muster quickly if we send word right away."

"Then it is decided." I rose and went to my chest of jewels, digging for my stash of silver and pulling it out, then stuffing the pouch into my pocket.

"Brodyn," I said, "lend me your brooch."

He unpinned the crest from his tunic and passed it to me.

"Gwenddolau must know this man comes on my behalf. Otherwise I fear his life will be in danger."

"Of course," he said. He watched the symbol of his loyalty disappear into my pocket, blinking.

"Aela," I called out, and she ducked through the door.

"Yes, my lady?"

"Will you fetch Cyan and Gladys? We have been cooped up too long. I'm sure the children are quite bored. We are going to feed the horses."

Gladys and Cyan were eager to go outdoors, even in the waning light, but the strangers skulking the grounds made them ill at ease.

Cyan narrowed his eyes, inspecting their plaids and their brooches, their unkempt hair and their brutish eyes.

"Where do these men come from, Mother?"

They'd built a fire in the pit just beyond the courtyard and were gathered round, drinking our ale moodily and stamping their feet against the cold. I could feel their eyes tracking us, wary. They knew just who my brothers were. To which family I truly belonged.

"They come from the south." I forced a smile. "And you must be polite, Cyan. These men are our guests."

"But what are *our* men doing out here in the cold?" Gladys asked, studying me. "Does this have something to do with the—"

"Gladys." I squeezed her hand. "Tell me which of the horses you shall visit first."

Gladys frowned but obliged, and as soon as we had passed out of earshot, I drew my children behind the cover of the orchard.

"I want to tell you the truth, but I need you to bear it well. Can you do that?"

My heart tightened as I watched their faces pale, but there was nothing to be done for it. Better that they knew the truth. They hesitated a moment, then nodded.

"That is very good, because I will need both your trust and your help. The king has called a war council. We do not know what he is discussing, and may not for some time, but I believe they plan to wage war on your uncles."

"But Angharad is with them," Gladys said. Cyan's chest began to heave, his freckled face reddening in anger.

"Yes, Angharad is with them, and too many others whom we love. We must warn them. I have a friend here, in the stables. But Tutgual has posted a guard at the stable door. He will not want any messages going in or out. And so you must act as if you are children feeding horses, and I must ask my friend if he will ride to the Borderlands with more haste than he has ever ridden before. If they have warning, if they have time . . ."

I trailed off. I did not know if a warning would do any good—whose life it might save, if anyone's—and I could not lie. I looked instead to Cyan, who was pressing his lips as he did when he was trying not to cry. "Cyan, my love. Tell me."

"And what of Rhys?" he said.

I reached to fold his trembling fingers into my steady hands.

"Rhys will ride with your father," I said.

Blink. Breathe. It must be done.

Gladys shook her head as the horror seeped in. "But Father would never harm our uncle Lailoken. And Lailoken would never harm Rhys . . ." Her eyes pooled with tears, and I kissed her quickly.

"Gladys, I know I ask a great deal. But right now we must complete this task. We must not cry. Back in our chambers, we will discuss this—all of it. We will cry 'til we are all wrung out. But right now we must speak with the guard, and he must admit us to the stable. Right now we must convince him that we know nothing of this, any of it, and that we are happy."

I waited, my stomach in knots as my brave son and daughter, far too young to face such a nightmare, wiped their faces and stiffened their spines. Cyan swallowed and looked across the courtyard to the guard who stood blocking the stable doors.

"I love you both so very much," I said to them, my voice wavering. "You make me so proud."

I had scarcely spoken when Gladys gave one last sniff and took off toward the guard in a run. I hesitated a moment, uncertain, and opened my mouth to call her back, but she turned, then called out to Cyan.

"Come, Cyan, hurry. I bet you can't catch me!"

Only a mother could hear the tin in her voice.

Good girl, Gladys, I thought. *You are such a good, good girl.*

I took Cyan's hand in mine and we hurried toward the stable.

Tutgual's guard did not smile, and Gladys stopped, unsure.

"My lady," he said.

"We've come to feed the horses," Gladys said as I came to stand beside her.

"And I've a message for one of our grooms," I said. "It seems his wife is in labor."

The soldier made a face at the womanly news, but did not move from blocking the door. He looked instead at me. The foster sister of Gwenddolau. The twin of Lailoken.

"I'll tell him, then," he said. "Which one is it?"

"Nay, I'm happy to do it," I said. "Truly. I promised the children they could see the horses in any case. I have no idea what they're speaking of in there, but my children have been cooped up for hours." I smiled. "Is it really too much trouble?"

"Sorry. I cannot admit anyone."

The children's faces fell in a show of disappointment.

"Surely the king's own grandchildren are an exception," I said. "Please. Even a few moments of distraction would be such a relief."

He scoured my eyes for a hint of fear but found nothing.

"Go on, then," he said at last, stepping aside.

"I thank you. We won't be long." I guided Gladys toward the grain, calling out brightly, "Go ahead, children, fill your buckets. The fillies carrying their foals are in the back. They'll be eager for some treats."

The stables were already in chaos, the horses of our guests having arrived muddied and in need of feed. Half of Tutgual's animals were being transferred to a pasture out back. I scanned the madness and spotted our groom tethering a mount by the wall to brush her and mumbling to himself. He looked up as I drew near, straightening in surprise.

"My lady!" He bowed. "My pardon. I did not see you."

I smiled in return. "Please, I can see you are busy. Continue your work."

"It has been some time since you've come to see the beasts," he said, continuing with his brush.

"And too long since I've spoken a kind word to you," I said quickly. "But I regret now I haven't much time."

"Something is wrong, then?" He glanced at my face with concern. "You need my help."

"Yes," I said. "Something is terribly wrong."

I drew him to the corner and told him what was taking place, of the war council and the cost to my family—and to all of us—should the Dragon Warriors not be warned.

"Will you do it?" I asked, my heart in my throat. "Will you ride to Pendragon and give him my warning?"

He stared a moment at the mount before him, her mane plaited and clasped with coils of gold.

"Aye, I'll do it. And I wouldn'a be sorry for it, neither."

"Thank you." I gripped his arm. "Thank you. You need only deliver the message and come back. But carry this. Keep it safe and produce it to Gwenddolau should anyone question you." I drew the brooch from my pocket and pressed it into his hand. "It bears my crest, the crest of my father. He will then know truly that you have come from me."

He nodded and took it, and I reached into my pocket to retrieve the weighty sack of silver.

"For your trouble. I will reward you double again when I hear you have dispensed with your charge."

"You needn't pay me." His expression was resolute. "The family of Morken's been good to me. I reckon I owe you my life."

"I thank you, but I shall pray it doesn't come to that. Deliver the message, then see yourself home. Your wife and your children shall be glad for it. And so will I."

"Yes, my lady." He waited a moment then threw down his brush with a shout. "Did ye hear that lads? I'm going to be a father again! Who'll take this horse? I'm off. You poor scags are on your own!"

The sun was just beginning to sink as I made his excuses to Tutgual's man at the gate and watched him ride off into the distance, his head bent low over the neck of Cyan's horse.

Cyan and Gladys wept themselves to sleep. I looked at them now, their goose-down pillows damp beneath their heads. Rhys's bed lay empty as the lords in the feast room plotted their attack with my son alongside them.

As my husband plotted the attack upon his very own daughter.

To keep my mind from preying upon what little strength I had, I moved soundlessly to the simple pine table where Rhys kept his possessions. There wasn't much. He was a simple young man, and pure, and, for the son of a prince, shockingly uninterested in material things. There was a comb, and I picked it up gingerly. It smelled of him, his dark hair, the fresh scent of soap and of leather. A vellum map of the tribal lands was stretched out here, too, the ink worn in the places where he'd traced his finger.

The fields and forests of Cadzow in the lands of the Goddeu. Clyde Rock and Partick, the seats of Strathclyde in the territory of the Damnonii. His mother's people and his father's.

I touched my fingers to the map, summoning the thread that bound mother to child, the one that could not be severed with a thousand swords. Rhys was sitting in the great room, his green eyes keen, watching the men who spoke all around. There was fear; I could feel it. What lies would they weave to poison the mind of Rhydderch's young son, to turn him against his very own uncles?

Against his true father?

What tales would they tell to incite Rhydderch to war?

There was so much sorrow, but whether it was Rhys's or my own, who could say? Where did a mother end and her child begin? I blinked the wetness from my eyes and looked down at the map. One route had been worn more than the others, and I moved my hand lightly along the trail of faded ink, collecting the dream fragments Rhys had left with his fingers.

The way traveled from our summer fortress at Cadzow, miles and miles through the verdant pastures of Liddesdale, to the place high above a gorge where the river Esk and the Liddel Water met. It was the site of a timeworn but magnificent fortress, fortified by the ancients, since charred and rebuilt. I'd never been there, but Lailoken had described it.

Gwenddolau's fortress. The fortress Pendragon.

The way the cliffs dropped a hundred feet below into the shallow rush of the river. Its ramparts made of monstrous oak, meters high and fortified with stone. The wooded emerald vale of the Esk stretched to the east. To the west, the glittering, salty vastness of the Solway Firth. Far below, the old Roman road skirted beneath its sentinel watch, but the men who built this fortress were no friends of Rome.

The little hall built within blazed with candlelight and smelled of hot baked bread and freshly uncorked ale, no matter the day. And if he closed his eyes in summer, when the wind carried the scent of creek leaves up off the water, Lailoken told me he could almost imagine he was back home.

It was this fortress in the lands of the Selgovae that Rhys had been dreaming of. Of his uncle Lailoken and the Dragon Warriors, his far-famed heroes. Of sitting at the table with a horn of ale beside one of the greatest warriors of all time.

The man the Song Keepers would remember as Uther Pendragon.

CHAPTER 46

R hydderch did not come to bed. What I mistook to be him, entering in the late hours of night, was instead only a sound that haunts me still: the ominous slide of wood accompanied by a thunk.

I leapt from bed and went to test the door.

Bolted from the outside. I was now a prisoner in my own chamber.

If they could have seen my teeth flash like a predator's in the dark, they would have known my fury. I wanted to fly at the door, to strike it, to scream. But the thought of Gladys and Cyan sleeping at last on the other side of the wall stayed my hands, as did the thought of waking them after sleep had finally found them, to have them worry for their mother, hearing her gone mad . . . I dressed instead and went to sit beside the glow of the hearth, my fury the only company apart from the rapid beating of my heart.

Was this to be it, then? Would my coward of a husband not even come to look upon my face before he left to wage war on my own brother? Did he not even possess the barest sense of honor and duty to look me in the eye and tell me the truth?

I had neither slept nor moved when the soft rap came at my door in the early hours of morning. I looked up slowly, preparing to face Rhydderch, but heard my eldest son's voice call out instead.

"Mother?"

I rushed to Rhys as the soldiers admitted him to my chamber, pulling him into my arms.

"Oh, Rhys, you've come. You've come."

I drew back to look at him, smoothing my hands over his face. The whites of his eyes were pink with exhaustion. Or with sorrow.

"You are a prisoner here," he said, green eyes darkening.

"Do not worry for me. Tell me what's happened. Have you eaten? Have you slept? Are you all right?"

An answer was on his lips, but then he could only shake his head, his mouth twisting in a futile effort to stifle his cry.

"Oh, love. It's all right. It's all right." I only meant to soothe him, but my mother's touch was his undoing. His strong shoulders shook and he leaned his forehead against mine as he began to weep.

"I can't . . ." he whispered. "I can't . . ."

The dam within me burst, my tears rushing to mingle with his.

"It's all right. You don't have to say. You needn't say a word. Just let me hold you."

We stood like that for a long moment, hearts hemorrhaging and foreheads touching, my hands bracing the back of his dark head, wishing I could pull him back into the shelter of my body where no harm could ever find him.

"Please," he said after a while, in a low voice. "Don't cry any longer, Mother. I cannot bear it."

I gave a soft smile and squeezed his head between my hands, one last blessing, before releasing him.

"That sound," I said, tilting my head. I could hear it now in the distance: the eerie scrape of metal over rock. The men of the war party were sharpening their blades upon the whetstone of the king. He kept it at the foot of his throne in the feast hall. The Song Keepers, long ago, had created its myth: that any brave man who sharpened his sword upon it was certain to deal out death, while the sword of the coward would be rendered as dull and witless as a reed.

I looked up. "Have you sharpened your sword on the stone?"

Rhys nodded.

"Good. Then you are ready."

"I am not ready," he said, his voice low. "The lords of the south say my uncle is a weak link in what must become a fortified chain. The strength of the Angle king Theodric grows in the east, and yet Pendragon will not swear allegiance. They plan to crush him, Mother, him and all his men, and create an unbreakable confederacy. And I—" His jaw clenched.

I could not let Rhys ride off into battle with a war in his own heart.

"Rhys. Listen to me now. You are strong and brave, and more skilled at arms than half your father's men. Be alert. Be ready for anything. And should the fog of battle come upon you, you will do what you must. War is not about victory. Blast what the Keepers say. War is about survival. Your only task is to protect yourself, to come home."

I looked into his eyes, lending him strength I did not have. "Do not worry for your uncles; they will look after themselves."

"And what of Angharad? I swear to you, if they . . ." He swallowed. "If they do not deliver her up, I will find her. Father and I—we're going to make certain Angharad is brought back home."

"Rhys"—I took his hands in mine—"do nothing foolhardy. You must keep your head. Promise me. Promise! You must promise me you'll come home."

He looked down, his handsome face full of shadows. "I promise I will."

The heavy clunk of the bolt sounded and the door eased open. Rhydderch's man gestured to my son.

"It's time," he said.

Rhys gave a nod.

"So," I said. "Your father will not come?"

He looked away. Gave a slight shake of his head.

"Then perhaps he is wise. For I cannot say what I would do."

"He no more wishes to see you a prisoner than do I. Do not be so unforgiving," he said carefully. "You know why he does this. If he wishes to become king, he has no choice." His face hardened. "I heard old Tutgual say it himself. If we succeed, Father will at last be named tanist."

So Tutgual meant to serve his faithful son one last task: win this battle, and Rhydderch would be promised his place as rightful king.

And I . . . I would become queen. Upon the spilling of my brothers' and my daughter's and my lover's blood.

The thought nearly made me retch. *Curse his kingship and curse him!* I wanted to scream.

But I feared what power my words might have, and here was my firstborn son, riding off to war.

And then, to my horror, I heard the ominous blare of the summoning horn, the call to arms no man could ignore. In the fields beyond the orchards of Partick, the tenants would be lifting their spears from the walls, embracing their wives and children. The people of town would be issuing onto the streets to hail their heroes riding off to battle.

I drew Rhys to me one last time and gave him a kiss.

"Be safe," I said. "May the Gods keep you."

I thought I knew pain. I had witnessed the murder of Cathan. I had lost my mother and my father. Ariane had left me. I had suffered a lifetime apart from my lover. I had sent away my youngest child to be raised by another.

But as Rhys looked at me one last time and closed the door, I discovered a pain unlike any I had felt before. I felt it rise like a looming tower of water, until the very pressure of my chamber dropped the way the air shifts when there is a storm out at sea. It made my ears ache. And then it crashed, rendering my body to splinters.

There is a place within pain that exists beyond tears.

It is a bottomless black pit that sends men marching with their spears drawn into mill-grinders. It is a beast with a thousand heads that rips at your entrails.

Languoreth.

Hadn't my mother warned me all those years ago that this day would come? She had tried to warn me, but in doing so she had only ensured that the creature knew my name.

The beast had been hunting me the whole of my life, and it came this day to finish me in my chamber. I closed my eyes and offered up my veins. The beast had a name I never truly knew until that moment.

The beast who came was called War.

Aela was there. She told me Brodyn had been taken sometime after midnight to the prison pit beyond Tutgual's hall, where he was being held for "safekeeping."

I did not wash. The room began to smell sour. Water came, but it made me retch. Food came but I could not eat. I tracked the hours as the sun shifted across the floor. The men had long since left. My groom would deliver his warning first. Even so, Rhydderch's cavalry was fast as well; they would likely arrive right on his heels. Darkness fell, and I began to feel as though my body were a shell. I was already drifting someplace above myself, when I heard the far-off unbolting of my chamber door and blinked into the lamplight to find Elufed bending over me.

"That will be all," she said to the guard, then turned to me. "Have you eaten?"

She looked at me expectantly but my mouth felt too heavy. I did not answer.

"She has taken neither food nor drink since the war party left," I heard Aela say.

"Good," Elufed said. She bent over me once more and peered into my eyes.

"I cannot free you, but I can offer you this." I felt her press something fat and fibrous into my palm. "The blood of a Wisdom Keeper flows through your veins. Eat it. Your body will know what to do."

Then she was gone. My tongue was welded with dryness to the roof of my mouth and I swallowed to wet it, struggling to sit up.

"My lady!" Aela came to assist me, and I could almost see my reflection in her eyes, hair dirty and limp in strings, my eyes hollowed out.

"What has she given you?" Aela asked protectively.

"Never mind it," I said. "It will not harm me." But I knew what Elufed had given me would come at a cost. Clasped between my fingers was the power to see.

"Leave me," I bid Aela. "And no matter what you may hear, do not disturb me."

Aela hesitated and I looked up.

"You must do it. For I am too weak, Aela, to ask you again."

She stood a long moment, then dipped her head.

The guard let her out. With her absence my chamber fell silent as a tomb. But tombs were sacred places, portals to the dead. I took a little water and opened my palm to look at the little red mushroom cap before placing it on my tongue.

It was spongy and raw, not dried, but earthy. And bitter. So bitter, my mouth began to water and my nose began to run. I swallowed it down and waited for the memory in my bones to aid me in what I needed to do.

My husband and the king had locked me in the blinding dark.

Now I called upon my ancestors to give me the power of Sight.

Drowsiness soon overtook me. I succumbed to sleep and woke, my chest damp with sweat. Yes, the room was a tomb. Or was I dreaming? The fire had gone out and my body shivered, yet I did not feel cold. My eyes were closed and around me was only darkness, and yet I could see each fleck on the floor's planking with such clarity. My body was parchment, skin like vellum, and I peeled it away, left it sleeping on the bed.

And then, it seemed, I was dreaming of the forest.

This time no rustle of wind, no call of birds, no sliver of sunlight, could penetrate the thick boughs overhead. I did not know these woods, but I could smell them. I could smell that dawn was coming though the woods were yet dim as twilight. I could smell men in their battle armor, hiding in the bushes, the sour scent of violence clinging to their skin.

A shuffle sounded. My ears pricked. I whipped my head round to see a soldier standing only paces from me in the underbrush, his spear raised and a hungry glint in his eye. My muscles tensed and coiled, ready to spring. But just as he thrust his arm back to let his weapon fly, another man came and swiped at his shoulder.

"Leave it," he barked. "Now's no time for hunting. Later there'll be plenty of venison to eat."

But I had already fled: up over fallen trees, up the hill, away from the gloom and the weight of the silence rushing in, stifling, thundering in my ears like a band of warhorses. Higher I raced with the grace of a deer, 'til I came to the top of a hill and could go no farther. Here a timber lookout was posted, surrounded by stakes. But it was empty now, abandoned, save for the remnants of a signal fire, forgotten woodsmoke.

Across the valley rose the ramparts of a fortress, surrounded by mountains of brush piled up, ready to be lit. The smoke of battle would soon be upon them. The banner of the Dragon flapped in the dawn from the peaked roof of Gwenddolau's hall, and below, between the ditch and the rampart, an army of Dragon Warriors the size of ants, their bodies facing the forest. I tried to make them out: my brothers, my love, searching with keen sight for any sign of my daughter. But the eyes I was looking through were scanning the woods, and the heart that was beating was not my own. It did not register anything beyond the terror of the battle cry that rose up, the harsh blare of the carynx, the roar of the men, discordant in their chaos, as they swept through the forest, their boots snapping twigs like slender bones lying in the underbrush.

Two armies standing, two armies racing, horses charging through the water of the river, swords drawn to slash and spears poised to tear, shield walls digging down into the dirt, bracing for the blows that would come, and I woke, vomiting, my stomach seized with cramps.

I was bent over the floor, feet tucked beneath me, my body obeying the expulsion of the toxin that coursed through my blood.

"No," I begged, swiping at my mouth. "Take me back, please. Take me back! I was too soon. I was too soon!"

But there was more, I could feel it; all was not done. A spark caught my eye and I looked to the hearth. Where the fire had gone dark, a new fire blazed, seeping past the weariness and into my bones, until where I had been shaking, I was suddenly warm.

I saw then, too, not just what was taking place but also what was yet to come. The fortress was burning, and yet there were men escaping through flame. I saw a mountain capped in snow, Dragon Warriors retreating into the forest. I saw my Angharad standing before me, so beautiful, beautiful but grown. I saw Cyan as a man, on the heights of Clyde Rock.

And then I saw further, further than I had ever imagined one could see.

I saw army upon army, foreign men with black banners pouring from the sea, a greater danger than any civil war of Britons. There was the clashing of steel and the spilling of blood 'til it ran through the grass like a red rushing river. I saw a hut on a hill and recognized my brother. His wild hair was white, his back hunched in age, traveling over cobblestones as children jeered and threw stones, calling him names. Disgraced. Forgotten. All his wisdom and kindness, the great deeds of his life—they had all been for naught.

Myrddin, they jeered.

Myrddin.

In the end I slept, my body worn out. When I woke it was daylight. Aela had come and sat at my bed. The battle was raging even as I stood.

"Fetch me some food, Aela. I wish to eat."

Her eyes widened but she raced to do my bidding, returning in moments with butter and bread. I bathed, took food, and drank, all the while lost in my thoughts. There would be no word for some time yet, I knew. But I would not lie there like a husk, waiting to be buried.

I had seen it: what would come. Not all, but enough that I knew. And there was something important that I must do.

On my table beside the window I found parchment and quill.

I sat and dipped the feather in ink, bending my head over the blank skin of parchment, and began to write.

There are those who will argue such things should not be written.

The songs are for the Keepers. Have I, of all people, forgotten the written word is sacred?

But who am I, if not a keeper of the Old Way? My name is Languoreth, daughter of Morken. I write because I have seen the darkness that will come. When we will no longer gather to share the sagas of our heroes, our gods. When our people flee into forests in the blackness of night and our histories burn along with the bodies of our Keepers. We will scatter their ashes back to the earth. And when the last of them are gone, who among us will remember our stories?

The shifting of the sun, the medicine of the plants, the lines of lilt and language; without our tales, our lives will be forgotten.

Already there are those who seek to tell a new history.

They will taunt and jeer, until my brother's true name is lost, and he is called only "Myrddin."

Madman.

But my brother is no madman.

He is cunning and brave. Kind and fierce. My brother is far-
famed: he whispered his wisdom at the shoulder of Uther Pendragon.
He fought to salvage the bones of a kingdom.

I write these words now on parchment because we live in such
times that must be remembered.

My brother's name is Lailoken.

NOTE FROM THE AUTHOR

Many of us grew up on tales of the wizard Merlin, the gnarled, white-haired mage who stood beside King Arthur of legend. As a child, one of my favorite movies was Walt Disney's *The Sword in the Stone*. But it wouldn't be until I was an adult that the mythos of the Arthurian saga would truly consume me.

Having written a travel memoir that required research into the Celts, I'd been studying Celtic history intensively for nearly three years by the time I wandered into a tiny bookshop in Glastonbury, England. Browsing the shelves, I came across a copy of Adam Ardrey's non-fiction book *Finding Merlin* and bought it on a whim. In it, Ardrey, a lawyer from Glasgow, presents compelling evidence that the legend of Merlin is based on a man named Lailoken who lived in sixth-century Scotland.

Finding Merlin contains several revelations. For me, perhaps the most intriguing was the fact this man Lailoken had a twin sister. Her name was Languoreth. She would go on to become a powerful queen, likely one of the most influential women in early medieval Scotland— but, tragically, she's been largely forgotten. *The Lost Queen.*

Though Languoreth may be lost to modern consciousness, her memory is preserved in several places: a Welsh poem copied down in the fourteenth-century *Red Book of Hergest* entitled "The Dialogue

Between Myrddin and His Sister Gwenddydd" (her family name) and a piece of Glasgow folklore known as "The Fish and the Ring."

We find Languoreth recorded in ancient king lists as the wife of a ruler named Rhydderch Hael, who scholars believe ruled from Clyde Rock in the late sixth to early seventh centuries. There are children descended from the union of Rhydderch and Languoreth; their names are recorded in ancient Welsh triads as well as historic genealogies. But who Languoreth truly was—and what she experienced in her life-time as one of the most powerful women in her era—has been buried under the weight of passing centuries.

The Battle of Arderydd, one of the most violent and least remem-bered civil wars in Scottish history, took place in the year AD 573, ac-cording to the *Annales Cambriae*. It pitted Languoreth's husband against her own brother. It pitted Lailoken against his own young nephew. I couldn't stop thinking about Languoreth and the epic times she lived through: the battle that tore her family apart, the Anglo-Saxon migra-tions, and the first ever politico-religious acts of violence that the Brit-ons of Strathclyde would have likely experienced. Moreover, in today's world, powerful female role models must be brought forth and honored now more than ever. I thought it a travesty that Languoreth had been written out of history, her powerful story never told.

When I first began researching Languoreth, there was a passion that ignited me, but mostly my work was driven by a visceral sense of sadness over the difficult times in which she lived and a great sense of injustice that her life had been forgotten. I don't believe writ-ers find stories. I believe stories find us. And the way in which this story found me left me with little choice as to whether or not I was going to write it. I believed it was time Languoreth stepped from the mists of history to take her place in our hearts, our minds, and our memories.

• • •

To the Celtic people, names were sacred. As a culture that lived and remembered via oral tradition, the Britons occupied a world where the spoken word held tremendous power. The son of a petty king or chieftain, Lailoken was (as Tolkien's Gandalf would say) "no conjurer of cheap tricks." He was a warrior, a druid, a scholar, and a powerful politician. As such, Lailoken made powerful enemies in his lifetime, especially in the burgeoning Christian church—enemies who, toward the end of his life, sought to obliterate his influence by doing the thing any honorable Celt feared most: erasing his name from the public record.

Lailoken's adversaries in the church began, in an effort to discredit him, to refer to him as *Myrddin*, which means "Madman" in Old Welsh—pronounced *"Meer-thin."* (Old Welsh is a language directly descended from Brythonic, the language of Lailoken and his people.)

As Adam Ardrey discovered, Lailoken means *Chief of Song*: it is in actuality a title, not a name. Just as Morken means, loosely translated, *Great Chief.* "Song" as the Celts referred to it, is a figurative word for a vital component of their culture lost to us now. We can only make educated guesses as to its true meaning. *Song* was not only singing, or oral history, or genealogies, or stories, or entertainment. It was also religion, power, mystery, and preservation of ancient knowledge regarding the natural world, healing, philosophy, and the very nature of human existence. I disagree with academics who assert that the idea of *Song* refers strictly to a role or tradition upheld by Celtic "poets," as well as that the term "poet" (as it is understood today) is even a word that can accurately describe the power, influence, and position that those involved in *Song* possessed in Celtic society. *Chief of Song.* Lailoken's sister or father would have called him by a family name, rather than by this title, but whatever Lailoken's real name was, it's been lost. Nonetheless, the title tells us that whoever Lailoken was, he was a leader of the Old Way, and someone of great importance to the political world of his time.

There is reason to believe the process of obscuring Lailoken's name began in his own lifetime. But certainly by the time Lailoken became known as *Myrddin* in lore and literature, the slander begun by his adversaries was complete. However, in what is perhaps one of history's sweetest ironies, only in the hagiography of Lailoken's greatest enemy (Glasgow's patron saint, Mungo), written nearly six hundred years later by Jocelyn of Furness, do we learn this insane fellow called *Myrddin* had another name by which he was known: Lailoken. And so "Lailoken" became the best name to use in trying to resurrect a more accurate memory of an epic ghost.

For hundreds of years, scholars and writers have obsessed over the Arthurian legends, seeking to unearth a kernel of truth about the magnificent men and women that color the pages of the epics. But surprisingly few have sought to overlay human migratory patterns in search of answers. When you examine what was happening historically during the times these stories were first taking root, it's easy to see how the tales of Myrddin could have migrated from their place of origin in southern Scotland down into Cornwall, Wales, and Brittany. In fact, there is much evidence for it.

Within the Celtic language, there is a linguistic split that occurred well over one thousand years ago. The Britons, including our people of Strathclyde, spoke a dialect called "P-Celtic." Their Celtic brethren the Scotti (or Westmen, as I also call them), spoke a variant called "Q-Celtic." We tend to think of history as static, and are quick to enclose events within parameters that give us an understanding of a beginning and an end. In reality, conquerings are seldom truly infinite, and history is fluid. The Anglo-Saxon "invasion" was—rather than a single event that can be set to a specific date in history— a series of migrations, battles, raids, and power grabs that went on for many decades in many different parts of Scotland and England. (These events also happened much later in Scotland than in England, where Romanized towns were taken over much earlier and seemingly with more ease.) In fact, there is evidence that Clyde Rock (today called Dumbarton Rock) was still a stronghold of the Britons well into the ninth century, a date which does not hold with Anglo-Saxon occupation as it is claimed to have occurred in the rest of the country.

When the Angles made Strathclyde and the other Brythonic territories uncomfortable enough to live in, migration took place. Britons from Scotland fled into what is now Wales, Cornwall, and Brittany, where other Brythonic populations still possessed the land and military prowess to offer them a better way of life. The Arthurian stories belonged to the Britons, and they took their stories with them.

This is how the Arthurian tales became geographically misplaced.

Ardrey is not the first author to place Merlin and Arthur in Scotland (although he is unquestionably my favorite). There are a few other books that present very good arguments, Nikolai Tolstoy's *The Quest for Merlin* being one. I agree with these writers that it is no surprise that scholars trying to place a historical Arthur and Merlin in the south of England or in Brittany come up with so little evidence. It's only when you return Lailoken and his contemporaries to their natural geographical home that the place names, family names, battle locations, and legends all fall perfectly into place.

I spent nearly six years immersed in the research and writing of this novel in an effort to present as accurate a portrayal of sixth-century Strathclyde and the world of the Britons as possible. When I have taken leaps, it has been with the archaeological and anthropological evidence in mind, but I don't doubt there will be argument as to some of my choices, and I've likely made some mistakes. In places I've taken the fiction writer's liberty of condensing the historical time line for the sake of story flow or infusing romance. For a more accurate time line pertaining to the events in the book, as well as a much more detailed account on the truth behind the legend, I encourage you to read Ardrey's works.

The post-Roman and Early Medieval time periods are among the least archaeologically represented periods in all of the United Kingdom. In southern Scotland, houses were almost exclusively built from timber, which is easily burned during times of war and rots away, leaving little more than postholes. Many lived in huts of wattle and daub that had changed little since the Iron Age and left few traces. Things were built on top of these sites by conquering peoples and subsequent generations, further obscuring any archaeological record. We don't know if Early Medieval noble houses had second stories, or stairs, or windows at all. (Many think likely not.) But we do know that, several hundred years earlier, Roman houses built in what is now the UK were multistory and had indoor plumbing and an early form of centralized heating, as well as paned glass, and so I have allowed for some Roman influence where there might have been none.

Much of what we know from this time period comes from the work of a monk called Gildas, who recorded maddeningly little in relation to dates. There is argument as to *where* Gildas was writing as well as when. Many scholars place Vortigern's betrayal much earlier historically than I have placed it in this book, and think him a man of England.

Given the dust and grime of the Early Medieval period, it's not likely druids (I call them Wisdom Keepers) wore the white robes first mentioned by Greek chroniclers daily; they were more likely reserved for ceremony and special occasions. To give them an immediately distinguishable feature, I've taken some liberties here. The brown hoods worn by monks were woven, tasseled pieces that slipped over the head, not full cloaks. A magnificent example can be seen today at the National Museum of Scotland in Edinburgh.

The sites in this book are characters that deserve unearthing themselves.

Bright Hill is my name, but in Mungo/St. Kentigern's hagiography it states that the hill in Glasgow where the saint buried the body of Fergus was indeed a hill sacred to the druids. It is Mungo's biographer, Jocelyn of Furness, who relates that any who tried to remove the "offending body" were punished with severe beatings and even death. Today Mungo's Glasgow Cathedral sits near the spot, and the hill of the druids has become Glasgow's Necropolis. Old Glasgow city records recall a natural spring near the bottom of that hill, and on a visit to Glasgow, author Adam Ardrey was kind enough to point out the road to me that now runs between the cathedral and the hill that used to be the Molendinar Burn, a freshwater stream that would have flowed from the base of the hill down to the river Clyde. There was an ancient spring there that would very likely have been sacred to the Britons, especially given its location so near their druid hill. I've called it the White Spring. "White Isle," near Partick, was most recently known as Whiteinch, and was demolished when the river Clyde was dredged to enable the passage of larger ships. Any archaeological remains of Cadzow Fortress are very likely buried beneath (and beside) the ruins of a much later medieval castle. You can tour the grounds, which have been blessedly preserved by the wonderful people at Chatelherault Country Park in Hamilton, Scotland. There you can walk the same woods that Lailoken and Languoreth walked, and you can visit the mysterious "Roman" earthworks nestled among an ancient stand of oaks. A special place.

Clyde Rock is now called Dumbarton Castle, found at the mouth of the rivers Leven and Clyde. "The Beak," where some early medieval buildings might have stood, was leveled in the seventeenth century to house a powder magazine, obliterating much of what might have been found there. But several ancient sources name Rhydderch and Tutgual (under various spellings) as rulers of Strathclyde at Dumbarton Rock. Fragments of glass and jewelry dating to the sixth and seventh centuries have been uncovered there. The museum there is excellent, and the enchantment of the place remains. VisitScotland now offers tours of many of the locations featured in this novel and in Adam Ardrey's books.

Linguistically, I've taken liberties when faced with the struggle of maintaining a sense of historic integrity while ensuring the names and places in this book are accessible to readers less familiar with P- and Q-Celtic. Sometimes choices I made were for the sake of ease of pronunciation. (Partick is modern, *Pertnech* is old.) Other times, one word was chosen over another, perhaps more accurate word to better convey a sense of atmosphere for readers. "Aye," for example, is a form of assent still used in Scotland today but thought to belong to the late sixteenth century, making it technically quite non-Brythonic and one thousand years too late for justifiable inclusion in my book. However, one word for "yes" in Welsh is *ie*, and Welsh descends from Old Welsh, which descends from Brythonic. Since *ie* is unfamiliar to most readers, I've used "aye" instead, as it perfectly captures the spirit of the expression and how it might have been used. *Alclud* and *Alt Clut* translate into "Rock of the Clyde" or "Clyde Rock." The historic site is found in the town of Dumbarton, which comes from the Q-Celtic "Dun Breatainn," or "Fort of the Britains." To keep things simple, I used the more colloquial English name of Clyde Rock. In a land of territories and shifting languages over time, some words were lost in one dialect and are remembered only in another. Rather than invent a word in these instances, I chose to use a more modern remembrance.

My hope is that these novels will encourage you to undertake a journey of your own. For although the legends of Arthur and Merlin have their roots in events that took place nearly 1,500 years ago, their enchantment and ability to enrapture us has failed to diminish over time.

Who was the man known as Lailoken? And what of our lost queen, Languoreth? The times this brother and sister lived through, the battles they fought, and the beliefs they fought for, may be obscured by deliberate slander and veiled by the fog of history.

But their magic is still accessible to any who seek it.

ACKNOWLEDGMENTS

These novels would not exist were it not for the great mind of author Adam Ardrey. Any who admire this trilogy should seek out the roots of the story in his nonfiction books *Finding Merlin* and *Finding Arthur*, which not only inspired me but also provided an incredible foundation for my own research. Adam has been not just a good colleague but also a very good friend, taking me to sites and spending the accumulation of many hours with me whether it was virtually, on foot, or in cars. Adam, thank you. And to Adam's lovely wife, Dorothy-Anne Ardrey, for making me feel so very welcome across the broad sea.

To my editor, Trish Todd, at Atria, for her keen eye, unparalleled historical fiction and writing acumen, and incredible belief in this book. You make me believe in publishing magic. Thank you for helping me bring Languoreth and her complex, sixth-century world back to life. To assistant editor Kaitlin Olson for her dedication, kindness, and time in shepherding this work. My sincere thanks to Susan Moldow, as well as copyeditor David Chesanow and the phenomenal team at Atria for their passion, talent, and support.

To my agent, Faye Bender at the Book Group, for her smart editorial feedback, guidance, encouragement, and all-around amazingness. She's a rare human being.

To Mary Alice Monroe, who not only prodded me to write these books but also delivered my own private MFA crash course in writing fiction. Your wisdom, mentorship, and belief have changed me. Julie Beard, Patti Callahan Henry, Patti Morrison, and Marjory Wentworth provided endless encouragement. I'm grateful to the rest of my Lowcountry tribe for their friendship and support: Dorothea Benton Frank, Ellie Maas Davis, Nathalie Dupree, Nicole Seitz, and Cassandra King Conroy. To Ronlyn Domingue, whose brilliant early read brought the book to another level. Thanks also go out to Lynne Fraser and Dr. Arlene Oldham.

Bobby Smith at Chatelherault Country Park in Hamilton, Scotland, has provided tremendous research support as well as friendship, car-repair advice, and lattes since 2013. He's made Chatelherault feel like a second home to me, the very woods where Languoreth and her family once walked. Martin Fitzpatrick's archaeological background and time spent touring Chatelherault with me was vital. To Paul Broadfoot at the Hamilton Library in Scotland for his research help concerning later medieval Cadzow Castle and Chatelherault. Warren Bailie at GUARD Archaeology Ltd. in Glasgow gave generously of his time, resources, and expertise. The National Museum of Scotland in Edinburgh has built a magnificent collection concerning Scotland's early people, and I'm incredibly grateful for their dedication, knowledge, and passion for history.

The Armstrong family in Scotland are the keepers of a very significant site, and were generous enough to allow me and Adam Ardrey to visit. Thank you for permitting me to tromp through your farm.

To Franciscan Brother Richard Hendricks of Ireland for his friendship and sharing his wisdom on the early Celtic Christian world, and to Father Guerric and the Trappist Monks at Mepkin Abbey, South Carolina, for the enchanted silence they provide seekers of all faiths. To Kyle Grey for playing tour guide on my first visit to Glasgow and Dumbarton Castle.

Deepest thanks to my big (and bighearted) family—Pikes, Johansons, Liebetraus, Leightons, and Johnsons—who have loved and encouraged me for more than a decade. I'm so grateful for you all. To the Whitmires and my best girls Liv Cook, Elizabeth Butler, Laura All, Stephanie Higgs, Liz Paulson, and Lea Beresford for epic friendship and support. To Eric Liebetrau, whose support and expert spelling ability made this book a reality. No question was too small. Thank you, Eric, for believing in me.

To my mother, Linda Johanson, who's read this novel countless times and offered unthinkable amounts of input and assistance, whether it was in phone calls at all times of day and night, the brainstorming of titles, the sounding out of plot threads, or flying to Scotland to play nanny to my toddler so I could visit ancient sites. There are no words. And to my sister, Kirsten Pike, the cornerstone of my foundation.

ABOUT THE AUTHOR

Signe Pike is the author of the travel memoir *Faery Tale: One Woman's Search for Enchantment in a Modern World* and has researched and written about Celtic history and folklore for over a decade. A former book editor, she lives in Charleston, South Carolina, where she writes full-time. Visit her at www.signepike.com.

THE LOST QUEEN

SIGNE PIKE

This reading group guide for *The Lost Queen* includes an introduction, discussion questions, ideas for enhancing your book club, and a Q & A with author Signe Pike. The suggested questions are intended to help your reading group find new and interesting angles and topics for your discussion. We hope that these ideas will enrich your conversation and increase your enjoyment of the book.

INTRODUCTION

Ever since Languoreth was a child, she's dreamed of becoming a Wisdom Keeper, one of a group who were the doctors, jurists, political advisors, teachers, historians, and diviners of the ancient Celtic world. But as a woman in sixth-century Scotland—and the only daughter of a king—her life's path is not her own. She has been promised in marriage to Rhydderch, a Christian prince whose kingdom and new religion threatens violence and conflict in the land of the Britons.

Despite knowing the important role she will play as a future queen, Languoreth cannot forget the connection she has to her family and the gods of her ancestors—nor can she ignore the intense attraction she feels toward Maelgwn, a Dragon Warrior from the Borderlands. Most of all, Languoreth cannot set aside the bond she has with her twin brother, Lailoken, who is destined to become the Wisdom Keeper Languoreth has always hoped to be, as well as a leader of the community her new family opposes but she still longs to join.

TOPICS & QUESTIONS
FOR DISCUSSION

1. In part one, Languoreth's family sees trouble stirring on the horizon as the Christians threaten a long-standing peace. Nevertheless, their father, Morken, advises Lailoken not to act, telling him, "This is not yet our war" (p. 20). What do Languoreth and Lailoken think about this conservative strategy? How might Lailoken's approach to the encroaching threat have been better? Worse?

2. When Morken first hears about Emrys Pendragon, he is skeptical of his ability to lead in such troubled times, but his counsellor, Cathan, claims, "When the people need a hero, so are such heroes made" (p. 21). What does Cathan mean? How does the world in which we live contribute to or hinder our ability to cope with our difficulties? Is the Pendragon the only such hero made in this book? Who are the others? How are we to define a hero based on this statement?

3. After she first meets Ariane, Languoreth tells her she has a funny way of speaking, and Ariane replies, "Perhaps it is you who has the funny way of speaking" (p. 38). How does Ariane's influence assist Languoreth during her development? How does her perspective change, as Ariane suggests here, after she becomes one of the few people from her house to live in a Christian kingdom? What effect

does living in a place so different from one's home have on one's understanding of the world and oneself?

4. Languoreth reflects on her mother's death by wondering if every time tragedy befalls a person it is excused by the saying, *"This is the way of the Gods"* (p. 47). Is accepting tragedy as destiny beneficial or detrimental to the people it's meant to comfort? How does Languoreth adopt this philosophy later in the novel, and is it effective for her?

5. When her mother told Languoreth she would be forced into an arranged marriage, she thinks: "In that moment I understood I would never belong to myself" (p. 52). What does that mean? Discuss the ways in which Languoreth belongs to herself and the ways she doesn't. Do women today still never completely belong to themselves?

6. Echoing Languoreth's commentary, Ariane tells Languoreth that she will not be like someone else, but rather, "I am always myself" (p. 56). How are being oneself and belonging to oneself distinguished as being different in the book? Despite serving Languoreth, does Ariane still belong to herself? Do other characters ever truly belong to themselves?

7. Languoreth often has doubts about her Gods, though Lailoken does not. Languoreth notes, "The Gods did not protect Mother. The Gods did not protect Bright Hill. Yet they will come to Cathan's aid?" (p. 122) How is Languoreth's understanding of faith different from Lailoken's? In what ways have their individual experiences shaped these separate versions? Is believing fate is on your side dependent on having faith? If so, faith in what?

8. Tutgual is never able to announce his decision about the Christian burial that sets off so many of the conflicts in this book. What do you think his decision would have been? Would a decision have made a difference in delaying the conflict? Does the inevitability of fate in this

moment outweigh the consequence of a human decision, even one from someone as important and powerful as Tutgual?

9. Ariane attempts to empower Languoreth before her arranged marriage by telling her, "Nothing can be taken from you that you do not freely give" (p. 146). To what extent is this true in the story, and to what extent does it prove false? What is taken from Languoreth and others that they do not freely give? What was given freely but reluctantly, as in a sacrifice? What is the benefit of such sacrifices?

10. When Languoreth finally recognizes herself as a grown woman, she thinks, "The woman who stood before me was untamable. Timeless. She was mother, crone, maiden, and beauty" (p. 175). These female archetypes become sources of power for Languoreth. What female role models does Languoreth have throughout her life? Discuss whether all these women are both untamable and timeless. How do they all embrace and/or reject these stereotypical female identities?

11. When reflecting on the Dragon Warriors, Maelgwn says, "I fear our love of freedom is also our greatest weakness" (p. 184). What does he mean? Why do other people in the novel sacrifice their freedom and those they love to be part of a unified kingdom? Are these sacrifices worth it?

12. Languoreth's decision to execute Desdemona is not an easy one, but once she makes it she never looks back. To what extent is Desdemona's betrayal understandable? How do class structure and sibling rivalry figure into her treason to make the political in this novel deeply personal? Is Languoreth right to execute Desdemona? In what way can this decision be seen as another of Languoreth's sacrifices?

13. In the end, Languoreth must say good-bye to her son, and she "discover[s] a pain unlike any [she] had felt before" (p. 509). Why is this final loss more monumental than all the others? What does

this say about the bond between mother and child, and about what is freely given versus what is taken? In what way are Languoreth's sacrifices greater than others' in the novel? Are women's sacrifices greater than men's? How?

14. In the first part of the novel, Languoreth often reflects on missing her mother, thinking, "What was the sense in loving if all those you cared for were taken away?" (p. 61) How do Languoreth's feelings change throughout the story as more and more is taken from her? Does the novel ever offer an answer to young Languoreth's question? Can Languoreth's entire life be interpreted as an answer to this question about loss, love, and the meaningfulness of life? How?

15. In her final letter, Languoreth foresees "those who seek to tell a new history" and writes her letter in order to "remember our stories" (p. 514). How is history equated to storytelling here? Who has the power to craft our understanding of history? Does a revisionist version of history, such as Languoreth's letter and this novel as a whole, help give voice and agency to those who are overlooked?

ENHANCE YOUR BOOK CLUB

1. After being abused by her father-in-law, Languoreth demands to know where her husband's loyalties lie, to which he responds, "My loyalty lies with you and with this kingdom" (p. 352). Ask everyone in your group to bring a list of where their top priorities or "loyalties" lie. For example, are they with their children? Their friends? Their religion? Do these loyalties ever come into conflict? Have everyone pick five core values from a list of options like this one prepared by Carnegie Mellon University (https://www.cmu.edu/career/docu ments/my-career-path-activities/values-exercise.pdf) and discuss how you all incorporate these values into your personal and professional life. What differences do you see emerging in what people feel matters most? How does this change the way you each interact with the world?

2. In part one of the novel, Languoreth and Lailoken make wishes on pieces of amber, then cast the amber into a pool. Bring some pebbles or beads to your group and have everyone select one to imbue with a wish. Discuss your process for choosing your item and your wish. Was the wish for yourself or for someone else? How would your wish have been different if you'd made it when you were a child or a teenager? How do you anticipate your wish changing in the future? Is it pos-

sible to craft a timeless wish? Take the stones or beads and toss them into an ocean, river, or stream, or set them beneath a special tree, perhaps with an offering of flowers.

3. Ask everyone to think of a story from their family history to discuss. It could be something from their childhood that now gets told at family gatherings or an infamous story they've heard about another family member. After sharing the stories, discuss how events become stories. What details have been added over time? Who likes to tell these stories, and why? From what perspective are the stories told? What messages do the stories convey? What would the stories look like if told by different family members?

4. Write down the names of famous male historical figures on slips of paper and put them in a bowl or jar. Have everyone in your reading group pick a slip of paper, then try to imagine and describe what the life of this man's wife, daughter, or sister was like. What would it have been like for women during the period each man is from? How would the women have been involved in the conflicts experienced or decisions made by their famous husbands, fathers, or brothers? What unique challenges would the women have faced when confronting these same difficulties? Later, research to see if anything is known about the women from these men's lives and what they might have been like.

A CONVERSATION
WITH SIGNE PIKE

How did you first discover Languoreth, and what compelled you to research her further?

I first came across Languoreth's name in Adam Ardrey's nonfiction book *Finding Merlin: The Truth Behind the Legend of the Great Arthurian Mage*. I was leading a retreat in Glastonbury, England, at the time, and the book caught my eye in a local shop. I'd just come from Tintagel, in Cornwall, where I was intrigued by Merlin's Cave beneath the castle ruins. As a nonfiction writer, I've spilled a good amount of ink tracing the threads of myth and folklore down to their origins, and I've discovered that within nearly every legend lies a kernel of truth. It fascinated me to learn that Languoreth was a historical queen. She was someone we could root in history, yet her brother was considered mythological. I realized that I wanted to learn more about the real people who potentially inspired the Arthurian legends.

At what point in your research did you realize that Languoreth's story required a novel, and then a trilogy? Is *The Lost Queen* the kind of story you originally envisioned? If not, how did it change during your research?

As I discovered that Languoreth had lived through such devastating events as the destruction of Bright Hill, the raiding of her father's granaries, the Anglo-

Saxon migration, and the Battle of Arderydd, I couldn't stop thinking about the nature of this woman and her incredible human experience. I began my own research and found that Adam Ardrey's work was not only sound, it was transformative. Yet still his book (and those of other authors like Nikolai Tolstoy) was being overlooked. As a former book editor, I understood that sometimes the only way to truly popularize new scholarship was to fictionalize it. I was determined to create an opportunity for people to remember Languoreth and others who lived through such monumental events in the sixth century.

Originally I wrote from multiple perspectives, not just Languoreth's, but it wasn't working—the writing just wasn't coming through. By this point I also knew there were too many important historical events to fit into one book. When I realized that this subject longed for a trilogy, I understood that *The Lost Queen* was meant to be *her* story. In book two, we experience much with Languoreth but also get to travel the broader world through the eyes of other characters.

Tell us a little bit about your research. In your author's note, you mention that you spent six years researching and writing. What resources were the most helpful in crafting such a detailed account of what Languoreth's life might have been like?

The first thing I did was to focus on historical sources, examining every ancient text that mentioned Languoreth or Rhydderch. Languoreth appeared in ancient kings' lists, in Mungo's hagiography, in the Glasgow folk legend "The Fish and the Ring," and in some Welsh poems attributed to Myrddin (regretfully, these have been heavily tampered with and appropriated by later medieval writers). The Welsh triads contain some maddeningly elusive references to major historical events, and we catch glimpses of Gwrgi and Peredur there, as well as Angharad, Aedan, Rhydderch, and Gwenddolau. I studied the Celtic culture from its origins up to modern times. I visited the historic sites in Scotland where we know Languoreth would have lived, went to museums, watched documentaries, and spoke with both archaeologists and modern-day Christian monks; I also read scores of books, including other contemporary theories about Arthur and Merlin and any academic papers on the subject and time period I could find.

Before becoming a writer full-time, you worked as an acquisitions editor for Random House and Penguin. How did this experience affect your writing of the novel? Did it help or hinder the process?

Editorial experience comes in handy when revising, but is entirely detrimental to the creation of a first draft, I discovered. Without a first draft, you have nothing. I had to learn to silence my inner critic long enough to create something that I could build upon. There's an incredibly good video featured on the Brain Pickings website in which Neil Gaiman gives advice on writing a first draft and finishing a novel. I watched it on repeat. I learned that if you can simply stack word upon word, again and again, that's how you build something. As an editor I was always so certain; it was simple for me to see the direction a story should go in or how to express something more powerfully. But I was always working behind the scenes. As a writer, I felt too vulnerable. I still do. But perhaps in this I'm a bit like Languoreth. Painful experiences are part of living. I can't allow myself to shy away from something just because it scares me.

The ending of *The Lost Queen* leaves us with some tantalizingly unanswered questions. Was planning the whole trilogy part of your process for crafting this first novel?

Yes. I created an extensive timeline of historical events that included battles and dates of noble rule and of the births and deaths of all my historical figures. I knew that, given how much I had to cover in three books, the Battle of Arderydd would be the natural climax of *The Lost Queen*. Everything hangs in the balance. A drive to reawaken people to the occurrence of this great and horrible battle was foremost in my mind in writing these books, so to move beyond it was inconceivable. (Book two picks up right in the middle of the action but provides new readers with substantial grounding so they can get their bearings even if they haven't read *The Lost Queen*.)

The Lost Queen includes many questions about faith, destiny, sacrifice, and the creation of historical narratives. What themes from your research about Languoreth were most compelling to you when you first started writing? Were there any that developed out of the story as you wrote that surprised you?

When I first started writing, the theme that loomed largest was that of historical narratives: How can we unearth the whole of what is true when history is written by the victors? Another that still consumes me is the concept of endings, especially the perceived endings of societies. Languoreth's experience of this was twofold: the rise of Christianity in a pantheistic world, and the Anglo-Saxon power swell that would eventually subsume the whole island, save for places like Wales, Cornwall, and across the Channel in Brittany. There is an epic, painful, and tragic expansiveness in fighting for one's beliefs in a time of great change. These are the times that create heroes, heroes who deserve to be remembered. Sadly, they can also create fundamentalism. That there were so many other themes that emerged as I told the story was, in and of itself, surprising. I thought I had quite enough to grapple with already!

Languoreth and many of the other female characters prove to be strong heroines. In what ways do you feel that Languoreth's story is still applicable for women today, particularly considering our current political moment?

Languoreth lived fifteen hundred years ago, and we're still carrying on the battle women like her began: to have influence in a world of men. However, as someone who's preoccupied with history, I tend to see human history in epochs. There was the time of the matriarch, embodied by the mother goddess, which stretched on for millennia. The emergence of Christianity ushered in the time of the patriarch. Compare the two on any timeline, and the patriarchal epoch is a blink. Astounding, then, to consider the damage. We've been brought to a precipice, a breaking point, and now more than ever women are being called upon to prove ourselves fit to run our government, our businesses, our environment, and even our own bodies. Languoreth's story is more applicable than ever because today we are each of us being asked, "What, to you, is worth fighting for?"

Your first book, *Faery Tale: One Woman's Search for Enchantment in a Modern World*, is a memoir about your travels—both physically and spiritually—through some of the lands described in *The Lost Queen*. To what extent did you find resonances between the projects? How was the experience of writing a memoir different from that of writing a novel?

In both, when I was "on the ground" conducting my research, I followed where I was led. Writing and researching *Faery Tale* taught me a new way to live—that synchronicity in life could be real, and that it *is* possible to find a sort of everyday enchantment that manifests in both subtle and astonishing ways. There is much to be said for locating and then listening to your gut instincts. I had many goose-bump-inducing moments in Scotland while visiting ancient battle sites and fortresses, and always the feeling that I had come home—that my "characters," for lack of a better term, had been waiting. When it came to the nuts and bolts, there was a lot of hard work. I had to teach myself how to write fiction, which is a colossally different beast. From my editorial experience I also knew that this could prove an impossible thing to do. I was fortunate to have some incredible mentors, and that made a world of difference.

***The Lost Queen* recalls many influential Arthurian and medieval myths and legends. What books were instrumental to you growing up or during your writing process in helping you capture the atmosphere of this world that has become so pervasive in the popular imagination?**

I grew up on Tolkien, C. S. Lewis, and Madeleine L'Engle. I've always been fascinated by old things and old places. As a girl I can remember the distinct and lamentable feeling that I'd simply been born in the wrong time. When I was fourteen or so, I read *The Mists of Avalon* by Marion Zimmer Bradley. There was something so much more authentic in that book than anything I'd previously come across in relation to the Arthurian legend. I'd never been particularly taken by it before then, in fact, aside from being fond of Disney's *The Sword in the Stone* as a child. Though Bradley's book tells a very different version of the tale and is more fantasy driven, it brought that world into sharp focus for me.

During your research, was there a part of Languoreth's story that puzzled you or never made it into the final draft of the novel? How difficult was it to decide which parts of her complex and eventful life to highlight?

Languoreth's relationship with Rhydderch is complex. I believe she married him around (or even before) age fifteen, and they remained married until his death. I'm interested to see how their relationship may evolve over the course of these three books. When it comes to what to include, the events that needed to be retold stood out clearly. They were large, emotional.

Considering the lengthy research process, the presence of previous scholarly and fictional work on this topic, and the complexity of writing a three-part epic, what did you find to be the greatest challenge in creating this novel? Which part felt the most rewarding?

The greatest challenge was creating the pieces of narrative that take place between the actual historical events. What story arc leads from one event to another? How would Languoreth speak? How would she think? How would she feel? These are things no one has recorded. They bring to the forefront larger questions about humanity and daily life. It was essential to craft scenes in the most authentic way possible, but given how little writing and remembrance we have of her, I had to rely on fiction writing and instinct to try to accomplish this.

I also had to tune out or ignore much of what deviated from my own conception of how the story went. There were certain shows or books that just didn't jibe with me. They gave me a visceral feeling, so I honored that. I kept my head bent to my own work.

What did you interpret your responsibility to be to Languoreth and her family in writing the story of her life? Relatedly, what do you believe Languoreth would think about the way you depicted her in the novel?

Oh goodness. The responsibility! Serving Languoreth and her family some justice is the most elemental aim of my writing. When I'm in my writing shed, I'm sitting with them, and it comes only to that. I come back to it again and again, asking for things to become clearer. So much of their real, human existences are shrouded in mist. I will never know if I've accomplished what I set out to do. Only Languoreth can be the judge of that. But it helps to know that I'm not the first person to write about Merlin and Arthur and the times they lived in—even if I am the first to envision the life of Languoreth—and I know I won't be the last. Writers and scholars have been seeking them and writing about them for hundreds of years, and I hope they will continue to do so for many hundreds of years to come.

Turn the page for a look at Signe Pike's new novel,

The Forgotten Kingdom
Book Two of the Lost Queen Trilogy

available now from Atria Books.

PROLOGUE

Lailoken

Hart Fell, the Black Mountain
Kingdom of the Selgovae
Late December, AD 573

The snows have come.

The cold seeps into my bones. Winter cuts into the mouth of this steep and dead-grassed valley, and the men huddle closer to the hearth, but no fire can warm us—winter in its bleakness leaves us shut for too many hours within these squat, wattled huts. We cannot escape the ghosts that followed as we fled, friends and fellow warriors. Cousins. Nephews. Brothers.

I wake in the night to the haunting blast of a battle horn. To the sound of a thousand feet rushing toward the fortress through the river below. In sleep, I see bodies piled in heaps, bloodied. Sightless eyes. In sleep, my heels are slipping once more in mud, sliding backward into the muck, spears thrusting at my legs and swords battering my shield as I brace myself in the shield wall. "Hold," I cry. "Hold!"

I wake to find only hollow-eyed survivors, their eyes understanding in the dark.

When the cavalry charged, the thundering of horses swallowed our battle cry. Never had I seen an army so vast—an angry horde of Britons, my own countrymen. We shared ancestors with even the most despicable among them; cowards who would not join us to fight the Angles came now, to finish us.

We watched from high atop the fortress walls as they crept across our fields like so many fleas. We lit the brush fires. Let the smoke sting their eyes and clog their throats—let them taste our bitter battle fog.

And as we stood, grim-faced in our armor, spear shafts in hand, a moment before the nightmare began, a single red deer fled from the forest below.

A doe.

A shaft of sun caught the glory of autumn leaves and her sleek, tawny pelt, and for a moment I was a boy again, standing with my twin sister, Languoreth, on the banks of the Avon Water as we watched a stag drink in the shallows of the river.

A moment of grace before the horror of destruction.

Now it is Yule, the day of the longest night.

There are twelve days in winter when the sun stands still, and we warriors with our night terrors and our ill-knitting wounds and our bloody-faced ghosts need to conquer the darkness or we will be consumed by it. And so, at sunset, the men stood or propped themselves up as I spoke the old words and lit the Yule log.

The woman who minds the goats had come the day before to take the stale mats from the floor, laying down clean woven rushes that smelled soft and sweet, a distant memory of summer. She brought with her the charred remains of a new year's fire, an offering to bless our hearth. "For luck," she'd said, "so far from your homes."

Her gaze lingered upon the mottled scar upon my cheek that runs from temple to chin, the welt I'd borne now for eighteen winters, half-hidden by my beard.

"Christians," I'd said.

She'd nodded as if I needn't say more. Here in the lands of the Selgovae, Christ had not yet taken hold. Perhaps his priests were too frightened by the shades and sharp-toothed creatures that frequent the vast Caledonian Wood.

Now my beard grows long.

I think of my wife and her thick, honey-smooth hair, the way she tilted her head to gather it, sweeping her fingers across the back of her neck. She is yet alive, I can feel her across the distance.

I can feel she is breathing.

She tethers me to my body when my spirit wants to flee, for as the days pass, my mind turns dark. When I sit in contemplation, my mind begins to slip. There is a beast that stalks in the pit of night.

I fear it will take me.

On the bleakest mornings, I climb the icy path up the valley to seek solace at the spring. The trickle of mountain waters is speaking.

Iron in blood, iron in water.

My sister's husband hunts us with dogs.

Old Man Archer says, "Rhydderch may have dogs, but we Selgovae are wolves. He will never catch you out, not whilst we conceal you here."

It is true—no one steps foot in the Caledonian Deep without being seen. The Selgovae have watchers who appear and disappear as if made from mist. And we warriors of Pendragon can climb quickly, those of us who are sound. We can slip into the deep chasm of these hills while Rhydderch and his hunters are still specks far below.

And yet one ear is ever pricked for the crow sound of our watchmen.

I do not know whether I fear him or am calling him as I stand upon the boulder, high above the iron salt waters, looking out over the winter hills.

I stand upon the boulder and wait for Rhydderch and his men.

I wait.

I watch.

And I remember.

CHAPTER 1

Lailoken

Strathclyde to the Borderlands
Kingdom of Strathclyde
Late Summer, AD 572

I t was the time of year when daylight stretched long. Travelers were often spied long into the lingering hours of dusk, yet on this day, the moors still blazed hot beneath sun when we stopped to make camp for the night.

We were bound for the Borderlands, two days' ride from my boyhood home, the fortress of Cadzow. We'd followed the wide and glittering twists of the river Clyde south and east, through lofty patches of oak and ash, past merchants rowing upstream in their currachs and men fishing from little coracles. We passed timber-built grain mills and neatly thatched tenant crofts as we traveled through the villages of my distant kin: men and women yet loyal to me and my sister, the children of Morken. Our father had been a fierce and honorable king. But as the people gathered to greet our caravan along the road, it was not me alone they cheered. They rushed from their huts to catch sight of the man who rode by my side—Uther Pendragon. Though he was not their ruler, he and his warriors had fought for many a winter to keep the Angles of Bernicia at bay.

Gradually, the terrain shifted, and we left the villages behind. Soon hills rose turtle-backed in the distance, where pastures gave way to the wild, boggy expanse of moor. It was this land that spoke to me, for it led into the heart of the new kingdom that had become my home. The kingdom ruled by my foster brother, Uther.

But Uther had not always been my foster brother's name.

He was a boy of fifteen winters called Gwenddolau when he first joined Emrys Pendragon. Emrys was a leader who'd inspired a brotherhood to rise up against the Angles, invaders from across the North Sea. The Angles had gained footing on our soil as hired mercenaries, but before long, through violence, they'd carved out a kingdom from stolen land and named it Bernicia. In resisting them, Emrys and his men became known throughout our land as the Dragon Warriors. There were battles, and then there was peace for a time. But when Emrys was murdered, war stirred once more. We chose the man best suited to defend Emrys's lands. In becoming Pendragon's successor, Gwenddolau became something more than a man. He became hero, protector, king.

He became *Uther Pendragon*.

The Other Pendragon.

And I . . .

I'd become more than a warrior, or son of Morken. I was a Wisdom Keeper, trained from a boy to be a king's counsellor, his most trusted advisor. We defended our stretch of the Borderlands through the vigilance of our scouts and the brunt of our swords. Our tenant farmers were grateful. The Gods protected us. The land produced. All we required, we possessed in bounty.

We traveled fast on fleet-footed horses. We traveled light, with thick cloaks and thin bedrolls, with little more than the sack full of oats each man strapped to his horse to be fried with water or blood from wild game. Thirteen leagues in a day we passed with ease.

And yet on this day, we'd scarcely traveled through Hawksland and the Blackwood when my young niece bolted upright in the saddle before me and cried out, "Stop!"

My horse tossed his head as I yanked back on the reins, gripping Angharad to keep her astride as the caravan came to a halt. "Angharad. What is it?" I asked.

The Dragon Warriors drew up their mounts, restless and questioning.

They'd never traveled with a child. Who among us had? Now we traveled in the company of a freckled girl of eight winters whose gray eyes were yet swollen with tears. At sunrise, Angharad had left all she had known to train with me as a Wisdom Keeper. That I was her uncle was little consolation.

"The feathers," she said now, pointing to the ground.

"Feathers." I followed the line of her finger to the place where, indeed, a cluster of crow feathers lay, their ink glinting rainbows in the sun. "And so they are."

It was this child's curiosity about the natural world that had first endeared her to me, and now I was to foster her. Yet despite my reassurances to my sister, I was still learning the way.

"Angharad. Surely you've seen crow feathers before." I leaned forward only to see her brow furrow.

"But I want to pick them up."

"Well, of course you may. But you must take more care when alerting me to feathers on your next sighting. You nearly tumbled from Gwydion's back."

Angharad's face flushed scarlet, her voice a whisper. "I'm sorry, Uncle."

There'd been little admonishment in my tone, yet my words alone were enough to flatten her. She pursed her lips in an effort to hold back tears, and guilt struck, pointed as a spear. "Oh, no, Angharad. Please. You mustn't cry."

The warriors looked baffled as I glanced round in search of aid. Gwenddolau sat mounted at a distance beside my cousin Brant, expressions vigilant yet uncertain.

"She's your kin as well," I grumbled, then motioned to Maelgwn, who already trotted toward us on his horse, green eyes alert.

"What's happened?" he demanded.

"She's weeping," I said.

"Aye, I can see." He dismounted and went to her, taking her small hands in his. "Angharad, what is it?"

"I didn't intend for all the men to stop. I only wanted the feathers," she said.

"Tell me why."

She took a breath, searching the sky. "My mother told me our hearts are like birds, pricked full of feathers, and that each time we say good-bye, a feather will fall. One for a friend, two for a sweetheart. Three for a child."

At the mention of Languoreth, Maelgwn's gaze softened. "And here you spied three feathers, just as your mother said."

Angharad nodded. "She promised if I found a feather, it had fallen from her heart. She promised if I picked it up and held it close, it would keep me safe."

"Then you must have them," Maelgwn said.

I watched as he handed Angharad the cluster of crow feathers. Long had Maelgwn loved my sister, Languoreth.

As Angharad drew them to her chest, I searched for the right words.

"I know your sadness, little one," I began. "Languoreth and I, we lost our own mother when we were no more than ten winters—"

Angharad's eyes widened at the very thought. "But my mother is not *dead*."

Fool, Lailoken.

"Aye. I mean, nay! Of course she isn't." I reached for her. "I only hope to say I know how your own heart must feel. We may collect each feather you see. But you need no such talismans to keep you safe. I swore to your mother—and I swear the same to you—you are safe with me, Angharad. I'm your uncle, your own blood, and . . . I love you." The last came too gruffly, and I cursed myself again. Maelgwn frowned.

But Angharad only wiped at her eyes, casting a weary look over her shoulder. "You're not terribly good with children, are you?"

I smiled in spite of myself. "You're right, then," I decided. "We've traveled far enough. We shall stop here for the night."

Gwenddolau approached, swinging down from his horse. "A rest is fine, but we cannot yet make camp. We haven't passed more than five leagues, Lailoken."

"Well enough," I said. "But 'tis only the first day of our journey, and Angharad is unaccustomed to long days upon horseback, brother. You cannot expect her to last from dawn 'til dusk in the saddle."

Gwenddolau's clear blue eyes swept the broad expanse of moor, resting on the grassy mound that rose in the distance. "Surely it is ill luck to make our camp so close to a hill of the dead. I have seen enough shades in my day."

"Aye, we all spied the mound, and many a time have we passed it," I said. "But the hill lies upstream, and the ashes within it are sleeping. Besides, we are not far from the old ring of stones. I'm certain Angharad would wish to see it. If you'll not brave the shades for me, brave them for your niece, eh?"

The look I received was one of predictable gravity—Gwenddolau's humor had gone with seasons past. "I feel no more ease bedding beside a stone ring than I do a mound of the dead."

Brant drew up his horse, his brown eyes touching on Angharad with concern. "The ring will make a good enough boundary for the horses," my cousin said. "They'll not stray beyond it."

"Aye," Gwenddolau agreed at last, signaling for the men to dismount. "They're ill at ease, as I am, round places of the dead."

In truth, I knew rest would suit Gwenddolau as well, whether he cared for it or not. His old battle wound was on the mend, with thanks to Languoreth's remedy, but he needed to recover his strength. Thirteen leagues in a day or half that, what did it matter? Angharad was ours now—all of ours—and I meant to tend to her as best as I could.

The thought seemed to weigh upon Gwenddolau, too, for as I watched, he placed his sunbrowned hands round Angharad's waist, lifting her from my horse with a smile at last. "Well enough, Angharad. Come, then. Let's find a suitable place to make camp."

I dismounted, following behind. "It's bound to be boggy. I'll fashion a bed so Angharad might sleep in the cart."

Next to me, the old warrior Dreon chuckled.

"Oh, go on, then, Dreon. Let's have it," I said.

"Well. I have naught to say but this: a handsome lord, in his prime at thirty-two winters—a Wisdom Keeper to boot—already become staid and matronly as an old mother hen."

"An old mother hen?" I said. "You should mind you don't choke on a chicken bone."

Dreon lifted his hands. "Eh, now! There's no need for bandying curses about."

"When I curse you, you shall know it."

"I believe you." The warrior clapped me upon the shoulder. "Whatever you may do, you mustn't fret, Lailoken. I have bairns of my own, and I'll lend you some wisdom—children are like wolves. They can smell your fear."

I'd met Dreon's offspring. A wild pack of stoats, more like.

"Well," I said, "seeing as you're such a master of your own fine progeny, perhaps you'd like to try a hand at fostering mine."

"Nay." He frowned. "And rob you of the joy?"

I waved him off and found Gwenddolau and Angharad crouched at the water's edge, looking upstream.

"We call this water Wildburn," Gwenddolau said, bending to splash his face. Droplets clung to his golden beard, and when he stood, he shook the water from his head like a dog, smiling at his niece.

"Wildburn." Angharad looked about. She'd drawn the black feathers from her cloak and clutched them like a doll. "Uncle." She turned to me. "Is it true there's a ring of stones nearby?"

"Aye. Just beyond that rise."

Her face brightened, a joy to see. "May we go there? May we go now?"

"Indeed," I said. "I'm to train you as a Keeper, am I not? Here you are, eight winters, and you haven't yet stepped foot in your first ring of stones. Come now, and we shall see them."

"The midges will be upon us," Gwenddolau called after us. "Mind that Angharad has some salve."

"Seems I'm not the only mother hen," I said beneath my breath. Stopping at my horse to take the ointment from my saddlebag, I smiled at Angharad and dropped it into my satchel.

The Dragon Warriors were moving through the rhythm of setting up camp: laying out bedrolls, watering the horses, and rinsing in the burn, while the youngest men gathered fuel for the fire and unpacked the cook pots. My twin sister had sent us away with great flats of dried beef and a bounty of summer crops, perfect for a stew of wild game, but her face had been ashen as we said farewell that morning. And as we'd ridden off through

Cadzow's gates—I with her youngest child before me in the saddle—I'd looked over my shoulder to see Languoreth standing on the platform of the rampart, watching us depart. It was enough to wound her that I was taking Angharad away. But her lover, too, traveled in my company.

"No ale before supper," Malegwn called to the men. His jaw was tight as he joined Gwenddolau beside the stream. Each of us had left Cadzow carrying our burdens, it seemed.

Yet Angharad was no burden. Languoreth and I had been so very close when we were children, before our fates had compelled us to live kingdoms apart. Now, with her daughter at my side, I felt the rift somehow mended. Angharad threaded her fingers in mine as she so often had upon my visits, when she and I would walk the woods together, naming things. She had my sister's tawny-red hair and the winter-gray eyes of her father, Rhydderch.

It felt right, in that moment, that she should be with me. That I should be training her in the way of Wisdom Keeping, raising her as my own. I felt my confidence return, pointing as we drew close. "See it there? The ring of stones lies just beyond that rise."

But Angharad had already spotted them. "Oh," she breathed. I wondered if the ring was quite what she'd expected.

Far to the north, I'd visited the ancient, imposing stones of Pictland—towering behemoths that brooded against molten silver skies. I'd sat within vast circles of sixty stones or more that rose amid thick sprays of heather. I'd walked, enthralled and nearly seduced within intimate stones, places where the rocks had been weathered so round that their curves resembled the finest bits of a woman's body.

Each circle felt different, and rightly so. For buried deep at the root of the stones were the ashes of men and women who had come before, awake and then sleeping with the shifting of stars and the rise of the moon. Though flesh had failed them, rock had become their new earthly body. Now their spirits were ever present. I could feel them regarding us now, as if the stones themselves were breathing.

These stones were not set in a circle. They formed instead the shape of an egg, sunk into the moor in perpetual slumber, rimmed protectively by a gently sloping dyke. The tallest among them was scarcely the height of a man, while the others stooped, irregular and hobbled. Still, they beckoned with their own particular enchantment, and Angharad made to enter swiftly before I caught her hand.

"It is ill luck to enter without seeking permission," I said. "These stones are guardians—men and women of old. They do not take kindly to trespassers and can cause all sort of maladies if they wish."

Surely your mother has taught you as much, I nearly said. But Languoreth was no Wisdom Keeper. There was a time when she'd wished more than anything to train, as our own mother had. As I was Chosen to do. But Languoreth was not Chosen. The gift had fallen instead to her youngest daughter. Languoreth had known Angharad was marked. That the child possessed gifts was evident—a thought that stirred excitement in me even as it raised protectiveness in my sister.

But I, too, had seen things as a child. Things that frightened me. Things I could not understand. It was enough to make old spirits out of young ones. Perhaps this was the reason I felt so compelled to teach Angharad how to wield her gifts—so they would not become a burden. So they could not break her.

"Some Wisdom Keepers are showmen," I told her now. "They would have our people believe that spirit speaks in great booms, like thunder. But spirit speaks in whispers. The best Keepers understand this and keep quiet so they might hear. Close your eyes and be still."

Through the joining of our hands I could sense her, alert as a rabbit. A little fearful. And beneath the surface, sorrow issuing in a foul and muddy water. I could take it from her if I wished. Draw it into myself, and she might experience some relief. But the source of such wellsprings ran deep. Water will find its way—it would only rise up again. Better to let her come to it in her own time. Her own way.

"Be still," I repeated. Angharad's eyes flared with frustration, but she closed them, her cinnamon-colored lashes settling against her freckled cheeks.

I waited until her face began to soften. She had found her way to the quiet, the place where deeper meaning could reside.

"I will teach you the blessing Cathan once gave me," I said. "Commit it to memory. The words will serve you well." I moved through the old chant twice, then once more for good measure. "Tomorrow we will return, and those words will be yours to speak. Yes?" Angharad nodded and I released her hands. "You may enter now. Touch the stones if you like."

"Sunwise?" she asked.

"Aye. Isn't that the way of it all?"

A summer wind played, flapping at the corner of Angharad's gray cloak as she stepped into the stones—a gentle sort of greeting. As she began to explore the circle, I told her what I knew of their story.

"This ring was built by your ancestors, those who came to this great island and first dwelled in the north. I speak of a time long ago—time out of memory. What you see are not only stones. They are your people, your clann. Their alignments track the course of moon and sun. The sunrise at Midwinter, the movements that mark the quarter year, too. In this way they are Time Keepers. Cathan brought me here—to this very circle— when I was but a boy. I saw for myself how this stone pairs with yonder hill." I pointed to the slope that rose in the distance. "If you stand just here on Midwinter sunset, there is a cairn upon the summit that marks the grave of an ancient king. You can watch the evening sun slip down its curve like the yolk of an egg, until it disappears into the earth."

I turned back to find that Angharad was not listening and fought the compulsion to throw up my hands. Such inattention from a novice was inexcusable. But Angharad was my kin, and the girl had never before visited a circle. I held my tongue and watched her explore, fingers tracing the pale lichen that bloomed from the speckled skin of a stone.

But then.

It was as if the air around us had gone cold. I looked up, expecting to see a swift-moving storm, but the sky was cerulean, dotted with fat, friendly clouds. Strange. Yet there could be no question—the atmosphere had shifted. I could scarcely focus on Angharad's form, my sight gone blurry.

Stones had a particular fondness for the attention of children. But with Angharad in the stones, this was something more. Ill at ease, I closed my eyes and turned inward, searching for the cause of such a shift, and felt suddenly as if I were being observed.

Nay, not observed.

Stalked.

My blood beat against my temples. These stones were born of my own kin. Never before had I felt such malevolence. What dared stalk me now? What dared stalk my niece?

Angharad stood with her palms pressed flat against a stone. I strode into the ring, but she did not notice my presence. The wind shifted again, but now the smell that met my nose was rank, like flesh gone rotten. I did not wish to speak, fearful of lending more power to this unnamable thing, yet I could sense it, a shadow approaching, traveling across the ages. Ancient. Such power stirred I nearly reeled.

A strange look had come over Angharad's face.

"Angharad, step back." I spoke evenly, not wishing to cause her alarm. But the child did not hear me. It was as if she were entranced. "Angharad. Step back, I said."

Pulling her from the rock was a danger, too abrupt. She had clearly joined some part of herself with the stone. There was risk in tearing her away that all of her might not return. But I could not wait. Reaching out, I yanked Angharad's hands from the granite and drew back, startled, as she rounded on me, crying out as if wounded.

"It is coming for you! It comes for my mother!" she cried, then slumped against me, boneless. I caught her limp body in my arms. She weighed little more than a sack of feathers. Her freckled skin had gone waxen.

"Angharad. Speak to me. Are you all right?"

Even as I held her, even as I questioned, I knew what had taken place. Angharad had experienced a Knowing.

My tutor Cathan was wont to have them, but he'd held such mastery over himself, his utterances were more akin to a common suggestion than a vision arrived from beyond the veil. Few Keepers I'd known had possessed sight equal to his. For me, divinity spoke through nature. Augury and rhetoric were my skills. Book learnings and king lists. Strategic maneuverings. I was a counsellor—an advisor—not a priest as such. Yet I knew some Seers suffered exertion from their visions, and I imagined the effect could be more taxing on someone young, one who did not yet know how to wield it.

The girl was far too open. Angharad had opened herself and something had come, something unbidden. And I had unwittingly placed her in danger.

I should not have brought her here, I thought. Not without yet understanding her. Then she stirred in my arms and my shoulders dropped with relief. Angharad looked up at me, blinking.

"I'm all right, Uncle. Truly."

I studied her. "Nay, not quite. But do you think you might stand?"

Angharad nodded and I placed her down gently, searching her eyes. Her gray eyes were stormy, but thank the Gods, wherever her vision had taken her, it seemed all of her had returned.

"Angharad. You must tell me what happened," I said.

"What happened . . ." She spoke slowly, as if only just remembering the use of her mouth.

"Aye," I encouraged, and her gaze turned distant.

"The stone felt soft. Soft as a sea sponge. And empty. Hollow. As if I might push it. As if I might push it and fall right through."

"And did you? Did you . . . fall through?" I watched her intently.

"No, for there was something else then. Something coming as if through a tunnel deep in the earth. It rushed toward me like a wind, fast as a thousand galloping horses."

"And then? Angharad, I do not wish to press you, but I must know the entirety of what happened so I know you are now truly safe. This spirit. Did it feel an evil thing? A . . . beast of some kind? What did you see?"

She frowned, frustration mounting. "I saw nothing, Uncle! It was a feeling, that's all." She struggled to find the words to explain it. "It was . . . a Thing."

"A Thing." I drew her to me. "I should not have brought you here. Not so soon. There are things I must teach you. I made an error, one I shall not make again. I am sorry you were frightened."

"But I was not frightened."

I could not hold back my surprise. "Were you not?"

"Nay. The Thing did not come for me," she said simply. "It came for you."

A shiver traced my arms, and I pressed her more tightly. Then quite suddenly Angharad's face shifted and she drew away, laughing. "What is it, Uncle? Why do you embrace me so?"

"I—I wish to comfort you." I blinked.

"Comfort me? Whatever for?" She smiled. "I am sorry, Uncle, for I must not have been listening. I cannot recall what you did say! Tell me again what such stone rings were built for. I do so wish to explore."

The child had no memory of the events that had taken place only moments ago.

"Nay, Angharad." I reached for her. "Perhaps tomorrow. But the stones are before you. Now you have seen them! You will be hungry. Come, let us return to camp. The air grows chill. It will soon be time for supper."

She furrowed her brow but followed nonetheless. As we picked our way back over the grassy tufts of moor, I puzzled over what had taken place. I had spent time in shadow. In caves and underground pathways. In ancient stone chambers built for the dead. I'd faced my own darkness and my share of shades—in this world and the other. Yet never had I encountered such a . . . Thing.

At our camp beside Wildburn, the night fire was crackling. We slathered on ointment to fend off the midges that swarmed with a vengeance. Dreon whittled a shaft of ash with his blade, shaping a new spear. We filled our stomachs with hot stew, and the men took turns recounting tales of the woods until Angharad's lids dropped and she slept where she sat. I picked her up and laid her gently on her bedding in the cart, tucking the sheepskin round her face, so peaceful now in sleep.

But I did not close my eyes that night for fear that the Thing, whatever it might be, should return, that Angharad would somehow be lost to me. I sat awake the long night, spine slumped against the wheel of the wagon, watching the shadows cast from the fire as they flickered and shifted, growing in the dark.